A TOUCH *of* STARDUST

ALSO BY KATE ALCOTT

The Dressmaker

The Daring Ladies of Lowell

A TOUCH OF
Stardust

*

KATE ALCOTT

Doubleday

NEW YORK LONDON TORONTO

SYDNEY AUCKLAND

Copyright © 2015 by Kate Alcott

www.doubleday.com

DOUBLEDAY and the portrayal of an anchor with a dolphin are
registered trademarks of Random House LLC.

Jacket design by Lynn Buckley and Emily Mahon
Jacket photograph Carole Lombard © Getty Images

LIBRARY OF CONGRESS CATALOGING-IN-PUBLICATION DATA
Alcott, Kate.
A touch of stardust / Kate Alcott. — First Edition.
pages ; cm
ISBN 978-0-385-53904-3 (hardcover);
ISBN 978-0-385-53905-0 (eBook)
1. Gable, Clark, 1901–1960—Fiction. 2. Lombard, Carole,
1908–1942—Fiction. 3. Motion picture actors and actresses—
Fiction. 4. Hollywood (Los Angeles, Calif.)—Fiction.
5. Gone with the wind (Motion picture: 1939)—Fiction. I. Title.
PR6101.L426T68 2014
823'.92—dc23   2014020972

MANUFACTURED IN THE UNITED STATES OF AMERICA

1 3 5 7 9 10 8 6 4 2

First Edition

For my father:

You always loved a good story.

This one's for you.

This is a work of fiction, although the central structure of the saga of making *Gone with the Wind* and key dates are accurate. Scenes using actual dialogue from the movie have been shortened.

A TOUCH *of* STARDUST

CHAPTER 1

*A*tlanta was exploding right on schedule.

Small darting figures danced across the lot, lighting fuses, jumping back. A single column of flame roared toward the night sky, joined quickly by another and then another. Bits of blazing debris broke free and floated upward. Houses, barns, wagons—everything ignited like parched underbrush.

"God, look at it burn!" yelled a man in a Confederate uniform. The sky above Selznick International Pictures was now a frighteningly brilliant, ferocious orange, and while men in business suits on a high platform above the fire cheered, residents of Culver City, California, huddled in their houses, wondering briefly if this was Armageddon.

Julie Crawford kept running, stumbling every few feet in the ridiculous high-heeled pumps she had thought would give her confidence on her first substantive assignment at the Selznick studio. She tried to turn her face from the blaze as she ran, but her skin felt seared with heat anyway. She risked a quick glance upward, toward the observation tower. David O. Selznick, bathed in searchlights, stood like a king, surveying his flaming domain.

Suddenly two huddled figures in a wagon pulled by a galloping horse loomed into view. Thugs swarmed forward, trying to grab the horse; the animal reared in fear. A man in a wide-brimmed hat jumped down and threw a shawl over its head; then, silhouetted against the vivid sky, flames licking at his clothes, he pulled horse and wagon to safety.

For an instant Julie felt she was actually seeing and smelling the burning of the Atlanta depot, not just imagining it. That was Rhett pulling the horse. Scarlett huddled on the buckboard; hidden from view were Melanie and her baby. Julie's heartbeat quickened. Good Lord, that man at the top of the tower really *was* bringing *Gone with the Wind* to life, and who wouldn't be enthralled?

*

"Damned if that wagon thing don't look pretty good," said the fake Confederate soldier in high excitement, pointing. "Old Sherman ain't getting those munitions now!"

A roar of whooping and hollering grew as people clapped each other on the back and laughed, relieved—though still casting nervous eyes at the fire engines encircling the lot. There was no way they would be needed, they told each other. Selznick was audacious, but he wasn't stupid. These flames would stay locked in his Technicolor cameras even as they devoured old scenery, making way for Tara, and it would all work, because this was Hollywood.

Julie stared down at the message clutched in her fist. Why was she standing here, gaping? Her instructions were to deliver this into Selznick's hands *before* the fire began. Her first chance to escape the mimeograph machine, and she had botched it.

But it was too soon to concede defeat. "I have to get to Mr. Selznick," she said loudly, pushing toward the tower, straining on tiptoe to see above the crowd, trying to ape the tone of self-importance everyone else on this set seemed to have mastered. "I have a message for him."

A fireman—a real one from the Los Angeles Fire Department

or a studio extra, she wasn't sure—glanced at her with exasperation. His face looked boiled red from the heat. "Honey," he said, "can't you see he's busy keeping *us* busy? Stay back—that's an order."

Somebody hooted. Her own face grew even warmer.

"Who gave you the message?" asked a male voice.

She turned and saw a man leaning against the side of the wooden observation tower, wearing a black suede jacket, a rumpled shirt, and scuffed tennis shoes. His hair was dark and on the long side, as if he had postponed a haircut or two. His hands were strong and freckled; his face glowed with the usual California tan. What struck her was the level gaze he was casting in her direction, a gaze managing to juggle amusement with gravity. Not old, not young. Julie wished suddenly that she had remembered to check her lipstick.

"One of his assistants," she said.

"Who?"

"I don't know his name."

He tossed the stub of a cigarette to the ground and shook his head. "Must be your first day," he said. "You don't bring a message to Selznick without knowing who sent it. Give it to me; I'll take it to him." He reached out his hand, eyes cool, a small smile pulling at the side of his lips.

"I'd rather deliver it in person," she said warily.

His hand paused in midair, then dropped to his side. "Good, you passed that test. Never give a Selznick message to anyone else." He grinned now, a friendly grin, beckoning her forward, pointing to the tower's ladder. "I'll take you up to the platform, I'm supposed to be there anyway. What's your name?"

"Julie Crawford. I work in the main office." She didn't have to say she worked cranking out press releases on the mimeograph machine. He seemed very sure of himself, totally part of this new world, and it would be nice to at least give the impression she knew a *little* about what she was doing.

"So—not Irish. Probably of good Protestant stock. Where did you get that red hair?"

"From my mother," she retorted. "And it's not red, it's auburn, and I'm not feisty or tempestuous or any of the other things red hair is supposed to signify. Anyway, as I said, it's auburn." She bit her lip, annoyed with herself. Once again, saying the wrong thing at the wrong time.

His grin widened. "My, my: touchy. You must watch a lot of movies. But I'm wondering, every girl in Hollywood these days wants to play Scarlett O'Hara. She has black hair, so Margaret Mitchell tells us. Even the fake blondes in this town are willing to be reinvented once again. Planning on a dye job?"

"No. I'm not one of them, thank you."

He shrugged, then started up the ladder. "Okay, natural is good. Follow me."

Julie climbed, glad she was wearing trousers. Mother would faint, but better slacks than having that Confederate soldier peering up her skirt. Even though the ladder looked sturdy, it made her nervous. The whole plywood structure felt slapped together, like everything else in this wonderful, scary place.

She stepped out at the top onto the platform and was surprised to see a good twenty people or so milling about, all looking very important. A glance at the surrounding landscape took her breath away. The fire roaring across the lot was devouring everything that had been there this morning: all the old sets for *King Kong* and *The Thief of Bagdad*. Tomorrow, after clearing debris, Mr. Selznick would build Tara right here. Julie couldn't imagine Scarlett O'Hara's majestic home rising from the land beneath this inferno.

"Young woman, you've arrived too late," a strong voice boomed out. "Your message preceded you."

She whirled around and found herself staring into the face of the man who ruled this world of make-believe—everything and everyone in it.

David O. Selznick. Nobody called him David; he was too magisterial for that. He wasn't an exceptionally tall man. His brows were thick and dark; his hair was receding. His steel-rimmed glasses had slipped down slightly onto his nose, which gave him a kind of professorial look. But the eyes behind those glasses would have burned through mere students; there was nothing benign about them.

And right now, they were staring at her. All Julie could do was stutter.

"Not her fault—the fire department wouldn't let her through," said the man who had brought her up here. His tone was casual but matter-of-fact.

"I'm sorry, Mr. Selznick—" she managed, thrusting forward the message.

Selznick glanced at it, frowning impatiently; he raised his hand, to bat away her words like so many flies. He turned, facing out toward the sky turned orange by the conflagration consuming the back lot of Selznick International Pictures. His chest swelled; his expression turned into pure delight.

"Great scene, isn't it?" he said happily, sweeping a wide arc with his hand to take in the scope of the fire.

All the observers crowded on the platform clapped in approving unison. Selznick had done it again, crazy though he might be. Brilliant, of course. But crazy.

"And how about *this* lovely lady?" Selznick turned his back on the inferno and gazed with calculated appreciation at a woman standing next to him. "Just so you know," he said, with a nod in Julie's direction, "this message was supposed to alert me to the visit of my young British beauty here, but she arrived before you did. Usually, I don't like surprises. Tonight was an exception. May I introduce England's treasure, the stunning Miss Vivien Leigh?"

Oh Lord, was he talking to her? No, he was addressing the crowd. Julie stared at the actress. Everything about her was tiny— her features, her limbs. Her skin was as luminous as a bed of pearls, and her eyes—almond-shaped, with artfully applied green eye shadow—gave her the appearance of a sleepy cat. The sensuous beige silk dress she wore embraced her amazingly slender waist, then swept out halfway to the floor in sinuous folds. Her smile, as she peeped slyly from under her velvet cloche, was dazzling. With the flames behind her casting their flickering light, she could have just stepped by magic from the pages of a Civil War history book.

"Scarlett?" Julie breathed.

A titter of laughter from some of the people on the platform greeted her words. Julie flushed. She had assumed too much. The part of Scarlett O'Hara in *Gone with the Wind* was not yet cast.

But Vivien Leigh's delight at her blurted response was evident. Who here could know how many hours she had spent in front of a mirror, while coming over from England to America on the *Queen Mary,* practicing the expressions of the imagined Scarlett, coaxing her alive? "I hope you're listening, David," she cooed, flouncing her skirt in a saucy gesture. Her dress billowed out, forcing some on the platform—slightly nervous about being swept over the side—to move out of the way.

Selznick laughed hugely, then tossed a dismissive glance at Julie. "You can go, my dear. The fact is, I don't tolerate tardiness, not among the employees of my studio. But I'm sure you'll find work somewhere else. And you can tell your friends back home you met the very beautiful and clever Vivien Leigh."

Julie turned to go, mortified. She was fired; he had just fired her. She straightened her posture, willing herself not to cry. No, she wasn't going back home. Not even the famous Mr. Selznick could make that happen. She was here to make a new life for herself, away from the stifling proprieties of Fort Wayne, Indiana. She mustn't buckle with the first setback.

As Julie reached for the ladder, she caught sight of a blond woman slouching casually at the railing. Beside her was a man with dark, thick hair and a carefully clipped mustache. His arms were folded tightly in front of a formidable chest. Julie registered a quiver of recognition, but her attention turned quickly back to the woman by his side. There was something about her—her demeanor, mainly. She seemed indifferent to the congratulatory hum of the crowd around Selznick. Her honey-colored hair looked real, not from a peroxide bottle, and obviously no stylist had dressed her. The linen shirt and wrinkled slacks she wore were probably from Bullocks Wilshire, but they looked as casual as the ones Julie bought at Ayres's department store back home.

"Friend of yours, Andy?" the woman asked her guide up onto the platform, nodding in Julie's direction. Her eyes were kind; her voice was throaty, amused.

"From childhood," he said with a straight face. "Very talented."

"Then get her a typing job. You've got plenty of people churning out scenes."

"They rewrite too fast—clean pages are useless. How about her helping out you and Clark?"

She shrugged. "If you can sneak her past David."

"Maybe with a black wig?"

She laughed. "That's a guaranteed disguise; do it."

"I don't want to wear a—" Julie began, confused.

"Just a joke," she said.

"Okay," Julie said, now thoroughly embarrassed.

"Just do what Andy tells you," the woman continued. "He'll put in a word with the right person. Right, Andy?" This was said in a casual tone, and the very self-confident Andy answered just as casually:

"Right," he said.

She turned to Julie. "Don't despair, sweetie. Everybody gets fired by David sooner or later, but Andy is his right-hand man, and he'll get you fixed up. At the rate our Mr. Selznick is going, this movie might provide all of you with lifetime jobs of one sort or another."

"Doesn't mean everyone gets what they want," her companion interjected.

The blonde shrugged and gifted him with a tender smile. But that didn't stop her from casting a scornful glance at Selznick. Not quite daggers, but definitely scorn.

"I'll handle it," Andy said, then tugged Julie away and down the ladder before she could say another word.

They faced each other on the ground. "What just happened?" Julie asked.

"You won't be fired—you'll see. Just toss out the name of your glamorous protector tomorrow and Selznick's office will have you back delivering messages in no time. A piece of advice, kid. Don't ever apologize to Selznick—he hates that. Meeting her was a stroke of luck for you."

"Who is she?"

His eyes widened, and then he laughed. "You *are* a babe in the woods. She's actually quite an innovator—one of the first to avoid getting her head chopped off by the studio heads for living in scandal. Around here—don't you know?—the morality police rule everything. They'll drop an actress whose love life gets exposed by the nasty gossip columnist Louella in a minute. This one is a star member of Hollywood's Unmarried Husbands and Wives—they actually call it that in *Photoplay*—haven't you heard of it?"

Julie shook her head. She had a lot to learn, even if she had no silly dream of tap-dancing her way to stardom. *That* small fantasy had disappeared the first time she smeared orange Tangee lipstick on her lips. Quite an experience—staring into a mirror and seeing a Kewpie doll staring back. That sight made it easier to accept her mother's verdict that she was neither beautiful nor talented. A relief, actually. It had given her permission to be a campus bookworm at Smith and ignore the absence of handsome suitors from Princeton or Harvard. There was, of course, always in the back of her mind the safety of the high-school boyfriend back home. She still felt a stab of guilt at the outcome of that.

"I'm no babe in the woods, and I'm out to learn as much as I can," she said as firmly as she could. "In my world, if you don't ask questions, you stay ignorant."

He seemed delighted with her defense. "Julie, my dear young, fresh Julie"—he paused, rolling her name experimentally over his tongue—"that was Carole Lombard, the Queen of Screwball Comedies. Excellent actress. You're right: keep asking questions. But don't feel too sorry for yourself—she was turned down for the role of Scarlett, so how do you think she feels?"

"Not good, I suppose."

"Right. And the man standing next to her is the King of Hollywood—the future Rhett Butler, otherwise known as Clark Gable. She's long divorced, so they can marry, but his decoupling is still dragging on. Drives Selznick crazy. He's afraid of scandal, but he wants to keep Gable happy. He invited Carole up today to mollify both of them."

"He looks different than he does on the screen," Julie said. Not recognizing Carole Lombard and Clark Gable? It branded her totally.

"They all look different when you see them in the flesh. Thinner, fatter, shorter—lots of the men are shorter. They stand on buckets for love scenes."

"Not Gable—he's tall."

"A mark of authenticity. And, as further introduction, I am Andy Weinstein, an assistant producer working with the amazing Mr. David O. Selznick, here to work on the as yet nonexistent *Gone with the Wind,* which is a sloppy monster of a movie with an unfinished script that lots of people predict will go down as the biggest disaster in film history. Got that?"

So he wasn't just handsome, he was smart and sort of funny; she was intimidated, so her instinct was to push back. "Well, I loved the book, just like everybody else in the country, and I think it will be a magnificent movie," she said.

"Ah, a contrary streak. Well, let's hope you're right. Now, before you slink away to nurse your wounds, will you let me take you to dinner?"

He really did have a jaunty smile; it warmed the shadows in his eyes.

He probably wouldn't pass muster back home in Fort Wayne, Indiana. But she wasn't there, she was here, so she could toss *that* bit of caution into the trash. Adventure and opportunity—wasn't that what she was looking for? She could either have dinner with this man and learn something, or declare herself a coward and go back to the rooming house and eat tuna fish on toast—the posted dinner for tonight.

"Yes," she said. She sounded a little calmer than she felt, or—at least—so she hoped. And, as he was to tell her later, she sealed the deal by lifting her chin high and adding, "Just as long as it's somewhere glamorous."

CHAPTER 2

They drove up from Culver City to Sunset Boulevard, then east toward Vine Street. It was a balmy night, once they were past the haze of the studio fire. Julie cranked down the window of Andy's gleaming blue DeSoto coupe and peered out at all the glittering neon signs looming above the palm trees, trying not to appear too awed by it all.

"See over there?" he said, lifting one hand from the steering wheel as they turned off Sunset, pointing. She spotted a huge billboard of a woman's head illuminated over a darkened building. People on the street were slowing their pace and staring upward. No wonder. An even larger neon sign next to the one of the woman proclaimed THROUGH THESE PORTALS PASS THE MOST BEAUTIFUL GIRLS IN THE WORLD.

"That's Earl Carroll's latest supper theater," Andy said. "He went broke in New York, but we're all about second chances out here. They don't open until after Christmas, or we'd go there and take in a show."

"So does that mean if I walk in there someone will wave a magic wand and turn me into one of the Most Beautiful Girls in the World?"

"All you have to do is believe," he said lightly. "Is that a little skepticism I'm hearing in your voice?"

"Do you believe?"

He laughed. "Well, I gave up a long time ago on Santa Claus, so you may have spotted something. All I'm doing is showing you the different kinds of magic we of the entertainment industry can offer."

She liked the dryness of his tone, which was somewhere between rueful and sarcastic. And also, she realized, quickly changeable.

"So you're a good Protestant girl? And not put off by my name?"

"Why would I care about that?" she retorted, imagining what her father would say right now. Something like, "Weinstein, huh?" Then he would snap his evening paper smartly and frown his disapproval. He was good at that.

"No reason," he said. His tone became playful. "You know, my mother always used to say, 'Why can't you meet any nice Jewish girls out there in Hollywood?' and I told her, 'Ma, all the girls here are Gentiles, and they all want to be actresses, and they all want to live in Beverly Hills.' Most of the Jews are writers or film editors and still live in West Hollywood. Some of us have worked our way up to the Hollywood Hills, but give us time."

He gave such an artless, loose shrug, she laughed. "Thank you for helping me out today," she said.

"No problem. It was quite a sight, wasn't it?"

"The fire? Oh yes."

"Nobody but Selznick would have attempted that," he said. "He hasn't even got a full script or a leading lady yet. You can't help being impressed by his chutzpah."

"Chutzpah?"

"Audacity. Nerve. It's Yiddish." He seemed resigned as he swung a hard right. "We're going to a place I like on Beverly Boulevard," he said. "Do you want to be an actress? Please say no."

"No."

"Really?"

"Why would I want to be?" she said. "I can't act."

"That hasn't stopped most of the girls out here."

"At least they're all gorgeous. I'm not even garden-variety pretty."

"That may be your good fortune," he said.

That stung a bit. He could have pretended.

"Where are we going?" she asked.

"We're going to dine with the stars and eat chili," he said. "At Chasen's. It's classic Hollywood, not too many gaping tourists."

"Are you really that contemptuous? I'm still a tourist, myself."

"They spoil the story," he said. Whatever that meant.

Chasen's was a modest-looking stucco building with a jaunty green-and-white-striped awning, not the type of place she would glance at twice in any other town. They slipped into an oversized booth covered in thick chocolate-brown leather that felt like soft butter. Julie peered around, wondering if she would see any movie stars, and tried not to appear to be looking.

"Think you would have recognized Gable in this setting?" Andy said lightly.

"Sure," she said, a bit affronted. "I was too flustered up there. I'm really not just a hick from the sticks, or whatever you're thinking. I go to movies all the time."

"I don't think that," he said. "And I'm not out to mock you. You have a spark to you. I like that. Look, you're new to town. There's nothing wrong with being green. Pretty much everybody here was green once."

She could not imagine that being true of him, but she wasn't going to say so.

*

They did eat chili that night. And drank several martinis. And Julie did catch a glimpse of Humphrey Bogart—sitting at the bar, nursing a beer, and slurping spoonfuls of chili from a bowl. But by then Julie was more interested in the man sitting across from her in the booth. All she knew about him so far was that he worked directly for Selznick as an assistant producer.

She told him about growing up in Fort Wayne, graduating last June from Smith College, and going home, resigned to the predictability of soon having a diamond engagement ring on her finger. It was all laid out, really. Her high-school sweetheart, a sweet, affable man, was already scouting neighborhoods for their first home—one big enough, of course, for a family. Christmas would be a really good time for an engagement party. The engagement ring, he declared, would be a full carat, which pleased her mother. He was a man on the way up, but not too ostentatious. What a wonderful son-in-law he would be, her mother enthused. Reliable, a good provider.

And then how jolted Julie was to realize that she no longer wanted the same things he did: That being the wife of a proper lawyer from a good family, totally content to forge a career drawing up wills for rich Fort Wayne people, wasn't her dream. That being on charity boards providing for the victims of the Depression was worthy, but not enough. Something in her needed to fly. How hard it had been to tell him, and her parents, the truth.

"You felt like a complete jerk," offered Andy.

She nodded. "Plus, I didn't know what I wanted."

"You just wanted to run. No"—he smiled—"fly."

"Yes," she said. "Now it's your turn."

"Born in Germany, American mother, German father. Parents divorced. Grew up—sort of—in New Jersey."

"Don't stop there," she said, laughing. She loved the energy in his voice.

"Okay. Columbia, then taught awhile, wrote an unpublishable novel, grew bored." He paused. "My grandparents stayed in Berlin, and my older brother moved to France, married a French girl, and became a citizen. I went over in the summer of 1932 to visit them all, harboring the stupid idea of nostalgic hours of bike riding, particularly through the German countryside. It didn't turn out that way."

"What happened?"

Andy looked away. "Nothing much good," he said.

She wasn't sure how to respond to that, but he quickly brightened.

"Anyway, I went home," he said. "I dumped the idea of teaching and moved on to Hollywood, dreaming of glory. Oh, and making some real money."

His first job was with Louis B. Mayer's stable of writers. "We were the joke of Hollywood," he said, leaning his head back, holding a cigarette, blowing wispy smoke rings up to the ceiling. He laughed. "They bunched us together in a room filled with typewriters, and when the signal came that Mayer was approaching, we all started typing. Quite a clatter as we all hit the keys and puffed away. You were fired if your fingers weren't moving." He gave a comical shrug. "Mayer never did understand that writers need to *think* once in a while, too. That was it for me. No more writing. So—are you nearsighted or farsighted?"

"What?" He did switch topics a lot.

He pointed. "Your glasses," he said.

"Oh." She touched the horn-rimmed frame and told him the truth. "Neither."

"So why do you wear them?"

"So people will take me seriously, mainly."

He stared at her. "Around here, everybody is taking their glasses *off*. Are you sure you aren't waiting for someone to lean over, remove them from your face, and tell you you're beautiful?"

Why did he try to rankle her every few minutes? "I told you, I want to be taken seriously."

"What do you want to be taken seriously *for*? And I'm really listening."

"I want to be a screenwriter," she said, taking a deep gulp from her martini glass. "And don't tell me that's crazy."

"I'm not laughing," he said. "What got you to that?"

"Frances Marion." She paused, waiting for his reaction.

"She was at the top, once. Worked a long time with Mary Pickford. One of the few women still holding on. Good dame, though."

"You're not making some dismissive comment?"

"No, I'm not. Frances Marion's one of the best writers in the business, but it's tough for women now. There's a lot of money to be made here, and men are taking over the jobs. That probably annoys you."

She ignored the gibe. "She came to Smith and gave a wonderful speech. All about taking chances, trying for something different."

Julie couldn't possibly convey how the Hollywood writer's words had inspired her—given her a lifeline, really. Or how appalled her parents were, and how her father roared that she should never have been allowed to go to a women's college like Smith.

"So you dumped your boyfriend and came to Hollywood. How do you know you can write?"

"I've got some ideas. I did some work at school." She refrained from telling him that her work had won admiring praise from her teachers. A classroom was no credential for Hollywood; he wouldn't be impressed.

"How did your parents react to all that after getting you tucked up and ready for a good marriage?"

"Not too well," she confessed. "I've got one year to prove I can do something."

"Then they pull the plug financially?"

"Well, yes. I intend to be fully self-supporting. I'll figure something out." The whole truth? If she wasn't, they would find a way to pull her back home. And she had no intention of going back, which she figured he probably guessed.

He gave her a wry smile as he lifted a hand to signal the waiter to bring yet another round. "One thing you should know up front: most writers you meet in this town are embittered, live in the shadows, are totally undervalued, and have probably never seen a single thing they've written make it to the screen."

"It can't be that bad or they would all leave, wouldn't they?"

He raised his almost finished martini, eyes lively, and kissed her glass with his. "Ah, the reason they stay is simple. They write a few second features, get screen credit once or twice—but there's always the big one just ahead, that plum script that brings an Oscar. Like the donkey, they keep following the carrot ahead of the nose."

"Andy, you really are pretty cynical."

"The truth? It's just a form of self-protection," he said. "I'm rooting for you." He looked at her, his eyes thoughtful.

*

She laughed a lot that night. Andy was funny and smart, and he actually did listen, and she could relax and enjoy herself for the first time since she had stepped off the train four weeks before and found her way to Selznick International.

"What's the best thing about Fort Wayne?" he asked as he polished off his bowl of chili.

It took a minute. She was still too involved with what was the worst—probably the consistent disapproval of her very proper and dusty-dry relatives. You didn't ask *why* things were done a certain way in Fort Wayne—like *why* Negroes were expected to "know their place," or *why* a girl was an old maid if she wasn't married by the age of twenty. Her mother had almost fainted when she gave away her so carefully chosen but unwanted wedding dress to a classmate.

"Catching fireflies in a bottle on a hot summer night," she said, and decided it was true.

She told him about her roommate, a girl from Texas who wanted to be a movie star, and how they'd met while they were both trying to fit their hands into Norma Shearer's prints at Grauman's Chinese. How they had snagged menial jobs in the studio copying room, but Julie wasn't fast enough to type stencils for press releases, only to mimeograph them.

"And why is that?"

"I didn't want to be stuck as a secretary, so I didn't take typing in school," she confessed.

He burst out laughing. "Calculated ineptitude—I like that," he said.

Then it was his turn. He told her he grew up with his nose in books, and cried only once that he could remember, when he was twelve and his dog died. He told her he tried to be popular in high school by telling jokes, and the worst humiliation of his life was when classmates dug into his pockets and found he wrote them all down on scraps of paper so he wouldn't forget the punch lines. He confessed this in such a boyish way, she felt she was the only one who knew. She loved the way his eyes crinkled up when he laughed.

Most of all, the way he looked at her. There was more there, a play of light and shadow, but for now it was enough to dance happily on the surface, sipping martinis with Andy. Hollywood was scary and exciting, and she had no idea what was to come next. But she was here; that alone was a victory. Her parents wouldn't approve, but she was pretty sure Andy was the best thing that had happened to her in a long time.

*

He drove her home; it was quite late by then. She kept the window open, closed her eyes, and inhaled the lush scents of California's sultry evening perfume. She loved that smell. She knew that, wherever she might be from here on, one faint whiff of anything similar would bring her back in a rush to this night, this night when she first met Gable and Lombard and a man named Andy Weinstein.

She thought he was going to kiss her. Surely he started to, simultaneously turning off the engine with one hand and reaching out to stroke the nape of her neck with the other. She imagined it would be as delicious and heady as the air, and she closed her eyes. She could feel his breath.

"Tomorrow morning," he said instead. "Nine o'clock, no later. And the woman to see is Doris Finch. Plain-Jane name, smart woman."

"What?" Julie's eyes flew open.

"The publicity office at the studio. And have your wits about you this time, kiddo."

He got out of the car, came around, and opened her door.

"And by the way—you are pretty, you dope," he said after walking her up the path; he was watching as she turned her key in the lock of the rooming house on Fairfax Avenue. His smile this time was almost mischievous. "How could you not know it?"

She slept well that night.

*

The next morning, Julie arrived early. She walked slowly up the drive of Selznick International Pictures in Culver City, savoring the beauty of the gleaming white building with its graceful pillars. Selznick's mansion was supposed to be a replica of George Washington's Mount Vernon, but she imagined it as Tara, and played with the idea that she was walking toward home, feeling the gentle swaying of her skirts, hearing the bustle of the plantation. . . .

A sudden sharp honk blared, and she jumped away from a fast-approaching car. It passed unnervingly close, close enough for her to catch a glimpse of the man she had so stupidly not recognized yesterday on the platform. Clark Gable did not look happy. Julie caught a quick flash of a blond head next to him, but whether it was Carole Lombard she couldn't tell.

*

Voices were muted in the crowded publicity department. That was because there was a great deal of shouting coming from Selznick's office down the hall, and all were pretending not to hear. But the voices were reverberating too loudly through the main corridor for the pretense to work.

The only person who looked unconcerned was Andy. He sat casually on a desk, twirling a pencil in his fingers, talking to a smiling woman with long legs and dark hair pulled back in lush, sculpted waves. Julie had tried for that style, but she couldn't make it work—her hair was too thick. She knew instantly this was Doris, and she had better stop thinking about her hair if she wanted to make a decent impression.

Andy looked up and beckoned. Doris swiveled in her chair and met Julie's eyes with a cool gaze that told Julie all she needed to know. This woman was not her friend.

"Well, hello there. You're the girl who got in trouble with Selznick yesterday? Good thing you met his favorite protégé—our golden boy here." She tossed a grin at Andy.

"She's got more going for her than I do," Andy cut in as the shouts from Selznick's office grew louder. "Lombard is in her corner. Doris, meet Julie, and vice versa."

They stared at each other. Doris blinked at almost the same time Julie did.

"Well—" Doris began.

The door to Selznick's office suddenly blew open, slammed back with enough force to crack the plaster. Gable straddled the entry, his physical presence stopping all conversation. Nothing quivered on the man except, oddly, his pupils. They seemed to be part of the audience to his indignation, just like all the other eyes in the room. He strode out, his face registering fury, which only made his presence in the room more powerful. Julie drew in her breath— could there be a more masculine man than this one? Probably every woman in the room would consider succumbing, even now—when he looked ready to kill somebody.

He strode past them, head up, moving toward the front door. Behind him, framed in the doorway, Selznick stood with arms folded, watching coldly—the man in charge, made of stone. Next to him, Carole Lombard, dressed again in flowing pants and what looked like the same wrinkled shirt from yesterday, stared after Gable.

"Hey, Pa!" she yelled.

Gable stopped and looked back.

"Sweetie, you're the King," she called out. Her voice was so huge, so soothing, it swallowed the air in the room. Even the phones, respectfully, went silent. "And every fucking person in this building knows that," she continued. "Not to mention everyone in the fucking country. So why don't you come on back here, and we'll work this little squabble out? Come on, Pa. For me."

Gable paused near the door, the muscles of his handsome face working. Pulling himself up straight, he slowly pivoted, a full theatrical turn. He glared at Selznick, then walked with measured steps through the silent room back to the producer's office. Lombard reached out and tweaked his ear, grinning. Turning, all three retreated and closed the door.

A collective sigh of relief stirred movement, followed by the hum of business as usual. The phones were ringing again; permission had somehow been granted to resume.

"Same problem?" Andy asked, looking singularly unimpressed.

Doris leaned back in her chair, picked up a nail file, and drew it sharply across a broken nail. Julie winced at the sound.

"Same as before. He isn't getting the royal MGM treatment here, and he's afraid he isn't up to the part," she answered. "And you never heard it from me."

"He wouldn't derail this movie."

"Of course not. But he's still scared, and he doesn't want Cukor."

"We both know why."

"Well, the *public* reason is that Cukor is masterful at directing women, not so good at directing men." She paused, then added, "Gable needs Lombard more now than ever."

"When is his divorce final?"

"When his wife finally gets the money she wants and settles. MGM is sweetening the pot. Couldn't be soon enough for Carole."

They both chuckled companionably, and Julie felt frustrated.

"Excuse me," she began.

Doris looked up with a faint smile, and Julie had the distinct impression she hadn't been forgotten at all. "Well, since you're such a favorite of Lombard's, we'll have you escort her to this afternoon's interview," Doris said. "You go with her and we'll see how you do. There'll be someone with you to show you the ropes."

*

The "someone with you" turned out to be Rose, her roommate and partner in the mimeograph room. Rose was just as bewildered over what "the ropes" were as Julie was.

"Just you and me?" she said with astonishment. "What are we supposed to do?"

Julie had no answer. She and Rose shared a mutual low-grade desperation because neither was good at her job, but this was worse.

Rose could type a little, though she was always dabbing correction fluid over her pages, and when Julie copied them, the corrections turned black and looked terrible.

"Kind of moth-eaten," Rose had admitted one day when Julie showed her a particularly messy page. "They're going to fire me, I know."

"Retype it and let's try again," Julie said. This was one way to forge a friendship, and it worked.

But now they were at a loss.

*

Andy was heading out the door of the studio office when Julie grabbed him. "What do I do?" she asked. "What do they want?"

He looked a little surprised. "You'll figure it out," he said. "You're there to keep the reporter on his toes—just look stern and clear your throat once in a while."

"Andy, please, be serious."

He now looked fully astonished. "What are you worried about? You've got access to Lombard, so now figure out how to make the best of it. Dinner tonight?" He plucked his hat off the rack by the door, adjusted the brim, and put it on.

"I'll think about it," she said.

"Suit yourself."

Was that a flicker of disappointment in his eyes? Well, if he couldn't give her a little more support, it was too bad.

He turned the door handle and was gone before she could change her mind.

CHAPTER 3

*J*ulie and Rose made their way past the scorched back lot to get to Lombard's dressing room, an opulently outfitted trailer, which was on the far side of the studio grounds. Dozens of trucks filled with brick dust were lumbering one by one onto the field, dumping their loads as crews on the ground armed with rakes combed the coppery-red silt into the scorched soil.

"Someone told me it's to make it look like Southern clay," Rose said. "Mr. Selznick wants every detail to be perfect. He's amazing."

"How can they work so fast? And to start building Tara on top of this tomorrow . . ." Julie shook her head, squinting into the afternoon sun as they walked along the edges of the lot, steering clear of the powdery brick dust curling into the air.

"It is kind of magical, isn't it?" Rose said shyly. "Aren't we lucky to be here?"

Julie nodded, grateful that Rose felt the same thump of excitement in her breast. Maybe they were just starstruck newcomers. Maybe seeing the mechanics of it all might eventually drain the magic out. But they were here, right now, part of the movie world— albeit on the edge. Anything could happen.

"Afraid we'll get disillusioned?" she asked, thinking of Andy's wry, almost mocking take on his own world.

"Not me," Rose said firmly. "Anything I don't want to see, I'll just close my eyes."

Julie pondered that briefly, wondering if she could do the same.

And there they were again, the two voices inside of her, one arguing for reality and the other for dreams. She had to fly *somewhere*.

She glanced at Rose with a touch of envy. Rose might look fragile, but she probably knew how to set boundaries and lock gates better than Julie did.

*

They reached the dressing room next to the soundstage where Lombard was wrapping up her movie *Made for Each Other.* Sitting on the trailer steps was an impatient-looking reporter in baggy pants who made a point of staring at his watch as they walked toward him.

"Our appointment was one o'clock," he said. "It's five after. I've been waiting for you studio people, but I do have a deadline and—"

The door to the dressing room burst open, and there was Carole Lombard. She wore a shimmery satin gown that all but slithered across her body, barely covering her breasts. It could have been a nightgown—Julie wasn't sure—but it took her breath away to see how confidently Lombard wore it. She looked amazingly beautiful.

"Oh, quit complaining," Lombard said brightly to the reporter, beckoning them all in. "I saw you out here and figured you could toast your heels for a while. You'll get a good interview." She laughed. "For starters, I'm wearing nothing under this dress; want that for your lead? Where are you from?"

"The *Reading Eagle,* Pennsylvania," he said, brightening considerably. "I hear you're signing for a new movie?"

"In negotiation," she said. "But I'm signing a helluva lot of autographs. When I think of the bunk I've written on them, I get sick."

It was too late for Julie to clear her throat.

Lombard's sitting room was simple but quite elegant. Not that Julie had ever been in a star's dressing room, of course. But the carpet, a deep forest green, looked lush and expensive. The sofa and two chairs were covered with a muted brocade fabric, and the coffee table was sleek and white. Screens hid the makeup room, but she could see past them to an array of mirrors over the dressing table. Large bouquets of ivory-cream roses were everywhere.

The reporter—his name, he told them with a certain huffiness, was Jeff Malone—settled on the sofa. Julie and Rose perched on the chairs, trying to look businesslike.

"First time doing chaperone duty, girls?" Lombard said, flopping down on the sofa next to Malone. "Good luck—nobody shuts me up."

The phone on the table beside her rang. She picked it up, listened for an impatient second or two, then rolled her eyes. "Me, play a violin? I'd look like a screwball. Now, if you want someone who can shoot a .410 shotgun, I'm your woman." She hung up.

The reporter said quickly, "I didn't know you hunted . . . ?" The phone was ringing again.

"Skeet shooting," she said as she picked up the receiver. "Clark likes to kill birds; I prefer to kill clay disks. Less blood. Though I wouldn't mind taking shots at producers." She listened for a second to the new voice on the phone. "Can we please get these details wrapped?" she said. "Yes, I definitely want the fucking house; sweetheart, I'm planning on giving a party there next week—you're invited. The guest of honor is going to be either a bear or a lion. Haven't decided." She all but tossed the phone into its cradle this time.

"You and Gable are officially a couple?"

She laughed. "Of course," she said. "Okay, let's get to it—you want me to talk about sex. I think sex is wonderful and therapeutic, and girls here in Hollywood should quit being obsessed with losing their virginity. And no double standard. Men who stray should be forgiven, and I want the same freedom for myself. That cover it for you?"

Malone's jaw dropped. He nodded.

Rose glanced at Julie, clearly horrified. Julie kept her face serene, but her thoughts were spinning. Were they supposed to do something? Did Lombard mean all that? Wasn't her relationship with Gable still sort of a secret? Then again, how could it be, since they were so openly and exuberantly a couple?

"Miss Lombard reserves the right to make that off the record," Julie blurted out. "It's, um, required for the interview." She had no idea what she was doing, other than trying to protect the actress somehow. Probably more like stepping in front of a speeding truck.

Lombard looked at her with interest. "That's all right, kiddo," she said. "Thanks, though, for putting your fists up."

Malone was in a daze. He scribbled away for half an hour, his questions interspersed with Lombard's phone calls, before Lombard told him briskly, "Time's up. You satisfied?"

"Yes, ma'am," he said.

"Send us copies," she said, and then glanced at the younger women with amusement. "That's what you're supposed to say, girls."

"Of course." Julie flushed. "Please send copies to our publicity department."

"Sure." Malone got up, opened the door, and started to leave. He turned around with one last question: "Do you ever get tired of the pace?"

Lombard didn't respond immediately. The phone was ringing again, but she didn't seem in a hurry to answer it this time. "Let me put it this way," she said. "I want to live a natural life before I'm an old lady."

"And what does that mean?"

"Eventually, I'd like to get off the pogo stick."

"How do you do that?"

And her answer, which stuck somewhere in the recesses of Julie's mind: "When I make my last movie, I'm going to tell them to bill it as 'Lombard's farewell appearance,'" the actress said matter-of-factly. "And I tell you, when they put that on the billboards, it will be true."

Malone left, a very happy man with a full notebook.

Lombard started to close the door after him, and stopped. She peered down the path and let out an impatient sigh. "So here comes another visitor," she said. "Have you girls met Jerry Bryant yet?"

"Who is he?" Julie asked.

"Unofficially? He's head morality cop for Selznick International

Pictures and the Legion of Decency, rolled into one." She smiled at Julie's confused look. "He's the head studio publicist. His job is to keep trouble and scandal out of the papers, and right now I'm not one of his favorite people."

The man climbing the stairs to the door was buttoning a suit jacket that strained across an ample belly. His hair, a bald patch at the crown, was gray. He didn't look happy. But as he stared up at Carole, his round face took on an expression of rehearsed cordiality.

"Well, well, Carole, another unsupervised interview? Why didn't you call me, sweetheart? Remember me? I'm here to keep you out of trouble." He flashed a stiff grin, revealing a mouth of unusually small, sparkling teeth.

"Actually, my dear Jerry, you're here to keep Selznick International out of trouble. Too late. The world's most scandalous interview is over, and now we can all cower, waiting for the deluge. How can I help you?"

"What did he ask you?"

"My opinion, of course, on whether that handsome Mr. Roosevelt is sitting in the White House plotting ways to drag us into a European war. Well, I told *him* a thing or two."

Jerry hesitated. Then, "You do like your jokes," he muttered as he stepped into the trailer—and noticed Julie and Rose for the first time. "Who are these?" he said.

"Really, Jerry. Where are your manners? 'These' are the two young women your girl Doris sent over to supervise the interview. They did a fine job. Anything else? I'm shooting a scene in a few minutes."

Uninvited, Bryant sat down, ignoring the pair. "This must be Doris's idea of a joke, sending two copying room girls to supervise. They're as green as Hollywood grass," he said, irritated. "But that's not important. I'm here on another errand—it won't take too much of your time."

"And what is that?"

He pulled a notebook out of his pocket. "Routine information," he said.

Carole remained standing, folding her arms. "What?"

He flipped open the notebook, pulled a pen from his breast pocket, snapped it open, and said, "I need to know your menstrual cycle."

"*What?* You can't be serious."

Julie and Rose looked at each other in astonishment.

"Carole, let's not make a major issue out of this. Your menstrual cycle, understand? That should be easy enough. We keep records on all the actresses; every major studio does." He tapped his notebook with his pen and waited expectantly. "It's important, sweetheart. For water scenes, cramps, mood problems—those things."

Carole started to laugh, a from-the-belly laugh. "Jerry, you dirty dog—do you want to fuck me?"

Bryant paled, then blushed scarlet before recovering. "I'd love to, dear, but I know I haven't got a chance," he said. "This is just routine. What if we have to shoot an ocean shot? Claudette Colbert had no objections. For heaven's sake, we don't need shooting schedules ruined—that would be a disaster."

Carole was laughing so hard she could barely speak. "Jerry, you're just doing your job, though the mandate seems a bit twisted, but how convenient this information must be for the studio brass. Somebody's planning for fucking, and I know it. Sorry, my menstrual cycle is privileged information. I wouldn't even give it to President Roosevelt."

Bryant didn't protest. "This will go higher up," he warned.

"I don't care."

Resigned, he closed his notebook and sighed heavily. "You are not easy, sweetheart."

"You're damn right." She leaned close as he prepared to step out of the trailer and kissed him on the forehead. "You're not a bad egg," she said. "Thanks for giving us a good laugh."

He worked hard trying to rearrange his face, but it wasn't quite in place as he hurried away.

Lombard's energy seemed to leave her as abruptly as air from a balloon. She sat on the sofa, swung her legs up, and plopped her head into the pillows. She reached for a cigarette. "Don't look so shell-shocked, girls," she said with a grin. "It's okay. They call me the Profane Angel, right? It's a smoke screen. It keeps men a little scared of me. I assume you both want to be in pictures?"

Julie shook her head in the negative. "Not acting," she said.

"I do," Rose allowed. She said it quite calmly, and Julie was struck by how large her friend's eyes were. Her mouth, full and pink, was parted in an uncertain smile.

Lombard nodded slowly, looking Rose up and down. "You are gorgeous, dearie—so why not?"

Rose blinked. "Why not?" she repeated weakly.

"I'll see what I can do. What's your name?"

"Rose Sullivan."

"You'll have to change that, of course. I shed mine as fast as I could when I got out of Indiana. Who wants to drag around a dreary moniker like 'Jane Alice Peters'?"

"I'm from Indiana," Julie volunteered.

Lombard looked at her with a curious smile. "You're the messenger Andy Weinstein took a shine to. Where in Indiana?"

"Fort Wayne, just like you."

"Well, well. We tend to speak our minds, we girls from Fort Wayne. Did you think that reporter could harm me?"

"I didn't know. I wanted to tell him he couldn't just write anything he wanted to."

"And what drew you to Hollywood?"

"I want to write movies."

"Like Frances Marion?"

"Yes." There, she had put herself with one word in the company of her role model, someone who was brilliant and had made it here, and she was thrilled that Lombard knew her name. Nobody at home did. And for just an instant something shimmered in her mundane connection with the star. Maybe it was because she had already decided she really liked this casual, profane woman who said what she wanted and did as she pleased.

"Are you any good?" Lombard asked.

"I don't know. My college English teacher thinks so." It was restful, just stating it that way. She sensed Carole wouldn't laugh.

"That plus a helluva lot of determination might get you somewhere someday."

"I hope so." She felt almost giddy. In a world of make-believe, maybe she had met a woman at the top who was real.

*

"Your friend Rose got touched with a magic wand this afternoon," Andy said, walking up behind Julie in the publicity office as she was stapling the last press releases of the day. "Lombard got her an interview—and a tryout for Scarlett."

"That was fast," Julie said, surprised.

"Selznick is auditioning every promising actress he can find. Your friend from Texas will be lacing up a corset in a couple of days. Want to watch?"

"Yes, I would love to." Could it really work like this? Did it mean Rose had a chance?

"Any feeling of being left out?"

Julie thought about it. "No," she said. "I would if I had the same ambition for acting that Rose has, I guess."

He smiled; she liked his smile when it came from the warmth of his eyes.

"A nonglamorous dinner with me as a booby prize?"

She nodded. Why had she been so prickly earlier? Two amazing days in a row, and a sanity check with Andy Weinstein after each one. That really wasn't a booby prize.

"I've got another piece of news for you," he said later, as they settled into a booth at a cheerfully noisy place on Wilshire with red linoleum and greasy menus.

"Something good?"

"Carole Lombard wants you to work as her personal assistant."

Julie dropped her menu, which landed dangerously near the flickering candle in the middle of their small table. "She does?"

"She told Doris late this afternoon. Said she liked the idea of having a hometown girl on her staff. Especially one with the guts to speak up."

"Oh my goodness, she makes fast decisions."

"You're not unhappy about that, are you? This gives you a nice edge, but I'm sure Doris would love to stick you back into the mimeograph room. She was not pleased about losing both you and Rose at one whack."

"I'm thrilled, Andy." She meant it fervently.

Andy looked at her with an expression she couldn't quite fathom. "I like bearing you good news," he said.

*

It didn't take long. Rose was called for her screen test only two days later.

Julie scrambled to help her get ready, both of them breathless and nervous. "Green eye shadow," Julie advised, remembering Vivien Leigh's makeup. "Lots of it."

When they reached the soundstage, which was cluttered with hovering cameras, they saw a row of bright-faced women sitting in chairs, all dressed in Civil War gowns of the 1860s.

"An assembly line," Rose murmured, and some of the light faded in her eyes.

Julie thought she recognized Paulette Goddard, who Andy said was still Selznick's favorite for the part. But maybe it was Jean Arthur—Julie wasn't sure. Sitting in a canvas chair behind the cameras was David O. Selznick, tipped back, glasses on his nose, staring straight ahead. Once, he glanced at his watch. Julie could have sworn everyone around him began moving faster.

"Rose Sullivan."

Rose squeezed Julie's hand and, following an assistant, walked through a door leading to the wardrobe department.

Only minutes later, she emerged, caught Julie's eye, and gave a wide smile.

Julie gasped. Her friend looked beautiful. Wardrobe had dressed her in a cream silk gown with a frothy tulle bodice cut very low, and Julie could see the modest Rose trying discreetly to pull it higher. She shook her head warningly in a quick motion, and Rose dropped her hands.

Do it their way. That's what the two of them had whispered to each other late into the night. "The truth is, I have nothing to lose," Rose had said, sounding far more sensible than Julie feared she would be if she were the one trying out for the part.

Again someone called out Rose's name, beckoning her onto the set.

Rose lifted her head high and walked gracefully before the cameras, appearing totally serene. A slightly bored-looking actor playing Ashley for the screen tests stepped up next to her.

"Okay," Selznick said. His voice was strong and brisk. "Rose—it is Rose, right?—in this scene, you are confessing your undying love for Ashley Wilkes, exposing your heart and soul. We're only doing one take per actress, so let's see what you can do." He signaled his assistant. "Roll cameras," he said.

The clapperboard went down.

Rose clasped her hands together, looking up at the stand-in, bursting with barely contained emotion. "I am in love with you, Ashley," she began.

The cameras rolled for fewer than five minutes, but it was long enough to impress Julie. Rose, without artifice, had transformed herself for those brief moments into Scarlett O'Hara. She really *was* a natural actress. Had Lombard sensed that?

"Thank you, young lady," Selznick said when the cameras stopped. "We'll get back to you. Next!"

And that was all.

*

Those first weeks working for Carole Lombard increased Julie's heart rate permanently, she was sure of that. To be around such a whirlpool of energy was to spin in the dizziest orbit she could ever imagine. She had no chance to slip into melancholy at Christmas, what with helping Carole swathe her trailer in festive red and green garlands and trying to keep propped up a slightly dizzy-looking tree adorned with lights and mounds of tangled tinsel. She was grateful to be able to pour out the stories to Andy. Not every night, but often now they had dinner together, either at Chasen's or at the cozy greasy spoon with sticky menus. Julie loved both. Andy would chuckle as she described how Carole burst through doors rather than walk through them. How she laughed, how she swore—as *Life* magazine put it—with "the expletives of a sailor's parrot." How she got up earlier than everybody else and played tennis with such ferocity she almost always won; how she never stopped moving. Her idea of a personal assistant was someone who paid her department-store bills, bought her Kotex, booked manicures, fed gossip queen Louella Parsons a few bright tidbits every week, glared at reporters during newspaper interviews, read to her, ran errands for Clark, and was ready for any kind of assignment at all.

That included negotiating with Gay's Lion Farm for the rental of a lion for her party, maybe a mountain lion—preferably on a leash? Like the one Herman Mankiewicz rented when the Columbia University football team played in the Rose Bowl? ("His alma mater, you know; the fight song is something like 'Roar, lion, roar.' If they don't have one, tell them a goat will do as well. Honey, whatever it is, will you pick it up?")

Andy loved that.

*

Carole surprised Julie one afternoon. "Any chance I can read some of your work?" she said.

"I have some essays; they're not really complete," Julie said, flustered.

"Well, get moving. You're too smart to be fielding Louella Parsons and hauling goats around town for very long."

She brought some material the next day, blathering something about how these were drafts, works in progress, that sort of thing, until Carole cut her off.

"Cripes, your English teacher liked it, right? Don't apologize in advance, just read." Carole did her usual, flopping down on the sofa, closing her eyes, and putting her feet up.

Julie chose a treatment for a story about a campus murder endowed with what her professor had called "unusual plot twists" that got her an A in his class. It didn't sound so great as she read. It sounded schoolgirlish.

She finished and put it down, annoyed with herself for ever having boasted to Carole about her writing prowess.

"Not bad," Carole said calmly. "Want to practice? Try writing a scene for *Gone with the Wind*. Lord knows, David has everybody else in town working on it."

"Are you serious?"

"Why not? Be audacious. You don't have to show anybody unless you want to. And don't wring your hands over it—it's not all about writing something brilliant. You have to put together a good act. Inhale the damn thing. Then become it. Hell, that's what actors do." She looked steadily at Julie, her expression thoughtful, and changed the subject. "Are you related to the Crawfords who used to own half of Fort Wayne?" she asked.

Julie flushed. She didn't want to be labeled again; she had spent enough time living down her lineage. She nodded reluctantly.

"Well, well. I'll keep your secret, dear."

"I don't have a secret," Julie said, startled.

"You're trying to unstick yourself from a pretty important and stodgy family and figure out your own life, am I right?"

"How do you know?"

"Honey, out here, we're all peeling off something. It's a toss-up over who has the most baggage—a high-school dropout like my Clark, or a girl from Smith."

*

The next evening, Julie ran the idea by Andy of writing a *Gone with the Wind* scene, knowing he would listen, but not sure whether she would get a funny, cynical response that would make her laugh. He had been too busy for dinner the past few days, and she missed him. Some dispute between the Screen Writers Guild and the studios, he said. Ostensibly about pay. Whether the communists were infiltrating the guild was the real issue. "We weave in and out of the real world in this racket," he said with a shrug. He was obviously not interested in saying more. The first day of principal shooting was rapidly approaching, and he was absorbed with work. Part of his job was tracking and organizing production logistics for the movie, and she could see the strain on his face.

He did listen, nodding with the gravity of any one of her professors, making no disparaging comments this time about a writer's fate.

"Carole's a smart broad," he said.

"Is that a compliment?"

"You better believe it."

She felt emboldened. "What about me?"

"If you weren't, I wouldn't be wasting my time with you."

"And if you weren't smart and funny and kind, I wouldn't be wasting my time with *you*."

A ghost of a smile—a flicker of that elusive shadow she could never quite pin down. "Good girl," he said.

It was late by the time Andy drove her home, taking the long way, along the undulating road known as Mulholland Drive, high above Sunset Boulevard. He had lapsed into silence. It was as if he were somewhere else, and she wondered if something had gone wrong between them.

"Andy, are you here?" she said, touching his shoulder after several moments of silence had gone by. "Everything okay?"

Without comment, Andy steered the car into a clearing that overlooked the lights of the city on one side, the San Fernando Valley on the other. He pulled on the brake. She loved this view—the sweep of the city, the glittering lights all the way to the unseen night sea at the horizon. She loved smelling winter wildflowers scattered through the dry brush. But right now her heart was hammering in a peculiar way, and she waited.

He clicked off the ignition. "I'm worried about *Gone with the Wind*."

She felt a guilty surge of relief. "What's happened?"

"I'm not sure this movie is ever going to get made," he said slowly. "Selznick is brilliant—he's the best in the business—but his need to control everything has gone past rational limits."

"Isn't that his strength?"

"Sure. And don't get me wrong: I love my job. Working with a genius like Selznick is usually just plain fun."

"Sometimes you hide that well," she teased.

"I'm part cynic and part schoolboy," he said with a small sigh. "But I'm worried that he loses perspective."

"Like when?"

"Biggest one? Ignoring the objections of Negroes—and their papers, like the *Los Angeles Sentinel*. Ever look at it?"

Julie shook her head, feeling guilty.

"It's not as if they're all angry because we're making the movie— hell, Negro actors are thrilled for the work. And their newspapers, organizations—they don't all want the same thing. But he's got to listen better."

Julie thought of the book. "They're all happy 'darkies,' and no one's too worried about slavery. Is that it?"

He looked at her and smiled. "Pretty obvious, isn't it?" His smile quickly faded. "That's just one example. He's obsessed with this story. He can't let a single detail go, and it could kill him. If this movie falls apart, we'll all crash." He put his head back and closed his eyes. "The damn script—all the different versions—fill four suitcases. Nothing is good enough for Selznick. Do you know how many women he's considered to play Scarlett? Just about every major actress in Hollywood, plus hundreds more. At least he isn't testing all of them. We're already two years behind schedule."

He didn't seem to need any further response from her, which was good, because she could think of nothing to say. But she felt comforted that he would tell her all this.

"Did you read what Gary Cooper told Louella this week? Said the damn movie was going to be a flop, and he was glad it was Gable who was going to fall on his face, not him."

"Maybe he just wishes he had accepted the part of Rhett Butler instead of turning it down," she said.

That brought another flicker of a smile. "Could be, but it feeds all the bastards who want Selznick to fail. You know how he got Gable for the part? Convinced MGM to ante up an extra fifty thousand to pay off that stubborn wife who won't give him a divorce. She says it isn't enough, she wants more—one reason Gable is always in a foul mood." Andy folded his arms across the steering wheel and stared at the glittering lights below. He looked so dejected, Julie reached out and touched his hand.

"Sorry, I'm not great company," he said, turning to her. "It's the cost of working with a true gambler who also happens to be a genius, I guess." He paused, then added, almost wonderingly, "You know, if one thing had gone wrong in the burning-of-Atlanta scene—just one thing—it would all have been over."

He was so close, and surely in need of comfort. Everything in her scolded against what she wanted to do, that it was not proper, but why shouldn't a woman act first?

She moved forward and kissed him hesitantly on the lips.

He didn't respond for a second or two. Then, with a sigh, he pulled her into his arms. The first thing she registered was that his lips smelled faintly of tobacco. The second was, how good they tasted.

He drew back sooner than she wanted. "Can't take advantage of a girl like you in the old Hollywood way," he said, cupping her head in his hands, dropping a gentle kiss on her nose.

"Why not?" she asked recklessly.

"It would be too much of a cliché," he said. "You know, don't you, this is the classic spot in L.A. for discreet deflowering?"

She started to speak, but he put a finger to her mouth. "Don't tell me, I don't want to know if you're a virgin or not."

"Andy—"

He kissed her again, and then slowly pulled away. "Time to take you home, Miss Julie Crawford," he said.

Julie didn't know whether to be embarrassed at her own temerity or hurt by his rejection. She was twelve years younger than he was, but she wasn't a child. They had only known each other for a month, it was true. She fought consternation as they made their way down the winding mountain road—he must be terribly worried, he was burdened by responsibilities, she wanted to help him—but concluded finally that he simply might not be attracted to her. That was devastating. She thought of him all the time. She stared out the window as he chatted about the weather, about the movie. She didn't look at him, just focusing instead on the headlights of drivers on the other side of the looping curves of Sunset Boulevard, growing increasingly miserable. Was this all there was?

They reached the rooming house. She turned to him, first putting her hand firmly on the door handle. "Don't get out," she said coolly. "You obviously don't take me seriously. I'm fine getting up to the door on my own."

"On the contrary, Miss Crawford," he said. "I take you very seriously."

"It doesn't seem like it to me."

He reached out and pushed back a lock of hair from her face, then traced her lips with a finger. "You'll either see it or you won't," he said. "Time will tell."

She couldn't think of a thing to say. "Good night," she managed lamely.

Rose was already asleep when she undressed and slipped into bed. Had Rose heard anything yet about her screen test? Julie wondered. She'd have to wait until morning to find out. Just as well. Her own thoughts were too mixed up for her to concentrate on anything tonight. Andy had invited her in, and then pushed her out.

The thought did occur to her later, just before she fell off to sleep, that if her father knew how properly Andy Weinstein had behaved up on Mulholland Drive, there might have been a faint thaw in what she knew would be his icy disapproval.

*

Somewhere near the end of the week, Selznick triumphantly announced his choice for Scarlett O'Hara: it was indeed to be that beautiful little English actress Julie had seen on the platform the night he burned down Atlanta, Vivien Leigh.

Rose was unfazed. "I never dreamed I would get it," she said, "but I've had a wonderful time."

"You're handling it much more calmly than I would," Julie said.

"Better not to want anything too much," Rose responded. Still, a flicker of wistfulness tugged at her face. "You know who was tested just before me?" she said. "Vivien Leigh. The wardrobe mistress told me they sneaked her in, hardly anybody knew."

"Did you see her?"

"No. But they put me in the same dress; the wardrobe lady told me that. And you know what? It was still warm." Rose lifted two delicate fingers, pressing them together. "I was that close," she said, beaming.

*

The red earth of the Back Forty rumbled with the sound of trucks and hammers and the shouts of workmen hauling paint and plasterboard and roof tiles and paper chandeliers and everything else Selznick demanded. Julie often spied Susan Myrick, a Georgia journalist and friend of Margaret Mitchell's, who was here to make sure Hollywood didn't tamper too much with her old friend's depiction of the antebellum South. She was a woman of serious demeanor, never without a copy of *Gone with the Wind* in her hand, and Julie was too much in awe to approach her. Myrick had already objected to a proposed scene of slaves cutting cotton in April—wrong time of the year, she announced to Selznick. And Scarlett could not carry a bowl of olives into the dining room, because olives were not grown on Georgia plantations. But Myrick lost her fight to build Tara without columns—which were never envisioned by Mitchell—to a stubborn Selznick, who conceded only to making them Georgia style—square, not round.

And now here it was, in front of Julie—the home of Scarlett O'Hara, a pillared white mansion standing proud and seemingly unbreakable. Unless you blew too heavily. That was the joke, but you only heard it from the construction workers.

A fairy-tale city was taking shape on this sweep of land, so amazing that Julie could, at least once in a while, get Andy out of her thoughts. The rapidly growing set was impervious to the honking horns and grubby hurrying of Culver City. It wasn't just Tara: a network of the streets and houses of Atlanta was springing up, and the scene expanded every day.

Each morning, she pulled herself from bed and joined the cleaning ladies and the plumbers and other sleepy travelers on the 5:00 a.m. bus to get to the studio early. That way, she could step onto the back lot alone and be in the old South and feel the magical world of *Gone with the Wind* come to life. In front of Tara, the trees that had been fashioned over telephone poles looked real, and if she hadn't known the dogwood blossoms were made of white paper, the illusion would have been complete. It just took believing. She loved watching it grow—over fifty building façades now, and two miles of streets. It didn't matter that she walked in a landscape of glued plasterboard, a place of fake structures held together by little more than Selznick's frenzied dreams. It was vividly real.

And—if she came early enough—deserted. So the morning she saw a sole figure standing in front of Scarlett's home, hands shoved in his pockets, hunched forward, collar up against the cold, it almost felt like an intrusion on her personal territory. Until she realized who it was.

David Selznick glanced up and saw her. She was shocked at how strained and spidered with red his eyes were. He looked like a man who didn't sleep. There were rumors that he was living on Benzedrine and gambling every night until three in the morning, and that his marriage was shaky. All this before principal filming had even begun. But his passion for perfection was legendary: Horses' tails had to be cropped in exactly the fashion of the Civil War; furniture had to be aged so it looked authentic. The gowns and uniforms had to be exact replicas of Civil War clothing, and not just the clothing that would show. Vivien Leigh was complaining vigorously about the dauntingly rigid whalebone corset she would be forced to wear, to no avail. The edict from Selznick was firm.

"Spectacular, isn't it?" he said, looking at her without a glimmer of recognition.

"Yes," she said.

"Every goddamn critic in town says I'm a jackass for taking this on. So what do they think gets accomplished if somebody with guts doesn't roll the dice every now and then?" He was staring at Tara now.

Was he talking to himself? She stepped back, sure now she had intruded on a soliloquy.

"We start shooting tomorrow," he said. "Right here. Scarlett will sit on those steps. I'm going to make a movie nobody will ever forget." He beckoned to her. "Come on, take a peek at history in the making."

There didn't seem to be any option, so Julie followed him up the stairs. He reached out to touch the knob on the door that was supposed to open onto the front hall of Tara, then pulled back.

"It's not much more than cardboard," he said with an offhand shrug, "but more real to me than a lot of damn things around here."

Julie stayed silent. He wasn't expecting a reply.

"Hell, nothing wrong with a good façade," he continued. "Just like everything else in Hollywood. It's enough for me."

Without another word, he turned, walked slowly down the steps, and strode away.

CHAPTER 4

JANUARY 26, 1939

*N*othing nervous about this happy crowd, I'd say," murmured Doris, surveying the field where she and dozens of others stood waiting. Her speech had its usual cynical tone, delivered with a roll of the eyes and a wry, impatient twist of the mouth—not quite a smirk. It occurred to Julie that Doris sounded a little too much like the wisecracking, flip Rosalind Russell. Maybe it wasn't just coincidence. Lots of girls here were walking around emulating some star they wished they could be. Why not tough, sexy Doris? Thinking about it made her less intimidating, if not more likable.

Still, she was right. A roll of jittery chatter was threading through the huddled crowd of people on the edge of the Back Forty.

Selznick had invited everybody who worked at the studio to watch the "festivities" of the first day of shooting, a word that had produced a fair number of snickers among those who knew how fraught with problems this venture was. You could see it in the director George Cukor's rigid stance. He held himself immobile in the restless crowd, arms folded, a set expression on his face.

Julie scanned the crowd, trying to pick out the critics and journalists, several of whom looked enlivened by the prospect for disaster. It wasn't hard to recognize the columnist Hedda Hopper. She had the alert, bright-eyed face of a parrot as she darted here and there; her lips were heavy with bright-red lipstick; her eyes—lined in black makeup that looked as permanent as cement—missing nothing, peering out from under a flamboyantly feathered hat.

"Look at her glare at Louella," Doris said, amused. "Probably thinks she muscled herself in to get a better spot for watching the filming. She'll have something to say about *that* in tomorrow's column. Those two could kill each other."

Julie's gaze turned to Louella Parsons. By contrast, she looked like a proper matron heading for a proper afternoon tea. She was much shorter than Hedda, her plump body encased in something made of heavy, dark wool with glittering no-nonsense gold buttons the size of Ping-Pong balls. Her face was set on dignified affability, but her eyes looked like small rocks.

Julie knew this was the one to watch. Louella had hinted in her column today that the careers of several important people working on *Gone with the Wind* were about to be destroyed. It was a tantalizing, airy warning, meant to send shivers down the back of anyone who tried to withhold a scoop from her.

So that was in the buzz circulating through the crowd—who was at risk?

And, Lord, there was the script. *Everyone* knew that was a disaster. Andy had said it was literally a mountain of paper with colored tabs marking the contributions of dozens of writers. The rumor going through the crowd was that Selznick was bringing in Ben Hecht for yet another rewrite. And what about the noises from the Screen Writers Guild? Were they really going to announce a strike?

And on it went. The less prominent reporters strained to hear it all, looking like fluttering crows as they hovered close to the cameras, trying to eavesdrop on Selznick's instructions to the crew.

Suddenly there was a furious shout.

"Look, there's Gable," Rose whispered. "What now?"

An angry-looking Clark Gable, jacket flapping, came striding toward Selznick, ignoring everyone in his path. "Those signs come down *now*," he shouted.

"What signs?" Selznick said, obviously startled.

Gable pointed to a nearby knoll where a long line of portable toilets stood ready. The usual necessity for movies shot with hundreds of extras, they had been placed a distance from the cameras, winding down the knoll like dominoes in a row. They were painted a dull green, a color that discreetly blended into the landscape.

Except for the signs.

In large block letters, they declared their instructions on each toilet: WHITE ONLY, read the first one; NEGRO ONLY, read the second. And on down the line, the declarative instructions repeated in calm symmetry.

"Where's the property manager?" Gable demanded. "David, I'm off this movie if those signs don't come down."

Selznick stared—and swore. He threw down the clipboard in his hands. A confused silence fell on the crowd.

"Who the hell put those up?" he yelled. His face was almost purple. "We're not in the Deep South, we're in Culver City, California!"

The reporters were scribbling fast, and the photographers were scrambling to take pictures of the toilets. In the jostling for position, Hedda lost her hat and sputtered in outrage. The "festivities" had taken an unexpected turn.

All Julie could think was, how could it be that no one had *noticed*?

Cukor jumped into action. "I don't know who authorized that, but yank 'em down," he ordered a maintenance crewman. "Right now, before one foot of film is shot." He cast a quick look at Gable. "Thanks, Clark," he said.

Julie now saw a small cluster of extras dressed as slaves standing to the side. As she learned later, one of them had gone up to Gable's dressing room, knocked on the door, and asked him to intervene. This surely took courage.

"They're no dumbbells," Doris chortled, nodding at the group. "They know Selznick can't fire them and replace them with Mexicans—not for this movie."

"Okay, folks," shouted Selznick through a bullhorn. "We've got *that* stupidity corrected; now let's get on with making a movie."

Julie craned to see Andy. She caught a glimpse of him staring at the scene as the signs were ripped down, a slight smile on his face. He saw her and gave a quick thumbs-up. Then he was back in conversation with the lighting crew, checking his clipboard, calling for the sound people. It was fun to watch him. He moved so easily, genially, talking to someone, scribbling a reply to a message, joking with the messenger, listening intently—and making it all look so relaxed.

Gable stayed briefly in place, the fury on his face fading into a kind of vague puzzlement, as if he wondered where he was. He had made no secret that he would not hang around for filming *Gone with the Wind*'s inaugural scene. Then, frowning, he turned on his heel and strode back to his dressing room.

"Julie honey, David's got one reluctant Rhett Butler, and he'll stay away as much as he can," Carole had said with a sigh earlier that morning.

Selznick's shouted order accelerated everything. Cameramen were wheeling their cameras into place. Gaffers raced about checking electrical equipment; soundmen adjusted their instruments; secretaries were scribbling notes and running errands.

Julie went on tiptoe, peering at Tara. The first scene to be shot would be the opening one of the movie. Scarlett was to sit on the steps of her grand Southern home, flirting with two of her swains. She was to pout when they spoiled the mood by telling her that war was coming—and they were enlisting.

Vivien Leigh, escorted by George Cukor, was already draping herself carefully on the steps of Tara. He held her hand, gently moving her into position. She leaned her head back against a pillar, listening to his soothing words, giving small, birdlike nods of assent. A makeup person armed with a soft powdered brush, intent on reducing the shine from the lights on Vivien Leigh's face, dabbed at the actress's nose. A wardrobe assistant fussed over her flowered muslin gown, fluffing the rich folds of material and spreading them wide. "I can't breathe in this corset," Leigh complained loudly, but no one was paying attention.

Finally, all was ready.

"Quiet on set!" a production assistant bellowed. Looking quite solemn, he lifted a black-and-white clapperboard high. On it was scrawled in chalk:

SCENE ONE, TAKE ONE—GONE WITH THE WIND

He clapped the boards together, producing a sharp, command-ing sound that brought immediate quiet. *Gone with the Wind* was about to be brought to life.

Up the gravel path, across the green lawn, the cameras travel to Tara. Scarlett sits framed beautifully on the graceful porch. Her voice is deli-ciously lilting and teasing as she begins flirting with the Tarleton twins, scolding them for their talk of war. Vivien Leigh—with her boredom and corset complaints—has disappeared. Scarlett O'Hara is sitting there now.

To Julie, all seemed perfect. To be drawn into this scene so quickly, in a way that was both the same as and yet different from when she burrowed into Margaret Mitchell's magical book, was enthralling. The colors, the clothes, the mood—

"Cut!" Selznick barked.

Cukor glanced at Selznick in astonishment. His usual amiable smile vanished. A producer didn't issue orders on the set: that was the job and prerogative of the director. "What's wrong?" he said. "The scene was perfect."

Selznick shoved his hands into his pockets and strode up to the waiting actors, frowning. "The dress isn't right," he said to Cukor, pulling one hand out of his pocket and flipping disdainfully at a sleeve of Scarlett's gorgeous gown. "Call Wardrobe. I want her to wear pure white—not the same damn dress she wears to the barbe-cue. That's not acceptable."

The crowd of workers and onlookers froze.

Cukor responded levelly, but the strain showed. "David, that's wholly unnecessary," he said.

"I'm sorry, George. That's how I want it." It was Selznick's flat-as-stone voice, the one no one dared question.

"You want to stop production for a *dress?*" Cukor said incredulously.

"Get Wardrobe on it," Selznick said, then walked away before Cukor could respond. The director stood frozen.

"So much for the celebratory first day of shooting," said Doris in a low voice. Even she couldn't manage her usual sardonic tone.

"All the equipment, the people, everything," Julie said in surprise. "Everybody packs up?"

"Everybody except Cukor. He's going to need some time to get his pride back. Selznick's making it pretty clear already what he's after."

"What's that?"

Doris's eyes conveyed more than just a tinge of superiority. "Julie, Cukor's the director, not Selznick. He's the one who usually makes calls like this one. Selznick is obviously ignoring him. Setting him up."

"Setting him up for what?"

Doris shrugged and turned to leave. "You'll see. Better hurry on back to Lombard's dressing room with news of Gable's defense of the working Negro. If she doesn't send you off to some zoo to rent an old lion, maybe you'll be able to pick up gossip for the rest of us. Something spicy."

"Working for Lombard is better than the mimeograph room," Rose said loyally.

"Oh, please. *Work?* For Lombard?"

The two women watched Doris walk away, her long legs drawing glances from the men she passed.

"Not a wrinkle in those silk stockings, and the seams are perfectly straight. I think we're entitled to hate her," Rose murmured.

Julie laughed, feeling better. "Well, at least we don't have to worry about becoming friends with her," she said.

✳

Andy joined Julie briefly in the commissary at lunchtime. Gloomy, he chomped away on a turkey-and-cheese sandwich, barely speaking, to the point where she pushed back her coffee and started thinking about going back to answering Carole's mail. She was getting good at copying the actress's signature—and if there were any mangy lions needed in the future, she would recommend Doris for the job.

"I'm meeting a friend for dinner tomorrow," he said abruptly. "A novelist."

"Anyone I would recognize?"

"Maybe. Scott Fitzgerald. He's working on the script."

"I thought Ben Hecht—"

"Yep, him, too. Everybody. Even though Sidney Howard did a great preliminary job."

"I've read *The Great Gatsby,*" she said.

His face relaxed for a moment into a faint smile. "I should've known you'd be a woman who actually reads. Pretty rare out here."

"I can spell, too. Better than Fitzgerald."

He laughed this time. "God, a college girl. I must be out of my mind."

"Do you think he can help with the script?"

"He's got some good ideas. Thinks we should use as much of Margaret Mitchell's dialogue as possible, but cut a lot of the redundant material. Selznick is resisting, naturally." Andy sighed. "I don't know what Scott's doing out here," he said. "He's got real talent, if he'd control his drinking. He should be writing novels, far from Hollywood. No reason for him to sell out."

✳

The next day's shoot went well, even though Julie heard that Scarlett's hastily constructed white dress had to be held in place with clothespins at first and Miss Edith Head's seamstresses would sew it up in back between takes. Julie had hoped to watch, but at Carole's request, she worked that day from Carole's Bel-Air home on Cloud Road. Here she would have a respectable-sized office to handle publicity and secretarial work when Carole didn't need her on the Selznick lot. There was plenty to do, but Julie feared life would be far less exciting.

That was before a studio messenger showed up at the door at lunchtime with a package for Gable from David Selznick.

Julie accepted the package and held it out to Gable as he came in through the back door, his trousers muddied from working in the garden he and Carole were trying to nourish.

"What the hell is this?" he said, puzzled, when she handed him the package. "Kind of heavy." Absently, he tossed a trowel he'd been carrying onto a sleekly immaculate beige sofa. Julie picked it up quickly as he took the package into the dining room.

Silence at first. Then a barrage of curses, which brought Carole hurrying to his side.

"Selznick is crazy," he sputtered, showing Carole the contents of the package. "Ninety-two pages of instructions on how he wants me to play Rhett Butler. What kind of maniacal character *is* he?"

He paced, looking worn. "He doesn't trust me to play this stupid part," he said.

"He's not the director—" began Carole.

"Cukor? He's worse," Gable snapped. He began clawing through his pockets, pulled out a wrinkled cigarette pack, and rescued the last one. He crushed the empty pack into a ball and threw it at an ashtray. He missed.

Carole handed him a lighter, the silver one he had given her as a birthday gift.

"He'll lavish attention on Vivien—I can see that already," he said, inhaling deeply. "Look, it's obvious. The man's a fag, and I don't like fags, and I'm never going to like him. Selznick knows that."

He said the word so flatly. Of course, plenty of people felt the same way, but Julie couldn't help remembering this was the same man who spoke up for the Negro extras yesterday.

"You're not going to pull out of the movie," Carole said quietly. "You haven't even done your first scene yet."

"Presenting Scarlett with a fancy Paris hat," he scoffed. "There are probably ten pages in this crap devoted to how David wants it done." Suddenly he seemed more weary than angry. "This isn't my type of part, Ma," he said.

"Okay, tell me the worst. Wait—let me guess. Leaning forward and finding your costume is cut too tight in the crotch?" she teased.

He smiled reluctantly. An almost sweet smile out of that handsome, clouded face. "Okay, Ma. But I'm still complaining."

*

"Dinner on Saturday next week? Somewhere special."

Andy was calling on the rooming-house phone. It was after midnight, and Julie had been summoned from bed in her pajamas by a somewhat cross and sleepy fellow resident. Yet, even at this late hour, his voice lifted her spirits.

"Why are you calling so late?" she asked. "Anything wrong?"

"Just rolled home after my evening with Scott," he said. His voice was relaxed.

"I hear today's shoot went well."

"Yep, Edith Head can do anything. She whipped up a white gown in about three hours, and Selznick was placated. Even though he didn't get as big an audience for the reshoot. What happened up in Bel-Air?"

"Gable was furious when he got Selznick's package of instructions for playing the part. The whole thing was over ninety pages; I could hardly believe it."

"That's vintage Selznick. No matter, kid. He counts on Carole to calm his big star down, though he would never admit it. Anyway, Gable will be very happy pretty soon, I guarantee it."

"Why?" she asked.

Andy chuckled. "Not telling you, not yet. Money buys everything, Miss Crawford. Loyalty, love—"

"You can't buy love."

"People do it all the time."

"They think they do, but that's not what they're buying," she said quickly.

The phone line hummed in the silence.

"So don't you want to know where we are going Saturday night?" he said finally.

"I didn't say I was free." She smiled to herself. It was fun again; she liked this play of theirs.

"Are you free, Miss Crawford?"

"Yes," she said, yawning. "Where are we going?"

"To the home of a very classy writer. Herman Mankiewicz."

*

Julie collected a heavy satchel of fan mail from Publicity a few days later and stopped back at Carole's dressing room, where, as usual, the actress was talking on the phone nonstop. Julie picked up a stack of already autographed pictures. They were of a smoky-eyed Carole offering the camera a lazy smile, a very popular pose with her public. Julie began stuffing them in envelopes and addressing them to the eager fans who had written the actress; she got dozens of letters a day. Easier to do it here and mail them quickly, Julie decided.

She was halfway through when the door was suddenly pushed open with such force the trailer shook.

"Ma, we got it." Gable's familiar baritone voice was actually trembling as he bounded in and slammed the door shut behind him. His eyes were wide open, like a child's.

Carole dropped a silver tube of lipstick to the floor and rushed forward. "Oh my God, she took the money?" she said breathlessly, her arms wide.

He laughed, grabbing her shoulders. "It's done," he said, sounding stunned. "God, I can't believe it; it's actually done. Rhea took the extra fifty thousand."

"Whoopee!" Carole shouted. "My God, Pa, you're almost free! How soon?"

"Early March. She's been in Vegas, waiting for the pot to sweeten." His voice actually shook. He ran a hand through his thick hair, now all askew, not doing its essential job of hiding his ears.

"So the extra cash Selznick got Mayer to dig up was finally enough." Carole shook her head. "I never could fathom how a woman would keep hanging on when a man didn't want her anymore. Well, this is a fair trade—you get the divorce, and David gets a less grumpy Rhett Butler."

"Hell, I'd even play a fairy if I had to," he said huskily. He took Carole into his arms, his hand grazing the small of her back before gliding downward.

Julie rattled a few papers to remind them of her presence, but they were oblivious. "Miss Lombard, I'll come back later," she said hurriedly, gathering up the stack of photos and fan letters, figuring she could finish them over at the publicity office. They seemed to have almost forgotten she was there.

"Shut the door tight when you leave, honey," Carole said with a giggle. She and Gable were already intertwined on the sofa. The actress thrust one long leg upward and began peeling off a stocking.

"I'm really happy for you both," Julie said, a bit flustered. She stepped out into the sunshine, pulling the door closed behind her, feeling she had somehow intruded on their obviously heartfelt delight. A fleeting thought startled her: had she doubted before? Maybe that wasn't the right question. Could true feelings in Hollywood be explainable in Fort Wayne terms? She hurried up the path, past the commissary, the carpentry shop, the foundry, the studio florist; over there, to her left, was the upholstery shop where fabric was aged chemically to make the *Gone with the Wind* furniture as weathered as possible; behind that, the barber shop where stars like Clark Gable were cut and manicured every day into replicas of authenticity for the film. Wasn't this real? What was she mulling all this over for anyway? Maybe there was some barrier—something ordinary people put up between themselves and celebrities that didn't *allow* the celebrities to be real.

It was such a bright, sunny day; the light was hurting her eyes. There was a harsh quality to L.A. sun on a winter afternoon. People said you ceased to notice it after a while, but it still bothered her.

Maybe it was time to get a pair of sunglasses. She could imagine what her friends would say at home: the middle of winter and you need sunglasses? Only a few weeks ago, she was laughing at the idea herself—too stagey, she had proclaimed to Rose. But it didn't seem that way anymore.

*

Carole, in high spirits, was bubbling over with things to do in the wake of Clark's news.

"First we've got to get this divorce *done,*" she said the next day. "*Then*—we're buying a ranch." She was pacing back and forth across the Bel-Air living room, barely able to contain herself. "I'm looking for just the right place. I think Encino; Clark will like that, and it will be perfect. Julie, oh, there's so much to *do.* Horses. Horses—do you know anything about horses, dear? You know, riding, equipment. . . ." She waved her hand vaguely. "Clark loves horses, and I'm going to be the best damn rider you've ever seen, in about a month. I'm buying matching saddles, found some good riding pants—no fancy jodhpurs, no fancy *anything*. Rocking chairs. I want two, one for him and one for me, and we'll put them on the front porch and watch the world go by!" She laughed and did a quick pirouette, almost stepping on a cat that was darting through.

"What front porch?" Julie asked.

"The one that will come with the house that comes with the ranch that we're going to buy," Carole said calmly.

"When is the divorce final?" Julie asked, smiling.

"Don't have the date yet. You'll be among the very first to know. Now, will you find out for me where we buy those horses? Brown ones."

"How many?"

"Forty or fifty, I suppose."

"Will do," Julie said.

*

Andy let out a deep, amused chortle when she told him about Carole's plans Saturday night as they drove to the Mankiewicz home. "She's a crazy one, the best kind of crazy," he said. "I won't be surprised if she does it all."

The sun was setting as they pulled up in front of 1105 Tower Road, their destination in Beverly Hills. The fading light briefly kissed the terra-cotta roof tiles on the Spanish-style home, turning them a glowing red. It was not a dramatic house—no splendid arches or rolling driveway. The one touch of glamour that Julie noted was the oval entrance of dark stone, flanked by elaborately carved torches.

Julie fingered the shimmering blue silk of her borrowed blouse, hoping she was dressed properly. This was her first Hollywood party, and nothing in the closet of an Indiana girl who'd gone to Smith College seemed quite up to such an event. So she wore Rose's blouse, a serviceable serge skirt that had sat through many lectures on European history, and the good pearl earrings her parents had given her for graduation.

"Eye shadow," Rose had said, squinting at her critically, wielding a makeup brush. "For you, blue, not green. And brighter lipstick."

"I don't want to look like Doris."

"Don't worry. Like this. Now look at yourself."

Julie stared at her reflection for a long moment. Maybe she was pretty, a little. Her eyes, with the help of the blue shadow, looked larger than usual, and she actually had a rather nicely shaped nose. Whether it was enough to keep her from fading into invisibility at a Hollywood party was the question.

"You have beautiful copper-colored hair," Rose had said admiringly. "And that blouse is perfect with it."

*

Andy opened the car door with an elaborate bow, clearly in a good mood, as he surveyed the neighborhood. He looked strikingly handsome tonight, Julie thought. His suit was one she had not seen, a fine wool, polished and crisp. Just looking at him made her heart beat faster.

"If you're looking for glamour, Oscar Hammerstein lives next door," Andy said, nodding at an elaborately large home partially hidden by high hedges. "If you're looking for intellect, you find it here."

"Maybe a mix? Being dazzled is fun," she teased as they walked up to the front door.

"You dazzle me." He bent swiftly and kissed her on the forehead, obviously in high spirits. "I've got a girl who reads, and I'm giving her more than movie glitz."

Before they even knocked, a maid in a starched white cap and apron opened the door and ushered them inside. To Julie's left was a spacious living room, dominated by an ebony grand piano. The sofas and chairs—precisely placed—were plump and inviting, covered in a calm floral print, with ruffles at the bottom. They weren't Hollywood, they were Fort Wayne, which was a relaxing thought.

To her right, through glass doors, the house opened onto a patio. Beyond that was a languid pool, the water a vivid blue, fed by a lazy waterfall. All the doors were open, and a soft evening breeze flowed through the house.

Guests were gathering—some in conversation by the fireplace, others flowing onto the patio, strong masculine hands as well as polished, tapered fingers lifting from time to time a glass of wine from the silver trays passed by the butler.

"Look at the pool," Andy murmured. "What do you see?"

She peered. "It's shaped like a frog," she said, surprised.

Andy chuckled. "Good, you noticed. That's one of Herman's jokes. He can't take this town seriously. Would you like to hear the one he's threatened to pull on his wife? Say yes."

She laughed. "Yes."

"Sara's crazy about Clark Gable, thinks he is the handsomest man in the world. Herman's threatened to invite Gable to dinner and then have him play a joke on her by taking out his false teeth at the table."

"Oh, Andy, Clark wouldn't do that," she said.

"You can be a bit literal," Andy chided gently. "No worry—most actors don't get invited to dinner in this house anyhow. Herman doesn't think they're smart enough—with exceptions." He nodded in the direction of a tall, handsome woman who had just arrived and was slipping out of a camel-hair coat with easy, sinuous grace. "There's someone you might want to see," he said, smiling.

Julie glanced curiously. The woman at the door was chatting now with Sara Mankiewicz, her face animated, her attention focused. Her eyes were not swiftly surveying the room, the standard gambit for party newcomers. A tingle traveled down Julie's spine. It was Frances Marion. How could she be fifty? Her skin glowed as if scrubbed for a Noxzema ad.

"Go claim your destiny, Miss Crawford," Andy urged with a wink. "Or at least take a peek at a living, breathing version of what you want to be."

*

Julie wondered later at how easy it had been. Did she walk over to talk to her heroine? No, she floated. Something like that. At first she stood there awkwardly, not sure what to say to get the screenwriter's attention. She felt like a schoolgirl again, but she was no longer part of an eager crowd, thrusting forward her autograph book for a precious signature.

She cleared her throat. If she didn't say something quickly, she would look like a fool. "Miss Marion, I met you briefly at Smith College last year. I would love to know what you think the future is here for women writers," she said.

The screenwriter turned in her direction and smiled. "The realistic one or the ideal one?" she said.

"I'm hoping there's a way of combining the two," Julie replied.

"If there is, maybe you'll be able to find it," Marion said, looking at her now more closely. "Not easy. Are you writing now?"

"Not yet. But as soon as I find a typewriter, I will be."

"You sound determined. When you have something to show, come see me." Marion's words were warm and she smiled again before turning away to chat with the easily recognizable actress Helen Hayes.

Julie instinctively felt the invitation was real.

So she was flushed with pleasure as she turned to look around the room, now rapidly filling with guests. Andy was in his element here. Introductions were casual, but there was the editor of the *New Yorker* magazine, in deep conversation with Mankiewicz, who jumped up and exuberantly shook hands with Andy. Standing by the fireplace was a restless man with a gaunt, worried face who she soon learned was Scott Fitzgerald. And she caught the name of Bennett Cerf, who had started Random House, the book-publishing firm. Other introductions blurred—there were two other writers from the East Coast—but when Julie saw David Selznick, she figured he was the reason this evening seemed especially important to Andy.

Selznick actually looked genial tonight, laughing at someone's joke as he tipped a glass of Scotch to his lips. Julie, cradling a drink in her hands, tried to imagine how victorious he must feel about the Gable deal right now. She began talking to the woman with him, who turned out to be his regally elegant wife, Irene—a lady with a cool smile and reserved eyes who warmed up perceptibly when she learned Julie was a graduate of Smith College.

"I would have liked to go to college," she said matter-of-factly. "But Father felt it was bad for girls, that it would expose me to outside influences."

"Where did you live?" Julie asked innocently.

"Here, of course." The woman's eyes had widened slightly. "Ah, I see, you are new to Hollywood. My father is Louis B. Mayer. He always said other girls *had* to go to college: they didn't have my advantages."

Julie almost giggled; if only her parents could hear that. She glanced over at Andy and saw him and Scott Fitzgerald in sober conversation with Selznick. She strained to hear.

"So what do you think of Mitchell's writing?" Selznick was asking.

Fitzgerald shrugged his shoulders almost wearily. His left hand was shoved deep into the pocket of his rather shabby jacket; his right hand cradled a glass of bourbon. "It's okay. Not very original," he said. "Workmanlike."

"So you're polishing it up, right?" Selznick said.

"I'm using her own words mostly," Fitzgerald said. He did not seem intimidated by Selznick's brusque tone. He was only one of many writers Selznick was bringing in to work on the script, and he knew it.

"Andy, you'll stay on top of this?" Selznick said.

"Of course," Andy replied. He saw Julie and grinned, then winked. She smiled back and turned away; she would tell him what Irene Selznick had said later. She knew now from studio gossip that Selznick valued Andy highly—that his ability to keep track of all the elements and egos of this massive project had made him invaluable. She felt wonderfully proud.

What she didn't notice right away was a tall, dark-haired woman with long, graceful fingers curled tightly around a crystal glass, who was staring at Andy. Only when she strode forward in Andy's direction, her expression stony, did Julie register that she was quite beautiful.

Julie remembered later that Andy looked up, saw the woman approaching, and appeared first startled, then resigned.

"You bastard," the woman said. She took her drink and threw it into his face. Bourbon dripped from Andy's hair as ice cubes clattered against a glass coffee table on their way to the floor. The woman put down the glass and stalked toward the front door, followed by a small, nervously apologetic-looking man with a very flushed face.

The room went silent for a brief moment before the murmur of conversation resumed. Andy took a napkin offered by a maid and wiped his face, then dabbed calmly at the stains on his shirt. He looked up at Julie and walked over to her.

"Who was that?" she asked, stunned.

"You might say a former colleague," he said. "We're not on good terms."

"I could tell," she managed. She tried to keep her voice calm, not quite sure what to say next. Irene Selznick had quietly drifted away to the other side of the room.

"I'm sorry you saw that—it's the postscript to an old story," he said.

"Please, tell me."

He sighed. "Julie, it's all old news."

Was she supposed to stand there and pretend nothing had happened? She glanced around the room and was suddenly struck by a realization. "No one seems surprised," she said. "Please, explain."

His face seemed to close up. "I'll tell you later. I assure you, it's nothing for you to worry about."

"Don't bother my pretty little head, is that it?" She mustn't cry. She mustn't look dismayed or scared or confused, all of which she was. Andy. What made her think she actually knew this man, knew his character, in not much more than a month? She couldn't stop her voice from trembling. Tears were forming in her eyes.

The stiff expression on his face softened slightly. "Okay, I've shocked you enough. I'll take you home."

She looked around. They were being serenely ignored. No tension, just life as usual. She knew this might likely end up as an anonymous tidbit in Louella's column tomorrow—anything about anyone connected with *Gone with the Wind* was fair game now—including something tongue-in-cheek about the clueless girlfriend who stood there barely holding back her tears. How was she supposed to act?

"Dinner is served," Sara Mankiewicz announced at that moment, with what appeared to be a quick, sympathetic smile in Julie's direction.

That did it. Julie straightened, lifted her head high. Through the dining-room doors, she could see a table glistening with silver and crystal. A maid was lighting tall cream-colored tapers. "Not at all, Mr. Weinstein," she said calmly. "We've been invited to dinner, and we will stay." She turned and preceded Andy into the dining room.

She peered at the place cards, each name in elaborate script.

Would they have remembered hers? There it was. She was seated between Ben Hecht and a magazine editor from London whose name—she peeked at his place card—appeared unpronounceable. Elegant bone-white china, succulent prime rib; jokes, laughter. Conversation. Ben Hecht, blowing smoke rings to the chandelier between courses. Easy engagement. The magazine editor ("Call me Bernie, forget the last name") chatty and pleasant. Sparring over the possibility of war.

"Roosevelt is trying to get us into it," Mankiewicz declared, slicing vigorously into his meat. "It's Europe's war, not ours."

"Mank, the Germans are out to own the world," argued the magazine editor. "For God's sake, they won't show any of your movies in Germany unless your name is taken off of them."

"They don't like me, I don't like them," Mankiewicz retorted.

"Hitler isn't going to invade the U.S.," Hecht broke in. "No reason American boys should go over there and get killed by the thousands."

A producer from RKO growled, "We'll have to get in it sometime," he said, waving his fork.

The conversation stayed juicy and lively, bouncing from topic to topic. Julie felt energized just listening. From across the table, Frances Marion smiled and lifted her glass, that small, universal gesture that held various meanings. And then dessert, a berry tart with ice cream; coffee; after-dinner liqueurs served in tiny crystal glasses. The mood was mellowing. From her seat at the table, Julie could see the lights shimmering blue in that jaunty frog-shaped pool. David O. Selznick, usually intense and focused, lounged back in his chair, chortling over one of Herman's jokes.

And when dinner was over, goodbyes said, coats donned, and she and Andy stepped from the house and out into a Hollywood night complete with a crisp midnight-blue sky and sparkling stars, Julie realized—to her pleasure and astonishment—she had had a good time. Even if Andy seemed weighted down with gloom.

*

They drove to the boarding house in total silence.

"Goodbye." She opened the door, feeling proud of herself. She had carried it off. "It was an interesting evening, though I feel I've been cast as an extra in a detective story."

"I'm sorry." The words obviously came hard to him.

"That's not enough."

"I was involved with a friend of hers, and it didn't work out." He really seemed to be struggling. "I want to leave it at that, if you'll let me. It was—bad. Maybe sometime. Not now."

"But I need to know more now."

"Sorry."

She could think of nothing further to say. "Goodbye," she said again.

"Goodbye, kid." His jaw set, he turned his eyes to the road. He already had the car in gear.

CHAPTER 5

On Monday, Carole pulled the bright-red scooter resting against the side of her trailer upright and paused, looking back at Julie. "Why don't you go watch Cukor do the birthing scene? Huge moment, and he'll get everything possible out of it," she said.

Julie tried to smile, but without enthusiasm. The chatter all morning on the studio lot had been about Olivia de Havilland's big scene to be shot today, one of her most important. Julie remembered it vividly from the book: Melanie, carrying Ashley Wilkes's child, goes into labor just as the Yankees march into Atlanta, and there is no one to help her except a reluctant but determined Scarlett. It would be a harrowing scene, and it had to look authentic.

The actress had never given birth, but Cukor had been working with her for days, calming her, encouraging her. The plan was, he would sit at her feet, out of camera range, and when she needed to scream with labor pains, he would pinch her feet. Hard. It would hurt. And she had agreed.

From what Julie was hearing, Clark wasn't wrong when he said Cukor favored actresses, and they bloomed under his tutelage.

"I don't know—" Julie began.

"Oh, for heaven's sake, you can keep an eye on Clark for me. Don't let the girls flirt with him. If Lana Turner sneaks onto the set, let me know." Carole tossed this over her shoulder with a grin as she swung one leg over the scooter, sat down on the seat, and prepared to take off. Julie wasn't sure if she was joking or not.

"But he won't be on the set for this one—"

"I know that; it doesn't matter. I'm just giving you an excuse to think you're working. And you'll see some good directing. Cukor could pull a good performance out of a giraffe, I swear. Anyhow, it's a better way to spend an afternoon than signing pictures of me, right? And you need some cheering up."

She gave Julie a wink and threw the scooter into gear. "Oh . . ." She paused, a slight wrinkle on her brow. "Don't tell Clark I praised George." Then she took off, hair flying, dodging pedestrians and delivery trucks, waving at everybody.

Julie, watching her go, managed a wave herself. Carole on that scooter was a familiar sight now on the Selznick lot, and everybody waved back at her. She could also sniff out trouble in a swift minute, and had known instantly this morning that Julie was depressed.

"So what terrible thing did Andy do?" she had demanded, while applying a sloppy coat of red nail polish, repeatedly thrusting the brush deep into the bottle and then dabbing it in the general direction of her fingernails. Precision and patience were not Carole's style.

Julie scanned the array of bottles on the dressing table, hoping to find nail-polish remover, but saw none. "It isn't anything he did, it's what he didn't do," she began. Recounting the incident, describing Andy's stubborn withholding of an explanation for what happened, felt somehow flat and pedestrian, like shaking out wrinkled sheets in the light of day. She couldn't quite muster the level of indignation she had felt initially.

Carole listened closely. "You are upset because he didn't explain why someone would toss a drink at him? Things get pretty dramatic in this town, dear. Isn't that up to him?"

Julie felt jarred. "But why would he withhold unless—"

"Unless it was something he isn't ready to talk about?"

"He treated me like a child."

Carole had a thoughtful look on her face, as if she was weighing choices. "He's a decent type, from all I know," she said. "But he's got a history. We all do. And it sounds like he's not ready to talk about it."

"But it puts a rift between—" Julie began.

"Honey, would you expect a list of all the women he's slept with?"

"Of course not. I . . ." She reached out and pushed back the bottle of red polish as it teetered on the edge of Carole's dressing table. She shouldn't have to defend a perfectly logical reaction.

"Then my advice is to leave it alone for now."

"So why did no one seem surprised?" Maybe that's what was truly bothering her—everyone knew something, and she was being kept in the dark.

Carole shrugged. "I think I know who she was, actually. She's pulled that stunt before." She had lost interest in her nails. "If you want him, go after him. He's respected and liked by everybody."

"I don't know if I do. It's all too fast."

"Hurry up and figure it out. Or he'll get away."

"You make him sound like a fish."

"Honey, he is. And it's a small pond with lots of women fishing, so make up your mind. Whoops, I'm late for the shoot." Carole jumped up, this time sending the open bottle of polish over the edge, glancing casually as it dribbled down the table's white eyelet skirt. "Never liked this pouffy white thing," she muttered. "Looks like something Scarlett O'Hara would wear."

"Your nails—"

"Makeup will fix them. They don't really belong to me anyway— they belong to the character I play."

＊

"I'm probably expecting too much," Julie said under her breath now, watching Carole chug breezily away. She turned in the opposite direction and trudged off to the soundstage in an increasingly glum mood. That scene at the Mankiewicz party would not have happened in Fort Wayne. But she was in Hollywood now, and the rules were different. Back home, she would have every right to expect a full explanation. Maybe here she *was* being childish.

She thought back to her conversation with Rose last night. Both of them were in pajamas, each on her own bed, as they talked. She told her eager friend about the dazzling array of guests at the dinner party, about meeting Frances Marion. About swallowing her anxieties and trying not to care about Andy's refusal to explain. In this setting, she had felt uncomfortably like a college girl again, sharing confidences with a friend in her college dormitory. She had found herself wondering, wasn't she growing beyond that?

Until Rose brought her wandering thoughts up short. "I think you're scared of him, and you care more about him than you want to," she'd said.

"I'm not scared of anybody, certainly not Andy."

"Oh, don't bristle. You just need to figure out what you really want here."

"Have you?" Julie asked. Things were happening fast for Rose. She was about to sign a contract now with Selznick, earning fifty dollars a week and taking diction lessons to scrub away her Texas accent. Every six months she'd get an extra twenty-five dollars a week. Officially, she would soon be a starlet, and pretty soon she'd be able to afford something better than this rooming house. Acting lessons were next, but Julie found it puzzling how unexcited Rose seemed about all her good news.

"Yes, I have," Rose replied.

Said so calmly. Julie saw the invited question in her friend's eyes. "You've met someone, haven't you?" she said.

Rose blushed and nodded.

"Is it serious?"

"Oh, I think so. I'm sure he's ready to propose, and I think I'm going to marry him."

"Oh my goodness, so soon? How can you be sure?"

"I am," Rose had answered calmly, lifting her head high. "I knew from the first day we met."

A sudden stab of envy. "But how can you be so sure?"

"We're very alike, and he's from Texas. He's starting his own construction firm here, like my father," she said with a contented smile. "I know it's fast. But I think you will understand when you meet him."

"What about your career?"

"He's fine with that, you know, for a little while."

"Until you get pregnant?"

Rose blushed, but answered soberly: "I'm having fun, and I like what I'm doing, but—you know what Selznick told me? He said my name was all wrong. That it sounded like the name of an Irish scullery maid, and I have to change it. That the minute anyone called me 'Rosie' I was finished."

"They do that a lot, I guess," Julie said.

"I told Jim—that's his name—and he said my name was beautiful, that he wouldn't change anything about me. And I knew then that, well"—she was struggling to find the right words—"most likely, even if I changed my name, I would always be doing try-outs, putting on still-warm dresses that other girls wore." She added softly, "I can see, that's the way it works in Hollywood."

Julie scrambled for words that wouldn't show her surprise. "I guess I've seen you as more like me—" she began.

Rose shook her head. "You're more ambitious," she said. "Can we still be friends?"

"Of course we can."

"You want to be a screenwriter, and I want that for you. But it's not going to be easy."

"I know." Julie couldn't say the rest of what she was thinking—that she wasn't ready to give up, not in the least; that she didn't see herself in Mayer's writing stable, pounding aimlessly on a typewriter; no, she saw more than *that* ahead.

Rose gently broke her train of thought. "When I say you're 'scared' of Andy, do you know what I mean?"

"I'm not sure."

"You know—that he might dissuade you from doing what you want. Think about it."

*

Julie pondered that question—so engrossed in her thoughts, she almost walked by the soundstage. But there was George Cukor, hurrying up the steps, hands in his pockets, head down. He waved at a gaffer who gave the well-liked director a shout of greeting. Julie hurried in behind him, unsettled by her own distraction. A few moments later and the massive soundproofed doors to the stage would have been locked; she wouldn't have been able to get in.

She blinked as she entered, disoriented by the sudden darkness of the building's vast interior, and grabbed for something to hold on to until her eyes adjusted. Those miraculous new boom microphones hung high, ready to move with the actors when filming began. Such a simple technological development, these movable mikes, Andy had told her—but they made it possible for the actors' movements to look natural on film, a seismic shift in film drama. The set was eerily quiet. All sound seemed sucked away into some sort of vacuum tube as she moved toward the set.

Below the booms, the staircase of Aunt Pittypat's house. Julie drew in her breath with surprise—this was no façade, it was the believable interior of an elegant home. The banisters were intricately carved. The tall window on the staircase landing was swathed in heavy olive-green velvet draperies. The lighting, the carpeting—everything seemed inviting yet oddly somber, fitting the tense scene about to be played. A person could walk into this re-created entry hall and believe herself in a real room.

There was a restlessness on the set. Crew members fiddled with equipment, casting wary glances at the figure of a woman sitting alone on the staircase landing. Julie had to glance more closely to recognize Vivien Leigh. The actress looked tight and distraught, rocking back and forth, whispering to herself.

Right then, Cukor emerged from the shadows and walked slowly up the stairs to where she sat. He was not a tall man, somewhat settled and rounded, with dark-rimmed glasses that kept falling over his nose. But when he knelt down before Leigh, took her hand, and began talking, she seemed mesmerized: Listening, nodding. Finally, smiling.

"There he goes, working his magic again," whispered a cameraman. "That guy knows women."

After a few moments of Cukor's soothing assurances, Leigh stood and smoothed down her gown and slowly took position at the foot of the staircase. Her expression changed. She leaned into the banister, exhausted and defeated.

It wasn't the actress standing there, it was Scarlett; Vivien had once again disappeared.

Cukor signaled for silence, and the cameramen crouched behind their cameras. A technician lifted the clapperboard high and looked to Cukor. He nodded. The sharp sound of the boards hitting made Julie jump.

Scarlett, her dress both torn and dusty from the streets, starts up the staircase, her shoulders heavy with the weight of the horror she is witnessing. Atlanta is falling. Melanie is about to give birth, but the busy doctor has refused to come. Scarlett tells the maid, Prissy, they will have to deliver the baby themselves.

Playing Prissy, Butterfly McQueen reacts with horror. "Oh Lordy, Miss Scarlett! We've got to have a doctor!"

Scarlett grabs her, sweat glistening on her face. "What do you mean? You told me you knew everything!"

"I don't know why I lied!"

Scarlett is furious. Propelled by despair and fear, she raises her hand high to slap the boastful maid. Her hand comes down with a swift swing to Prissy's bandanna-covered head. The girl lets out a spiraling, frantic scream.

"Cut," ordered Cukor loudly. "Good, deep-throated yell, Butterfly. We'll dub in the sound of the slap later."

Butterfly McQueen nodded, patted her bandanna back in place, and sat down in a canvas chair off set. Vivien Leigh said something to her, lowered herself into the adjoining chair, and took a glass of water offered by the script girl. She and Butterfly began chatting about the weather.

It was such a switch to normalcy, Julie felt a bit dizzy.

"So did you think Scarlett was really going to whack Prissy over the head?"

A familiar voice. Julie turned, suddenly flustered. Andy stood next to her, looking his usual wry, relaxed self. His shirt was rumpled, unbuttoned at the neck, with no tie. His hands were shoved into his pockets, his eyes steady on hers.

"I thought she was about to."

"McQueen told Cukor flat out that she wouldn't scream if she really got slapped. She hates the weak-minded part of Prissy anyway, and she wasn't going to stand for suffering that indignity, even for the role. Easy call, don't you think? Especially when Cukor will redo this scene another dozen times or so. Poor girl wouldn't have a brain left in her head—and right now, I'd say she's one of the smartest people on the set."

"Andy—"

"I know. Maybe you're thinking you overreacted?" He raised a finger to stop her from responding. "Okay—I accept your apology. Will you accept mine?"

She looked into his eyes and saw a flicker of something—humor? She wasn't sure. Andy had a way of dancing around with jokes when he was totally serious.

"I don't know what to say. I didn't overreact."

"Okay, I'll concede that. It just makes my apology more sweeping than you might expect. It's for everything that I have done or will do in the future to embarrass or hurt you. Is that covering enough ground?"

He reached out his hand and touched her cheek.

"I don't see a loophole in that contract," she said, heart thumping.

"There is one out—I may well make you angry, even furious. Neither hurt nor embarrassed, you may still at some point want to kill me. You okay with that?"

She nodded; no words seemed needed right now.

A cameraman whistled in their direction, then laughed.

His hand dropped away. "I can't kiss you here, Miss Crawford," he said. "But I will tonight, if you let me."

*

His house, all dark wood and sweeping glass, sat perched on a cliff in the Hollywood Hills, overlooking the night lights of Los Angeles. It had a stark, almost spartan façade, but Julie had been out here long enough now to know many homes balanced on the cliffs were deliberately built to vanish visually into the hillside.

She stepped inside, onto a sleek marble floor, curious to see what Andy's home might say about him.

It was small and spare, but arrestingly furnished—a black suede sofa, a dark oak writing desk, lamps with bold geometric shapes. Julie was drawn to the desk, tracing its clean, polished outline with her hand.

"Le Corbusier dubbed the style 'Art Deco,'" Andy said.

"It's beautiful," she said. "Very modern."

"Thanks." He moved across the room to a small, mirrored bar, looking a little uncomfortable, and took a crystal flask of brandy from one of the shelves. "You'll have one with me?" he asked.

She nodded. Feeling less awkward in motion, she moved over to the window and stared out at the city below. She had imagined him in something like this: something touched with Hollywood sophistication; something that spoke of intellect and style; something different from the antimacassars pasted over the backs of chairs and the brocade drapes, hung so heavily they shut out light, that spoke of home. She glanced around for photographs, seeking something personal, and saw nothing except a strikingly beautiful painting of a girl in blue holding a mandolin. The lines were bold, spare, and yet sensual. "Who did that?" she asked, pointing.

"Tamara de Lempicka," he said. "Polish, lives here. A Hollywood favorite. They call her 'the baroness with the brush,' so you can see, this little number of mine is already a Hollywood cliché."

"Not to someone seeing it for the first time," she said, taking the glass of brandy he was handing her.

His glance flickered. He liked that. As she looked around, she noted a very sober-looking magazine on a side table. It was clearly not a copy of *Photoplay.*

"*Contemporary Jewish Record,*" she read out loud with a touch of surprise.

"You don't think it fits the atmosphere?"

"It fits this atmosphere if it reflects you."

"It does. You do remember I'm a Jew?"

There was a slight challenge in his words, though spoken lightly.

"You don't have to ask that."

He picked up the magazine, flipped its pages, and put it down again. "It keeps me up to date on what's happening in Europe."

She thought of the grumblings at home, the rallies at Smith, all centered on the worries that the United States might be pulled into one more European war. "You've been there. You've seen more than most of us," she said.

"I've seen only a quick glimpse of what's going on."

"What happened when you went back?"

He stared out the window, taking a moment before answering. "Something was slipping away and being replaced by something else," he said. "You could feel it in the air—you couldn't smell it or taste it, but it was behind all the smiling faces. Then it got plenty tangible."

He was riding his bike on a sunny day in Berlin, he told her. Turning a corner; a group of Hitler's storm troopers swaggering up the sidewalk. People moving out of their way. The bullies his grandparents deplored, the thugs in dirty brown shirts—they were always roaming the city, shoving people, mocking them, forcing them to give the Nazi salute. An old man approached, eyesight and instincts dulled as he blinked into the sunshine. They tripped him. And laughed. Stopping his bike, ready to confront the pack. Bullies, just bullies, his grandparents said. They don't like Jews—stay out of their way. But they go after anyone with a big nose, so be careful.

"They had their sport, then laughed and walked on. I stood there, a stupid American."

"Why didn't—"

"Why didn't I go after them?" He shot her a melancholy smile. "Because nobody around me reacted. Oh, I ran over and helped the man up, walked him home. People hurried up and down the street, barely glancing at what was going on. Including a few cops. Just a normal street scene. *Nobody thought it unusual.*"

"What about your grandparents?"

"I tried to get them to come back to the States with me. They said I was overreacting—the government was reining in the Brownshirts—and Berlin was their home." He looked down at his drink. "They're still there. And my brother said there was no problem like that in France, so he's still there, too."

She reached for his hand, remembering the friendly but fervent exchanges at the Mankiewicz dinner party and realizing that Andy had stayed silent during most of it. "What do you think should happen?"

"Look, I know you don't mean it, but, please, don't give me a politely guarded question," he said quietly. "I'm sick of them. Jews are being evicted from their homes; they're losing their jobs. The Nazis are ordering boycotts of their stores. Breaking windows, clubbing anyone out too late at night—the usual thing. It's getting worse."

"Are you saying Roosevelt should declare war on Germany?"

"Hell, yes. Hitler will take over Europe. I wish I could protect my grandparents."

"Any chance of that now?"

He smiled a bit wearily. "Sweet Julie."

"Please"—she was stung—"don't dismiss my question."

"I'm sorry. Okay, it may be too late. But I'm hoping to get my brother out of France. I can get bribe money to Vichy officials and sign affidavits of support for his family, but getting the United States to issue visas for Jews is tougher and tougher. Nobody wants to face what's going on. What makes me angry are the Jews in this town who don't want to talk about it. People like Mayer want to pretend they aren't Jewish—might hurt business."

"That's shameful."

"The sad part is that it's pretty sensible. It's not just the Jews in Europe who are disliked—we're disliked here, too. Americans just hide it better." He pulled a cigarette out of a pack in his breast pocket, lit it, and inhaled deeply. "And I'll bet that doesn't surprise you one bit."

He wasn't looking directly at her, which was just as well. She feared that her memories of all the comfortable jokes about Jews she had heard through her life, even at her family dinner table, might show on her face. She felt a sting of shame.

"Sorry, I didn't mean to give a speech."

"You didn't. You were just giving me facts I should know anyway."

"Your parents wouldn't approve of us, would they." It wasn't a question.

"Andy, please—I'm me, not my parents."

He sighed. "Julie, Julie."

They both fell silent for a long moment.

"Maybe it wasn't a good idea to bring you here," he said. He sank down into the sofa and took a deep gulp of his brandy.

She sat down next to him. "Why not?"

"Too much exposure."

"Of what—or whom?"

"My house tells secrets I prefer to keep."

Julie answered carefully. "It says you like modern living, and it says that you like simplicity, and"—she rubbed a finger over the black suede—"you like good fabric, and you don't have a dog."

He raised an eyebrow. "How do you know I don't have a German shepherd sleeping in the kitchen?"

"No dog hairs."

He laughed. They were both relaxing a little.

He added slowly, "It also says we're different, and we live in different ways."

"We're not here to eat dinner, are we?" She could stop avoiding as well as he could.

"Would you be disappointed if we were?"

She didn't want to keep playing; it was too tiring. "Andy, we're not reading lines for a movie. Please, kiss me, and mean it."

He let out a sharp sound, and pulled her close. His kiss was slow and searching, a leisurely invitation to a tantalizing and unfamiliar kind of lovemaking. When his hand slipped down her throat to her breast, cupping it, she wondered if he could feel her heart pounding. She wound her arms tighter around his neck and hoped he did.

"Are you sure?" he asked.

Yes, yes. "You are so polite."

"What happened to the proper girl from Indiana?"

"She packed her bags and left." Julie arched her back, moving closer.

"Then who's here in my arms?"

"Me."

Gently he pushed her down into the soft pillows of the sofa, his hand moving inside her blouse. He was on top of her now. She could smell the sharp scent of his aftershave, feel the smoothness of his skin. Somehow her blouse was unbuttoned; she felt his mouth close over her nipple. He moved slowly, still inviting her consent, as she blocked out the echoed warnings of her parents and home.

His hand slipped farther down her body. She had no interest in objecting.

"Okay, I guess you mean it. Let's go." He stood and picked her up in his arms, and walked toward the bedroom.

Julie shut her eyes; her heart was pounding so hard now, she felt it trying to jump from her chest. This was Andy, and she knew what she wanted; it had been true since their first dinner at Chasen's. Everything felt blazingly hot and delicious. Would it hurt? It didn't matter—she didn't want to be a virgin anymore.

*

The sound of the ringing phone slowly penetrated sleep, first as a buzz in her ear. Emerging to consciousness, she savored the feel and taste of Andy's skin, the heaviness of his body on hers; slowly, slowly, rising from a peaceful fog.

"Andy, your phone is ringing," she said.

"Sure." Groggily, he reached out for the phone on the table next to the bed.

"Hello?" he said.

"It's done," a familiar voice replied, loud and clear enough so Julie could hear it, too. Doris? Suddenly Julie felt wide awake.

"Shit," Andy said quietly.

"What's done?" Julie whispered. She clutched the sheet tight to her naked body, feeling oddly vulnerable to that confident, harsh voice crackling over the phone line.

"Somebody with you?"

Andy ignored both questions. "What happens now?" he said.

"Production shuts down in the morning. There's no way Gable didn't know this."

"Probably not."

Andy was making no attempt to move the phone away from Julie. But he was making no effort to include her, either.

"Well, I've got a lot of work to do," Doris said. "The *Examiner* will be on the streets with the story in a few hours, in time to spoil everybody's breakfast. Then probably a slew of heart attacks at the studio."

"To be expected," Andy said with a shrug.

A sharp cackle from the other end of the line. "Selznick will have his next hire in pretty quick."

"Firing is a habit of his," Andy said with a quiet chuckle. "You and I know that. See you at the office." He hung up the phone and stared for a second at the ceiling.

Julie sat up, flustered. He seemed to have forgotten she was here. "What happened?" she managed. "Why is Doris calling so late? Don't you get any private time?"

He ignored her tone as he reached for a cigarette and lit it, then sat up next to her. "Cukor's been fired," he said quietly.

"Oh my goodness," Julie said, genuinely shocked. "What happens to the movie?"

"We're about to find out." He touched her hair and kissed her lightly on the forehead. "Let's get dressed," he said. "I'm taking you home, kid."

*

She couldn't sleep that night. Andy had been kind, but obviously preoccupied when he dropped her off. Rose was sound asleep. So Julie was left alone to think about her evening in Andy's bed. She shivered with a mixture of delight and awe, remembering. When she shut her eyes, she could hear her mother telling her the perils of not keeping one's virginity. When she asked, "What does sex feel like?" her mother had pursed her lips, obviously struggling to find an answer that would neither disgust nor tempt Julie, and finally said, "You will feel fully that you are a woman."

So she had retreated to erotic novels about bohemians in Paris to find the answer instead.

What *did* she feel right now? Daring, fulfilled, delighted? Had she expected something glorious that would take her to heights of ecstasy? She buried her head in the pillow. Be honest—it hadn't been like *that*. She felt admitted to some new place, but she must make her way in it awkwardly. The language was foreign. The thought of Andy holding her, the feel of him touching her body, that was wonderful, and he had been tender. But it had hurt—well, just a little. Had it lived up to those delicious descriptions of sex in the novels she read so hungrily in high school? Well, maybe not.

Maybe she could admit she was a little disappointed—not that she wouldn't do it again, with Andy, in a minute. She tossed, then turned, wondering if her feelings about the first time were normal. The only person she could imagine talking to about that was Rose. But, then again, Rose might be shocked.

Whenever her thoughts turned to Doris, she forced them out of her mind. Too much. Dutifully, around six in the morning, she began thinking about George Cukor.

CHAPTER 6

ulie's eyes were stinging and her head throbbed the next morning as she dragged herself from bed and made her way to the bathroom. She stopped, toothbrush in hand, staring at the windowsill of the common room. Shoved up against the glass was an old Standard Corona typewriter someone had decided to discard. Its keys were yellowed and the return bar was hanging by a single screw, but it sat tall and unbowed in worn dignity, waiting to be picked up by the trashman.

It was like getting a late Christmas present. She reached out and punched a few keys. The ribbon, though faint, still had ink. There was a desk below the window, and, tentatively, she opened a drawer. Yes, paper. Bright, shiny, empty white paper. Very carefully, she rolled a sheet into the typewriter, stared at it for a moment, and then began typing. Slowly.

An hour passed before, with a start, Julie checked the time. Lord, she was late; she still hadn't brushed her teeth or showered.

But, even hurrying for the bus twenty minutes later, she had to force herself to push away her own thoughts and try to focus on the latest travails of *Gone with the Wind*. Pay attention, she told herself. This might be Selznick just getting rid of Cukor to please Gable, but the ramifications were huge. Unless Selznick named another director quickly, there were going to be some decent people fired today, people without the high salaries of actors and actresses—secretaries, script girls, gaffers—all of them in jobs that put food on the table for families no moviegoer would ever know.

She walked up the driveway to the antebellum headquarters of Selznick International, seeing small knots of workers clustered together on the grounds outside, some glancing over their shoulders, as if waiting for a blow. Several women held handkerchiefs to their eyes.

Inside the central publicity office, everyone moved back and forth aimlessly. Through Selznick's open door, Julie saw Olivia de Havilland and Vivien Leigh standing in front of the producer's desk, alternately crying and pleading for Cukor. Both were dressed, head to toe, in black.

"They heard the news while getting ready to film the scene in the Atlanta Bazaar," Rose whispered. She made no mention of Julie's late arrival; it occurred to Julie that her friend might not have been fully asleep when she tiptoed in late last night.

"David, David, *we need George,*" Olivia said, weeping, raising her voice so all could hear. She tore off her somber black bonnet and threw it on Selznick's desk. "We thought we were dressing for a movie scene, and now we find we are mourning our *director?* For God's sake, David—George is the heart and soul of *Gone with the Wind*! You can't fire him!"

"I believe I have that prerogative," Selznick responded dryly. He walked to the door and shut it, gently but firmly.

"He won't budge," Doris said. She was sitting at her desk, staring at the door, a tight smile on her face. "They can plead all they want; nothing will change. He's shutting down production for now. Just to scare everybody." She turned her head; Andy was standing behind her. "So who do you think?" she said.

"That's easy. Fleming. He's wrapping *The Wizard of Oz.*"

Doris nodded, satisfied. "My call, too."

"Want to bet how soon?"

"Two weeks. Ten gets you a hundred."

"And a side one on whether Vivien and Olivia donned that funeral garb purposely to make their plea more dramatic?"

Doris laughed. "Yeah, I thought of that."

Julie felt suddenly impatient with their insider smugness. "Well, may the best man win," she said. "Obviously, you don't need me for this conversation." She turned to leave, and made it to the front door before Andy caught her by the hand.

"Hey, what's the matter?" he said.

"I'm tired of being ignored by the two of you."

A slow smile spread across his face. Making a fist, he gently tapped her chin. "What's this? A little jealousy?"

She flushed. She tried to tell herself she had no claim on this man. But her eyes filled. "We shared something. . . ." She stopped.

He stared at her reflectively, his eyes traveling over her face. "You are a decent kid," he said.

She could think of nothing to say.

"Listen, I've got an idea," he said. "Let's get out of here for the afternoon. I want to take you somewhere, somewhere special. Anything on your list?"

"You're serious?" Carole had told her she could take the day off.

"They don't need me here for the lamentations. George will survive. So will the movie. Give me some glamorous destination and I'll take you there. Lawry's? Du-Par's? Brown Derby? Malibu? Gilmore Field? It isn't officially open yet, but The Hollywood Stars are practicing today. Somewhere you haven't been before. What do you say?"

"Okay." She loved his sudden animation. Her uncertainty began to lift. "Let me think. . . ." But she knew. "You're going to laugh," she warned.

"No, I'll hide my amusement, I promise."

"The sign. The one on the hill that says *Hollywoodland.* Can we get close to it?"

For an instant he looked surprised, then wary. "Is that really what you want to do?" he said.

"Yes. I want to see it up close."

Was it her imagination, or did he seem to waver? "You wanted me to choose Gilmore Field?" she teased.

"It's more impressive than the sign," he said.

"But not as glamorous a place to a girl from Indiana."

He hesitated a beat or two longer than she expected before reaching out and taking her hand.

"Okay, kid, your choice. Let's go."

*

Within an hour, they were winding and twisting up a hillside, along Beachwood Canyon, into the Hollywood Hills. "If I'm your tour guide, want some statistics?" he asked. He seemed to be forcing an effort to exhibit his earlier buoyancy.

She nodded. She was catching glimpses of the sign as they rounded curves, and realized already that it was larger than she had expected. Maybe she was showing her provincialism, but it was a thrill to get up close to this Hollywood icon.

"Each one of those big white metal letters is fifty feet high and thirty feet wide. Put up in '23 as a sales tool for a subdivision. Don't know how many lots they sold, but it was a great promo for the movies," he said, pointing. "Just around another curve or two and you'll see what I'm talking about."

She looked around. What a beautiful, deserted place this was—holly bushes clustered close to the road, oak trees, even scatterings of bright-red poppies. Everything seemed to thrive here, without the bleak, snowy winters of the Midwest. She was not going back. She would find a way to become a screenwriter. Her thoughts returned to the pages she had banged out that morning on the old typewriter. How amazing and exciting it was to see a wisp of an idea take shape.

Andy pulled abruptly to the side of the narrow road. "Look up there," he said. "Close enough?" His voice was trying to lighten. "Can we go now? I'm getting hungry, and there are no restaurants up here."

She peered through the windshield glass. HOLLYWOODLAND. It was bigger than she had expected. Its size was like a shout, a bellow of grandeur. It dwarfed the few homes on the slope of the hill, diminishing them into dollhouses. It was stunning.

"Can we get closer?" she asked.

Without answering, Andy put the car in gear and kept climbing. Then he suddenly twisted the wheel, turned off onto a dirt path, and pushed down hard on the gas pedal. "Sorry, it'll be a bit bumpy from here."

The sign loomed over them now, so close Julie could see the tangle of worn wiring that held the metal squares to each other. Some of the squares, shabby and dented, dangled precariously in place, shivering with every breath of wind. At the far end, a tall ladder in back of the "H" reached a full fifty feet to the top.

Andy pulled up in back of the sign and turned off the engine; he stared at the ladder, his face still.

"It doesn't look cared for," she said, disappointed.

"The real-estate company isn't bothering anymore. Doesn't matter—not many people get this close up. Seen enough?"

She was determined to hold on to her initial mood. "I'll bet it still has the best view in town." She pointed to the ladder. "Somebody must climb up there; otherwise, why the ladder?"

"There's a caretaker. He's around here somewhere, old guy who lives in a shed up the hill. He'll probably be out of a job soon."

She cast him an arch look. "You seem to know quite a lot about this place. Been here often?"

He shook his head slowly. "Once was enough."

"You can be as terse as a real cowboy," she said. She opened the door and jumped out of the car, beckoning to him. There were too many constraints in her mind and her heart; she felt like defying them. "Come on, let's do something adventurous—just a little daring?"

He got out of the car as she ran over to the ladder. "What are you doing?" he asked.

"I'm going to climb the ladder," she said gaily. "Come on, Andy, do it with me!" She put a foot on the bottom rung and started climbing. "Have you climbed it before?"

He leaned backward, staring up to the top. "No."

"Well, why not? Anyway, it's my turn. Let's go, okay?" She went up a few more steps, then paused a bit as she stared upward, determined not to dissolve into a nervous Nellie.

Moving swiftly to her side, Andy put his hand on the rung over hers. "No," he said, more forcefully than was necessary.

"Why not? Fear of heights?"

He managed a taut smile. "What proper young lady from Indiana wants a man climbing a ladder, looking up her dress?"

It didn't quite come off as a joke.

"Look, let's sit in front of the sign instead and wave to all the scurrying masses below who will be—coincidentally—looking up at us. Must be a metaphor in all that," he said. His hand still gripped the rung, blocking her path up.

She wanted the lighthearted Andy back. "Okay," she said, stepping back to the grass.

His face relaxed. Gently, he took her hand and led her around the shaky bottom plates of the first "O" to the steep rim of the cliff; here they settled in, backs against the scaffolding.

"I don't want to spoil this for you, but I have to tell you something," he said.

Her voice caught. "What is it?"

"A woman climbed up that ladder and jumped off this sign a few years ago. Killed herself."

"Oh God, Andy, that's terrible. Who was she?"

"Just a young kid dreaming of making it big in Hollywood. She got turned down for a part in a big movie and some say she couldn't take the pressure."

"Did you know her?"

"Saw her around the studio, said hello a few times." He looked up at the flapping letters above them. "This place is such hokum. The whole town is hokum."

A slight wind curled through the brush and up to the sign, setting the loose panels behind them flapping against each other in a tinny cacophony of sound. They sat quietly, listening to the wind, staring down to the valley.

"Are you still enamored with Carole and Clark?" he asked.

"I think they'll get married as soon as they can," she said. "They truly are in love."

He was silent for a moment. And she realized how she yearned for that word to mean something to him. "Please, don't mock," she said.

He squeezed her shoulder and pulled her close. "I'm not saying they aren't, but that doesn't mean much here. Actors pay attention to each other for a while, and then they get back to feeding their public selves."

"God, Andy—"

"Look, hunger is real. But hunger here is different."

She sat in silence. It made little sense now to tell him about her idea this morning that had turned into twenty pages of typing. She had felt inspired; he would roll his eyes and laugh. Maybe later. After she wrote another draft. Maybe his attitude was exacerbated by Cukor's firing.

"Are you worried about your job?" she asked.

"Sometimes. But I stay sane by not believing anything here is worth getting frantic about," he said. "Do you understand how this works? Selznick wants to scare the hell out of everybody; he wants the town to hold its collective breath. Then he'll hire Victor Fleming. Louella and all the other sycophants will hail it as a brilliant decision, and *Gone with the Wind* will sail through, with hosannas to Selznick. His whole goal is to take over the movie himself. Listen"—he chuckled—"if he could, David would play Scarlett. Anything to give him total control."

"He's your boss. I don't care about the movie, I care about you."

He gave her a light kiss on the forehead. "So are we done with this little venture?"

"You're changing the subject."

"What's your wish, my lady?"

"I'm thinking about that poor girl who jumped off the sign. How alone she must have felt."

"Right. The fact is, despair comes too easy here." His hands cupped her head, his face leaning close to hers. She could have sworn

87

he moved to cover her ears against the almost seductive, rhythmic sound of the wind on the metal plates of HOLLYWOODLAND.

"We did share something special last night," he said quietly. "I'm not good at saying that kind of thing. But for you, yes. Julie . . ."

She closed her eyes. It wasn't going to vanish; she would not have to pretend their lovemaking had been casual or even unimportant. "It meant a lot to me," she whispered.

"I know," he said, his voice gentle. "Tonight?"

"Yes."

"And—"

"What?"

"You don't have to be so determined to lose your virginity this time. Relax."

She giggled. And relaxed. And as he kissed her, with a moan of what could be pleasure or sadness, as the wind coiled past them, with the city at their feet, she wondered about all the girls who came here with plans and dreams, and whether hers were as unreal as theirs.

*

Carole's Bel-Air home was in its usual chaos Wednesday morning. Julie couldn't imagine anything else, not with the two dachshunds, a Pekingese, a cocker spaniel, a rooster, two ducks, and a cat named Josephine who insisted on sleeping with the dogs, whether they liked it or not. All had the run of the house except in the living room, with its white carpet.

"I do have my standards," Carole said to Julie without a trace of self-mockery. One of the ducks quacked and fluttered across her feet. Laughing, Carole scooped it up and surprised the poor creature with a kiss. The duck fluttered away, and Carole turned to Julie. "You're gonna get tired of hearing it, but I'm in heaven," she said.

Julie couldn't resist. She reached out and hugged this ebullient woman who never spoke in riddles, dissembled, or dodged a question—a hug immediately and exuberantly returned.

"Let's talk about your job," Carole said, stepping back as the cocker spaniel streaked past, chasing the cat. "Are you happy with it?"

Julie smiled. "I like working for you," she said. "The truth is—I don't have much to do."

"You're promoted now to companion, secretary, adviser—"

"Adviser?"

"Okay: should the living room remain off-limits to the animals?"

"Yes."

"See? You just advised me. Have you started writing something?"

Julie nodded, suddenly shy.

"For *Gone with the Wind*?"

"No. It's something different."

"Can I press?"

"I don't know," Julie said, groping a bit. "It's about surviving in a fantasy world. I'm not sure myself yet."

"Don't show anyone yet, but keep at it. You're not going to hang around here forever."

"I'd rather be here than in Fort Wayne," Julie said.

Carole smiled. Their mutual distaste for their hometown had already formed a bond. "Honey, me, too," she said, then added, more slowly, "I still see the faces of those poor devils begging on the streets in '29, when I went back to see my grandparents. Half the country was out of work. What are your parents like? They did send you to a fancy college, right?"

Julie's thoughts briefly took her back home. Her parents were good people; they had done their best. She would not have gone to college except for her father's determination to shape her as a son, not as a daughter, and she would not be here if her mother hadn't dreamed of making it in the movies herself. That revelation—the day she left—had come as a surprise. And so did one more. As her mother kissed her goodbye at the train station, hugging her tight, the scent of Chanel N° 5 wrapping around Julie, she had whispered, "They are all Democrats in Hollywood, dear. Don't tell your father, but I voted for Mr. Roosevelt."

"It was kind of abrupt," Julie said after relating this to Carole, starting to laugh. "It was as if she had just told me her innermost secret."

Carole hooted at the story. "So your mother has a mind of her own," she said, "even if she has to hide it."

"Were you sorry to hear about Cukor?" Julie asked tentatively.

"Nope." Carole was brisk. "George will be fine, but David will get a better performance from Clark with a new director, and that's good for the movie." She shook her head. "God, my man is so wonderfully clumsy. You know he can't dance?"

Julie shook her head.

"I sent him a full ballet outfit with oversized toe shoes when he was making *Idiot's Delight* to help him laugh and loosen up for the dancing in that one," Carole said. "But he's terrified about the ballroom scene in *Gone with the Wind*. I've been trying to teach him, but he is so adorably shy." She began a mock waltz around the room with an imaginary partner: "One-two-three, one-two-three," she intoned, dipping and swirling. Then a sudden squawk. "Clark, you're stepping on my foot!"

Julie started to giggle, but suddenly there was the sound of throat clearing. They both looked up, and there was Clark, standing in the doorway. His cheeks were red. "Am I that bad?" he asked in an embarrassed voice.

In answer, Carole threw out her arms and walked toward him. "Julie, turn on the phonograph, will you?" she said gently.

Julie moved quickly to the new Decca console next to the sofa. There was a Bing Crosby record on the turntable. She switched the phonograph on and carefully put the needle on the disk. The singer's lazy, velvet voice immediately swirled into the room, crooning a familiar song. What was it? It was "The Shadow Waltz." Clark had his arms out awkwardly now, clutching Carole as she coaxed him into a dance. He swore under his breath, looking down at his feet. "Can't get the damn things to move properly," he said.

"Look at me, not the floor," Carole commanded. "Just listen to the music; I'll dodge your feet."

Julie sat quietly and watched Carole gently guide Clark around the room, murmuring encouragement. It took a few minutes, but his rigid shoulders finally began to relent. Yes, he was listening to the music. He pulled Carole closer, kissed her ear. "Only for you, Ma," he mumbled. "Only for you."

When the record was over, the needle kept scratching back and forth. Julie lifted the arm up and put it back in place.

Clark had a devilish look in his eye as he glanced at Julie. "So— you think I'm ready to twirl Scarlett around in the ballroom scene?" he asked.

"Um . . ." Julie tried not to smile.

But Carole was already laughing. "Julie, you ignore him; he's teasing. Anyway, it's all been resolved." She beckoned to a servant who appeared at the door carrying a tray of tea and cookies, and sank into a chair, rubbing her feet.

"It has?"

"Victor is having a rotating platform built," she said. "All Clark has to do is stand there with Scarlett in his arms and twirl away."

"Victor?"

Carole shot a quick glance at Clark, who shrugged his shoulders. "Whoops, not announced yet," she said. "Victor Fleming, of course."

Just as Andy had predicted. They both looked a little chagrined at the slip.

"That was quick. When was it decided?" Julie asked.

"Oh, a long time ago. It's just that nobody told George."

"But that's not fair."

"Don't feel too sorry for him," Clark broke in. "Vivien and Olivia are already sneaking over to his house for private coaching. Everybody catches their breath, I'm happy, and the movie gets made."

"Andy said the same thing."

"He's seen a lot of scenarios play out," Carole said. "An interesting man, even if he carries something of a burden on his back."

"Something of a burden? What do you mean?"

"Oh, the usual Hollywood angst. You've had a peek at it." Carole's tone turned brisk and bright as she went on to chatter about the stack of bills mixed in with the fan mail, and how glad she was that Julie would sort through it and make sure she didn't send a signed photograph to the electric company and fifty-five dollars to a movie fan.

"I don't know which would be more surprised—it might be fun to find out. Then again . . ." She laughed and beckoned Julie to follow her outside. "Let's pot some chrysanthemums; isn't that a ridiculous name for a flower?"

Julie smiled, but wondered. This was the first time she had sensed Carole dodging a topic. And it was about Andy.

CHAPTER 7

*E*ven though everyone seemed to know the director's mantle was about to be draped around Victor Fleming, life at Selznick International Pictures stayed uncomfortably on hold until the end of February. Extras in Union and Confederate uniforms huddled together in the commissary, smoking furiously, scratching at unfamiliar beards, and laying bets on how long it would be before *Gone with the Wind* was back in production. They were at ease in their Civil War costumes—too much so, the costume manager grumbled. Ketchup and mustard stains from nonexistent Civil War food such as hot dogs were collecting on their jackets at an alarming rate. Sending everybody home wasn't an option. Getting them all together to start up in a hurry would be like scrambling to rebuild and launch a battleship. That's what Andy said. His tone was light, but—since he was Andy—his eyes were watchful.

＊

"One, two, three, go," Doris said on the first of March, grinning, looking at her watch. And, yes, a beat or two later, David O. Selznick came out of his office, beaming, his arm around a smiling Victor Fleming. *Gone with the Wind* was once more alive. It was all a bit too dramatic, but Julie was running errands at the studio for Carole that day and felt her pulse quicken as the lot exploded again

with energy and life. Writers—pinched faces, furrowed brows—
hurried back and forth with edits and script possibilities. Publicists
in broad-shouldered, pin-striped suits chatted animatedly with the
universally dingy press corps, and faceless "assistants to everybody,"
as Andy described them, scurried from set to set. Only the camera
crews looked bored.

*

"Want a verbal snapshot of the battlefield?" Andy said at the end of
the first week of Fleming's tenure. "Wardrobe is stitching and alter-
ing, schedules are being waved about, Fleming is already threatening a nervous breakdown, meetings are droning on, and our most
British of British actors, Leslie Howard"—he rolled his eyes—"is
yawning his way through his lines again, letting everybody know
how bored he is with playing Ashley Wilkes." He laughed, a full-
throated laugh. "Could be the Mad Hatter's tea party, but it's working. So far."

Julie laughed, too, delighted to see Andy so buoyant. They were
at their favorite booth at Chasen's on a rainy night, exchanging their
news of the day in the comfortable manner of married people, or so
she liked to imagine before pushing the idea away. This was enough
right now. She gazed around at the familiar surroundings. Snack
plates of tiny sausages, deviled eggs, and spoonfuls of black caviar
on tiny triangles of toast were before them on the table. The crisp
smell of sizzling steaks being delivered to other tables floated in the
air, mixing with the always present aroma of Camels and Lucky
Strikes. The photos of celebrities on the walls offered a sense of
belonging somehow to an exclusive club. And on a chilly night like
this—with people stomping their feet and shaking wet umbrellas
when they came in the restaurant—she felt she could pull the warm
ambience of the dark wood walls and deep-brown leather upholstery around her like a cozy wrap.

Her eye caught the lazy circling of the model airplane hanging
over the array of liquor bottles above the bar. A man with the con-

centrated body of a prizefighter and the hands of a stevedore sat alone, under the plane, talking with the bartender. Once again, a vague sense of recognition—she didn't want to ask.

"James Cagney," Andy said, following her gaze. "Not as tough as he looks. Hates the Nazis, which makes him a great guy."

She smiled. Andy cared about bigger things than who was playing what in the latest movie. In one way, he was her touchstone in this town; in another, he could be the first to disappear. Put *that* thought away, she told herself. She was her own touchstone; that's the only way it could be. Because, if it wasn't, then she had made this leap in her life for all the wrong reasons. Anyway, everything was going smoothly: Andy was back on the job, Carole had found the perfect ranch, Clark's divorce decree would be final in a couple of days, and she was working on her screenplay every chance she got.

"So what's happening at the House of Two Gables?" Andy asked.

She told him about exuberant shopping trips with Carole, delighted that she could make him laugh at stories of Carole's one adamant rule for her decorating scheme: every piece of furniture for the new ranch had to be custom-made and giant-sized.

"Even the drinking glasses are the size of Mason jars," she said. She ran her finger around the rim of her own glass. She had ordered something called a sloe gin fizz, and was feeling a bit light-headed already.

"I gather you're glad that drink of yours isn't in a Mason jar."

"You don't miss anything," she said with a smile.

"When do I get to see the script you're writing?"

His habit of switching gears always caught her unawares. "I don't have it finished yet," she said. "It's still rough."

He looked at her inquiringly. "I might be able to help," he said gently. "I'm not going to tear apart anything you write."

"I know." Why *was* she hesitant about showing it to him?

"Is it funny? Sad? Scary?"

"It's about two famous people in love who figure out how to live blended lives that don't turn phony."

He lifted an eyebrow. "A version of Carole and Clark?"

"Yes, a little. I haven't tried a full screenplay before, and I have to get the dialogue right." Talking about it felt a little like prancing naked onto Wilshire Boulevard. Even with Andy.

"Dialogue won't save a story like theirs. People can say anything they want, but it's what they do, not what they say. They may get away with it for a while. . . ." He stopped.

"Are you talking about a screenplay or real life?"

"I'm saying it's only part of the story."

"Without it, there's no story."

"Maybe."

"Maybe you've worked in Hollywood too long." Why was she angry?

"Remember, it hasn't all played out yet," he said.

Whether he meant Clark and Carole, *Gone with the Wind,* or the two of them, she wasn't sure. But she had a sudden fear that Andy would not believe a story with a happy ending. It made her feel oddly lonely.

"I'll have another drink," she said, slipping what remained of the sloe gin fizz down her throat.

"Julie, sweet Julie—"

"Don't call me that, I don't like it."

He sat back with a puzzled frown. "I should call you 'nasty'?" he said calmly.

"I didn't mean to snap, I'm just—"

"I know. You're a writer and you're feeling fragile and you're not ready to talk about your work and I should shut up. Right?"

The lonely feeling was lifting. "Right," she said.

With an easy, graceful gesture, Andy signaled for a waiter. "Let's you and I skip the chili and chow down on some hobo steak tonight," he said. "The wonderful thing about it? They burn it at your table."

She laughed, easy again.

✳

Whisperings. Julie stepped into Carole's trailer and heard whisperings from behind the partition dividing the private section from the front room. She tried not to listen, but nothing quite alerts a person's hearing more than the sound of whispers.

"I won't do it."

"Pa"—Carole's voice took on the cajoling tone of a purring kitten—"it will work, you don't have to be afraid."

"I'm not afraid, damn it. I know what my image is with the public, and I'm not jeopardizing it."

"Look, you're a very masculine guy, and everybody knows it. I—"

"It took me a long time to get there, Ma."

Julie rattled papers, cleared her throat; they were too absorbed in their argument to care.

"So you had a father who didn't mind you dropping out of school at sixteen, and who was a lot happier when you worked as a logger than when you read Shakespeare and played in the town band, right? Pa, let that stuff go."

"I can't. People will laugh."

"Shit, honey." The curtain separating the two spaces was suddenly swept back. "Hi, Julie," Carole said. "What do you think? You know what we're arguing about."

Her sudden inclusion in the conversation made Julie stammer as she mustered her thoughts. Of course she knew. It was the latest gossip wafting out from the *Gone with the Wind* set. Clark Gable would not cry on camera, and Fleming was insisting he would ruin a key scene if he didn't.

Impasse. Ordering, yelling, pleading—nothing so far had made Gable budge.

What did she think? Had she ever seen her father cry? No, not even when her grandmother died. Manly men didn't cry.

"It seems natural in the book," Julie began, then stopped. She could almost feel herself turning the pages again, reading once more how Melanie tries to comfort Rhett Butler after Scarlett has miscarried their baby. Inexorably, believably, Rhett's crust of swagger and self-assuredness falls away as he blames himself. And then, in front of Melanie, he cries.

"I cried myself when I read that scene," she said. "It was perfect."

"See?" Carole said, spreading her arms, palms up. "Pa, the world is ready to cry with you."

Clark looked tired. The sleeves of his fuzzy black sweater were too short, exposing knobby knuckles and calluses on his fingers, the legacy of his gardening efforts. There were spider veins under his eyes and a droop to his mouth. He looked exhausted, but adamant.

"Not my father."

Julie remembered Carole telling her that Clark's father used to laugh at his son's high-pitched voice. Only years of training had lowered it. "That's one thing he can thank Rhea for," Carole had said of his second wife. "She paid for all the lessons."

There was a sudden, sharp knock on the door.

"Here come the troops," Carole muttered as she opened it.

Victor Fleming stepped in. A handsome man with high, arched eyebrows that gave his face a formidable, ironic frame, he could make his smile easy, lazy, or quick, as the need might be. He looked as if he would be equally comfortable at a black-tie dinner or tramping through fields hunting deer.

He knew the language of masculinity, Julie thought. If anyone could sway Clark, it would be him.

"Are you still resisting this, Clark?" he began. "This will be your most powerful scene ever."

"I don't believe that. Strong men don't cry, goddamn it. They'll laugh at me." He sounded like a twelve-year-old.

"Honey, Victor's right," Carole said.

"Don't get into this, Ma." Clark's voice had an almost desperate quality now. Some nerve was being touched.

The trailer was getting uncomfortably warm. Clark sat hunched over on the sofa, methodically punching one solid fist into the other.

Another knock on the door. Julie opened it this time, and stepped back as Selznick walked in. He stood in the doorway, glaring at Clark.

"Okay, Clark, here's the deal," he said slowly.

"Don't make me do this," Clark interrupted. "Rewrite the scene; I'll walk off the movie if you don't."

Nobody spoke. Julie tried to squeeze back against a wall, to move away from the tension. It was as if an electric cord had flamed out and gone dancing around the room.

"You don't mean that," Selznick said.

"Try me."

Silence.

Selznick glanced at Fleming, and the two shared an almost imperceptible nod. "We've got a compromise to propose," he said. "We'll shoot the scene two ways—with tears, and then with you turning your back and bowing your head. People can know you're crying without seeing it. You get to choose after you see both versions."

They all waited in silence as Clark surveyed them cautiously. His fingernails were digging into the palms of his hands.

"Is this on the level?" he asked.

"Yes," said Fleming promptly. "But remember, I reserve the right to tell you what I think—and by God, people are going to feel deep sympathy for your character if they see his humanness. Tears won't wipe out manliness, they'll make it stronger."

A small, wintry smile from Clark. "Okay, you've made your point." He stood. "Let's go." He stopped at the door and turned to Carole. "Ma, I don't want you there, okay?" His voice had a slight pleading quality.

"That's okay, Pa," she said, the bounce back in her voice. "I'm actually doing a scene today myself. See you at dinner." As the men filed out the door, she swept up a manila folder from the lamp table and handed it to Julie. "These need to get over to Publicity right away," she said casually. "Why don't you hitch a ride with Clark and deliver them for me?"

Julie took the envelope and nodded a bit nervously. But at the studio, Doris handed the envelope back to her and said with exasperation, "There's nothing in this. And we didn't expect anything from Miss Flighty Bird, either."

So she had nothing to do except go watch the filming of Clark's scene. Which, obviously, was what Carole had intended all along.

*

The set was stiff and silent; the actors, standing on their marks, were as rigid as paper dolls. Olivia de Havilland, as Melanie, nervously pursed her lips, watching Clark. He was staring out of a fake window, waiting. Rhett Butler had not emerged yet, and everyone knew it.

"Waiting on lighting," barked a crew member. "Get that glare off of Gable's face."

Victor Fleming leaned forward, watching Clark.

"Roll sound," he ordered smoothly.

An instant later: "Roll camera."

The paper dolls came to life.

Melanie walks toward Rhett, clutching her blue shawl close. She tells him Scarlett will survive. Rhett is bereft over the miscarriage that his actions provoked. He puts his head down and turns his back to the camera.

"Cut," Fleming ordered.

"That worked," Clark said, turning to walk off the set.

"Okay, Clark—our agreement, remember? Let's try it the other way." Fleming seemed to be doing everything he could to keep his tone relaxed.

For a few seconds, Julie wondered if Clark would back out of his promise. But Olivia stepped forward, walked up to Clark, and put her hands on his shoulders. "Clark," she said. "You can do it, I know you can do it, and you will be wonderful."

He stared at her, then looked past the lights to the shadowed figure of Victor Fleming. "Okay, Vic," he said. "I'll let it go." He turned away from all of them for a long moment, then turned back.

"Ready?"

"Ready."

Melanie tries to comfort Rhett. Rhett sits down, looking past her, his face devastated. His hair is falling onto his sweaty face, his shirt crumpled, his face worn. The tears begin to flow.

"Cut. Clark. That was magnificent." Fleming's voice was choked, then almost drowned out by the spontaneous applause from the cast and crew.

Olivia ran up to Clark and put her arms around him. "We all know that was hard," she murmured. "But it might be one of the best scenes of your career."

Clark gave a weak grin, looking at Fleming. "And it took this tough guy to pull it out of me," he said.

Fleming looked abashed, then slapped Clark on the back. "Thanks," he managed.

Julie quietly retreated from the set and stepped outside into the bright sunlight. It was only make-believe, of course, but she felt oddly thrilled, because she had witnessed something more than that. How hard it must be for an actor—lights blinding him, cameras so close he could hear the crew breathing, people watching his every move—to be able to offer something true. Clark had overcome the fears of the lonely boy with bad teeth who lived inside of him, always had, and always would. Carole loved that boy as well as she loved the King. That's what made them real.

CHAPTER 8

*Y*ou're waiting for the phone to ring, aren't you?" Andy stretched out on the bed, propping his head up on a pillow, and cast an amused glance at Julie.

"Oh, not at *this* time of night," she said quickly. In truth, she was waiting. It wouldn't be tonight, of course, not now, but Carole was mum about when and where. The divorce decree had finally come through in the mail. Carole was the one who had torn open the envelope when it was delivered to the house in Bel-Air. She'd let out a huge whoop and exuberantly waved the official document like a flag of liberation. She and Clark were free.

"But I'm sure it will be any day now," Julie added as she turned to cuddle closer to Andy. It was three in the morning—time for sleep. Her thoughts drifted; her eyes closed. The phone rang.

Andy picked up the receiver.

"Tell Julie I need her tonight; it is wonderfully urgent, and hurry up!"

"Carole?"

"Of course, sweetie, who else?" Carole's voice was jubilant.

Andy handed Julie the phone.

"It's time—it's all planned! Hurry over here, and bring Andy with you. It will be loads of fun. But come around to the back; I'm afraid word will get out pretty quickly."

"You're getting married? Now?"

"Well, of course! Now, hurry!"

*

Hollywood, at three in the morning. Even now, deep into the night, Wilshire Boulevard looked wide awake and filled with light and energy. Nobody was on the sidewalks, but, then, people rarely were; instead, they trundled around sardinelike in the metal capsules called automobiles: skimming past places like Simon's Drive-In at Wilshire and Fairfax, with its neon sign and glittering metal canopies and girls in short skirts and ponytails usually tripping from car to car, bearing burgers and shakes, snapping small metal trays onto the frames of open car windows. Julie felt she sailed between day and night, thinking of all the wonders of Los Angeles—the cars, the women and men in sunglasses competing for attention on the beaches, volleyball at Playa del Rey. The restaurants, the palm trees . . .

"I went down to the beach at Santa Monica and got tar between my toes," she said sleepily. "That stuff's hard to scrape off."

Andy laughed, keeping a heavy foot on the accelerator as they drove, following Julie's instructions for navigating the path of twists and turns that led to the much quieter terrain of Bel-Air. The route was familiar to her during the daytime. Now the ride felt different— mysterious, almost—in the hovering darkness of early morning.

A wedding, they were going to a wedding. She switched on the radio, and the quiet air was filled immediately with the soft, swinging beat of Benny Goodman's clarinet.

" 'You Turned the Tables on Me.' I like that song," Andy said.

"That's the first line," she said playfully. "Do you know the second?"

He smiled, and sang awkwardly, " 'And now I'm falling for you.' "

She pulled closer and rested the side of her face on his chest, breathing in the comfort of a new intimacy. She could not be imagining this. It was real. All of it. Her hours in his arms, his kisses; the magical ebullience of Carole and Clark—fairy tales could come true.

Andy was slowing down, peering ahead, looking for a street sign.

"Is that it?" he said, pointing to a rambling two-story house at the corner. "If it is, they've got company."

Julie peered out. Yes, reporters and cameras were camped on Carole's lawn. News *had* leaked out, but how could it not? They were here to do their jobs, weary but expectant looks on their faces as they patrolled the grounds, their hats pulled tight against the night chill, the glow of their cigarettes dancing across the wide lawn like fireflies. Covering the glamorous was not always glamorous.

"Keep going, and turn at the corner."

Andy drove even slower, past the house, to the intersection, where he turned left into a driveway hidden by thick foliage.

They slipped quietly out of the car. Holding hands, the two of them ran for the house, Julie trying to stifle a giggle.

Carole, dressed in dungarees and an old shirt of Clark's, threw open the door. "Wonderful, we're ready. How's your gas, Andy? Enough till daylight?"

Andy, looking puzzled, nodded. "I thought—"

"Right, you're going to a wedding. Did I forget to tell you where?" She threw on a coat and grabbed a suitcase, then beckoned to Clark, who was right behind her. With no makeup on and her hair tied in pigtails, she looked like a Girl Scout.

"Okay, where?" Andy said.

"Kingman, Arizona," Carole said. "Don't worry—we've been fixing sandwiches, and my cook filled a couple of Thermoses with coffee. Let's go; the clock is ticking."

Clark looked a bit abashed as he grabbed his coat and followed Carole out. "It's about eight hundred miles round-trip, and I've got to be back on the set Monday morning. But we're doing this our way—you two with us?"

Andy started to laugh. He looked at Julie and shrugged his shoulders. "Up for it?" he said.

"I'll have to ask my boss for time off," Julie said, straight-faced.

"You've got it," Carole said with a snap of her fingers. "And don't worry, when we have to stop for gas, we can squeeze in front and Clark will hide in the rumble seat so nobody recognizes him. I'll tuck my hair up and pull a hat over my head."

*

Night gave way to sunrise as they drove. Carole spelled Andy at the wheel first, then Julie. Clark pored over a map. "We should get there by afternoon," he said, yawning. "Ma, pass me that coffee."

Julie could still hardly believe her own presence in this bizarre, totally unglamorous elopement. She stared out the window as she took her turn driving inland, past San Bernardino, through Apple Valley, then into the heat of Barstow. Andy was dozing; she could hear him snoring faintly in the rumble seat, and see through the mirror the wind blowing his hair. A crazy picture flashed through her mind: Andy asleep in the rumble seat, she on top of him, waking him up. Surprising him. It made her smile.

"God, this place is flat and dry. We could've shot scenes for *The Painted Desert* here," Clark said at one point. He was sitting by the door, next to Julie and Carole in the front, ignoring the fact that one well-muscled shoulder was squeezed tight against the half-opened window. He tried in vain to stretch his legs. His face was covered with dark stubble. "Maybe not such a bad place to live, though. I like driving through the country, wondering about what living in different places would be like."

"Where did you grow up?" Julie asked.

"Ohio. Neither bad nor good. Got out of there as soon as I could and eventually got to Hollywood. Bad teeth, afraid to smile. Yeah, an instant hit."

"Tell her the story, Pa," Carole said.

"Sure. Jesus, this car is cramped." He groaned, managing to roll down the window to give his arm more room. "I tested for *Little Caesar,* which would've been a great part to land. Zanuck didn't waste any words. He told me my ears were too big and I looked like an ape." He sat there for a moment, saying nothing. Then, "Most of us start from nothing, with plenty of rejection. I remind myself of that whenever I get to feeling too important."

A giggle from Carole. "Honey, face it. Those ears of yours still make you look like a giant sugar bowl."

He turned his head to look at her. "I'm a lucky man," he said, almost somberly. "I got you, even though I can't act worth a damn.

You know what I want on my tombstone? 'He was lucky and he knew it.'"

Andy was banging on the back window now. "Okay, Miss Craw-ford, pull over—I'll take it from here," he shouted.

"Should we stop in Vegas and give your ex-wife a hug, sweetie?" Carole asked as she tied the strings of a sunbonnet on her head and took Andy's place in the rumble seat.

"Sure, if she gives back the money."

On they drove, as the sun rose high. They sang songs, with Andy belting out an impressive baritone leading them all in "I've Been Working on the Railroad," Carole and Clark harmonizing on "Sweet Rosie O'Grady," shouting themselves hoarse, laughing to the sky. When they tired of singing, they dozed, stopping from time to time to change places in the rumble seat. Julie knew she would long remember the lazy hours of that trip—the jokes, the songs, the scraps of talk as they chugged along the edge of the Mojave Desert, bouncing over tired roads toward Needles, a town that straddled the borders of California, Nevada, and Arizona. A place called Needles? What a wonderful, crazy name!

"Goes up to a hundred and twenty degrees here in the summer," Andy said, swinging the wheel, pushing hard on the accelerator. "Even the rain is hot. You're getting quite a tour of the neighbor-hood, kid."

"How's the gas?" Carole yelled.

Andy looked at the gauge. "Low," he said.

"Okay, Pa, we've gotta stop at the next station. Time for you to hunch down in the rumble seat."

With Clark curled head-down, out of sight, they stopped at a dingy gas station boasting one tired-looking pump. DAN'S GAS, HIGHEST OCTANE EVER, read a faded sign on top of the station. The attendant, who had a tanned and weathered face, hitched up his grease-stained trousers, looking bored as he slowly approached the car.

"There better be gas in that thing," Andy muttered.

It was the only moment of worry. And when it turned out there was plenty of gas, they roared off, releasing Clark after the gas station was safely out of sight. From there, they began climbing; soon Julie could see the lower elevations of the Hualapai Mountains. Another hour ticked by.

"Almost there," Carole said encouragingly.

Around one in the afternoon, after making their way down a flat stretch of straight, dreary road, they saw a tall, ungainly water tower emerge from the horizon.

On it was a sign: WELCOME TO KINGMAN.

"Doesn't look like much," Clark said, squinting at the sign. "But you can go anywhere from here."

"Pull over," Carole demanded unexpectedly.

Andy obeyed. "Where to?" he asked.

Carole folded her hands almost primly, pulling herself straight. "The courthouse, and then the church. But brace yourselves, gentlemen—I want flowers first."

"Flowers?" Clark sounded flabbergasted. "Here?"

His astonishment was understandable. Looking at the terrain could make anyone wonder whether flowers actually grew here.

"I'm getting married, and I want flowers." Carole's voice was quite calm. "Pink roses, please."

They all looked at each other. Carole was not joking. Her chin was thrust forward, her hands were still folded, and she looked quite determined.

"That makes perfect sense to me," Julie said finally. She peered ahead at the tiny town, hoping she wasn't promising too much. "Andy and I will find a florist; stay here."

"Pink roses," Clark mumbled. "God help us if they only have red ones."

*

The hunt for a florist in a town the size of Kingman was astonishingly easy. Either it would be on the main street or there wouldn't be any at all, but there it was: a small shop with a white-and-black sign over the front door saying FLORIST—with some straggly-looking daisies in the window. Amazingly, they had pink roses. After a second of hesitation, Julie ordered a carnation boutonniere for Gable. That would please Carole.

From there, everything went smoothly. Signing the documents at the courthouse didn't take very long, though the clerk on duty in the marriage bureau blanched when she recognized Clark, who gave his age as thirty-eight. Amused, Julie noted that Carole shaved a year off her age—declaring she was twenty-nine—on the wedding license.

The next stop was the First Methodist Episcopal Church. A solemn-faced minister with graying hair greeted them calmly at the door. There were no widened eyes, no stuttering, no surprise. Of course, Carole would never have left the details to chance. This seemingly madcap trip was not just a lark, it was tightly planned. Carole might be funny and a little crazy, but she was smart.

"Come help me get dressed," Carole whispered to Julie. Her eyes were very bright, and her skin was flushed. "I can't wear white, but damned if I can't wear a really pale gray."

The two of them, hauling Carole's suitcase, entered a changing room off the church vestibule. Carole opened her case and pulled out a beautiful dove-gray suit of soft flannel, fashionably padded at the shoulders. Julie reached out to stroke the supple wool as a beaming Carole held it up for appraisal. "Irene made it for me, and never asked a question," she said. "She's wonderfully discreet. Do you like it?"

A suit made by Irene Lentz, the fabled designer of magical gowns for the movies?

"I love it," Julie breathed.

Carole stepped out of her rumpled clothes, tossing her shirt and pants and her chemise and panties into the now empty case. She stood naked for a moment, totally still. Julie had never seen the constantly mobile actress silent. In those few seconds, she could have been a goddess carved from marble. There was almost a look of wonder on her face.

"This is truly happening," Carole said, breaking the spell. Suddenly she was tugging on fresh underwear, snapping the tops of her hose into her garter belt, wiggling into the suit skirt, and grabbing from the pile of clothing on a chair a gray-and-white polka-dotted vest in the most delicate of silk fabrics. Then the jacket.

"How do I look?" she asked.

"Beautiful," Julie answered sincerely. "And so happy." She handed her the bouquet of fragrant pink roses.

And for just one brilliant moment, she saw another girl from Fort Wayne, Indiana, looking back at her, her heart in her eyes—no artifice, no humor.

"I truly love him," Carole whispered.

✳

The ceremony was brief. Carole cried. There were no lines to memorize, no rehearsed cues; maybe that was what made it so tender and real to Julie. And Clark, rattled, gave the minister the platinum wedding band instead of slipping it on his wife's finger.

"Ah, Mr. Gable," said the unflappable cleric, handing the ring back to him, "it goes to her."

"Yes, of course."

"You'd think you hadn't been married before, dear," Carole teased, eyes dancing.

Later, what Julie remembered most was the feel of Andy's hand holding hers. The strength of his grip said more than words, though it almost made her wince. For those moments in that church, watching that marriage take place between two stars who could dazzle the world, anything seemed possible. A bubble of happiness surrounded them, and she and Andy were part of it. She wondered if he felt the same way.

✳

After taking care of the necessary details—Andy telegraphed the announcement of the wedding to the MGM publicity department, and Carole made sure to send a separate telegram to Louella Parsons—the four of them climbed back into Andy's DeSoto coupe and headed, weary but exuberant, for home. "Louella will hate me for not tipping her off." Carole sighed. "But she'll get over it, I hope."

They made one stop, at a Harvey House restaurant, for their wedding dinner, surprising a roomful of customers. Murmurings as they were recognized rippled from table to table, with small cries of astonishment and scattered clapping. They sat at the lunch counter, and Clark ordered steaks for everybody in the room.

A young waitress in her Harvey House uniform—crisp white bow on her head, and an immaculate white apron over her black dress—was the first to approach Carole. She was so nervous, the bow on her head wobbled. "Miss Lombard, could I have your autograph?" she asked timidly.

"With pleasure," Carole replied. And, flourishing the pen so dramatically Julie feared she would splatter ink on her wedding clothes, Carole scrawled on a proffered menu, "Carole Gable."

*

They reached Lombard's home close to three in the morning, almost twenty-four hours from the time they had left. MGM had policemen already standing guard, and several dozen reporters were trampling the lawn. Julie thought some of them looked tired enough to be the same crew to whom they gave the slip last night.

"Okay, a press conference," Carole said sleepily, suppressing a yawn.

"Miss Lombard!" yelled one of the reporters. "Are you married?"

"Yes!" she yelled.

Louella, the formidable Louella, broke from the pack and marched up to Carole, glowering. "Why didn't you tell me?" she demanded.

"Oh, don't be angry, this felt so private," Carole responded soothingly.

"My dear, you made a mistake."

Carole was too happy to take the columnist seriously. And the same demand was coming from the other reporters now, as they shouted over each other.

"Why didn't you tell us? Gotta say, you've disappointed Hollywood!" bellowed one. "Where's the drama in a plain little elopement like this?" yelled another.

"I've got all the drama I need," she said cheerfully. "I'm married to the guy I adore, and that's all that matters. Whoopee for love!"

Even the reporters had to laugh. Julie looked around for Andy, wanting to share the excitement, but he had moved away from the crowd. Her stomach flipped a little when she saw him standing under an orange tree by the side of the house. Next to him was Doris Finch. Whatever it was about, the two of them had their heads together, talking animatedly.

She had no interest in feeling closed out again. Shoulders back, she walked over. "Anything wrong?" she asked.

Doris seemed delighted to be bringing a new round of bad news. "There's trouble with Fleming now," she announced. "This time, it's Vivien who's ready to quit."

"Why?"

Doris was pleased to enlighten her. "He told her she wasn't playing Scarlett bitchy enough; Vivien said she *couldn't* be a bitch, and he said—wait until you hear this—'Miss Leigh, you can stick this script up your royal British ass.'" Doris began to laugh.

"Is this serious?" Julie asked.

Doris laughed harder; Andy joined her.

"The whole project will lurch on," he said. "Julie, don't let a frown wrinkle your pretty face—none of this matters; it's all part of the game."

He spread out his arms, taking in with one sweeping gesture everything around them. The trampled grass, the swarming reporters, the flashbulbs exploding, Carole in Gable's arms, one slender leg lifted for the cameras. Soon the sun would come up; paperboys would be out in the streets, shouting about the magical marriage of glamour to glamour for the edification of ordinary people drinking their morning coffee and heading to ordinary jobs—wistful for the perfection of celebrity, for the lives of Hollywood's reigning king and queen.

And Julie hoped, fleetingly, that all of what they felt for each other would stay real, and never become just part of the game.

he weeks passed quietly, the California sun making its way through the usual milky haze that draped itself like a blanket over Los Angeles each morning, shining brightly through the afternoon, and sinking promptly when it was supposed to. Carole was on a publicity tour for *Made for Each Other*. Andy and Clark were engrossed in the daily ups and downs of *Gone with the Wind*. This gave Julie hours of free time to work on her script, and she could hardly pull herself away from the old Corona typewriter that no one else seemed interested in using. Her story had a structure now—it was growing; it was getting better. She loved the work, the discipline. Every word had to be carefully chosen, had to carry forward the characters and the plot. Some nights she was excited; then, when day rolled around again, she would find herself seeing all the faults, all the stupid words, and she would tear the latest draft to pieces.

She mentioned this to Carole in a low moment.

"Nothing bad about that," Carole said with a bright smile. "You'll throw away garbage that you first thought was profound, and on you'll toil until you create something decent." She started laughing. "Honey, that's the way it works for all of us."

Sometimes Julie was able to go on set and watch the filming of the movie that anchored all of their lives. It was a chance to see Andy work, which helped her understand why he seemed more tense these days. She wondered what had been sacrificed by firing

Cukor. Fleming seemed constantly distraught—especially when he found out Selznick had planted a spy, the continuity girl. Her job was to report any deviation from Selznick's blitz of daily orders, but everyone knew who she was. She looked like a gray mouse trying to hide in the baseboards as she scuttled around the set.

Andy shrugged it off on the infrequent nights when he was free for dinner, but the tension didn't leave his face. "Selznick is up to his old tricks, complaining about everything, sending instructions to Fleming. He doesn't like the color quality of the takes; Fleming says it's those damn Technicolor cameras, can't get good angles using them. Doesn't matter—he's stuck with them."

"Do you actually like your boss, or not?" Julie asked. "I'm never quite sure."

Andy seemed surprised at the question. "Sometimes I do and sometimes I don't," he said. "But I respect him. And he's taught me a lot."

"Not to be an egomaniac, I hope," she said.

He raised a hand and gently tweaked her ear. "What do you think, kid?"

She laughed. They were at his house, in the kitchen, spooning spaghetti and meatballs into crockery bowls. To her surprise, she had found that Andy actually liked to cook. At some point, she should confess to him how much she hated dicing and chopping and reading recipes; she should admit that she always forgot something essential, like garlic, or even onion. It wasn't a character flaw a woman was supposed to admit to, but there it was. Confession would come later; right now, she was contentedly—and safely—slicing a loaf of French bread.

"Look, I know I've been pretty absent lately, but I've got a place I want to take you," he said. "Somewhere special."

"Don't tell me, let me guess—a movie premiere? A Hollywood party?" she teased.

"The new ballpark. I've got great tickets. Want to come?"

"For what?"

"Baseball, of course," he said, looking slightly surprised at her ignorance. "Don't you like baseball?"

She started to nod her head, and saw the sly gleam in his eye. "Absolutely," she said promptly. "I know what a home run is, and I know three strikes mean you're out. After that, what is there?"

The gleam in his eye spread to a full grin. "Good, you're not pretending. Listen, come with me. It's more than a Saturday game; it's the first time the Stars play in that ballpark." He was suddenly earnest. "There's nothing like it, Julie."

If she had hated the game, her answer would be no different. "Sure, I'll go," she said.

*

Saturday morning. Andy grabbed her hand, nodding toward the streetcar tracks. "Okay, kid, let's run like hell," he muttered.

They ran. Julie was grateful for the tennis shoes borrowed from Rose, which allowed her to keep up, jumping over curbs, dodging a few cars, gasping as they got closer and closer to the big red streetcar on the tracks ahead. They managed to scramble aboard the car, already jammed with jovial, shouting passengers, just as the bell clanged and the driver began slowly pulling out, to clatter and bump through the streets of Los Angeles to the newly opened Gilmore Field.

"If we'd missed this car, we would've missed the start of the game, which would be a disaster," Andy said with an excited laugh, pulling a handkerchief out of his pocket to wipe his forehead as they hung on to the overhead straps.

"No disasters today," Julie yelled over the clamor of the crowded streetcar.

"Not here anyway." Andy leaned over at that moment and kissed her on the lips.

So familiar now, the taste and feel of his mouth on hers. She swayed with the streetcar, inhaling the smoke and laughter all around her, glad she was here. Andy seemed to have shrugged off care. He was like a boy today, and she loved it.

Twenty minutes later, the streetcar bell clanged loudly, and the driver lurched to a stop. Andy bent down to peer out the window.

"We here yet?" Andy called to the driver.

"You better believe it, buddy!" yelled a man up near the door. "Look at that ballpark!"

"Let's go." Andy took Julie by the hand, and they made their way down the streetcar steps with all the other baseball fans. She could see the Farmers Market, just off of Fairfax Avenue. She had once wandered around its array of tiny stalls with their bright canvas covers, inhaling the smells of fresh oranges, taffy candy, and enchiladas, amazed to find a market of such simple, rural nature in Los Angeles. Even now, she would have been tempted to suggest they stop for ice cream at one of the stalls, but that was before she looked up and saw the new stadium ahead of them. Who couldn't be impressed? It gleamed white, its walls rising high, and she imagined it beckoning seductively to the hordes hurrying toward its interior. She glanced at Andy. His face was open and expectant as he tugged her along, slipping them both expertly through the swelling crowd, turning one way, then another, to get inside faster. By the time they reached a ticket stall, the line of people filing into the ballpark was huge.

"Do you know what you're going to be seeing first?" he asked.

"Tell me," she said.

"Wait until we walk up the ramp—the one ahead?" He pointed. His face glowed with pleasure. "I love the moment just before I see any baseball field. It's wonderful. You hear the voices, feel the excitement. . . ." By this time they were walking up the ramp. "Now, watch," he said, his voice almost reverent.

Two more steps, and she saw. The shadows cast by the bleachers parted like heavy theatrical drapes, presenting the field in all its dazzling glory: a richly vibrant hue, as green as the finest emerald. White baselines cut crisply across the field, turning it into a Mondrian painting. The stands were filling with people, music was playing, vendors of beer and hot dogs were hawking their wares. All this, under a bright sun in a clear blue sky that seemed to touch the field with a kiss.

She heard Andy's sharp intake of breath.

"This is my way of going to church," he said. "Does that shock you?"

"No, not shock me." She thought about it. "But why?"

"Faith and religion, they're timeless, right? So is a baseball game. It's the only major sport with no time limit. No clock running out. I love that. I love the timelessness of it."

"Because it makes anything possible?" she asked.

"Yeah, I guess that's right." He looked at her with sharpened interest. "You get that?"

"It's new to me, but, yes, I think I get it." What mattered most was this precious glimpse of Andy unweighted by irony. It did occur to her that, if it took a baseball field to give her a peek inside this man, wasn't that itself ironic?

They were in the ballpark now, stepping carefully down the narrow steps to one of the front rows. Andy was whistling for the vendors even as they threaded their way through the crowd to their seats behind home plate—"Two beers," he yelled; then, "Two hot dogs!" as they settled in. "Look how close we are," he said happily. "This is going to be a great ballpark." He sat down, pushing back unruly hair. "See anybody familiar down on the field?"

She peered and saw a man dancing around the field, pretending to hit an invisible ball with an oversized bat. "Who is he?" she asked.

"Oh, just some actor mugging for the crowd. He's doing warm-up, Hollywood style—it's a tradition," Andy said, reaching into his pocket for money to pay the vendor. "Look around you, toots—this is going to be Hollywood's favorite off-duty playground."

Even as he said it, Julie realized that a frowning, slightly built man swearing and fiddling with a home movie camera in front of them was the singer Rudy Vallee. And two seats over, shouting encouragement, was Bing Crosby. Who was that next to him? She wasn't positive, squinting into the sunlight, but she thought it was Jack Benny.

"Crosby needs a shave, wouldn't you say?" Andy asked.

She nodded and smiled as she tried to balance a cold beer in one hand and her hot dog in the other. Except for the actors around them, they could almost be in Fort Wayne. "Why so many movie people?" she asked.

"Because a lot of the big guys own a small piece of the Stars. Bob Cobb—he owns the Brown Derby—bought the team and figured he could get it going by selling stock to DeMille, Crosby, and a lot of others. Team isn't too good yet, but everybody wants a bite."

"Do you own a piece?"

He shook his head, pausing for a brief second. "It's not my crowd," he said with a certain deliberateness. His eyes brightened. "By the way, want to know who gave us these great tickets today?"

"Sure."

"Lombard slipped them to me, and there's the reason why." He pointed to a tall woman with a set smile sitting a few rows ahead of them. "That, my dear Julie, is Rhea Gable. She got an extra set of tickets in the divorce settlement. Your happy couple will stay happier away from her." He let out a whoop. "Okay, here we go! Let's play ball!"

✳

The home team players—dressed in white knickers and socks—were jogging out on the field to the cheers of the crowd. To Julie, they looked oddly pristine for men about to play a running, sliding game like baseball.

"Why are they wearing white?" she asked.

"Home team always wears white," Andy replied. He gave her an exuberant kiss on the cheek, almost upsetting her beer. "Glad you came, kid."

She glowed at that. It was proving to be a delicious day, even though the Stars started their decline in the first inning. But in the stands? No posturing, no acting, just half of Hollywood looking as if it belonged more in Fort Wayne than in the movie capital of the world.

✳

The sun was dipping toward the west. It was the top of the ninth, and the Stars were losing, but no one seemed too unhappy, even after the Stars' hapless pitcher walked a man with the bases full, bringing in a run for the other team.

"Yep, no mirrors, no cameras, except for Vallee's sixteen-millimeter contraption. What are those guys behind us arguing about?" Andy turned and groaned. "Oh God, politics."

Two men, a skinny one with a nervous tic that kept his narrow mustache twitching, and a burly type whose bleary eyes reflected the consumption of too much beer on a hot day, were arguing at the top of their lungs over whether President Roosevelt was trying to get the United States into a European war.

"He'll sneak us into it, you just wait," said the skinny one.

"He hasn't got the balls," scoffed the other. "We're not going over there."

"Are you kidding?" The man with the twitching mustache was turning red. "He's gonna get pushed to it by the goddamn Jews! Why should we go to war for those kikes?"

"Yeah, and what about the kikes over here?" said the one with bleary eyes. He tipped up a can of beer, draining the last of it. "They should go back where they came from."

Their voices had muted the chatter in the seats nearby. A few people glanced quickly around and then turned away, to stare at the field.

Julie felt Andy's body tense. "No," she whispered. "Ignore them. It's not important."

But Andy was already on his feet. He turned slowly, took one step up over the seat to the next row, and grabbed the skinny man by the collar. When he twisted his fist, the man's face turned an even darker red.

"Like to repeat what you just said?" Andy asked.

"Leave me alone." The man twisted to break free of Andy's hold.

"Oh, maybe you want to apologize?"

"Get your hands off of me," the man hissed. "Jew."

For just a few seconds, the world seemed to stop. Andy's face was darker and colder than Julie had ever dreamed it could be. He looked capable of anything.

"Andy, no—" she heard herself say.

Suddenly two stadium policemen were on the scene, firmly pulling the man from Andy's grasp, each taking him by one arm.

"Cool down, mister," one of them said quietly to Andy. "We've had our eye on these two, we'll handle it."

"Hey, why don't you guys carry this on out in the parking lot?" the other policeman said loudly to the two drunks. "Maybe we can get a telegram off to Roosevelt, telling him what you've decided."

Someone laughed. A nervous, jocular titter. The stillness that followed settled around Julie like a heavy, smothering coat.

Nobody looked at Andy as the stumbling pair were escorted out of the stands and disappeared into the shadowed tunnel.

Andy stared after them, his jaw working.

"Okay, let's wrap up the game. We'll be back to fight another day," yelled a man two rows behind their seats. Then he lowered his voice, muttering to his companion, "The Jewish guy works for Selznick; I've seen him around."

Julie wasn't sure if Andy had heard. She turned and found him staring at her—still, oddly, with the face of a boy. But a boy hit by something; hit hard.

"*Ignore* them?" he said. "Did you say *ignore them*?"

∗

All the way back on the streetcar, Julie tried to find reasonable words to resolve this. The man had been a fool, but challenging him only underscored the ignorance of his words; surely Andy could see that. Besides, he could have been hurt.

Yet, each time she glanced at Andy's still face, she felt shut out. Oh, they talked. He told her more about the game of baseball, chatted about Fleming's irritation with Selznick's interference. He told her about the rapidly growing number of rushes he was viewing every day. "I'll be going over more of them tonight," he said easily, looking out the window. "Guess I won't see you tonight. I'll get the car and take you to your place."

"Okay."

"Anyway, you can use the time to work on your script, right?"

He was trying. Her eyes felt wet.

"Andy, I'm sorry. It was a terrible insult. I wasn't trying to diminish that, but, yes, I was trying to hold you back."

He gave her a bleak smile. "It's not your fault, kid," he said. "You've probably never even heard the word 'kike.' I'm the one with the problem."

She would not tell him, she could not tell him, that she did indeed know the word—had heard it in various settings, usually as a joke, accompanied by laughter. Even at Smith. Giggles, there; whispers, quickly evaporated. It was a hidden word, used only in certain company, never discussed. The man bellowing in back of them at Gilmore Field had roared it out with its full complement of hate, and if she ever heard it again, she would not smile faintly and walk out of the room, nor would she just declare it rude or stupid; she would—she hoped—toss it back, exposed for what it was.

How could she say all this to Andy?

"No, I am," she said.

He touched her hand then, stroking her fingers. But he said nothing.

CHAPTER 10

ndy's car pulled up to the curb in front of the board-ing house with a silky purr. As he reached to turn off the ignition, she noted for the first time a touch of gray at his temples. A few hours ago, she would have teased him about that and he would have laughed. Instead, she silently tucked her carefully folded program into her purse, wondering if indeed she wanted to save it after all.

"I'm fine; don't get out," she said.

"I always walk you to your door," he said gently. "Or at least I try to."

She smiled faintly. "No," she said, "it's okay."

"I'll call you."

She leaned close and kissed his cheek. There it was, in his eyes, just a flash of the boy she had seen at the baseball field. He turned his head—surely to kiss her—but then he quickly turned away.

And she was out of the car, and he was gone. Julie paused on the sidewalk, watching him go, and turned to survey the bleached stucco exterior of the place that was her nominal home. It wasn't anything special, just a tidy four-story building with the usual red clay tile roof. It had a comforting aura of respectability, promis-ing a haven of sorts. Like a blanket pulled up to one's nose, giving protection.

Somewhere between the sidewalk and the front door, it struck her that the voices of the girls here didn't yet have that recognizable crackle of hardness she heard all the time in Hollywood. Maybe most of them would get stuck on the mimeograph machine or settle for jobs as waitresses, and maybe that would happen to her. Maybe there were, as Andy liked to put it, only a few trajectories for star-struck girls, most of them downward. They argued about that in his kitchen, at times, over home-cooked spaghetti washed down with red wine. He didn't understand how this boarding house told both sides of the story. It was, indifferent food and all, their comfort—their security blanket. Pull up that blanket, pull it up high, high; reassure yourself you are not really one of the girls who fail. But always a cold draft worked its way through. What *did* come after this? Serving hamburgers at Bob's Big Boy? Marrying the first available man? Or maybe—just maybe—for her—selling a script and being launched as a writer?

One thing she knew as she reached for the doorknob: she wouldn't be going back to Indiana. No one who came here would go back home. It wouldn't happen.

*

Rose looked up from her perusal of the latest issue of *Photoplay* as Julie came in the door. "Carole called," Rose said. "She bought a tractor for Clark, a bright-yellow one, and wants you to help her get it gift-wrapped. A tractor, can you believe it? She's the wackiest—" She stopped, eyes widening at the sight of her friend's face.

"What's wrong?" she said as Julie sat heavily on her bed.

"I'm trying to decide if something broke in two today with Andy," Julie heard herself say.

"What happened?"

Julie told the story, quoting word for word the tirade of the man sitting in back of them at the game. It sounded worse when she heard herself repeating it.

"What you said wasn't so terrible," Rose said. Absentmindedly, she twisted the brand-new diamond ring on her left hand, stroking it from time to time with a caressing motion. "It sounds to me like Andy overreacted a little."

"It's more that I underreacted. I looked around and saw people averting their gazes as if . . ." Julie struggled for the right words. ". . . as if they wanted to pretend it wasn't happening. And I was one of them."

"Do your parents know he's Jewish?"

"No."

"They won't approve, will they?"

Rose had a knack, in her own direct way, of getting to the heart of things.

"No."

"Do you want to marry him?" Rose's words were matter-of-fact, her voice casually inquiring.

"I don't know," Julie said.

"Are you saying that because you really don't know, or because you don't know if he wants to marry you?"

"Rose—"

"I understand: you want a career."

"Yes. Why does it always have to be marriage?" She sensed Rose's kindly pity, and it made her uncomfortable. She knew they both had grown up with the same fears—warnings, really—stories about dried-up spinster cousins left alone and impoverished, and all those other terrible things, like losing one's virginity to a cad. Well, *that* part was done, which Rose probably suspected, but she wasn't going to mention it. And Andy was no cad.

"It doesn't, of course. But it is a natural outcome for two people who love each other."

Again, that vague pity. It made her defensive.

"Well, love gets made up. Somebody gets pregnant and rushes to the altar while her friends count off the months on their fingers until the baby is born. And if you don't get caught, you feel superior."

"I don't feel superior, and I am in love."

"I know, I certainly didn't mean you. But love gets made up."

"Oh, stop it, Julie. All right, sometimes love is made up. But security is real, and maybe that's better."

"So you're switching from being a romantic to a pragmatist?" Julie knew she was flailing.

"I can be both."

How could Rose be so content and sure of herself? Julie put her head in her hands, unable to spar anymore, letting the confusion of the past months wash over her. She was here to explore, to write, to fly. She was too absorbed with Andy. If a barrier like this could separate them so suddenly, what was at the core of their relationship? And even if she felt a gravitational pull toward imagining a life with him, what security could there possibly be with a man she had realized today she barely knew?

Rose reached out for Julie's hand. "You're coming to dinner with Jim and me tonight," she said firmly. "You need a change of scenery, something new to think about."

She couldn't decline; it would hurt her friend. "Thank you," she whispered.

*

Julie closed her eyes after sinking into the back seat of Jim's car, listening as he and Rose chatted, grateful for the respite from her own uncertainty; she blinked once in a while as she watched the blur of street and city lights roll by. It was now past twilight, into the early-evening hour when beautiful women in fur wraps and handsome men in snappy hats strolled the sidewalks of Highland or Vine toward their favorite restaurants. The better dressed they were, the more delectable and discreet their destinations, which were often tucked behind softly lit palm trees and lush hedges. What was that poem she remembered? "The Children's Hour," that was it. Here it was the cocktail hour. It tantalized, made her wistful. She rolled down the window and breathed in the air. She always felt she could smell the ocean at this time of night, which was ridiculous: it was too far away.

She came out of these drifting thoughts with a jolt when she saw Jim was pulling into a parking place in front of Chasen's. She opened her mouth to say something, then closed it. It was too late, too ungrateful, to protest that this was the last place in Hollywood she wanted to be tonight.

*

The host, giving her a swift, slightly surprised glance, escorted them to a booth near the back of the restaurant. Rose, chatting brightly, slid in from one side, and Julie from the other, as Jim, a bluff, take-charge man who clearly adored Rose, signaled for the waiter. Wine was swiftly delivered, and as Julie lifted her glass, she looked over Rose's shoulder. Her hand froze in midair.

Andy was at the bar. He sat with his back to her, staring down at what looked like his usual martini, which the bartender had just placed before him. He was hunched forward, his jacket bunched at the shoulders. He looked drained of energy.

She blinked. Sitting next to him was Doris Finch. Sitting very close.

Julie brought her glass to her lips, took a measured sip, and slowly put it down. As she watched, Doris reached up an arm and softly stroked Andy's neck, whispering rapidly.

Julie forced her gaze away and stared at the tablecloth. So her adolescent jealousies were not unwarranted. He had not wanted to be with her tonight. Why couldn't he have just said so? Was that too much to ask? She felt a tingling sensation spread through her body, from her scalp down.

"Are you all right?" Rose asked with concern. She had not yet seen Andy and Doris.

"I'm fine," Julie replied with a quick smile. She needed to get out of here. She quickly excused herself, saying something inane about powdering her nose. As she slid from her seat, she hoped Andy would not turn around. She wasn't ready to face him—not here, and not in front of Doris or Rose and Jim. She headed for the ladies' room, keeping her shoulders straight, grateful she knew the way.

She shouldn't be embarrassed; she hadn't done anything. But she was. Was she just impossibly naïve? The cozy little reality she had built in her brain for the two of them had not housed them both, only herself. He kept himself outside of their relationship, visiting—oh yes, with many visiting privileges, but holding back, always holding back. She kept thinking that one of these days she would find the key to opening him up, and now here she was, running to hide in the ladies' room. The door to the ladies' lounge was just ahead. What a cliché she was. The wronged girlfriend? She didn't even have that status. No promises had been offered, just a sweet, loving intimacy she had believed in.

Her hand was on the doorknob. Made of fancy cut glass. Don't cry. The door, tufted and plump, pushed quietly open.

Let the lounge be empty. Let there be no prying ears collecting morsels of gossip to buy favor with Louella or Hedda or to help tip the balance of power at a studio for a favored director. Why was she so fevered? She didn't matter to anybody here.

It was empty. Minus even the attendant in the starched white apron who usually stood silently, handing chattering women tiny linen towels to dry their hands. Julie took a deep breath, feeling oddly hidden in this sleek, modern room with its muted lighting and adroitly positioned mirrors that gave each primping woman multiple views of herself. All she had to contend with now, coming from every direction, was the sight of her pinched white face. She pressed her forehead against the cool glass of the mirror and took a deep breath.

The lounge door suddenly opened, its tufted leather interior thumping against the wall. Julie ducked her head, trying to dodge the mirror's reflections.

"Nursing your hurt feelings, just as I thought," a voice said.

Doris stood inside the doorway, arms folded, offering a small, taut smile.

"You don't know what I'm feeling." She was trapped for the moment.

"And maybe you don't know what he's feeling, either. Really, you are quite young. What are you hiding in the bathroom for?"

"I'm not hiding, for heaven's sake."

Doris let out an impatient snort. She opened the latch on her handbag and pulled out a pack of Lucky Strikes and a matchbook. A cigarette went swiftly between her bright-red lips. One snap of her bright-red fingernail dislodged a match, and she lit the cigarette. It occurred to Julie she had never seen Doris without one.

"Did you follow me in here just to gloat?" Julie managed.

Doris inhaled, looking at her with a world-weary expression. "I figured this would play out like some movie scene. Can you spare us both that? There are a few things you should probably know. Are you ready to hear them?"

Julie wanted to push her away, but all she could do was step back. "Does Andy know I'm here?"

Doris shrugged—a loose, lithe movement of her shoulders that was part of her casual sensuality. "He hasn't noticed," she said. "I made no mention of the fact that I spotted you coming in the door. Generous of me, don't you think?"

"He told me he was working late tonight, and obviously that wasn't true," Julie said with as much coolness as she could muster. "Whatever is happening between the two of you isn't my business. But I don't want to talk to you, and I don't want to talk to him."

Doris looked amused. "You are something of an ice queen, aren't you? He has an unfortunate tendency to be attracted to your kind."

Suddenly Julie felt tired, almost overwhelmingly tired. She wasn't going to play this game. "I don't know what that comment is supposed to mean," she said. "And I'm not interested in finding out."

Doris seemed abruptly at a loss. A large ash hung perilously from the tip of her cigarette. "He wanted company tonight, and I'm the one he asked," she finally said. For just an instant, something uncertain showed through her careful makeup. "Look, he's been involved with someone like you before, and it didn't work out."

"Someone like me?"

Doris hesitated. "I don't want to see him hurt."

"And you are so sure I will be the one to do that?" Julie felt a flare of anger.

Doris leaned forward, crushing her cigarette out in a crystal ashtray next to the soap bowl. Still looking uncertain, she stretched her mouth into something approaching a smile, turned, and started to walk out of the bathroom. She stopped. "Oh, two other things. Yeah, you shocked him with your reaction at that ballgame. And he heard a couple of hours ago that the Nazis have arrested his grandparents."

The door swung open again; Doris was gone.

*

Julie barely moved as she stood alone in the bathroom. What terrible news for Andy, just what he had dreaded. Why couldn't he have called? Did he really think she wouldn't understand or try to offer comfort? But then, beneath that, another voice: You're the one who counseled turning away from those bigots at the ballpark. He can't pretend not to see or hear what cuts into his soul.

Walk out of here, she told herself; you need time to think. Time, maybe, to grow up a little. She pushed open the door and stepped back into the lazy social world of Chasen's, filled with the murmurs of lilting voices and the sound of tinkling glasses. A place of mellow self-satisfaction, truly.

Say nothing to the man at the bar who rubs too close to your heart, leave him alone for now, respect this apartness. Ignore the woman next to him, who is claiming emotional territory with a triumphal glance over her shoulder. Give a kiss to your friend, sitting wide-eyed in a booth and wondering what is happening.

Hail a cab, go home; claim the modest little Corona, and start thumping out words. Stare at them, cut them tighter and stronger, jump over careful semicolons, and dump the protective adjectives. Fall asleep over the damn machine.

*

Oh God, the alarm.

Wake up. Time for work?

No. Time to go to Carole's.

CHAPTER 11

*C*arole's driver sat, patiently waiting, in a black roadster, the early-morning sun glistening off the polished top of the automobile. Julie glanced at her watch as she hurried out the door; stepping into the car, she finger-combed her hair. There had been time only to dress quickly and tell her puzzled friend she would explain everything later. She was supposed to meet Carole at the ranch to help her get the place ready for their move. She would keep her focus on that and not dwell on last night. She felt childish. It was too easy to fall into seeing everything only from her own point of view. If she was to think about anything right now, it should be what Andy must be feeling for his grandparents. That worry had opened a gap between them, and at some point she would try to breach it. Not today. No poor-me response. Over her long night of troubled dreams, head on the cold steel of the typewriter, she told herself she had outgrown that.

✳

Carole stood by the gate to the Encino ranch at 4525 Petit Drive, clad in dungarees and high boots covered with mud. Her blond hair was caught up in a rubber band, high on the crown of her head, and her face was without makeup. She looked joyous. With one foot, she kicked open the gate and beckoned the driver to inch his way in over the newly graveled driveway.

"Hi there, honey," she said as she jumped into the back seat with Julie. "Sam, find this girl some boots, okay? I think we've got some in the trunk." She turned her attention back to Julie. "I'm giving you the full tour first, but then we're painting fences. Redwood. Ever painted redwood? Very tricky, I'm told. It defies being painted green."

Julie shook her head and started to answer, but Carole was laughing, pointing to the sweep of land unfolding on both sides of the car. "Alfalfa fields, citrus groves," she said. "Twenty acres of everything. I can hardly believe it. Let's get out; I want to show you something. We can do the house tour later."

She jumped from the car before it came to a full stop. Julie didn't hesitate: she hopped out right after Carole. So what if her shoes got muddy? Carole's lightheartedness was intoxicating.

"We're putting in what some people call a chicken house and what *I* call a hennery, right here," Carole said, taking in a plot of land with a wave of her arm. "See? It's only a short distance to the house, so I can collect eggs in the morning. Just trot out in my nightie, no fans peeking out of the bushes, and scoop them up. Ever collected warm eggs straight from hens?"

Julie laughed and shook her head.

"Makes me feel quite motherly, like I've plopped them out myself." A touch of wistfulness crossed Carole's face. "Wish I could. But we're trying." Her mood switched again. "The pigsty goes over there." She wrinkled her nose. "I won't be visiting them. And I have a wonderful tractor that's coming—did Rose tell you I want it gift-wrapped?"

"Yes," Julie said. "We could wrap it in ribbon—"

"Oh no, hon, I want it *boxed,*" Carole said cheerfully. She grabbed Julie's hand and drew her through the field, pointing to the barn, then the stables. Together they stepped inside. Lining the walls was an array of equipment, all hanging neatly: shovels, rakes, brooms of all sizes. "Only thing missing is the horses," Carole said. "Clark is buying them; I can't wait. He doesn't want to clean out their shit, but I don't mind—just have to make sure I take off my pants before going back in the house." She laughed. "We'll ride in the mornings together; God, life will be wonderful." A second's pause. Then: "Even when it's not." She cast a quick glance at Julie. "Things don't stay perfect with any couple, you know."

The implied invitation to speak trembled between them.

"There was a scene at the baseball game yesterday—" Julie began.

"I know."

Julie felt a little rattled. "The news traveled that fast?"

"The movie business never sleeps," Carole said with a tighter smile than usual. "And Europe has everybody here on edge, Jew and Gentile."

"Did it hurt him?" Please say no, she thought.

Carole considered that. "He confronted a bigot, right? Let's be honest, people would rather sweep these things under a rug. But Selznick has big plans for Andy, and most people know it. So, no, I don't think it will hurt him."

"His grandparents—"

"I know that, too. You've been talking to Doris, right?"

Julie hadn't planned to say more, but changed her mind. "He's drawn away from me because I tried to stop him from reacting yesterday. He was out with her last night. And she told me there'd been another woman in his life, that she was like me."

"Doris is a protective sort." Carole let out a sigh. "Ah well. You're going to hear sooner or later, so I'll tell you now. There was a woman, yes. Not like you at all, by the way. And an accident." She peered into one of the stalls, surveying the clutter of saddle racks and horse feeders with studied interest.

"What happened?"

"Are you sure you want to hear more?"

"Of course I do."

"You know what that thing is over there?" Carole pointed to what looked like a cart. "It's a manure spreader. Amazing, the things a horse needs."

"Carole—"

"Okay. . . . It happened two years ago. Andy was dating a gal named Nicky who was blonde and pretty, and up for a role in an MGM movie. There were rumors she was diddling Mayer to get the part, but, hey, maybe true, maybe not. Anyhow, they were out drinking one night, got loaded, climbed into her car, and headed up Sunset Boulevard, going well over the speed limit, I'm told."

"Oh God."

"The car jumped a curb, just missed some guy walking his dog, and hit a tree." Carole said. "Andy wasn't hurt, but his girlfriend's face was badly banged up. She lost the part in the movie. Andy pleaded guilty to drunk driving, paid a fine, and spent a week in jail. She publicly blamed him, wouldn't talk to him. End of romance."

Julie looked down at her shoes, noting the caking mud, letting herself wonder if the suede would clean. Why was Carole sounding so casual? "That's terrible," she said, her voice shaky. "He could have killed her."

"Sure, if he'd been the one driving."

Julie cast Carole a look of astonishment. "He wasn't?"

"He said he was, but even the police had their doubts. She was a crazy driver, and most people think he took the blame to save her reputation. Not incidentally, he was supposed to be in love with her, from what I heard. He wanted to be a stand-up guy."

"She would let him do that?"

Carole's hand flew to the left side of her face. "Yes," she said softly. "She was a cheat. And a crybaby."

Julie's gaze followed Carole's hand to her left cheek. Even now, if you looked carefully, you could see a faint scar traveling the length of Carole's face, the legacy of an automobile crash when she was eighteen that left her with a devastating injury; it almost ended her career. One of the most impressive things about Carole was that she had elected to have reconstructive surgery without anesthesia, to keep her facial muscles from relaxing and thus risk a permanent scar.

Thinking of that gave Julie the shivers. "Did Nicky's face heal?"

"Yes. But she wasn't all that good of an actress, and it gave Mayer an excuse to dump her. She complained all over town that Andy had ruined her career. After milking the episode for all it was worth, she took a job as a stewardess." Carole shook her head. "Andy never defended himself."

Julie felt a rush of sadness—not for herself, but for Andy. "You know far more about his life than I do."

Carole shook her head. "Not really. I knew him first simply as the fellow with the quickest access to Selznick. I hear he's the guy you go to, to unscramble a production problem around here—though he underplays it." She gazed again at the equipment on the far wall, looking puzzled. "Why the hell do we need a manure spreader in here? Don't horses manage to spread it around on their own?"

Julie smiled. They left the barn and plodded on together, in rare silence. Ahead, behind the thick bushes and trees, Julie glimpsed the house. Wide and gabled, of white-painted brick, it exuded warmth and hospitality. The awnings were a faded, mossy green, and the generously scaled porch all but demanded that a visitor plop into one of its canvas chairs and lift her face to a blue sky and be happy. A sky that would always be blue—wasn't that the promise? Andy would say the promise was false. But this wasn't a movie set. Carole scoffed at movie sets. This was the place where she and Clark could unzip their glamour skins, crawl out, and be safe. If she could just curl up on that welcoming porch, maybe she could figure out how to find a haven, too.

"Talk to him," Carole said gently. "And figure out what you want."

"How? How did you get so sure?"

"Honey, I meant what I said when we met. Here's what I want: I want the ranch, I want Clark. Vivien complains that he has bad breath when she kisses him, but who the hell cares? Not me. I want a baby. I want family photographs everywhere. I want pictures falling off cluttered tabletops, some in fancy silver frames, some in plain ones, shots of babies growing up. Clark and I growing old . . . throw in some great horses and an antimacassar or two . . ." She paused to catch her breath.

Julie started to say something, but stopped at the sound of voices coming from the direction of the main house.

"Reporters," Carole said, squinting against the sun. "Fuck, probably another crisis on the set; they want Clark to respond. Vivien again, I'll bet. She cries every time they tape her breasts to give her a little cleavage. Wouldn't have had to worry about that with *me*. Bit of a wimp, I'd say."

They trudged forward in unison, and only at the moment when they came in range of the porch did Carole's step falter. Louella, plump Louella, the woman with eyes carved from stone, stood like a queen in the midst of her aides and cameramen, her placid body oozing righteousness.

"If you had told me first," she purred, reaching out to fasten one formidable claw on Carole's arm.

"Told you first about what?"

"When you learned the truth about Loretta Young's baby, dear. Young men will sow their oats, won't they?"

Carole stared at her, then scanned the busy, avid group of people there to chronicle her every expression and every word. She put her hands on her hips and gave a very unladylike snort. "For God's sake, that story has been whispered about for four years," she said. "It was all over when I came on the scene, so why should I care?"

"She's adorable," Louella said. "Cutest little thing—looks just like Clark. Loretta surely knows how to keep a secret, doesn't she?"

One crack in Carole's demeanor and Louella could send the story out of Hollywood and into the world. Julie felt blown apart by the eager hunger in the woman's voice, but Carole—the actress— emerged with perfect timing.

"Louella darling, are we still a little upset about not being included in the wedding plans?" Carole said lightly. "I was dying to have you there, but we had so little time. Now it's my job to make it up to you. I can tell you some wonderful stories about the trip— right, Julie?" She turned to Julie, who could only nod.

"I felt quite abandoned," Louella cooed. Nothing in her demeanor suggested a fragile waif. She turned with a whip-sharp motion and faced Julie. "By the way, your young man got himself into a bit of hot water yesterday. Any comment, dear?"

Julie opened her mouth but Carole spoke first. "Wasn't he brave?" she said brightly. "Standing up to some drunken lout who shouldn't be in our ballpark in the first place?"

"Some say that about our handsome Mr. Weinstein," Louella murmured.

Carole stepped in front of Julie and circled the pudgy columnist with her arm. "I'm going to whisper our moving date, if you promise not to tell," she confided. "I would just love to have you with us to celebrate. So many little tidbits about *Gone with the Wind* to share. You mustn't quote me, but I don't think poor Vivien could fill an A-cup brassiere."

Louella dug quickly into her snakeskin bag and pulled out a notebook. Julie could only watch in fascination, wondering how someone like Carole knew so instinctively the right twists and pirouettes that would keep her steady.

✳

Late that afternoon, with Louella and her entourage gone, Julie and Carole—both now in boots and overalls and armed with brushes—knelt on burlap sacks and slapped heavy coats of paint onto the seemingly interminable stretch of fencing that surrounded the stable.

"Louella is a viper, but she can't get me," Carole said calmly, brushing her hand against a stray lock of hair that had escaped her ponytail, leaving it streaked with paint. Her face was uncharacteristically still, and the tiniest of lines traveled down in soft curves on each side of her mouth. "I don't give a damn about Loretta Young and her baby. That all happened before I fell in love with Clark. I care about what could happen now."

Julie dipped her brush into the paint can, then slowly deposited a long swipe of thick gelatinous color onto a fence post. Now? "I don't think—" she began.

"Honey, there isn't a woman on that lot who wouldn't jump at the chance to fuck the King," Carole said. "I know better than to get complacent." A shadow crossed her brow, then vanished.

She glanced at Julie's surprised face and leaned over to pat her leg with a paint-stained hand. "It's a matter of protecting one's investment. In fact, I think I'd like you to spend a little more time on the set for a while."

"Doing what?"

"Oh, running errands for the dashing Rhett Butler. Once Pa peels off those duds at the end of the day and goes back to being Clark, I'm not worried."

Her tone was now so lighthearted, Julie wasn't sure how to respond.

"It's okay, Julie," Carole said quietly. "It's the price I pay for getting what I want. It's never free."

Julie nodded. She was learning more from Carole than she had ever learned at Smith.

✳

Daylight was fading when Rose met her at the door of the boarding house, an envelope in her hands, her eyes hopeful. "He left this for you about an hour ago," she said. "He said to meet him at the studio if you could. He looked sad, Julie."

Julie opened the envelope to find a single line in Andy's bold handwriting:

I saw you at Chasen's. Please.

It was late, and the main offices of Selznick International Pictures were almost deserted, but the guard at the front entrance seemed to be expecting her.

"You looking for Mr. Weinstein?" he asked genially. "He's been viewing rushes and checking out schedules."

She nodded, wondering how it looked for her to be here so

late—and then wondering why she cared. "Where will I find him?" she asked.

"He's over in the Twelve Oaks library now. They had some problems with the props. Lady, that is one beautiful set. Hard to believe people ever actually lived like that. You seen it?"

She nodded with a smile. The library of Twelve Oaks, Ashley Wilkes's majestic home—a perfect replica of a Civil War–era library, at least as David Selznick imagined it. One of Julie's favorite sets, actually. Twice, after a day's shoot, she had visited, imagining herself floating in silks and hooped skirts through this rich, elaborate space, so elegant with its arched windows and curved walls. Once she tried to pluck one of the hundreds of books on shelves reaching up to the elaborately molded ceiling, forgetting they were cardboard façades.

✳

Strange, on a spring evening, to be entering such a world of fantasy, wondering what reality was about to be played out.

Andy was sitting on the gold settee, staring into the nonworking fireplace, lost in thought. His dark hair lay still and heavy across his brow, obscuring his eyes. That alarmed her. She needed to see his eyes.

"I'm sorry I wasn't straight with you after the game," he said, not yet looking up.

"So Doris told you—"

"She didn't have to. I saw you leaving. She shouldn't have been the one to tell you about my grandparents. That's something I should have done. There are plenty of things I should have done."

Why was he not looking at her? She moved into the room, approaching him tentatively. "Andy . . ."

Finally, he looked up, and the weariness in his eyes made her take an involuntary step back.

"Come, sit down," he said. "I've got a couple of things to say."

She had an urge to push away his words. "Andy, I'm dreadfully sorry about your grandparents. That's what you've been fearing, and it has happened. I understand better now what prompted you to confront those people. I don't have to know anything about you and Doris, I just want—"

"Stop—"

She couldn't: it just poured out. "And I know about the accident, about the woman you loved. And I know you went to jail for her."

"No—"

"You don't have to deny it," she implored.

A sharp exhalation; he looked away. "So even *that* you've had to learn from someone else."

"I understand you better, knowing these things," she rushed on. "I can't begin to imagine how it must have felt, and I wish you had told me, but, please, don't let it change anything between us." She waited. Did he hesitate? Just for a second; then he placed his hands on both sides of her face and kissed her lightly.

"Okay, here's the rest of it," he said.

She sat numbly as he talked.

. . . They left the bar that night, arguing. Mayer was dangling a good part as a carrot to get what he wanted out of her, Andy said. There were tears, accusations, shouting when they reached the car. Why was she so intent on being an actress anyway? Forget it. Are you saying I don't have the talent? Maybe you don't, damn it. More tears; anger. You don't believe in me. Well, you'll do anything for a part; you care too much about your so-called career. She grabbed the car keys—Okay, I don't want you, and I don't want Hollywood if Hollywood doesn't want me—and jumped into the driver's seat. The engine roared, and he ran, scrambling, to get in the car on the passenger side. Tires screeching, the car headed out the driveway and tore up the road.

"I was angry and I said what I thought; I was afraid she wasn't above fooling around with Mayer to get that part. But I was too rough. I could have soothed her down. She was more fragile than I thought. Maybe I could have just said, 'Okay, fuck Hollywood, *I want you.*'"

She could think of nothing to say.

He didn't seem to notice. "I'll tell you why I didn't. Because at that point I wasn't sure I *did* want her. She was chewed up, obsessing over stardom."

Julie found her voice. "Like the girl who jumped off the *Hollywoodland* sign?"

His glance was startled, and he looked now straight at her. "Here's the truth, Julie," he said. "I figured when she crashed that car I owed her. Her face was cut pretty bad."

"That woman who threw the glass of bourbon in your face at the party—"

"She was a friend of Nicky's who still believes I was driving. I've never said differently."

"Why not?"

"You're asking that, as a woman? Look, if a man can't be a hero, he can still try to be noble. Or maybe just kind." He smiled slightly. "I wanted to forget it, stuff it away somewhere. I didn't want to be thinking about it or talking about it. I'm not sure what image of me I wanted you to believe. And maybe that's because I've known all along we were opposites. After what happened at the ballpark . . . Maybe I'm not a good match for you. I scared myself, Julie. Grabbing that guy—"

"That's ridiculous." She batted his words away. "We'll put this behind us."

He shook his head. "No, you won't forget it. And I'm too old for you anyway. We're not going to make it, kid."

Julie found emotional ground. "Don't call me 'kid,'" she said. "Don't call me 'kid' ever again, it's your way of making me less than you."

"Okay, you don't want to be called 'sweet,' and you don't want to be called a kid. God, can't you understand? You're not *less* than me, you're *different,* same as she was."

"Oh, I get it. She wasn't Jewish, either. Good excuse, Andy."

"It's about more than—her." He stopped.

"Now you're having trouble saying her name?"

"All right. It's about more than Nicky. There's a big divide between us, you know that. Just how welcoming would your family be if you brought me home to dinner?"

She had to fight. "You're not being discriminated against, you are discriminating against *me*," she cried. "I love you—there, I've said it. And I don't care if you still love that woman who let you go to jail for what she did, that's the past." She could hear it: her words were similar to Carole's. It wasn't by chance. She knew what she wanted.

There was no change in Andy's eyes. And then she understood. "You're afraid I'll prove fragile, too," she said with sudden astonishment.

His gaze faltered. Yes, that hit home.

"You're lovely and sweet and smart—and you believe in this place," he said. "If you crash, I don't want to be the cause of it."

"Not everybody does, for heaven's sake. Look at Carole; she's a strong woman who can stand up to anything."

He paused. His next words took all the fire out of her.

"She'll break, too. Most do."

"You are determined to believe that," she said.

"Experience, that's all."

They sat in silence, as if fixed in place—prepared for an upcoming scene, hitting their marks, waiting for the next cue. But no matter how intently Julie listened, there was no cue to be heard. She would have to find the right one on her own.

ulie saw Jerry Bryant coming onto the set, and burrowed as deep into the flimsy canvas chair she occupied as possible. This was no morning for chatter—not in her dreary state. The soundstage felt chillier than usual this Monday, and she pulled her gray mohair sweater close, hoping for invisibility.

Too late. Jerry had spotted her and was on his way over, flashing a big, toothy smile. Ever since that first awkward conversation with Carole about her menstrual cycle, he'd adopted her as his "pal." Julie figured he had a favor to ask. Somehow or another, he'd decided she was the conduit to the irrepressible Carole, who broke every rule he tried to enforce.

There was no use trying to replay the scene with Andy. He'd simply closed down. After a night of very little sleep, she was finally allowing herself anger. She would not beg anymore. She was ashamed of herself; she was not going to dissolve. She was going to keep writing. Now, if only Jerry would pass her by.

Beyond him, she could see Clark lounging in a canvas chair, waiting for shooting to begin. Victor Fleming sat next to him, the two of them laughing and drinking beer. He didn't need her to run errands, obviously. And yet here she was, on guard against something, feeling uncomfortable. Was no relationship ever secure? Well, she was doing this for Carole; that was enough.

It struck her suddenly that the atmosphere on the set was not as jumpy as usual. Nobody seemed to be in any hurry, which was odd.

"Good morning, pretty lady," boomed Jerry.

"Hi, Jerry, what do you need?" she said when the publicist stopped in front of her. He wasn't such a bad sort, really. Just annoying.

"A little help with Vivien, okay? Come with me, please?"

She stood reluctantly. Jerry cradled her elbow with one hand and began guiding her toward a door in the cavernous studio that led to the wardrobe department.

"This breastwork situation is out of hand. It has her in a constant fury," he explained, as if confiding something no one knew. "She's permanently angry about it, but today is the worst."

Julie needed no explanation. It was Jerry's job to keep as many gossipy items about conflict on the *Gone with the Wind* set out of the papers, and the "breastwork situation" was proving one of the hardest to control. Vivien Leigh was not to be appeased. Selznick hadn't helped matters by setting up a twenty-four-hour guard around her rented home on North Camden Drive. But with Clark and Carole finally married, he wanted no more "living in sin" stories, this time publicizing Vivien's relationship with Laurence Olivier. That enforced secrecy was not making for harmony on the set.

They walked into the wardrobe department, and Julie caught her breath. She hadn't visited here before. Everywhere she looked, costumes hung neatly on padded hangers—hundreds and hundreds of them, all made for *Gone with the Wind*. Under Selznick's exacting directions, bolts of luxurious textiles had been produced by small mills over two continents and delivered here to be shaped into gowns that would dazzle the eyes of any viewer.

Julie walked slowly down one row, resisting the temptation to finger the silks and velvet she was brushing by. She couldn't stop herself from touching a delicate lace petticoat that looked like gossamer, as silvery and fragile as a spider's web. Just the slightest of touches, she told herself somewhat guiltily.

Slowly, she became aware of raised voices at the far end of the room.

"I'm going to quit—I *am* going to quit!" screamed a voice. "They sit out there, laughing and drinking beer, those two, and they don't give a fig about this movie."

It was Vivien.

"Now, sweetheart—" soothed Jerry.

"Don't you 'sweetheart' me," she snapped. "I'm a prisoner in my own house, and they're binding me into these clothes every day, and I want it to stop." A cluster of fitters and dressers stood helplessly around her, waiting for a calm moment. She saw Julie and burst into tears. "You're Lombard's girl, aren't you?" she said. "Make those morons stop laughing at me." She held up a book. Julie saw it was a well-worn copy of *Gone with the Wind.* "You know what Victor said to me when I argued again for this dialogue?" she demanded with tears in her eyes.

"He told me to throw the 'damn thing' away. You know something else? He hasn't read the book, and neither has that mousy Leslie Howard. They don't care, they really don't care."

Julie did what came instinctively. She put her arms around the tiny actress and hugged her. "That's terrible," she said, ignoring Jerry as he blanched, gesticulating madly. Was she supposed to go along with Fleming's style of treating Leigh like a spoiled child? Not reading the book, indeed. Everyone knew the director was a rough-hewn man's man, just like Gable—but it was shocking that Fleming had never read *Gone with the Wind.*

Vivien quieted down almost immediately. Sobbing lightly, she sank into a chair; one of the fitters handed her a handkerchief right away. She smiled wanly at Julie. "Thank you. It's nice to have a non-patronizing response from somebody around here."

That was all she had to do. Amazed, Julie watched Vivien lift her head, stand uncomplainingly to be trussed up once again, and march out onto the set.

She was, after all, an actress, and a professional one.

"Julie, anytime you want to think about coming back to work in my department . . ." an impressed Jerry Bryant began.

"Thanks, Jerry," she said, mustering a smile. "I have other plans."

＊

A few nights later, she sat in Carole's Bel-Air living room, twirling a glass of white wine in her hand, staring at the prisms of light breaking and forming as she sipped, trying to look anywhere except at Carole. But she couldn't block out the sight of Carole's blond head bent forward as she silently read Julie's manuscript.

I shouldn't have given it to her, Julie thought. It's too soon, it isn't ready. This isn't a college class. I'll look like a fool.

Much of her time lately had been spent watching Clark and Vivien shoot and reshoot different scenes, take after take, for hours. At first it was fascinating. The two stars joked together off camera, feet up, swapping gossip, gulping coffee. But the minute the cameras rolled, the atmosphere around them crackled with tension and passion. How did they do that? How could actors step in and out of reality so brilliantly? Yet, by the end of this particular day, Julie felt locked in a vise as tight as Vivien's whalebone corset. She wanted to do something to push forward. There had been no word from Andy, not a whisper. She couldn't keep yearning for him to reach out; it was dangerous. If she didn't challenge his certainty that she was fragile, she would never be sure of herself again.

Carole turned the last page. She put her hand on the manuscript and looked up at Julie with a curious expression on her face, "It's good," she said. "Like a short story. Is it about us?"

"Not really," Julie rushed to say. "But built on the kind of lives the two of you want to live, I guess—with totally fictional people." Was she babbling? The curious look in Carole's eyes was still there.

"Is this what you want us to be?" she asked gently.

"No, no, it isn't like that. This is just a story." Or was it? Now she wasn't sure.

"Honey, there's nothing wrong with believing in fairy tales. And sometimes they do come true."

They sat in silence for a long, almost dreamy moment.

Carole broke the spell. "My advice is, take this to Frances Marion," she said briskly. "If nothing else, this is your admission card. Think of it that way; it will be easier."

"Is it really any good?"

"Yes. And it shows *you*. I'll give Marion's secretary a call in the morning. Seeing her won't be a problem. She likes helping young talent—unlike most everyone else here."

That was all.

That night, back at the boarding house, Julie lay in bed with the lights out, hugging her screenplay. The thick stack of papers on her chest felt both comforting and heavy. Her admission card. To something. Something that would not include Andy, no matter how much she yearned for it to be otherwise.

*

It had indeed gone swimmingly.

"Yes, Miss Marion said to come to tea at her home on Saturday," the metallic voice of Frances Marion's secretary said over the phone a few days later. "Two o'clock. You do know the way, don't you?"

"No, I don't," she said.

An indulgent little laugh at the other end. "Just come to the top of the Enchanted Hill; you won't miss it." The connection clicked off.

In a car borrowed from Rose's fiancé, Julie drove up Angelo Drive, peering ahead, looking for what Jim and Rose assured her was one of the more spectacularly gracious homes in Hollywood. "It's a true hacienda. It could've been plucked out of Spain whole and delivered to the top of that hill," Jim said. "They've got a hundred and twenty acres up there. She and her husband built it; he's dead now."

The hill was cresting when she saw her destination. A home of creamy stucco rose gracefully to the sky. She drove through an archway into a court built of cobbled brick, curved around a fountain made of richly vibrant Mexican tile. Beds of exotic flowers and plants, most of which she had never seen before, gave the setting an almost tropical beauty. She pulled into a corner and switched off the ignition as an aide hurried over to give her a grin and open the door.

"Miss Marion is expecting you," he said. "The seminar is about to begin."

Seminar? Puzzled, Julie walked into the house.

*

Julie peered into a sitting room adorned with high arches and beautiful leaded windows.

Perched in high-backed chairs arranged in a semicircle, and looking as nervous as she felt, were half a dozen other women, each appraising the others with quick, darting glances. They sat in silence. A maid in starched white had poured the tea and passed a plate of sugar cookies, announcing that Miss Marion would be with them soon.

Julie took the last available seat, trying to keep the cup of tea now in her quivering hands from rattling in its saucer. She smiled cautiously at the woman closest to her, who had lively gray eyes and seemed to be doing the best job of all in balancing her tea.

"Hi, I'm Emily," the woman announced in a normal voice. Her hair was almost black, and cut in a short, somewhat out-of-date bob, but it gave her a casual air that Julie wished she could emulate. "Can you believe where we are? Should we be pinching ourselves to see if we're awake? We're sitting in Frances Marion's living room! How did we all manage to get *here?*"

Two of the women looked shocked. The others pretended not to have heard. Julie, without thought, started to laugh.

"That's very flattering," a strong, musical voice responded from the archway leading to the front hall. "Let's be clear, ladies—not everyone these days would be so impressed. You're all here because you are talented, you want to be in the picture business, and I want to help you. Greetings."

Frances Marion walked into the room and reached out a hand to each of them in turn. She was dressed in a gray wool-crepe dress with white cuffs and collar that clung naturally to her body, managing to convey both sophistication and sensuality. She had a warm smile, but her handshake held brisk professionalism as well as graceful hospitality.

"Let's start with some perspective." She strode over to the mantel and picked up a familiar gold-burnished statue.

"May I introduce the glory object of Hollywood?" she said, eyes dancing as she thrust it aloft. "Meet the inscrutable, perfectly shaped gentleman we all call Oscar. He's much heavier than you would think. Here, see for yourselves." She tossed the statue to the woman named Emily, who grabbed it in surprise. "See what I mean?"

"Oh my," managed Emily, hoisting it with some difficulty. "Yes," she said, turning to hand it to Julie.

As Julie's fingers closed around the cold metal, she felt a shiver travel down her spine.

"What I want you all to know first is that Oscar is a perfect symbol for the movies," Frances Marion said. "He's a man with a powerful athletic body, clutching a gleaming sword, right? But half of his head, the part which held his brains, is completely sliced off. In other words, my dear ladies, this place called Hollywood is run by men, and they're not always smart. So don't be too much in awe of them."

They all glanced at each other, smiling, relaxing. This would not be a standard seminar. For the next forty minutes, Marion asked the women about their work and told them she would read whatever scripts they had to offer. "But to work here, you must understand— this isn't the world of literature. Writing a script is like writing a bugle call—there are just four or five notes, and you have to keep repeating them."

There was more, much more. Julie tried to frame the question foremost in her mind and finally voiced it. "We all admire you," she began, "because you've done such wonderfully creative scripts for Mary Pickford and just about everyone else in Hollywood. You aren't saying these didn't amount to much, are you?"

"No," Marion replied. "But this isn't the place for a novelist. Not if you require a symphony to tell your story. It will save some heartache. Cary Grant said it best: 'We have our factory, which is called a stage. We make a product, we color it, we title it and we ship it out in cans.'" She looked full at Julie and gave a small smile. "Even when it's a movie like *Gone with the Wind,*" she said quietly.

*

A full tea was served in the garden. Julie sat next to the woman named Emily and discovered she had offered a script to Selznick and heard nothing back. "Me, too," piped up a comfortably rounded woman, munching on a scone dipped in Devonshire cream. "They could at least have the courtesy to say no, don't you think?"

The response to that was a collective sigh.

The afternoon sped by. When it came time to leave, Julie put her script down on a table, letting go of a part of herself, hoping it would live and thrive. She looked at the others, each similarly leaving a script, knowing they all felt the same way. She felt oddly thrilled, not anxious. There were other women like her, and they weren't all deluded, starry-eyed females trying to have a voice in a man's industry. And as she drove down the hill, after saying goodbye to the others, she laughed out loud, thinking of Marion's Oscar. With half his head cut off.

CHAPTER 13

*H*eard anything yet? I've got champagne if you have; a stiff Scotch if you haven't."

Carole could make her inquiry sound casual, but, then, she was an actress. She and Julie were measuring the dining room at the ranch for a bear rug Carole had dragged home from an auction, besotted with what she called "the noble head" of the beast.

"Isn't it gorgeous?" she enthused as they pulled and shoved the dead bear to the middle of the room. "It will fit, of course it will. I want his head—look at those teeth—facing Clark when we're eating dinner; he will love it. This place is almost getting crowded! Okay, which is it, champagne or Scotch?"

"Scotch." Julie sighed.

Rain was falling outside. Julie could hear it tapping on the windowpanes, followed every now and then by a sleepy roll of thunder, echoing from somewhere off in the fields surrounding the house. Beyond the rain, on the horizon, a thin ribbon of fading light still glowed.

She looked around. Indeed, the rooms were filling up. Much of the furniture was Early American, mixed with Western notes—in one room, Clark's rifles were mounted all over the walls. As soon as Clark finished shooting the last principal scene of *Gone with the Wind,* they would be moving to Encino. Carole had two movies completed for the year now, including *In Name Only* for RKO, which meant no more opportunities to tease Cary Grant over his real name—"Poor man, Archie Leach? Everybody should be given a second chance on what to call themselves." She could pour her energies into scouring shops and secondhand stores for treasures sometimes only she valued. Like the bear rug, Julie thought.

Julie plopped down on the soft fur, avoiding contact with the bear's eyes. Spending time with Carole was like breathing in crisp, bracing air, sometimes too much at a gulp. But they were friends now. Just today, they had packed Carole's things on the Selznick lot, stripping away all the glamorous white sofas and lavish lamps in her dressing room, leaving it once again just a trailer. Even though she had finished filming *Made for Each Other,* that trailer had allowed her a presence on the Selznick lot—and, as far as Selznick was concerned, anything that made Carole happy made Clark happy.

"Poor David, I'm sure he thinks I'm not leaving a moment too soon," Carole said to Julie, surveying the cheap-looking ordinariness of the empty space. "That bright idea of mine yesterday was about as smart as my turning down the lead in *It Happened One Night.*"

That "bright idea" had involved launching a few hundred balloons at yesterday's picnic for the cast and crew on the Selznick International front lawn. Unfortunately, they floated out over the Atlanta sets, stopping the filming of a scene. The sun was bright and hot, and the balloons began to pop. Maintenance crews fanned out, frantically looking for all the bright pieces of latex scattering everywhere. Selznick had not been pleased. That Carole thought it was funny and didn't apologize hadn't helped. Clark later reported the hilarious sight of a cursing Selznick pacing the set, picking up balloon fragments himself.

"Only you would get away with that one," Clark said to his wife, chuckling.

"I wish I'd hear something," Julie said now. She flexed her fingers, which felt stiff from lack of use. They hadn't had a workout on the typewriter in what seemed like an eternity—in truth, more like two weeks.

"Sure, I understand. Creative people live in mortal fear of tossing their seed on barren ground."

Julie couldn't help it—she laughed.

"So I mangled the Bible this time?" Carole grinned. "Well, that's what happens when you leave school at fifteen." She leaned over the bar, belly first, and surveyed the various bottles, which were lined up like soldiers on duty. She picked up an already opened bottle of Johnnie Walker Black. "This is Clark's favorite—a bit strong, but you need it today," she said. She turned her attention back to the shelves of glasses on the other side of the bar. "Cut crystal or jelly?" she asked.

"It doesn't matter."

"We'll go fancy."

Carole picked up two crystal glasses with the bottle and sat back down on the rug. She poured a healthy-sized drink and handed the second glass to Julie. "So—what was it like to go to a high-toned college like Smith?" she asked. "Does everybody ride bicycles and wear walking shorts? Nobody to do your makeup before class?"

Memories of the wooded landscape, the tidy, carved paths, the sense of containment that marked her college life surged back. Julie blinked, suddenly nostalgic for all those middle-aged teachers in dark dresses and Peter Pan collars who laid out study plans, gave weekly tests, graded precisely. In college, rules were clear. "It was fun, but . . . it hugged too tight," she said. "Margaret Mitchell actually went there for a while, a long time ago. I heard she hated it and dropped out."

With a sympathetic chuckle, Carole handed her the bottle. "You stuck with it, and she's the one making a million dollars. It's okay to toss the first one down."

Julie filled her glass and took a big gulp, swallowed fast; then took another and started to choke.

"Drinking correctly does not seem to be a skill they taught you at Smith," Carole said, taking the bottle from her. "I've watched Clark do it, one healthy swig at a time. It builds fortitude." She poured her drink to the brim and drank, then handed the bottle back to Julie.

"When did you know you wanted to be an actress?" Julie asked.

"I didn't really; it just happened. I used to play baseball in the street with the boys after school, and a producer visiting his mother was out on the porch one day and saw me...." She shrugged. "I never got to geometry."

"Am I bragging if I tell you I got straight A's in geometry?"

Carole flashed a fake wicked smile. "Let's get to the important stuff," she said. "Did you ever play ball as a kid?"

"I couldn't hit," Julie confessed. In her neighborhood, the boys ran the night games out on the street. A girl who couldn't hit had to watch from the sidewalk.

"I loved it," Carole said dreamily. "I loved the feel of the bat, the sound when it hit the ball, that fabulous crack. And I could run; damn, I was a good runner. I was the best runner on my block. There were nights when I felt I could fly if I just ran a little faster." She lifted her arm, observing her muscles with detached curiosity. "I wonder if I could still do it?"

"I'll bet you could do anything you wanted to do." Julie meant it.

"Okay, here's my question." Carole frowned. "What the hell is a hypotenuse?"

"It's the longest side of a triangle."

"Well, we know a lot in this town about triangles. I'd guess the longest side is the guy."

Julie giggled as she poured another drink. "Are we really doing this? I feel like we're in some Western movie."

"Saloon scene, *Peril at Noon,* take one!" Carole gulped down a mouthful of Scotch and let out a whoop. "Good shooting, partner, we got ourselves a bear!" Her nose was getting pink.

"I've gotta ask you something," Julie began.

"Well, hurry up, we're both going to be too drunk to string two sentences together pretty soon," Carole said cheerfully.

"I think of you as fearless. Are you afraid of *anything*?"

"Live bears," Carole said. "I like dead ones." She patted the head of the bear lying so tamely beneath them.

"How can you be fearless unless you don't care what happens?"

"Honey, how can you be fearless unless you *do* care? I care like hell about some things, and the things I don't care about don't rank on any fear scale at all." Her forehead puckered into a frown. "Did that make sense?"

Julie wasn't sure now whether it did or not. The bottle was passed again. "I want to sell my script and I want Andy," she said. "Maybe I'm asking for too much."

"Oh, fuck that. Ask for the moon, why not?"

"We haven't talked lately." Julie's stomach ached, thinking about that. Or maybe it was the Scotch. "And maybe you're wrong about Frances Marion. Maybe she read my script and thought it was total trash."

"You're on your own with Andy, but I told you, you'll hear from Marion." Carole squinted, trying to see into the bottle of Scotch. "It's empty," she said in surprise. "Should we open another one?" She stopped, listening. "I hear something."

Julie nodded. "I thought it was my ears." The room was spinning.

"I think it's the phone." Carole started to get up and fell back down onto the rug. "My legs aren't working," she said, giggling. "Well, I can still crawl." Slowly she made her way to the telephone stand in the hall and tugged at the cord. The phone toppled to the floor. Carole picked up the receiver, holding it upside down at first, then cooed, "Hello?"

She listened. "Well, of course she's here," Carole said. "I'll tell her. What time? Who is this? The maid, honey." She hung up and crawled back to the rug.

"Speaking of the devil. That was Frances's secretary. She wants you to attend a story conference tomorrow morning in the Writers' Building at MGM. Nine a.m."

"That was for me?" The room swayed. Julie tried to stand up, but collapsed like a string doll. "They like my script?" She could hardly form the words.

"Well, put it this way—you have been invited to your first literary dissection. Now you will see how the creative process really works. Congratulations!" Carole struggled to her feet, pulling at the buttons of her well-worn gabardine pants. "These things are getting tight," she muttered. "Honey, it's time for the champagne. Just a little."

Carole's words floated in Julie's befuddled brain. She heard the champagne cork pop and felt the bubbles tickling her nose as she and Carole hoisted stemmed glasses this time. Carole was laughing and chattering, even as Julie, the room swaying even more, puzzled over one word. Dissection?

*

The morning sun was moving relentlessly upward. Julie stood staring at herself in the bathroom mirror of the Encino house. Before her, a can of Barbasol shaving cream and two toothbrushes—one red, one yellow—sat at attention on a thin glass shelf, signaling the beginnings of serious occupancy. No array of cosmetics yet; no brushes and creams and salves—those were all still in the Bel-Air house.

Was Carole the red one? Or the yellow? Julie ran her tongue over the mealy fuzz in her mouth; it made her think of mold. She gagged.

So this was what a real hangover felt like. She'd been high before, a little drunk, kind of tipsy, but never with an aftermath like this. Her mother would be in despair. Her daughter, the nice young Smith graduate, was truly, horribly hung over. Naturally— she was living in a city of sin. Julie frowned, pressing her forehead against the cold mirror over the bathroom sink. Had her mother ever actually said that? She couldn't remember. Well, anyway, she thought it.

Julie blinked, trying to clear the red from her eyes. What time was it? There was no way she could have made it back to the boarding house last night. Carole, all apologies, had given her a pair of pajamas to wear; they enveloped her. Were they Clark's? "They're the ones of his I could've worn if I'd played Claudette Colbert's part in that damn movie," Carole told her with a giggle. "Good night.

Set the alarm. Take my car. Wear something in my closet, but don't wake me up."

She then weaved upstairs and threw open the bedroom door, waking what sounded like a surprised Clark. Julie heard her giggling, teasing; then Clark's gruff, sexy baritone. The door closed.

Now all Julie could think of was brushing her teeth. I'm sorry, Carole. I'm sorry, Clark. She reached out for the yellow toothbrush, squeezed some Pepsodent onto the bristles, and brushed with one goal: get rid of the mold.

*

The sun glanced off the windshield of Carole's car as Julie drove to the MGM studio, the light stinging her eyes. She would never touch Scotch again, she vowed. She would never drink a glass of champagne again. Please, she would promise anything to make this appointment on time and standing up straight.

Finally, she was in Culver City, and there it was ahead of her, the central entrance to MGM Studios. Very grand—formidable. It made Selznick International look like a dollhouse. She parked on the street and presented herself to the uniformed attendant inside the guardhouse. He was wizened, dried up from too much sun. His hat, which once might have fit, settled low over his brow. He surveyed her with a critical eye.

"One of Marion's girls?" he said, raising his eyebrows.

"I have an appointment for nine o'clock."

The guard glanced at the clock behind him. It was now a quarter to nine. Julie felt a dampness under her arms and hoped she wasn't ruining Carole's green jersey jacket. He seemed to be thinking it over, playing with her. "Well, okay," he said, after perusing a sheet of paper. "You're on the list. Go to the Writers' Building. Room 632. It's a good walk down that way." He pointed.

Julie didn't care how she looked; she ran. Past a pair of clowns in full makeup, lounging against the side of a building, puffing away on cigars. Past a cluster of women in bright ballet costumes, practicing turns and pirouettes. Past a freckled teenager wearing braces and a cap pushed back on his head—was it Mickey Rooney? Hurry, hurry. She didn't know who would be there, what was supposed to happen; all she knew was, she had received a summons that might change her life.

*

The door to Room 632 was ajar. Julie hesitated, then stepped in. Half a dozen men sat around a long table covered with ashtrays full of cigarette butts. The walls, indifferently painted at some point in the past, were streaked with smoke stains. Frances Marion wasn't there; no women were in the room.

"Miss Crawford? Sit down, young lady," said a rotund man squeezed into an expensive suit. His hair, thin and graying, was combed carefully over an oily scalp. He did not stand up, just waved her to a seat next to him. His mouth somehow smiled while the rest of his face didn't move. He looked down at a stack of papers in front of him. "We've read your script. A lot of talent here, right?" He surveyed the others at the table.

"You said it, Abe." A man sitting across from her was nodding so vigorously that his head looked as if it might come loose. His complexion was sallow, the color of thin chicken broth. He was drumming a yellow pencil against the table with jittery fingers. "Wish we had the money for it."

Julie sank into the seat next to the man named Abe. "It's a very contained story, a love story," she said quickly. "It wouldn't require expensive sets." She knew a little something about that, having watched the creation of *Gone with the Wind,* she reassured herself.

They looked at her blankly, as if she hadn't spoken.

"I could see Hepburn in this," said a third man, sitting at the end of the table, cradling a cup of coffee. His face was puffy, his eyes bloodshot. He looked as if he, too, might have finished off a bottle of Scotch last night.

"She's box-office poison, too smart-ass," said Abe, thumbing through the script. He stopped and looked up at Julie. "Can you write for men? It's action, drama—not dialogue, you know."

"I think so," Julie said, wondering what that meant. "I'm sure—of course I can."

A fourth man, sitting at the end of the table, stared down at what Julie assumed was her script, shaking his head like a doleful coroner performing an autopsy. "We need a good detective story. No, we're *desperate* for a good detective story. Something gritty. Can we fold a murder in here?"

This time it was Julie who looked at all of them blankly.

Abe said, "This is very L.A. But we need more sophistication. I don't want to see any goddamn palm trees."

"Actually, this is set in the Midwest," Julie interrupted.

"Manhattan?" said the man drumming with the pencil. "We could do Brooklyn or Coney Island. Maybe a murder on a Ferris wheel?"

"Christ, no," said Abe. "There's no audience for Brooklyn." The drumming stopped immediately.

"What we need is a corpse rouger," the coroner broke in.

"What's that?" Julie asked.

"Somebody who can pump life into a dead script."

Surely she had heard wrong. "Are you saying—"

Abe brightened. "If I can just jump in here for a minute, I think what we need is a good woman's tearjerker. Broken love, a murder—juicy."

"That's it, Abe." Everyone around the table nodded in unison.

"Well ..." The man named Abe was pushing back from the table, signaling an end to the meeting. "How's three hundred for six weeks?"

"What?"

Again, it was as if she hadn't spoken.

"You okay with that? Wonderful! Welcome to the MGM family," Abe boomed, standing up. "We'll get this set up. Nice to have you on board." He reached out a hand. "Better check in with Marion before you leave."

Dazed, Julie took his hand, mumbled her goodbyes, and walked back out into the narrow corridor. Somebody would point the way.

*

"Miss Crawford? Miss Marion's expecting you," said a crisp-looking receptionist as Julie approached her desk. It had taken ten minutes of wandering from floor to floor to locate the right office, which, when she finally found it, was smaller than she had thought it would be.

Marion sat at a narrow, highly polished desk filled with papers. A transom window was open, but no breeze was circling today. Surrounding her in casual clutter were boxes of what looked to be scripts; behind her were shelves filled with randomly stacked books and several family photographs in gold frames.

"Some of us around here still read," she said with a smile, as Julie's gaze rested on the books. She waved her to a seat. "You've had your baptism of fire, or at least one of them," she said. "And you survived. Abe Goldman—he's a production head, by the way—gave me a quick call. He liked the way you stood up for your script."

"But he didn't want to talk about it," Julie said uncertainly.

"That's the way it works." Frances Marion leaned back in her chair. "Abe wants to *think* he values independent writers—encouraging creativity and all that—but, just between us"—she actually laughed—"he rules in a small universe, and values mostly his own opinions. Sound familiar?" She arched an eyebrow, but kindly. "Julie, you've been offered a job—just for six weeks, but you will know what you want much better after that than you do now." Her voice took on a wistful edge. "It's very different from what it used to be. Nowadays, you knit your story all day, and people like Abe unravel it every night."

Julie said nothing for a moment, gazing at her idol. Marion's dark hair was pulled back into a businesslike bun, with streaks of gray at the temples. Her hands, in this light, looked more heavily veined than Julie had noticed before, and sprinkled with dark spots. What her mother called liver spots, Julie remembered with a jolt of surprise. She thought of Frances Marion as ageless, but she wasn't.

"You were with Andy Weinstein at the Mankiewicz party, as I recall. Any news about his grandparents?" Marion asked unexpectedly, leaning back in her swivel chair, hands pressed together under her chin.

"They were arrested; that's all I know," Julie answered, feeling awkward. If he had heard more, he had not told her.

"Put in a camp, probably. I was in Berlin last year," Marion said. "Swastikas everywhere. Lots of strutting soldiers with guard dogs. We should be doing movies about that, but nobody—not L. B. Mayer or the Breen Office—wants to offend Hitler. Mank wrote a good script about Hitler in '33, which pretty much decided its fate. Breen's censors killed it."

"Why?" Julie was sure she was asking a stupid question, but Marion answered soberly.

"We make too much money over there. Forty percent of our revenue comes from foreign markets."

"What do you think is going to happen?"

"Eventually, war. The Nazis aren't going away. I have two sons. . . ." Her voice trailed off for a moment before she pulled herself upright into a more professional posture. "We'll take care of all the details," she said briskly. "Your job will be to sit in on story conferences and work with other writers and producers to develop various scenarios. Whatever Abe decrees. No credits are promised, and all rights fall to the studio."

"And I get three hundred dollars?"

"Julie, you get three hundred dollars *a week*. This *is* Hollywood."

Julie gasped. "Oh my goodness, I can't believe it." She could save, maybe even save up to buy a car.

"It's almost like play money out here, you know. That's what draws writers like Scott Fitzgerald. He gets twelve hundred a week."

"Miss Marion, what happens to my screenplay?"

"Just call me Frances, will you?" She smiled. "Miss Marion has a thing for Robin Hood, and I don't have a thing for Errol Flynn." She made such an unexpectedly comic face, Julie laughed.

"That's the girl," she said approvingly. "Tuck your screenplay away in a drawer, but don't throw away the key."

"Okay." Julie drew a deep breath; it was still hard to say good-bye to her labors. "Can I ask—does my story really need a corpse rouger?"

This time Frances Marion laughed—a hearty laugh. And when they were both laughing, Julie began to feel that something good might actually be happening. At least for six weeks.

*

"Three hundred dollars *a week*?" Rose screeched the words. "Julie, that's incredible, I'm so happy for you!"

Julie had come in to the mimeograph room at Selznick International in search of her friend, who was working her last day, and Rose, bless her, actually jumped up and down as Julie gave her the news. It made Julie a little dizzy to watch her. The throbbing in her head had definitely not gone away. The room was encased in glass to save the rest of the office from the sound of the rattling machines, but Julie could see a few curious glances thrown in their direction— including one from the always inquisitive Doris.

"When do you start?"

"Not until next Monday. I haven't the slightest idea what they'll have me doing."

"Have you told Carole?"

"She's the first person I called." The whoop over the phone had been such a pleasure to hear. "She told me not to forget to laugh."

"Does Andy know?"

"I haven't seen him," Julie said.

They stared at each other.

"I think he might be happy for you," Rose ventured.

Her coaxing was having an effect; why shouldn't she seek Andy out and tell him her news?

"They're viewing rushes today. Maybe—"

"—I could take a stroll over to the screening room?" Julie smiled at her friend. "Well, maybe I might."

"If you don't, you can mimeograph this big stack of releases," Rose said jokingly, gesturing to a basket full of paper, making a face. "No, I didn't think you wanted to do that."

*

A slight breeze was blowing, just enough to make Julie glad she could button up Carole's green jacket, which was indeed quite damp now under the arms. The path to the screening room was deserted, for which she was grateful. It gave her time to think.

It was all very well to get congratulated on landing a writing job at MGM, but the job didn't feel any more substantive than a cone of spun sugar. What was she supposed to do? She thought of Andy's story about Mayer's stable of writers, wondering if that was what lay ahead for her. Irritated by her own nervousness, she straightened her shoulders as she walked. For six weeks, she had a real job. Hard though it was to admit this, it had stung a little when Vivien Leigh called her "Lombard's girl."

Julie made her way to a graceful street, a street straight from the old Atlanta of the Civil War. No one was around—no technicians in overalls, no extras smoking cigarettes, no directors, camera crews—it was empty. Tempted, she decided to walk through it.

To her left was the façade of a redbrick building, with a large, bold sign nailed to the wall that read ATLANTA EXAMINER. And just ahead was the railroad-depot set, designed—at Selznick's insistence—as an exact replica of the actual train-car shed destroyed by Sherman in the Civil War. Up on the hill behind it was the Tara mansion. And there was the white-columned church that soon came to be a hospital for the sick and wounded soldiers. The wind whispered around the corners of the façades; here and there, a door flapped back and forth, exposing the sturdy plywood structures holding them up from behind.

What would happen to all this? Would it be left to burn in some future cataclysmic fire ordered by some future powerful producer? And what would rise from those ashes? Julie smiled to herself with a certain ruefulness. She was writing melodrama in her mind—at least, some kind of script.

She was reaching the end of the street. Ahead was the present— the projection building, a solid, sealed edifice that had no windows. It was totally without magic from this view, but, with luck, there was magic shaping up inside.

CHAPTER 14

he screening room, with its dark, fabric-covered walls and comfortable seats of thickly padded tan wool, was supposed to be a more relaxed place than most of the sets of *Gone with the Wind*. Andy, back when he was introducing her to the culture of the movies, described the screening room as a place where tempers could cool, anxieties abate, credit be given. All, of course, if the rushes were good. If they weren't, the tensions heightened.

She remembered the wry twist of his mouth as he chuckled. "But you get at least the illusion of progress."

There was a different kind of atmosphere here today; Julie felt it the minute she walked into the screening room. The curtains onstage were open, but the screen was blank. They hadn't started yet. The place was filled with people moving back and forth, restlessly connecting, talking in low tones. The smoke from their cigars and cigarettes was so thick, it was a wonder they could see each other. This was where a pimple on Scarlett's cheek or a drooping chin line on the aging Ashley Wilkes would be discussed for half an hour; where technicians would decide if some scratched footage could be repaired; and where the cinematographer could enjoy quiet satisfaction when a particularly good shot drew approving comments from his colleagues.

Julie had been here only a few times, enough to know that the gravitational center of the room was usually the frowning, exhorting David Selznick. Not today. Everything seemed focused on a short, squat little man in the back, puffing on a cigar, talking to a frazzled-looking Victor Fleming in a voice that screeched like a rusted bedspring.

"I want a happy ending," he sputtered loudly, "and I'm not settling for anything else. People going to the movies want a love story that ends good, hear me? And no more of those scenes like Cukor going on forever with Melanie eating the chicken leg—this is a big story and it's gotta end like a big story!"

This could only be one person. Julie hadn't seen him before, but knew immediately it was Louis B. Mayer, Selznick's father-in-law. The powerful L.B., head of MGM, who once sold scrap metal, often referred to in lowered, tense voices—and, in fact, Julie's new employer.

The rumor was, Mayer couldn't read very well. He hired women readers to outline for him the plots of books that he considered buying. And, as Andy had told her, the bargain Selznick struck with Mayer to get Clark from MGM was to give Mayer a big share of the film's profits. How strange to look at this legendary man radiating power and think of him as the father of the cool woman she had chatted with at the Mankiewicz dinner. A wealthy father who wouldn't let his daughter go to college? Her parents would scorn him.

"Julie."

She turned around, her heart thumping. And there he was, looking much the same as he had the evening when she first met him standing so casually against Selznick's tower. She could see it all again: his hands, his steady, amused gaze—taking in the plight of a scared messenger about to lose her job. Andy, you need another haircut, she wanted to say. But she wanted to say it while lifting a hand to push the hair away from his face, her lips close to his.

"How are you?" she asked. With a great effort of will, she stopped herself from moving closer.

"Good. And you?"

He seemed as uncertain as she was.

"I'm fine."

"I didn't expect to see you here."

She took a step forward. "I've got some wonderful news—"

A familiar voice cut through the room, knife-sharp. It was Selznick, his face flushed, arguing with Mayer. "I won't allow a stupid ending pasted on this picture; it isn't going to happen. We're getting close to wrapping this, and I'm not fucking it up."

Mayer's face turned purple. "The public wants these two to end up in each other's arms, do you hear me? *And so do I.*"

"Shit," Andy said quickly to Julie. He nodded to the back row of seats. "Get a seat, hurry. Save one." With that, he moved swiftly to the two titans of industry glaring at each other, past an apoplectic Fleming. Andy put an arm casually on Selznick's shoulder. He leaned close, murmured in his ear, smiled at Mayer, and tossed off something casual. A joke? Mayer didn't exactly smile, but his response sounded a little like a grumbled laugh.

The jittery atmosphere of the room began to ease. The men started drifting to their seats. Julie sat down; after a few more words with Selznick, Andy strolled back, all smiles, and settled into the seat next to her.

"How do you stay so calm?" she asked, knowing better.

"It's part of my job." His lips twisted in a cheerless smile.

The lights in the room were dimming as the film editor signaled the projection room. And then, large, startlingly vivid, the face of a steely-eyed Rhett confronting Scarlett appeared on the screen. It took Julie a moment to orient herself to which scene it was. None of the rushes were in sequence, of course, because nothing had been filmed in sequence, which drove the actors to distraction. Vivien Leigh had garnered much sympathy a few weeks ago when she lamented, "We're handed scraps of paper, scenes that don't connect; how does an actress know where she is in the story?"

But from here, in the dark screening room, those concerns seemed inconsequential. The images of Rhett and Scarlett filled the room. Julie almost had to remind herself who these two people were. Yes, that was Clark up there inside that ruffled shirt—

Clark, the man whose wife teased him for his big ears. And that was Vivien, who raged daily against the indignity of having her breasts taped together.

. . . Scarlett has been discovered embracing Ashley in the lumber mill, threatening a scandal. She defiantly refuses to go to his birthday party that night, even though her absence would raise more suspicion. Rhett tells her she must attend. They argue; he wins. . . .

The scene faded. The room stayed quiet, so quiet you could hear the whirr of the projector. They all waited; there would be more.

Julie didn't want to move. Andy's breathing, calm and rhythmic, seemed bound to hers. The warmth of his body flowed so close it rattled her. The plan had been to share her news and then leave, asking nothing, expecting nothing. But here he was, so very close.

"Take a look at this one." Fleming's voice cut into the silence. "Clark added a little juice to the scene. We've shot the alternative, but thought you'd enjoy this, L.B." He chuckled and glanced nervously at the diminutive, stolid Mayer. Placating him seemed to be a universal goal.

. . . Clark, in a velvet jacket, smoking a cheroot, is celebrating the birth of Bonnie Blue, his child with Scarlett. Triumphant, he offers a glass of sherry to the comfortably rotund, smiling Mammy, who is delighted to celebrate with him. Shyly she accepts, reaching for the glass. Rhett grins. . . .

. . . And then, suddenly, Mammy—no, now it is Hattie McDaniel— spits out the liquid, looking totally surprised. Loosening his Rhett swagger, Clark begins to laugh.

A collective guffaw from the crowd watching. "That's Clark, always the practical jokester," said Fleming, slapping his thigh. "He threw out the tea and snuck real whiskey into that glass. Hilarious. Hattie's a good sport."

She barely heard his words, for Andy's hand had settled over hers. Not holding, not stroking. Just resting. He didn't turn his head; she didn't turn hers. Slowly she moved her fingers, then shifted her hand palm-up. Their fingers intertwined.

He had asked, and she was answering.

*

It was another ten minutes before the lights went up, this time on a reasonably jovial group. The rushes today were good; Selznick was not demanding retakes. Julie slipped her hand from Andy's, and saw in his eyes something she had missed terribly.

"Dinner tonight?" His lips curved; this smile was genuine.

She nodded. Those two words—they were able to undo the heartache and uncertainty in an instant.

"What were you starting to tell me when you came in?"

"I've got a writing job," she said eagerly. "MGM hired me; it's a six-week tryout."

"Your script? It sold?" He couldn't hide his surprise, which rankled a bit, but she saw his eyes brighten, too.

"Well, no. But they said they like it. I'll be included in story conferences, maybe offering ideas, hopefully writing dialogue."

"Who hired you?"

"Abe Goldman. Frances Marion set it up."

People were standing, putting on jackets, putting out cigarettes in the ashtrays at each seat. Andy at first just stood there, gazing at her. Then he smiled. "I know that guy," he said. "You've got quite a ride ahead of you." He shrugged his shoulders. "Well, you're hooked now."

"Anything more to say than that?" She wasn't going to let herself get anxious.

"I'm happy for you; you've wanted this, and I know you'll work hard. Don't mind me—you know my sour views." He reached out, hinting at an embrace, but stopped and turned his gesture into a touch of her shoulder. This was enough to unleash her tongue.

"I've missed you," she said.

Someone was calling his name. He glanced in the direction of the voice, then back to her.

"Julie." His voice was an exhale, something between a sigh and a groan. Then he gave a deep breath. "Will you come home with me?"

She nodded. He flashed a quick smile and turned away.

She stood alone, wondering. If happy endings only existed on-screen, as Andy would say, maybe she needed to be careful. Maybe she was writing the story she wanted in sand. But maybe, for God's sake, Andy was wrong and just didn't know it yet.

*

Early summer in Los Angeles was hard to identify; it was so much like the rest of the year. That was the standard line to newcomers, always good for a roll of the eyes or a laugh. You looked for seasonal changes in the clothes on the mannequins in the windows of the May Company and Bullocks, and little shops with jaunty names—like Sporty Knit—on Hollywood Boulevard. It actually wasn't true, Julie thought as she settled into the passenger seat of Andy's car and unrolled a window, the better to breathe in the golden air of early evening. She felt the delicious change of seasons on her face, in her hair. Everywhere.

Andy made no attempt to head for one of the restaurants they usually frequented. They headed first for Julie's rooming house, where—without discussion—she hastily packed a bag. Then, back into the car. Andy turned off of Sunset and drove up the narrow, twisting road that led to his house, so discreetly tucked into a hillside. Their silence was comfortable. Anticipatory.

*

The car turned into the driveway, its tires crunching gravel. Andy flicked off the ignition and sat still for a moment, not looking at her. His hands rested on the wheel. She examined them. These were the very same hands that by now knew the private terrain of her body very well.

He opened his door; she opened hers. He fingered the house key on his ring, turned the lock of the highly lacquered black front door, and pushed it open. In the front hall, they stood close, not moving at first, just looking into the sleekly furnished living room and beyond.

"The first time you brought me here, you said you felt exposed—that your house would tell secrets you preferred to keep."

He smiled, still not looking at her.

"What are they?"

"Just one." His voice sounded as gravelly as the driveway.

"What is it?"

"That I'm a lonely man."

She turned to him. Gently, he pulled her close, then buried his lips in her neck and kissed her with an intensity that took her breath away. No tentativeness; no courting; just a hungry joy that came from him and was soon inside of her, moving through every nerve, tensing every muscle.

"Oh God, I love you," he whispered. He started to pick her up, but her legs crumbled, and soon they were in a heap on the floor, fumbling, unbuttoning, unzipping.

Had she heard right? Had she heard what he said, was it the truth? His hands were everywhere. She arched her back, all banal concerns such as words and what they meant evaporating from her brain.

*

The flick of a lighter; a spark of fire; then darkness again. They had never bothered to turn on a lamp. Andy leaned back, inhaling. "Are you hungry? I can scramble some eggs," he said.

She lay in the crook of his arm, somewhere between consciousness and a creamy form of sleep. "Hope you have some decent cheese to put in," she murmured.

"For God's sake, what kind of cook do you think I am? Of course I put good cheese in."

"Velveeta?"

"Never." He was kissing her neck again, licking her ear. "Tell me more about this new job of yours."

She regaled him with an account of the strange meeting at MGM she had joined as a bewildered participant, describing the room, Abe Goldman, and the others. What they wore, what they said; how they were talking about anything and everything except the script she had put before them like some orphan baby, watching it shiver on the steps of the great MGM.

He laughed—threw his head back and laughed. It was infectious. She found she could laugh, too. "I really don't know what I'm supposed to do, but, Andy, it is exciting, isn't it?"

He ruffled her hair and pulled himself up on one elbow. "Of course it is. You'll have a good run. Now, here is what I predict: Monday, they're going to assign you to some gangster-movie rewrite."

"That's crazy," she protested.

"Enjoy, kid." He paused, casting her a questioning glance. "Is it okay if every now and then I call you that?"

He could have called her a walrus on this wonderful evening and she wouldn't have cared. "Just as long as it doesn't get to be a habit," she said.

"Good." He leaned back. "I'm ready for a drink, aren't you?"

She winced. "Not quite yet, actually."

"Mind getting me one?"

"Nope." She kissed his cheek and stood up, walked naked over to the bar, aware that his eyes were following her all the way. The door to the liquor cabinet was ajar. She opened it. Inside wasn't just the usual bottles of wine; there was also a large bottle of bourbon, half full.

"Been having some parties?" she asked as lightly as she could.

"No," he said. "And no women, either, if that's what you're asking."

"Looks like you've upped your consumption of bourbon." She laughed, giving assurance that she was just joking.

"Yeah, I think I've been pushing it lately." He didn't laugh. He sat up, ground his cigarette into a glass ashtray, and reached to the end table by the sofa for his pack of Lucky Strikes. He quickly lit another cigarette. "Yeah, it's been different."

She pulled out the bourbon and poured him a glass. "Tell me about your grandparents," she asked, handing it to him.

"I like you walking around naked," he said, taking the glass. "Don't get dressed yet, okay?"

He pulled himself onto the sofa, and she sat down next to him, tucking her legs beneath her. She liked it, too. It was freedom. Where had the modest Julie from Fort Wayne gone? What would the teachers in high-necked navy-blue serge at Smith think of her now?

"Tell me," she said.

He took a deep gulp; she could hear him swallow. "You'll get bored in two minutes."

"Oh, shut up and talk."

"Is that Julie talking?" He grinned faintly. "Pretty assertive kid these days."

And then, in a ruminative tone that was new, he told her about his grandparents. "For me, they never can be just old people with white hair, hobbling around," he said. His grandfather taught history and wrote textbooks, and his grandmother—who loved reading— worked as a secretary in the local high school library. These were the two people he loved more than any, he said. He told of their home in a sleepy, neighborly borough of Berlin, where he had spent much of his childhood. Of the luxuriant fat maple trees that lined the streets. About a shallow river that ran through a meadow in back of their home. "I would take my grandfather's fishing gear and go try to catch dinner for the three of us." He smiled. "Never managed to catch a fish, but they never stopped me from trying. I caught on that there were none in that river when I was about ten."

"Were you there often?"

"As much as I could be. It was a happier place than with my parents. Anyhow, my mother died that year."

She heard the ache of memory in his voice, and waited.

With an effort, he lightened his tone. "You know the best thing? There was a chocolate factory nearby. On the days they were cooking it up, the kids in the neighborhood—including me—would sit on the curb, salivating at the smell, dreaming of gorging on it."

"Did you get any of it?"

"Well, sure. My grandparents weren't torturers." He took a lock of her hair in his hand and tugged it playfully. "Once a week, my grandfather and I marched down there, and I was given the excruciating pleasure of picking out a whole box of chocolate pieces. Damn, it was hard to choose. But I managed."

"You love them very much."

"When I was with them I was home," he said simply. "More than in New Jersey."

"You haven't told me this."

"I don't like nostalgia—and the Berlin I know is gone," he said. "Now I'm afraid they are, too."

She was silent for a moment. "What have you heard?" she asked.

"I've found out they've been sent to one of the camps. A place near Munich called Dachau. They were getting used to petty, harassing arrests, and I was hoping it was just another one." He reached for another cigarette. "Why didn't I haul them out of there? Christ, I knew the Nazis don't like any Jews, especially those who write history books."

She leaned closer, cupping her hand over his cheek. "Maybe because they were never doddering old people to you, and you respected their ability to determine their own lives."

He stared at her, at first almost uncomprehending. Then his face softened. "Thanks for trying," he said.

*

By ten, Andy was asleep on the sofa. She watched him, a little surprised at the number of drinks he had consumed. It wasn't his usual pattern. His mood had lightened as they put dinner together, making small jokes and passing on the latest gossip from the "*Gone with the Wind* wars," as he liked to put it. Selznick was complaining that Vivien's eye shadow wasn't green enough, and calling the makeup people at three every morning, demanding so much green eye shadow that it flaked into her eyes; she was furious. Andy made it funny, but his glass stayed refilled more often than usual.

She stared at the sink. The remains of their scrambled eggs lay crusted in a small iron frying pan. She would wash it later. Good thing she had brought clothes for Monday—Carole's car was in the Selznick studio parking lot for Clark to take home, and Andy was in no condition to drive.

Gathering her clothes, she looked ruefully down at poor Carole's rumpled and stained green jacket. Well, it had been quite a day.

She leaned over and kissed Andy gently on his eyelids. There was nothing to do but offer whatever meager comfort she could.

The house was silent now, except for Andy's rhythmic snoring. Her thoughts turned to Monday. She had a real writing job. She could breathe now; she could stop and absorb the news. She felt a pulsating surge of excitement. She would take whatever Abe Goldman pushed at her and she would do it well. She would make them sit up and take notice; she would make Frances Marion proud of her.

Andy turned on his side. Almost guiltily, she pulled her thoughts back and stroked his hand. Right now she was here, with this complicated, elusive man she loved. She curled up next to him on the sofa, pushing away thoughts about what was coming, about walking through those intimidating gates at MGM wearing a badge that would give her a professional identity for the first time in her life.

Think about it later, not now.

Truly, there was nowhere else at this moment she would rather be than here, with Andy.

CHAPTER 15

*I*t was the same guard at the gate of MGM as before, peering out at her on this drizzly Monday morning. But when she smiled tentatively, he gave back only a blank stare. "Name?" he barked.

"Julie Crawford. I'm supposed to get my badge from you." I work here now, she wanted to add, but restrained herself.

He shuffled papers, shaking his head. "No badge here with that name," he said.

"I'm sure there is," she said. "Frances Marion told me—"

"Oh yeah, you're one of her girls." He shuffled some more, then, almost reluctantly, pulled out a bright-red-and-blue badge with her name typed on it in uppercase letters. "Don't lose this," he warned. "You'll be thrown out in a minute if you do."

She assured him she wouldn't, pinning it to her jacket. It was her own jacket this time, not one cut as fashionably as Carole's, maybe even a bit staid, but at least it looked serious. She smiled to herself, thinking of Andy's advice this morning, when she pulled it from her bag.

"Wear it without a blouse. Abe Goldman would like that," he teased.

She'd laughed, touched at his effort to relax her. A whole weekend, most of it curled up with him in bed, not wanting it ever to end. But now it was Monday. Stockings; be careful, only pair; snap them into the garter belt. Wiggle into skirt; button blouse; don jacket. Buttoned or unbuttoned? Buttoned. Comb hair. Eye makeup. Rouge. Coral lipstick—or did the color look too bright?

"Go for it, Julie girl," Andy said quietly as she picked up her purse and gave him a smile. He yawned, reached for his trousers, and pulled them on. "If I can find my shirt somewhere in the bedding, your chauffeur is ready."

And now here she was, blinking at the red-and-blue badge, which had just torn a hole in her jacket.

"Don't you know how to put that badge on?" the guard barked again. "Jesus. Women."

"Where do I report?" she asked, putting a snap into her voice. She wasn't going to cringe before this bully.

"Same. Room 632, Writers' Building. That's where all you writers go."

As she turned away and walked through the MGM entrance, she consoled herself with the reminder that she didn't like the jacket anyway, and the badge would hide the tear.

The main street into the studio was almost deserted this morning, probably because the dreary rain falling from dull skies seemed to have no intention of stopping soon. She took to watching her feet after stepping into an unexpected puddle. She reached the Writers' Building, climbed the stairs to Room 632, took a deep breath, and pushed the door open. She wasn't late—in fact, she was early—but every seat at the table except one already held an occupant, and the haze in the air and the butts in the ashtrays confirmed they had been there for some time.

"Come in, come in, Julie, not to worry, we've been getting a little bit of a head start," boomed the voice of Abe Goldman. He leaned back in his chair, hooking his thumbs around a pair of bright-green suspenders pulled tight over his paunch. He wore no jacket. A large black dog lay curled at his feet, eyes closed, muzzle tucked deep into its thick fur. On a back table, Julie noticed for the first time an array of typewriters lined up and spaced precisely a foot or so apart, looking like soldiers at attention. "Okay if I call you Julie? We're all family here, hon. Right, Bill?" He looked to his left. Bill, the doleful one she had dubbed the coroner last time, nodded.

She sat down, to Goldman's left, folding her hands together on the table before her, not knowing what else to do with them.

"This is thinking-cap time, Julie," he said. "We need your ideas for our movie. Bill, hand this girl a notebook and pencil, will you?"

"What movie?" she asked, quickly taking the proffered equipment. She felt fully alert and ready.

"The one you've been hired to work on," Goldman said with a tiny tinge of impatience. "Gangsters, a sure bet."

Bill spoke up with a croak. "If we time it right, we can get Wallace Beery for this one."

Julie could almost hear Andy chuckle: this was just what he had predicted.

"He's too tough to work with," chimed in a new face at the end of the table.

"We can center it on a prison riot," said Bill.

"But wasn't that *The Big House*?" Julie asked, puzzled. That was one of Frances Marion's big successes years ago, and Wallace Beery had starred in it. Would they really be considering the same plot device and actor again?

"Nothing at all like that one," broke in Goldman, with a wave of his hand. "We've got something totally unique in mind. A breakthrough movie. Forget Beery—we'll get Jackie Cooper. This will be great; you're lucky to be working on this one. You can't imagine how many films made around here are so bad they're unreleasable. We just stash them away. So let's get some ideas." He looked at her expectantly; she noticed his nose had a greasy shine.

Julie took another deep breath. Four of the men at the end of the table were scribbling fast on their tablets, glancing up periodically, brows furrowed. Was she supposed to be doing the same?

"Well, I've been thinking, given what's happening in Europe, isn't it a good time for a war movie?" she said.

She saw their jaws drop, saw the glances shot in Abe Goldman's direction.

"Just what do you have in mind?" he said, his voice suddenly frosty.

"Nothing specific. Something on the Nazis, maybe from the perspective of an American caught there or with relatives there, maybe an updated version of *I Was a Captive of Nazi Germany*—"

Goldman cut her off. "That '36 disaster? The Hollywood girl caught by the Nazis? You think we're *crazy*? Heads rolled over that one. Look, the Nazis leave us alone; we leave them alone. Hey, honey, we need better than *that*."

She tried again. "I saw in the morning paper—"

"Look, let's get back to the real world. The papers deal with Hitler, not the movie industry. No war news." His eyes were narrowing.

"Okay," she said with a twinge of desperation. "So it's a prison movie. Maybe not just about bad guys, but there could be somebody unjustly convicted who is trying to get better treatment. . . ." Just throw it out; you can do this, she told herself.

"That's great," Goldman said. He looked at his watch. "Good. Just one favor before you get to work?" He smiled widely at Julie. "Old Sammy here needs to do his business. There's a path and bushes out the back door—mind taking him for a quick walk? Make sure he doesn't poop on the sidewalk."

Julie, flustered, looked at the dog, whose ears had pricked up at the sound of his name. He looked gentle enough. What could she say? "Okay," she managed.

Goldman pointed to the typewriters, nodding at the line of scribbling men before him. As one, they stood and moved over to the typewriters on the back table. The clatter of keys began almost instantly.

"See the end machine? That's yours," he said. "Let's get brainstorming; then we'll pound out the details."

Julie nodded silently. She leaned down, touching the dog's neck, feeling for the collar—hoping for a leash. The dog looked up at her with melancholy eyes. As if to apologize.

*

By the time Julie sat down in front of her designated typewriter half an hour later, the others were pounding away as if inspired. They're way ahead of me, she thought, feeling a rise of panic. What was she supposed to do? Somebody unjustly convicted. Her idea, right? Tentatively she tried a paragraph: Joe—that's a good enough name—Joe O'Leary is in prison for a murder he didn't commit. She paused. Maybe he was put in solitary after—after a food fight? She didn't know much about prisons or gangsters; she had to keep trying. If she sat here staring at the almost blank page, she would look like an idiot. Write something.

*

"Okay, gang, let's take a look." It was Goldman, who had disappeared for a long lunch and was now back in the room. He glanced at Julie as he petted the languid Sammy, again curled beneath his chair. "Sammy get his business done?" he asked.

She nodded.

Goldman started collecting the script drafts, chatting cheerfully, joking with the men as they rose and headed back to the main table. She handed him hers, which was barely three pages long.

He raised an eyebrow. "A master of brevity?" he said.

She managed a smile and took her seat at the table again.

"Okay, let's look at our little lady's first offering here; fine with you guys?"

The men all nodded.

"So we've got Joe O'Leary in jail for murder, getting into trouble after a food fight. . . ." He frowned. "Not sure about the name 'O'Leary.' The Irish all want to see themselves as priests these days. Food fight? Wouldn't a knife fight be better?"

A man at the end of the table—with a round face scorched an unhealthy shade of red—spoke up. "I envision a gang; they break out through an old sewage tunnel. They get caught—who ratted on them?"

Goldman smiled. "I like that."

Another voice from the end of the table: "Look, we've got a rogue guard who kills his best buddy from grammar school—he's in for robbery, and—"

It went like that for the next three hours. Two more trips to the typewriters. By the time the afternoon was waning, the idea intriguing Goldman the most involved three ex-convicts opening a grocery store in Abilene, Texas. Tomorrow they would probably be two cops.

It didn't feel like a job, it felt like a game. And maybe it was, she thought as she walked slowly out beneath the grand MGM arch. Maybe they were all acting, and Goldman knew the outcome already, and what was her role in all this, anyway?

She couldn't talk to Andy, not tonight. They had a date for Friday, but the pace on *Gone with the Wind* was growing faster and more fraught with tension every day. She was on her own for a while.

Julie climbed up the streetcar steps and was grateful to find an empty seat among the tired-looking commuters alternately dozing and staring out the window. The bell clanged; they were off. At least she was in a real world. Anyway, Rose would be eager to hear all about the enthralling start of her job as an MGM scriptwriter. So how would she respond?

That was easy: old Sammy had been the best part of the day. And for some tucked-away reason, that tickled her so, she almost had to laugh.

*

Andy arched an eyebrow and rolled his eyes. "Julie Crawford, screenwriter—whining about your chosen profession *already?*"

Friday night, her first week over—she had been looking forward to this. And here, finally, was Andy—she could tell him everything as they sat together in a Chasen's booth. One week now of learning how to read Goldman's mind and give him what he wanted. It was so crazy, wasn't it? She was trying to speak up in good old Room 632, but they all looked baffled when she threw out an idea.

Sometimes she wondered if anybody except Goldman actually *saw* her; besides, she didn't quite get the point of the constantly changing bad-guy script.

And now Andy was challenging her. "I'm not whining," she protested.

Andy swallowed the last of his martini and signaled the waiter. "Sounds like it to me. Look, it's been a rough week for me, too. Remember, you wanted this."

The words were out of her mouth before she could stop them. "That's your third martini," she said.

"Oh, I can do better than that. At least they're not doubles." He shot her a jaunty grin. "Sorry, but this movie is a bitch."

His rough-edged tone was new. Julie looked closely at him, realizing he had a twitch under one eye. His hand holding the martini glass was shaking slightly. She knew from Carole that everybody was expecting Selznick to fall apart any day, that only drugs and liquor were keeping him stitched together. Andy, too?

"How much longer until it's finished?" she asked.

"We'll wrap retakes by the end of August, I think."

She reached for his hand, wanting to still the tremor.

"Look, I'm not good for you," he said. "You shouldn't waste your time—"

"Don't say that again," she interrupted. "You get tired and depressed and then you think that I'm going to fall apart on you, and that's not going to happen."

The waiter was now hovering. Andy lifted his glass. "No doubts? Even if I order another one?"

It was a challenge, and it startled her. "I'm not crossing swords with you on this," she said.

The waiter took his empty glass and hurried away.

"You deserve better. You've had a rough first week, and you should be getting some sympathy, and I'm not giving it."

"Well, why don't you try?"

He looked her full in the face now, his eyes steady on hers. "Ah, a gauntlet thrown. Okay, I will, starting right now."

"Well?" She felt a nervous smile tugging at her lips.

"My dear Julie"—he reached out with his hand and cupped hers—"Abe Goldman is a jackass for not knowing how to use your talents best. And it will get easier as you get grounded. Honest."

"Thank you," she said.

The fourth martini arrived. He stared at it and then deliberately set it aside. "Would you like to come watch filming tomorrow? It's a big scene for Vivien," he said. "They won't have the theme music dubbed in yet, but it's going to be spectacular."

Julie nodded, feeling somewhat breathless. Being with Andy sometimes felt like swinging on a trapeze quite high above the ground.

*

Saturday morning, sunny, with a bite in the air. Appropriate. Once again, if Julie inhaled deeply, her throat constricted with the tension reverberating across the soundstage at Selznick International Pictures. It was only eight o'clock, earlier than most shoots, but Selznick was relentless in keeping up the pace—as everyone knew.

Andy's eyes lit up as he saw Julie slip into a chair. A dip of his head his only acknowledgment.

She spied Vivien Leigh standing aside, bedraggled, her clothes limp and dirty, her hands cupped over her mouth, eyes cast down. Behind her, a comforting hand on her shoulder, stood Vivien's lover, the dark-eyed, stunningly handsome Laurence Olivier. So Selznick had allowed him on the set this once; that's how important getting the right performance from Vivien was today.

Off to the side, Hattie McDaniel waited, arms crossed, staring at the floor. The set was a mix: a shambles of a wrecked house and, a few steps away, a flat piece of earth. A broken, skeletal fence. A stark, naked tree against a backdrop. Electricians were fumbling with floodlights.

"Move those spots; she's got to be in complete silhouette," Fleming ordered. The electricians hurried to obey. They tested the color.

"Intensify it," growled Selznick. "Make the light of that sun the color of fire. Flames, flames—everything has been destroyed. It's a sky of anger, the sun setting on a way of life. Get it right." The electricians nodded, adjusted again. Nobody questioned the orders of these two masters.

The hum of voices quieted. Fleming took his director's chair; Selznick, next to him, sat in rigid form, straight up, staring at the set. Julie knew what everyone was praying: Don't find anything wrong, not now.

"You ready, Vivien?" Fleming's voice, though not relaxed, was calm.

"Yes," said the drab, worn woman in the shadows.

The clap: *SCENE: HUNGER, TAKE ONE—VIVIEN*

Scarlett has escaped from the burning of Atlanta and made her way back to Tara. War has ruined everything. Her family and the remaining servants are all sick and starving. Dazed, she moves out to a barren stretch of land, a field scorched by war. The light glows behind her, casting her into stark silhouette. She leans down and pulls a root from the ground. A carrot, a turnip—withered, unedible. She crumbles, broken, her head down above the land, crying—finally, crying. And then she stands.

Vivien's voice cries out from the soundstage, filled with torment and ferocity. "I'm going to live through this. If I have to lie, steal, cheat, or kill, as God is my witness, I'll never be hungry again!"

"Cut," commanded Fleming.

For a long moment, no one said anything. Vivien was still standing in the makeshift field, breathing hard, and tears streamed down her face. She took a deep breath; wiped them away.

"Don't ask me to do that again, David," she said calmly, staring at Selznick. "You've got everything I have to give."

Selznick was motionless in his canvas chair. Olivier stepped forward, his arm around Vivien, staring at Selznick, silently daring him to try demanding his usual multiple retakes.

The set was very quiet as Selznick picked up the unnecessary bullhorn by his side and put it to his mouth.

"That's it for the day," he said. "Great job."

Vivien strolled off the set with Olivier, walking in the direction of her dressing room. Even with scraggly hair and a dirty face, she was beautiful. As she passed Julie, she winked. She was breathing deeply, almost defiantly.

Of course. As moved by the scene as she was, even with tears in her eyes, Julie couldn't help smiling: Scarlett's cry of defiance had come from a body unrestrained by a tight corset—and there were no tapings squeezing her two perfectly respectable-sized breasts together. You win this one, Vivien, she told herself.

Andy was at her side, looking tired and relieved. "We're getting there, we're actually getting there," he said. His shirt was damp with perspiration. "Pretty good, right?" He looked at her almost eagerly.

"It was terrific," she said.

"Wait until you hear the music. Max Steiner is working night and day; the one for this scene is called 'Tara's Theme.' Pretty damn good."

"How can he score the whole movie so fast?"

"He's got a couple of top composers helping, but if we run out of time, we'll take some scores from the MGM library," he said. "Look, we're done for today. We'll watch dailies after dinner. I hope there are no scratches on the film—I wouldn't relish the job of getting Vivien to do it again. Victor invited a few of us out for a couple of beers. Will you come?"

In the middle of the day? Fortunately, she bit her lip to keep from saying the words. God, maybe she was a wimp. A puritanical wimp.

*

The main street leading to the Culver Hotel at Washington and Culver Boulevards was dusty and hot. Such a strange, made-up town, Julie thought as they trudged toward the hotel. A faded sign hung high over the intersection, proclaiming in large red-and-black letters: THE HEART OF SCREENLAND. It was no idle claim. With two major studios in this town of nine thousand people at the foot of the Baldwin Hills, the movie business was both salvation and identity. The hotel—without its rotating glamorous guests—wouldn't have survived long.

"The *Wizard of Oz* gang finally cleared out of here. I'm told the Munchkins took their sweet time doing it," an engineer observed as the clearly exuberant Fleming beckoned them to follow him into a bar next to the hotel—a dark, narrow room with eight high bar stools covered in worn leather, lined up in a row, facing a mirrored wall half obscured by liquor bottles. Covering the window was a blinking neon sign for Schlitz beer. About ten people, all men except for Julie, had been invited along—a couple of electricians, another assistant director—male buddies clearly used to sharing the noisy camaraderie Fleming was famous for.

The bartender greeted the group with rigorous cheer; obviously, they were good customers. Andy helped her onto a stool, looking a little sheepish.

"Okay, we should be taking some kind of healthy hike along the beach, but, damn, everybody is tired as hell," he said, with a shrug of his shoulders.

"I don't begrudge you this," she said quickly.

"We'll stick around for just one beer."

*

Julie stared at the clock above the bar. It was already four o'clock. Andy and Fleming were in a long, slurred argument about whether Cukor should get any directing credit for the movie, which Fleming rejected out of hand. And what about Sam Wood, who took over for a while when Fleming was sick? "This is my movie," Fleming yelled at one point. The bartender turned up the radio to drown out their voices, but the two men still argued. The others had drifted over to a pinball machine, where they whooped and cheered whenever one of them won.

Julie kept a smile on her face, but her mouth was beginning to ache. She took a few bites out of a dry hamburger Andy had ordered for her; there was no ketchup to put on it, and just a darkened mass in the bottom of a mustard jar that looked as if it had been sitting on a shelf for a very long time. People didn't eat very often in here, the bartender confided. Sorry, lady.

"Can we go now?" she said to Andy, smiling brightly so the others wouldn't see her as trying to be pushy.

He patted her shoulder, and kept talking. Boxing now; they were talking about some boxing match.

"Well, look at all you bastards getting drunk," said a loud, familiar, cheerful voice. "Clark said he knew where you would be, and he's right! Anybody up for a game of darts?"

It was Carole, standing in the doorway, with Clark right behind her. She had a bright-green turban tilted rakishly across her forehead and wore a pair of beach dungarees that most women would scorn. On Carole, they were perfect.

"I am," Julie called out, sliding off the bar stool. She didn't have to sit here patiently waiting until Andy remembered she was with him.

The bartender handed her a box of darts and pointed to the dartboard. Ignoring Andy's startled glance, she joined Carole, and the two of them started a game.

"I was only planning to drop Clark off to toss a few with Fleming," Carole murmured to Julie. "But I saw you through the door, and you looked kind of bored. Everything okay?"

Julie threw a dart, keeping her hand steady. Bull's-eye. "Can I get a ride home with you?" she said.

Carole peered at the dartboard, impressed. "You're either really good at this game or mad at Andy," she said.

"Right," Julie replied. She already felt better.

Carole threw a dart. Again a bull's-eye. "Ready to go? Clark's settling in, and I've got stuff to do," Carole said, eyeing her husband. Clark was leaning jovially across the bar now, holding a beer, joking about Olivier's surprise presence on the set today.

"Sure." She was going home. Julie tried to muster some of Carole's lightness of being. So Andy drank too much; who in this town didn't? She walked back to the bar and tapped him on the shoulder. "I'm leaving," she said as casually as she could. "Big week coming up, and I've got things to do."

He looked befuddled, but showed a vestige of concern. "I'll drive you," he said.

"No, no, I'll go with Carole."

"I'll call you later."

She felt strangely serene. "Not tonight, Andy. I'm busy." And as she walked away, she felt some tangled threads loosening in her heart. Maybe she would be busy for longer than just tonight.

CHAPTER 16

Early morning at MGM was a lazy time, a waiting time. Julie was getting used to seeing actors, cameramen, gaffers, all lounging in chairs, talking, watching the parade go by. One time she saw two women chatting together, knitting furiously, fingers flying—and realized with a start that she was looking at Rosalind Russell and Paulette Goddard, two of the stars making a film called *The Women,* which—unbelievably—had no parts for men.

It also struck her that she was hearing more radios on her trek to Room 632. Roosevelt was announcing something about a commerce treaty—who with? She didn't catch it. The Nazis were signing a pact with Italy. There was talk of Japan; warnings of spreading war. Somebody yelled, "Turn that damn thing off; let's hear some music!" A sudden blast of swing replaced the broadcaster's sonorous voice.

None of the other writers was friendly. They all shot glances at the copy of the people next to them, short malevolent glares that hinted at much more than curiosity. They were probably all here on tryouts, all hoping for permanent jobs. And they were all dancing as fast as they could.

"Julie, honey . . ." Goldman touched her arm and guided her over to the door as the others stuffed rejected scenes into leather briefcases and packed up to leave. "I've got a plan for you that might help your creative juices flow faster."

He must be saying she wasn't performing well enough. Julie's heart missed a beat. Okay, she cared, she cared as much as all those other would-be screenwriters in the room. "I'm willing to work on any project," she said.

"Yeah, good." His eyes shifted restlessly. "Almost halfway already. We need to tap into your strengths more. You've seemed a little flat lately."

He was telling her she was finished; she was sure of it. Well, she wasn't going to blow her one big chance. "I'll do anything I have to, to give you the kind of work you want," she said quickly.

"Hey, I've got a great idea." His eyes lit up. "I've got a couple of movies at my place that you should see—they're more women's movies, anyhow. Why don't you come over tonight? We'll go through them, and I'm sure you'll get some real inspiration."

How could he be so blatant? How naïve did he think she was? Well, that was easy. He was a practical man who probably figured that, presented at the right moment of desperation, his sleazy gambit could work. She wanted to scorn this guy with his greasy nose, maybe even embarrass him—to stand up straight and say to his face, "I know what you're after, and I'm not that kind of girl." Corny, yes, but she could fantasize that. Yet that's not what came out of her mouth.

"Tonight?" She stared at him, her stomach sinking. "I can't tonight—"

"Then sometime this week." His voice was slightly edged now. "Time is running out, honey." He glanced at old Sammy, dozing under his chair. "Sammy would sure miss you, I can tell you that," he said.

*

The streetcar home bumped and rumbled over uneven pavement. Julie stared at the rounded back of the conductor, wondering how differently he and she experienced weariness. His arms were thick and strong. But he had to grip a wheel all day and watch for people darting across the rails in front of him. He had to swallow anger when riders snapped at him that he had missed their stop. Everybody had to contain feelings in one way or another; wasn't that what kept civilization working? Julie sat back and closed her eyes. The deal before her was pretty plainly drawn—nothing subtle about it. She couldn't imagine lying on a bed beneath that man. It was a dead end, this quixotic venture of hers. She couldn't talk to Andy; Selznick had sent him to Sacramento on some money-raising errand. What could he say, anyway? And since the afternoon at the bar in Culver City, she had felt a need to hold back a little, catch her breath.

His apology the next day had been both sincere and embarrassed. "Julie, I was a total jerk, and I'm sorry," he said. "The pressure here is getting to me, but I'm not going to let drinking run my life."

"It's more than the job, I think."

He blinked, paused. Then said, "Yeah."

"It's your grandparents. Your brother."

"I'm not denying it."

That was all; he said no more. But when she reached for him and kissed the tension lines on his brow, he held her very tightly.

So who else? Frances Marion was out of town, too; no chance to talk to her. She couldn't talk to Rose. Really, the only person she could talk to was Carole. But what could Carole do? Suggest she tell Goldman to go fuck himself? What a wonderful word "fuck" was. There was so much power in it. When Carole used it, with all her natural cheer, men froze—fearful or fascinated, it didn't matter— just definitely stuck in the headlights. Could she do it? Maybe. But, then, did she want to walk out on screenwriting and settle on a job imitating her friend's scrawling signature on high-gloss photos and taking them in batches to the post office? It wasn't enough to walk the sets of Hollywood movies and dream about somehow being part of it all.

The operator rang the bell. "Your stop, lady," he yelled.

Not tonight. "Drop me at Sunset," she said.

He shrugged, pulled on the bell, and kept going. There were only a few people left on the streetcar—the gray, almost invisible servants whose faces were always ordered and still, whether on duty or not. It depended on the neighborhood. Not many stayed on as far as the end of the line in Brentwood.

She walked up the hill, breathing in, calming herself down. From the outside, you couldn't tell that Carole and Clark were poised for an exuberant, chaotic move. All the terrain looked clipped and ordered and serene.

"Movies teach you how to do that," Carole had confided. "Create a set; who gives a shit if it's real? Just make it good enough to believe."

Carole opened the door. "Oh God, how did you happen to show up right now?" she said, grabbing Julie's hand and pulling her inside the house. She wore a terry-cloth robe. Her hair was divided into rows of thick pin curls held by glistening metal clips, her face partially covered in cold cream.

"I need some advice," Julie blurted, surprised. "What's happened?"

"Julie, hold on to your hat. Rose has been trying to find you."

Julie clutched the doorknob, her mind quickly spinning through a variety of catastrophes.

"No, no, not a disaster, come on in." Carole guided her into the living room and pressed her down into a chair. "My dear," she said solemnly, "your parents are in town. Your father had some business in San Francisco, and they decided to come here."

"What?"

"They showed up a few hours ago. Rose called me, I called Andy. He's been in Sacramento, didn't know where you were. What the fuck is up with you two? He sounded pretty tense."

"My parents are here?"

"Rose says they told her they intend to bring you home. And they're quite determined."

"What?"

"Honey, you said that already. Can we move the dialogue along?"

Julie leaned back in the chair, stunned. Her mother and father were taking charge again, just as they had always done. That bit of prosaic reality had faded in all the dazzling months since she came to Hollywood. She tried to catch her breath. She felt as if she were shriveling inside, getting smaller, younger.

"Okay, you have to go back to the boarding house and at least pretend that you live there full-time. What do you want to happen?"

Carole's voice sliced it, chopped it, served it to her, quivering, on a platter. *What did she want to happen?*

The tears began. Julie felt like an idiot. Her nose was running; she wiped it on her sleeve—a new jacket, bought in a proud blazing shade of red, not torn, but now stained and ready for the cleaners. Carole, silently, handed her a handkerchief.

"I can't face them. Everything is messed up; I can't face them."

Carole lit a cigarette and inhaled, oblivious to the blob of cold cream now quivering on her lip. "Sure, you can," she said. "You're no baby, or you wouldn't be here in the first place."

"Abe invited me to his place, and he's not talking about work," Julie said.

Carole let out a hoot, slapping herself on the knee. "It took him longer than I expected. Honey, he puts the move on every girl. Just blow him off; he's not powerful enough to make the difference between success and failure, but he sure wants you to think he is."

"Why didn't you tell me that before?"

"You have to find out these things yourself." Carole sat back, looking at her thoughtfully. She drew deep on the cigarette. "It's what you do after you find them out that matters." She suddenly jumped up. "I've got an idea," she exclaimed.

She went to the bottom of the staircase leading to the second floor, stepping carefully over packing boxes filled with dishes and bar stemware ready for the mover, muttering about all the damn junk that cluttered their lives and why didn't she get rid of it all.

"Pa!" she yelled.

"What?" came the raspy, deep-voiced reply.

"Aren't you doing a big scene tomorrow with Vivien?"

"Yeah, we fight and I sweep her up and all that. Why?"

"Julie has to keep her parents busy while she figures out her life; can we get them in to watch?"

Clark's head appeared at the top of the stairs. "Sure," he said. "At least I don't have to do any dancing."

Carole turned back to Julie. "Okay," she said briskly. "Bring them to the set tomorrow morning; everybody is impressed watching a movie being made."

"My father doesn't approve—"

"Oh, honey, bullshit. *Everybody* is—I guarantee it—even your father." She shook her head. "Funny, our parents are really different, aren't they? When my mother got divorced and left Fort Wayne, she headed right for Los Angeles so she could set out to make me a star in pictures. Big cheerleader."

"My parents consider everything here low-class."

Carole's face brightened. "You know what? We're going to have them to dinner tomorrow night. Relax them, talk about good old, fucking Fort Wayne. Right here." She looked around vaguely. "I'll just shove these boxes aside and fix something."

"Carole, you don't cook," Julie protested.

"Who said I'm going to cook? Now you've gotta get over there; my driver will take you. We can buy some time and keep them entertained while you decide what comes next in your life. And, honey . . ."

"What?"

Carole looked at her, and Julie saw in her eyes all that this other girl from Fort Wayne had mastered in herself: The sadness, the fear, the defiance, the strength to make it. And, always, the laughter.

"Toughen up," she said. "And don't cry."

✳

Jerome and Edith Crawford were seated stiffly on chairs that a flustered Rose had arranged for them on the front porch. Julie's mother held a teacup carefully balanced on a chipped saucer, sipping gingerly, listening to Rose chatter about the weather, and how nice it was this time of year, especially in the early evening. The light, you know.

Her father sat, simply staring into the distance. He had always disdained small talk, and as she stepped out of the car and started toward the house, it was clear to Julie that he was making no exception for the soft twilight of Los Angeles.

He looked older. It had only been some six months since she last saw both of them. Her father's paunch was larger, and her mother's hair was now quite thoroughly gray. Oh, please, don't grow old, she found herself thinking as she walked toward them. I love you both; go away and let me grow up; don't make me feel guilty so I do what you want me to do; but promise you won't grow old.

"Julie, darling." Her mother was on her feet, first carefully depositing the teacup on the windowsill serving as a table. "Wherever did you get that jacket? Darling, red? Red isn't your color, or—well—maybe it is now."

Julie put out her arms. Her mother was trying. "What a surprise," she managed, giving her a kiss.

Jerome Crawford was on his feet now, too. "This young lady gave us a tour of the boarding house," he said in a low, rumbling voice. "It looks quite well run, on the whole. She assures me there are double locks on all the doors."

Rose was smiling nervously. Chagrined, Julie remembered she hadn't bothered to make her bed this morning. Worse, she had left her panties and bra hanging on the shower pole in the bathroom. She cast a quick, imploring glance at her friend.

"The maid came early today," Rose said in a rush, reading her expression. "Did our room first, so your parents had a place to rest."

There was no maid. Julie wanted to hug Rose.

＊

Her father had already chosen a restaurant for dinner—nothing on Sunset or in Hollywood at all, but a steak house that a business partner had told him about where everybody seemed to be from the Midwest. A place where waiters gathered around different tables every ten minutes to sing "Happy Birthday" to a guest and present the celebrant of the moment with a vanilla cupcake topped by a candle.

"We've got one like this now in Fort Wayne," her mother said happily. "They are very much alike. It's quite pleasant, don't you think, dear?"

"Yes, Mother," Julie replied.

She told them about her writing job. About Frances Marion. About Carole and Clark, and all the glamour, and how exciting it was here. She apologized for not writing very often. She did not tell them about Andy. She did not tell them about Abe Goldman.

"Three hundred dollars a week?" her father said with astonishment. "That's insane. What work here can possibly be worth three hundred a week? What have you written?"

"Actually, I'm drafting a scene for a prison movie," she said.

"You?" Her mother looked stricken. "What do you know about prisons?"

"Not much," Julie said with a light, toss-away laugh that didn't quite work.

"Then why are you doing it?" Her father was known for his direct, no-nonsense questions: a man who got quickly to the heart of things, her mother liked to say.

"It's part of the tryout."

"Tryout? This is temporary work?"

By the time their steaks arrived, Julie had a headache. These two rock-solid people had shaped her: molded her values and given her an education; bequeathed skin color, bone structure, blue eyes, even her taste for chocolate. She could feel herself slipping back to all of this, to all of what was safe.

She was tired. Oh, she was tired. The hell with it—she ordered a martini.

Her mother's eyes widened. "That's quite a strong drink, dear. Isn't wine better? Or, I suppose, once in a while . . ." Mrs. Crawford looked helplessly toward her husband for aid.

Except there was something staged about her glance—something almost programmed for delivery—which gave Julie a jolt of surprise. What made her see that? Was it the world she lived in now? She felt as if she were viewing her parents for the first time from an audience. They were performing. Did they expect applause?

Mr. Crawford smiled benignly. "Nothing wrong with our little girl trying something adventurous for a change," he said, patting Julie's arm. "Never could develop a taste for them myself."

Julie smiled and took a sip of her martini, almost feeling it was the first one she had ever tasted. They were giving her permission to veer a little bit off-course. She found a twinge of contentment in that realization, which was insane: she was not a child.

Her father cleared his throat after the pear flambé, patted his mouth with a pristine white napkin, and started to speak. "Julie, we are here for a specific reason," he began. "I think you know what it is."

She wasn't up to hearing the inevitable. "Please, not now," she said, reaching for her father's hand. She talked rapidly, telling them she was taking them onto the *Gone with the Wind* set tomorrow morning; that they would see Clark Gable and the glamorous Vivien Leigh, and wasn't that exciting?

Her mother's eyes did light up, but her father frowned. "We anticipated leaving tomorrow," he began.

"No, no, you can't miss this," she said rapidly. "Plus, Carole—the actress, Carole Lombard?—my friend I told you about?"

Her father looked blank. She plunged on.

"She is having us over to dinner tomorrow night. It would be terribly rude to turn her down; I already accepted. . . ." She looked desperately at her mother.

"Jerome, it would be very impolite," her mother cooed. "Remember, she's from a good Fort Wayne family."

Julie resisted the impulse to hug her. "It truly would be," she pleaded. Out of the corner of her eye she saw a covey of waiters in white approaching their table—oh God, surely it wasn't her mother's or father's birthday—but then they rushed past; the lucky recipients were seated behind them, by the window.

"All right," her father said, giving her a keen look. "But don't think I don't see your delaying tactics, dear. You've had your fun out here, and it's time to grow up and get back to the real world. You won't have to exist on tryouts back home."

"We'll talk about it, okay?"

"Of course we will."

They all three smiled simultaneously.

CHAPTER 17

She couldn't seem to stop herself from nervously rattling on, but Julie was proud to be escorting her parents onto the *Gone with the Wind* set. Yes, what they *really* wanted was to pull her out of this so-called den of iniquity, but maybe she could divert them by offering them a peek into the dazzling world of the movies. Maybe.

It would have helped if her mother had read Margaret Mitchell's book. But she listened shyly as Julie told her the plot of the Civil War tale of love and carnage that had enthralled thousands—and, through the magic of cinema, would soon reach millions. Julie got so into her description that she flushed when Jerry Bryant, standing nearby, cast amused glances in her direction. She must sound as if she were auditioning for his job.

Jerome Crawford allowed himself to gaze with some respect at the vast paraphernalia necessary for filming a movie—the cameras, the spotlights, the electrical equipment, cables threading back and forth—and the dozens of people—assistant directors, wardrobe heads. This, he acknowledged, was a small army.

Clark—surely under orders from Carole—made a special effort to come over and meet her parents, walking a bit woodenly, of course—though not many people knew it was because of those tight-fitting pants he had to wear. Victor Fleming did a quick handshake, prompted by Clark. And Jerry Bryant provided a cheerful welcome, winking at Julie on the side.

As she turned to guide her parents to their seats, Julie saw Andy. He stood with arms behind his back, staring at her. She hadn't expected him back from Sacramento yet. He didn't move in her direction. He obviously hadn't shaved. His shirt was wrinkled and loose, with dark crescents of sweat beneath the armpits. Maybe he was waiting for her to act first.

She hesitated.

"Who is that rather unkempt-looking man staring at you?" asked her father.

"An acquaintance," she said. The words, packaged into her long ago, fell out of her mouth. As she heard her voice, she wondered how she could slip so quickly into such airy neutrality. But why today, of all days, did Andy have to look like *this*?

"Quiet on the set!" bawled an aide to Fleming.

They settled into their seats, and the lights began to dim. A tightness was beginning, spreading down to Julie's toes and up to her ears. She scrambled to figure out what she was feeling. Embarrassment? Relief? She was a coward; that was why she hadn't made introductions. Was she so bound to convention? Though she looked away, she could still sense Andy's stare. He wouldn't be shocked at her act of avoidance. He might even laugh and flip off some version of "I told you so." It confirmed his claim that she could move in his world but he wouldn't fit in hers. No matter how often she protested against that, what she just did—or didn't do—was what counted.

She hadn't focused on the scene being filmed this morning. But when she saw the magnificent, red-carpeted staircase of Scarlett and Rhett's home being slowly wheeled into place, her heart sank again. Of course, this was the one that some of the crew members laughingly called the rape scene. She squeezed her hands together, digging nail into nail. This wouldn't go down too well with her father—of that she was sure. One chance to charm him, and this was the sampling of Hollywood being served up today.

A sudden unexpected thought: here she was, once again, her father's daughter, dancing around the Maypole.

Both of her parents jumped visibly at the sharp sound of the clapper.

Vivien, a tiny figure dressed in Scarlett's red velvet gown, slowly descends a massive, graceful staircase. The rich burgundy carpet glows softly in the flickering gaslight. Scarlett looks toward the study, and hesitates.

"Come in, Mrs. Butler." Rhett's voice is heavy with drink and contempt. "Sit down."

She obeys.

"Observe, my dear," he says slowly, cupping her head with his hands. "I could tear you to pieces with my hands, and I would do it if it would take Ashley out of your mind forever. But it wouldn't."

"Take your hands off me," Scarlett snaps. "You drunken fool."

He does. She stands, turning to go, marching from the room, reaching the bottom of the staircase.

Rhett follows her, grabs her, and kisses her. "This is one night you're not turning me out." He lifts her into his arms and strides up the staircase; the figures of the two actors vanish into the dark.

"Cut!" bawled Fleming. "Let's do it again!"

Groans from the actors, but they obeyed. Another confrontation, another sweep up the stairs to the unseen bedroom.

"Once more!"

"Victor, that take was perfect," complained Vivien. But she took position as Julie wiggled in her seat. How many times would her father watch this scene without marching out?

"That's it!" yelled Fleming after the third take.

"Damn, I need a drink," Clark grumbled, heading for a chair. He cast a glance at his costar. "You don't weigh much, my dear violated Scarlett, but I wouldn't be hauling you up those stairs every night in real life."

"You sure wouldn't," Vivien Leigh said teasingly. "My Larry would shoot you dead."

Julie's father looked shocked and stupefied. He stood in full dignity, frowned at his daughter, and suggested lunch. A quick glance at Edith Crawford gave a different story: her eyes were unnaturally bright.

"Oh my," she breathed. "How handsome Rhett Butler is." Her face was pink.

As she guided her parents off the set, Julie looked quickly around for Andy, but he was gone. The three of them walked back into the relentless, cheerful sunlight as her mother chattered about what a lovely dress Scarlett had worn for the scene, and what a treat to see a movie being made, and you know, dear, I've heard quite a lot about this wonderful Bullocks Wilshire store you have here, what a treat it would be to peek in, we could find you some new clothes for the trip home. . . . And Julie kept nodding, not even registering her mother's last words, thinking about Andy, relief slowly sinking into shame.

"We can visit there this afternoon," she said.

"What a grand idea! Your father wants to look into buying up some orange groves somewhere. It's always business, business."

*

It was Julie's first visit to the famed department store. "Isn't it splendid?" her mother murmured, peering from the car up at the graceful tower sheathed in green-tarnished copper as they turned into the motor court. "If I lived in Hollywood, I would shop here all the time."

"A lot of actresses do," Julie said, as she pulled up to the curb, where an alert-looking valet in livery waited to take the car, a sturdy Ford her father had rented at the airport. It was not quite as fancy as most of the ones she saw in the parking lot, but renting cars was a brilliant idea, her father had proclaimed as he gave her the key. The man who founded the company, John Hertz, was ahead of his time. He, Jerome Crawford, just might make a small investment himself.

They walked through the entry into the Perfume Hall, which was cupped between walls of marble three stories high. The floors were of highly polished travertine. Women in soft, sheer wool suits gazed at flacons of perfume arranged under counters of sparkling glass, murmuring to each other from beneath wide-brimmed hats.

Edith Crawford smiled in appreciation and floated through, with Julie dutifully following her to the elevators in the center of the store. The elevator doors, closed, were stunning. Julie couldn't resist; she ran a hand over the paneling, which consisted of alternating vertical strips of ebony and brass.

"We don't have anything like this in Fort Wayne," her mother gasped. "Look, isn't that Greta Garbo at the lipstick counter?"

Julie glanced at the sultry-looking woman with long, dark hair peering critically into a makeup mirror as she tried out a lipstick. Yes, the famed actress.

"Mother," she said, a bit startled, "I think you see more movies than you admit to."

For the next hour, Julie wandered in her mother's footsteps as the older woman explored the store. Live models strolled through the aisles, silent and queenly in fur boas and jersey dresses and evening gowns of pale-pink silk. Edith Crawford was burbling with excitement. None of it caught Julie's interest; not today.

She was hiding Andy from her parents. If she had kept looking at him on the set, if the lights had not dimmed, she would have seen his sardonic smile; that look of: Oh yes, just what I expected, proper Midwestern girl. Forget her protestations of liberation from convention, propriety, and all that. When it comes down to a scruffy hungover Jew, she doesn't know him. Her cheeks burned. If she could write his dialogue in her own mind, she was acknowledging something. She felt a vague, meager sense of gratitude that her mother liked to shop, that she was enjoying this fanciful glide through Hollywood. She wasn't ready for the moment of reckoning that her parents, sooner or later, were surely poised to push.

"Julie, it's time for tea. Nobody comes to this place without visiting the tearoom," Edith Crawford said finally.

"How do you know that?" Julie asked, surprised.

"My hairdresser subscribes to *Photoplay*." Edith, her lips firmly together, put a striped cotton blouse back on its hanger. "This is far too expensive. Amazing, people willing to pay such prices—that's Hollywood for you. And here we are, barely out of the Depression." She clucked dutifully, then brightened.

"I love everything here, and I'm sure they have delicious sandwiches upstairs. Maybe we'll see some more movie stars. What do you think, dear?"

Julie smiled and said something innocuous. They entered one of the elevators. The doors closed silently in place behind them, and they rose to the fifth level of the store.

When the doors swept open, they stepped into a room as delicately appointed as a French boudoir. The walls were pale green, the chairs upholstered in a supple shade of salmon. So serene, so calming.

Julie followed the hostess behind her mother's erect, cheerful figure, wondering, How does she manage to make herself at home here when I can't? Maybe the answer wasn't so difficult. Edith Crawford was used to immediate entry into any world her husband's position and her own lineage unlocked. She brought her proper Fort Wayne identity with her when she traveled, snapped carefully and tightly into her purse. She was using it now.

Julie nibbled at tiny triangle sandwiches flavored with cucumber and sipped at tea that had barely changed color when the waitress filled her cup, wishing she could laugh with someone and say it tasted like hot water and nothing more—but very *good* hot water, of course.

"You don't know whether you're happy here or not, do you, dear?"

Her mother's calm question slid silkily through her thoughts, yanking her straight.

"You said one year—" she began.

Her mother waved her hand, the flutter of a butterfly. "Let's not talk about deadlines. That is such an awful word, isn't it? And you don't have to answer. I really do know what I see in my daughter's face."

She took a tiny bite of her sandwich. "That handsome, unkempt man this morning who was staring at you—he matters, am I right?"

Surprised, Julie began to stutter. "Mother—"

They were looking fully at each other now. No side glances. Julie saw the deep creases around her mother's eyes, the thinning hair, the loosening skin of her neck.

"No confessions are necessary; I saw what I saw. I saw it on his face, and I saw it on yours." Her mother was sitting achingly straight, bright in demeanor, so beyond language in the message she was sending.

"It's all mixed up," Julie managed. She wanted to say more, but the arc of connection between them was already wobbling.

"We'll discuss it later," her mother said briskly. "Shall we share a piece of cream pie? Or would that be spoiling the dinner your friend—amazing, my goodness—Carole Lombard is cooking tonight?"

"It won't spoil it," Julie said. She managed a smile, uncertain what was going to happen next.

*

Carole was dressed for the evening in black velvet sailor-style pants and a white cotton shirt tied in front, leaving her midriff bare. She opened the front door with full theatrical exuberance, sending out a wave of energy that seemed capable of lifting anyone off his or her toes, even as a new large German shepherd and a small, yapping terrier threw themselves at Julie's parents in a sloppy, hysterical welcome. They took an involuntary step back.

"Down, dogs; who taught you your manners? Well, hello, Jerome! Hi, Edith! Welcome to our home!" Carole gave Edith an exuberant hug, bussed Jerome Crawford on the cheek, leaving a bright smear of lipstick, and guided them into the house. "Don't stumble over the frigging packing boxes—we're moving as soon as that damn movie is finished."

Julie's mother handed her a box of Whitman's chocolates, tied in a red bow. "It's called the Sampler," she said. "You know, meaning samples of all their chocolates? It's all the rage at home, and my favorite, and I was delighted to find it here, too."

"Thank you!" Carole swooped up the box and looked at its design as if she had never seen the ubiquitous brand in her life. "How lovely! Come, sit down. Scotch or bourbon?" She turned her head and yelled, "Clark!"

From the porch, Clark Gable poked his head around the door, a big grin on his face. "Hi there," he said, waving a pair of tongs. "We're having steaks and burgers tonight. Anybody want a drink?"

"I'm way ahead of you, Pa," Carole said. "I think we've got a bourbon man here—right, Jerome?" She winked at Julie's father, who didn't smile, just nodded crisply as Clark, who, wearing a suspiciously clean white apron over khaki pants, swooped in and started mixing drinks.

Julie could have hugged her friends, right there; they were going to make this a Midwestern night with all of their acting skills. They were out to prove Julie had not fallen victim to the falsities of Hollywood.

She could tell immediately it was working with her mother. Within a few minutes, she was chatting with Carole about the variety of designer labels at Bullocks Wilshire. Her father seemed determined not to be taken in by anything; she could see that. But he stood more stiffly than usual, looking around, blinking, nodding formally when Clark handed him a glass of his favorite brand of bourbon.

"Want to check out dinner with me?" Clark said, nodding toward the porch. Jerome Crawford, still looking around with feigned lack of interest, followed Clark back out to the porch, where a servant was carefully placing hamburger patties on the barbecue grill. Julie could hear their voices.

"I turn 'em," Clark said with cheer. "You cook the burgers at your house?"

"Edith manages all the kitchen work," Jerome answered as he sipped his drink and stared out past the balcony at nothing.

Clark tried again. "I find them easier to eat than steak," he said.

Jerome shot him a glance and swirled the ice cubes in his glass a few times. "Why is that?"

"My plate. It gets loose."

"You wear a plate?"

"Sure. Lots of people do. Do you?"

Jerome paused, as if to consider whether this was an outrageous or a friendly question. "I do."

"Ever have problems with the damn contraption?"

"From time to time." The words came out like a forced confession.

"Yep, same here," said Clark. "Have to keep pushing mine back into place." He put his hand up to his mouth. There was an audible click. "That's better," he said. "Hate the damn thing, but I sure wouldn't be playing Rhett Butler without it."

Julie wasn't sure what to expect next as the two men walked together back into the dining room. Then she realized she was hearing her father laughing. Well, sort of. More like chuckling. A sound more relaxed from him than she had heard in years.

*

The kitchen crew worked silently and artfully as Carole went back and forth through the swinging door, kicking it with her foot, carrying in each platter of food herself. "I'm very good at scrambled eggs, but not much more," she said cheerfully as she passed around fat baked potatoes and a heaping bowl of peas. "Don't stint on the sour cream or butter—we've got plenty."

When it was time for dessert—apple pie à la mode—Carole shot Julie a wide smile. "Hey, hon, can you help me a minute in the kitchen?"

A bit baffled, Julie followed Carole through the kitchen and onto the side porch.

Carole put her hands on Julie's shoulders. "I hope you won't hate me for what is about to happen," she said quietly. "I thought you deserved a second chance."

"Me?"

The doorbell rang.

"I'll answer it," Carole yelled. She moved toward the front door. Slowly, Julie walked back into the dining room, stood behind her chair, and waited.

He looked achingly perfect: his shirt crisp and clean, his face shaven, his eyes seeking hers immediately, his expression searching but noncommittal.

"Edith and Jerome, meet a pal of ours. He works for Selznick—just stopping by to give me a package. Andy Weinstein, meet my friend Julie's parents; they're visiting from Fort Wayne, just here for a couple of days. Thanks for dropping this by. . . ." Carole spoke rapidly, too rapidly.

It was the first time Julie had ever seen Carole nervous. Yes, a second chance, not for Andy. For Julie herself. A second chance to stand up for herself and her choices, for the man who reflected the changing bits and pieces of who she was.

"That's okay, Carole," she said, walking around the table and reaching for Andy's hand. "Mother, Dad, Andy is my friend, too—my very good friend—and I'm delighted he can meet you and you can meet him."

His fingers touched hers, warming everything inside of her. She wasn't going to leave anything out. "He was on the set this morning, and I should have introduced you all then."

"I was working and traveling all night—sorry, not too presentable. But it's a pleasure to meet you both," Andy said calmly.

"Will you stay for apple pie?" a relieved Carole said.

He shook his head and smiled. "Not tonight; we're still looking at dailies. More trouble with Mayer: he wants expanded production control. But I'm glad I had a chance to meet you, Mr. and Mrs. Crawford," he said. He spoke warmly, confidently, and when he looked back at her, Julie felt a sturdiness building between them.

His visit lasted five minutes. Or maybe it was ten. "May I call you tomorrow?" he asked quietly as he prepared to leave.

"If you don't, I will be devastated," she said. She kissed him quickly, not caring if her parents could see them from the dining room.

And as the door closed behind him, and she thought of what this must have cost him, of the risk he took, of all he fought against, of the challenge he was presenting, of all of this, she almost didn't hear Carole's whisper.

"Julie." Carole was beckoning her into the kitchen.

She approached, standing still as Carole put a hand on hers. Julie had never seen her friend look so serious.

"Okay, I'm taking a chance, but here it goes," Carole said carefully. "I fought for Clark and I fought for my career. And I'm telling you, if you wait for everything to be just right in your life, you'll never get any happiness. You have to fight for it. And the minute you start fighting for something, you've won. The end doesn't matter."

Julie felt confused. "Are you talking about Andy?" she asked.

"I'm talking about *everything*. Are you listening?"

Julie nodded. She walked back into the dining room, slightly dazed, in time to hear her father's question.

"Weinstein, is it? Is he Jewish?"

She looked at him, her voice firm. "Of course he is, Dad. Most of the smart people here are."

For a few seconds, no one said anything.

And then Edith Crawford, her chin quivering a little but her head bravely up, said: "A very nice man, dear. I hear they are very good to their wives."

CHAPTER 18

They faced each other the next morning, the Crawfords, over a breakfast of eggs served sunny-side up, crisp toast, and sausage, in a small diner near Julie's boarding house where the waitresses wore tiny starched caps and sensible shoes. Jerome and Edith sat on one side of the booth, Julie on the other.

It was early; Julie had to report to work this morning. But with her help, Jerome and Edith were already packed up and checked out of their hotel. Edith had hinted at the possibility of staying a little longer, but Jerome was a man who stuck firmly to his plans, and he declined to consider another deviation—the plan was to leave for home on a noon plane, and they would be on it.

Julie was positive he held in his wallet a third ticket. No more waiting.

"I'm sure you both know by now that I am not coming back with you," she said, feeling very calm. She sipped her coffee, hand quite steady.

"Well, we understand you might not be ready *yet,*" her mother said quickly.

"No, Mother, I mean not at all."

"That's not acceptable," her father said. His authority reverberated across the table like an electrical pulse. "This is not a place for a young woman like you. And you know I am right."

"You might be, Dad. But you know what? I'm going to try to

make it my place." Another sip of coffee. Hand still steady. "Look, I love you both. I will visit—of course I will—and I hope you will come back and visit me. But I'm an adult now, or at least on my way to being whatever that is, and I'm going to do my best to make a mark here, and if I don't, I'll decide from there." It sounded good; she had rehearsed it all night, and she meant it. She'd spent hours staring at the ceiling, reflecting. Dawn had brought a steadiness to her thoughts, and even a major idea for a script. She couldn't wait to get to the grubby writers' room at MGM.

Her mother began crying.

"There will be no more money from us," her father said. He was white-faced.

"Then I've got to prove I can make a living on my own," Julie replied. "And if I can't, I'll get a job in a restaurant like this and keep trying." How strange it was to be looking steadily into her father's eyes without blinking.

"You can't possibly think your fallback position is marrying that Weinstein fellow," he said.

"You mean the talented, handsome Jew I'm dating?"

Her mother fumbled frantically for a handkerchief. "Jerome, don't you think you should eat your breakfast? The eggs are getting cold. Here, I'll butter your toast—"

Jerome Crawford reared back, shocked. He didn't look at his wife. He spoke very slowly, in that same deep voice that only a few years ago had signaled final parental authority. "I never thought I would have a daughter who would defy her parents and her values as flagrantly as you seem to be planning to do."

Anyone else, and she would say: How can you speak like this? Don't you know you can't veil bigotry by invoking values, it shows through? She deliberately had spoken the word "Jew." It wasn't quite like "cancer," the word always whispered. It was worse—a blunt word that said more up front than people like her father wanted it to. Better to slide into "Jewish," which took away the one-syllable harshness that made it all too obviously disapproving.

Her father, whom she loved. If only she could say it clean and clear. Root it out, look at it, turn it around: Dad, don't you know what is going on in the world? Don't you see the narrowness of our lives? Haven't you ever wanted to separate values from fear and rigidity? No, she couldn't say any of those things, not to her father. Not yet.

For now, it was up to her to give him a way out.

"Dad"—she reached across the table and took his hand—"I'm not trying to hurt or defy you. If I am dating Andy, it is because he is a good person. I know what I want to do, and you'll have to let me go sometime."

"It's too soon."

"It will always be too soon."

"You'll always be my little girl."

She must convince him to stop hanging on so tightly. "Will you settle for me being your big girl?" she parried.

His eyes—were they watering slightly?

Well, damn, hers sure were. And so were her mother's.

"I'll see you at Christmas," she said.

＊

If the waitress in the starched cap and oxford shoes clearing dishes at the next table noticed the three people with red faces and moist eyes by the window, their food before them as pristine as when she had placed it there ten minutes ago, she might have wondered: Were they mourning or celebrating?

Then again, this being Hollywood, they might have been rehearsing a movie scene.

＊

Julie was sitting alone at the table in Room 632 when Abe Goldman arrived, Sammy trudging wearily behind him. Goldman's eyes widened in surprise as he entered the room.

"What are you doing here so early?" he asked.

"I wanted to talk to you before the others arrive," she said. She saw in his face the fast sequence of thought—maybe she was accepting his invitation—no, shading into irritation—she had something else in mind.

He took his seat, pushed back from the table, and folded his arms. "What's up?" he said crisply.

"When I first came here, you talked about movies that were so bad they were unreleasable," she said. "It made me curious. I would love to see some of them."

"What the hell for?"

"Well, I was remembering something Frances Marion said in her speech at Smith: she said a good editor can save a film, even a bad one. So I began thinking—maybe there are ways to remake some of them. A good editor has to know how to build a story, and I think I'm a good editor."

He slapped his thigh and grinned. "For your college yearbook?"

She nodded, not backing off. "Plus other things."

"Come on," he scoffed. "Look, are you kidding? Heading off for glory with a pair of scissors and a jar of paste? That's a waste of time. I'm giving you the chance of a lifetime with this movie—"

Julie took a deep breath and plunged to where her instincts would normally tell her not to go. "I'm not offering any good ideas for your prison script, you and I both know it. There is no female perspective. But right now I would love the challenge of salvaging something and making it worthwhile. Let me try this, Abe. Then it's up or out, and I know it."

His eyes turned cool and calculating. She sensed him assessing his own advantage. If she succeeded, it might help his career; nobody was ever completely safe at MGM. "Okay," he said shortly. "I'll send a few of our crap films over to the projection room. You can go over there now—it's clear—and watch them. Waste your day, hey. You're making a mistake."

Julie smiled, relieved, and looked down at old Sammy. She rubbed his head. "I'll miss you, pal," she said. She picked up her purse. "Thanks, Abe. I'll do my best."

Goldman looked a bit befuddled as she exited. The other screen-writers began drifting in, casting her a few wary glances. Was she up or out? Sideways, she answered silently. For now.

✳

The projection room was gloomy and cold, and the seats here were not as plush as the ones in the *Gone with the Wind* screening room, where tension stayed high—and the seats warm—all the time. Julie settled in, pulling her sweater tight, and waved to the projectionist to start the first movie of the four Abe had sent over. It would be a long day.

✳

Hours later, freezing fingers tucked inside her sweater, she stared at the finally—mercifully—blank screen.

"One more to go. Hate to tell you, but the last one is the worst of all. I'm taking a lunch break—you ready for more when I return?" the projectionist bawled cheerfully. Julie had no idea what time it was. She simply sat, stupefied by the impossible plots, the terrible writing, the clumsy scene-cutting of what she was watching. It was as if these movies were expected to be terrible from the very begin-ning. What had she been thinking? These weren't salvageable, not at all. And one more to go.

"Go ahead, I'll watch the last one when you get back," she called to him.

She thought of strolling out into the sunlight and getting some lunch herself, but it seemed like too much effort. So she sat in semi-darkness, waiting.

A door opened behind her, letting in a sliver of light from the hall. She turned. Andy was standing silhouetted against the light.

"Julie . . ." He stopped, said nothing more.

She stood and slowly walked toward him. There would be no careful banter today. She knew it; she sensed he did, too.

"I'm sorry for turning away from you yesterday," she said. "I know what you thought. And you were right: I lost the courage to be honest around my parents."

He gave her a sheepish grin. "Don't be too hard on yourself. I looked at myself in a mirror after you left the soundstage. I saw why you didn't want them to meet me."

"Please don't be kinder than what you really believe," she said.

They were standing close now. He lifted one hand and tenderly smoothed back her hair. "Did I come off presentable enough?" he asked quietly.

Thank you, she thought. Thank you for not making it bigger than it was.

He wasn't finished. "There's more, though. We both know that, don't we." It wasn't a question.

"Yes. And I've never been more sure than I am right now that I love you," she said.

He gently kissed her forehead, every movement still slow, restrained. "I don't know where we're going, but I love you, too," he said.

"Don't say, 'but,'" she begged. "Don't start your next sentence with 'but.'"

"Funny about this whole insider/outsider thing," he said, his voice muffled by her hair. "When it comes to the movie business, you stand outside; I am inside. In your parents' world, you are inside; I am outside. Look"—he stepped back, cupping her head in his hands—"you're doing your best to get into my world and show what you can do. If you can push against that, then maybe I can push a little against what holds you back from me."

"That's why you showed up last night?"

"You bet. Carole gave me one of those get-your-ass-moving lectures she's good at. Are your parents still here?"

"They left on a noon plane."

They turned their heads at a sudden scramble of noise from overhead. "Hey, I'm off at four o'clock, and if you want to see this last movie, you'd better sit and watch it now!" yelled the projectionist.

"Yes, I want to see it," Julie yelled back.

"Mind if I stick around and watch with you?" Andy asked.

Really, with an audience of one peering down on them, she couldn't say what she truly wanted to say, which was, sure—and let's take our clothes off and make love right here, because the movie will be so terrible, we'll need diversion.

"I'd like it if you did," she said.

"What's the name of this one?"

"*Madhouse Nightmare*," Julie said.

Andy winced. "I remember that dog. L.B. had a niece acting in it; when he saw how terrible it was, he pulled the plug. MGM took a big loss." He settled into the seat next to her and kissed her hand. "So what did your father say?"

"He asked if you were Jewish."

"And . . . ?"

"I told him all the smart people here were. Don't you want to hear what my mother said?"

"Wouldn't miss it."

"She said Jewish men are good to their wives."

"An old canard if ever there was one."

She laughed, at ease.

The lights went down. The screen lit up.

※

The closing credits rolled, over an hour later—a very long hour. "Jesus," Andy muttered, "there's nothing anybody can do with that."

But Julie kept staring at the now black screen. Yes, it was terrible—a melodrama set in an insane asylum, and the worst movie of them all. Absurdly overacted. Yet she had an idea. "I think I can do something with it," she said slowly.

Andy shot her a puzzled glance. "What the hell can you do with *that*?" he said.

She was scribbling notes and didn't answer right away. "Do you think those actors would be available for a few scenes?" she asked.

"Probably. They can't be getting much work."

She frowned, nibbling on the eraser of her pencil. Melodrama, horrible melodrama, that's what it was. Obviously unsalvageable. But what if it were turned into a comedy? How could she do that? Her mind was dancing. She scribbled some more.

"You're looking absorbed, kid." Andy gazed at her thoughtfully.

She looked up. "Andy, I know what I can do," she said with a rush. "I've got to work on it right away. I really think I know what to do."

"Where shall I take you?" he said quietly.

"The boarding house. I've got a typewriter there; I don't want to work on this in the Writers' Building. I want to have it ready by tomorrow."

"No dinner at Chasen's?"

She tried to make her voice a little apologetic, but she was too excited. "Not tonight; I'll probably be working late."

He smiled, a slow-spreading quizzical smile. "Familiar words," he said.

CHAPTER 19

Julie hadn't expected to be climbing the stairs again up to Room 632 quite so soon, but she couldn't wait the next morning to show Abe Goldman what she had figured out. Once again, she was there first.

Goldman walked in, eating a doughnut, bits of powdered sugar clinging to his upper lip. He looked almost resigned when he saw her.

"Okay, what's your bright idea this morning?"

"I think I—" She stopped. "Where's Sammy?" she asked.

"Too old," Goldman said shortly. He avoided her gaze. "Spit it out, will you? I've got a busy day."

She put a stack of papers on the desk, taking a deep breath. Time to sell.

"This can be saved as absurd comedy," she began. "I've written a prologue and an epilogue which could be filmed with very little additional cost."

"How the hell do you do that?"

Trying not to speak too fast, Julie laid out her idea. She would open with a scene of a pompous writer announcing to his fiancée that he cannot marry her—he can reach higher as soon as he sells the weighty drama he is about to present to a top publisher. She cries; he pretends to care. In truth, he has his eye on the publisher's daughter. The meeting begins. He starts to outline the plot of his book, describing it in dramatic terms—and this fades into the movie itself.

"The audience already knows he's delusional about what he's written," she said. "They're primed to laugh; that's what makes this work."

What unspools on the screen is pure clumsy farce. A few cuts—easily done with scissors—break in, in which the incredulous publisher asks the clueless author, You are serious about this?—then back to the absurdity of the original movie.

Finally, the epilogue. The author, after being laughed out of the boardroom, gets on the phone, trying to win back his fiancée. But she cheerily turns him down, announcing she is eloping with the publisher.

"That's ridiculous," Goldman growled.

"Of course it is," she said. "It's supposed to be. Everybody ends up looking like they're in on the joke. And if it's done right, it can save the studio thousands of dollars."

"It's a stupid idea."

"Even if it rescued Mr. Mayer's niece's reputation from the trash barrel?" Don't shrivel, she told herself. It's dumb, it's stupid, but with some tweaking it could work.

He yawned, stretching back, tipping his chair precariously. "Honey, this isn't my kind of movie. Look, you've got a few more weeks—get something going soon or you'll be out of luck. A piece of advice? This kind of fanciful stuff will get laughed out of the only boardroom that matters, and that's the MGM boardroom." He rocked back and forth, clearly pleased with himself.

Julie collected the pages, cheeks flushed. What should she do now? She could see it in her head, just how this would work. It meant finding exactly the right tone to get a seamless blend between the original movie and her material, but she was sure it could be done. And cheaply.

"I'll think about what you've said," she managed, moving toward the door.

"Don't get too downcast. My offer of an evening watching some good movies is still open," he said cheerily.

She stopped, took another deep breath, and asked. "Where *is* Sammy?"

"Look, he's an old dog, and you probably won't be around to walk him much longer."

"You put him in a kennel?"

"Something like that."

She exited, slamming the door. He might think he had the final word, but not after that.

*

Frances Marion's receptionist looked up with a puzzled frown. "Do you have an appointment?" she asked a bit distantly.

"No, I don't, but I would like to see Miss Marion for a few minutes if that is possible." She was slightly breathless, swallowing back surges of panic and then frustration. Promising to talk quickly was almost an apology, she realized that now, a way of saying: This is not terribly important; I'll tell you about it as fast as I can, so you can move on to weightier things.

"She's leaving for the East Coast in a few hours." The receptionist was now speaking in a slightly consoling tone, a more polite way of being dismissive.

"Please, I have to see her," Julie said.

The door to the office behind the secretary's desk opened. Frances Marion stood there, not looking surprised to see Julie. "I heard your voice," she said. "Come on in; I have a few moments. You got here faster than I expected."

"You were expecting me?" Julie asked, as she walked in. Marion closed the door behind her.

"The telephone is faster than your feet," the older woman said, smiling slightly. "Okay, Julie—Goldman says you aren't going to make the grade as a writer working for him. So tell me about this wacky idea he was chortling over." Marion settled into her chair, folding her hands together on her desk, and waited.

Julie took a deep breath. "It's about saving *Madhouse Nightmare*," she began.

Marion chuckled. "God, that was terrible. L.B. was livid. Give me the details and show me the script. I tried this ploy once myself—not as easy to do with sound." She reached for the script. Julie handed it over silently.

Marion read, then looked at Julie thoughtfully. "Your writing is good." She tapped on the desk with one properly polished fingernail; for a few seconds, that was the only sound in the room.

Then Marion stood up, glancing at her watch. "Well, you're still on the payroll," she said. She gathered together the pages of Julie's script, slipped a rubber band around it, and held it up inquiringly. "Mind if I keep this, show it to a couple of people?"

"No, of course not."

"I'll send it around before I leave. In the meantime, I don't think you have to bother showing up at the Writers' Building. Better to avoid Goldman. We'll talk when I get back."

Marion put a hand on her shoulder. "Don't despair. Remember, we deal in clichés in this town. It's always darkest before the dawn. Isn't that comforting?"

Julie tried to smile and turned to leave. She hesitated at the receptionist's desk. "Could I possibly use your phone?" she asked.

*

"Alloooo? Nobody home," came a high-pitched voice over the wire.

"Carole, it's me; don't hang up."

A cautious silence. "Julie?"

"Yes, you don't have to pretend to be the maid."

Carole giggled. "I'm getting pretty good at it, aren't I?"

"Yes, but you're even better at something else."

"What's that?"

Julie took a deep breath. "Adopting animals. Dogs—"

"Let me guess, you've found one that needs a home."

"Yes, his name is Sammy."

"Young? Old? Does he shed or bite?"

"He doesn't bite. But he is old. Somewhat."

Carole sighed. "This is some ancient, mangy mongrel, right?"

She couldn't lie to Carole. "Yes," she said, "but he's a very nice dog."

"Okay, hon, bring him up. I'll be gone, but Clark is here."

"Thank you." Julie hung up the phone, hoping she wasn't too late.

The Culver City Animal Shelter—when she finally found it— was a decrepit building in back of a gas station. As she walked in, the smell and the noise of what sounded like dozens of barking dogs almost made her step back.

"Lady, you're too late today. We already did our rounds of picking up strays. We can come by tomorrow, but no sooner," said a wiry attendant with a missing front tooth. He squinted, looking her over, wiping his hands on a stained apron.

"How long do you keep a dog?" she said.

He laughed. "Do you know how many of those critters wander the streets these days? Twenty-four hours, max. Sometimes a little more, if they look cared for. Then it's the gas." He pointed to a shed sheathed in metal to the right of the front door.

"I'm looking for a dog," she said. "He—got lost."

"Breed?"

"I think a mix. Some golden retriever, I think, but he's black. Maybe a little collie."

"Okay, a mutt. Puppy?"

"No." The sight of Sammy moving slowly, his bones clearly aching, flashed through her mind. "He's actually fairly old."

The attendant shrugged. "Take a look at the cages, see if you see 'im."

Julie walked to the end of the hall and into a long narrow room with metal cages stacked halfway to the ceiling. There was a dog in each one, some barking and pressing frantically against the bars, others lying curled in a still heap.

She felt unnerved as she walked farther down the narrow aisle. If these animals could talk, she knew what they would be begging for.

"Sammy?" she yelled. "Sammy dog?" The clamor was harrowing.

Then, at the very end of the aisle, she saw him. Probably the oldest, droopiest dog of them all. Sammy wasn't barking, just watching her come his way. She reached a hand into his cage; he licked it.

"This is my dog," she said to the attendant.

"Good timing, lady. He was due to be put down tonight."

She exhaled a sigh of relief. Surely this particular mangy old dog, lucky enough to escape Abe Goldman's tender mercies, would be a welcome addition to Carole's menagerie.

*

Julie hadn't counted on Clark's reaction.

"*Another* one?" he said doubtfully, as she walked into the house with a clearly doddering Sammy by her side. Clark looked bleary-eyed, and she saw by his chair a stack of typewritten notes, obviously from Selznick, probably filled with another manic round of acting directives. He was wearing a torn tee shirt and a baggy pair of blue jeans, and sneezing, obviously fighting back a cold.

"He's a gentle dog," Julie said quickly. She pushed Sammy closer, hoping he would win Clark over by licking his hand.

"She'll love him," Clark said with resignation. "But we sure have a lot of animals around here."

"She's got a generous heart," Julie ventured.

"Yeah, that's for sure," he said. He reached down and stroked the back of Sammy's neck; the dog gazed up at him with a soulful expression.

"Okay, old guy," he said. "As long as you know I'm the primary beneficiary of that." He straightened, looking up at Julie. "Oh hell, one more animal isn't going to make a big difference."

Maybe it was an expression of relief, but Sammy promptly let go and peed on the floor.

*

Andy laughed when she told him the story. "So what happened?" he said.

"Well, Clark wasn't fazed. Then Carole came in while we were cleaning up, took one look at this doddering old creature, saw the pleading look in his eyes, and immediately rushed to give Sammy a hug and a bowl of milk—which the cat took over immediately."

"Good for you; you saved the dog."

"Lucky for you I didn't bring him here first," she said with a small grin.

But she was too anxious to savor that triumph for long. Three more days of her six-week tryout gone. Julie couldn't get that thought out of her head as she stood in Andy's kitchen, scrubbing potatoes to bake for dinner, reminding herself to prick them so they wouldn't explode in the oven. That had happened a few weeks ago. And even though Andy laughed at the time, it was embarrassing.

"Still pretending you know how to cook?" he said, giving the back of her neck a quick kiss.

"Please, one thing at a time. Next week I'll try boiling eggs."

He smiled, but he wasn't quite up for their usual banter. He looked tired—worn, really. He was nursing along a single bourbon and water to please her, she knew. The pace of filming *Gone with the Wind* was always frantic, but it was getting worse and worse as they approached the last scenes. The NAACP had won the fight weeks ago to get the word "nigger" out of the movie, and the United Daughters of the Confederacy wanted the scene where Scarlett slaps Prissy taken out—because no well-bred Southern lady would do such a thing.

"They lose," Andy said, suppressing a yawn. "I was afraid the Breen Office's ruling against the word 'damn' was going to hold, but David hauled out the Oxford Dictionary and convinced those damn—okay, laugh—censors that it wasn't an oath, it wasn't a bad, bad word, it was a *vulgarism*. That's this week's triumph."

"It's a good one." Julie wiped her hands on a towel. The potatoes were in the oven with the roast; now all she had to do was remember when to take everything out.

"We'll never get rid of the censors." He paced back and forth. "And here we are, ready to shoot the final scene of the movie, and still nobody knows what the script is until everybody is on the set and ready to go. And Mayer is going to screw up everything if he doesn't stop fighting for a happy ending. He's driving Selznick crazy."

"So what's going to happen?" she asked.

"He'll shoot something that hints at a reconciliation between Scarlett and Rhett, but nothing more than that. Christ, Selznick was rewriting the shoot for tomorrow a couple of hours ago. Right now, it ends with Scarlett imploring Mammy to tell her how to get Rhett back, and Mammy comforts her and says he will return. Fade-out, with lots of hope and music."

Andy leaned against the kitchen door and closed his eyes. "Julie, I'm beyond tired," he said slowly. "I love my work—I feel excited when it all comes together, when something special comes out of the whole messy process. But what good is it? We pump out movies on anything and everything. Here we are, doing a romance set in the Civil War, but we aren't doing anything about Hitler."

"I ran an idea by Goldman, but he was almost horrified at the suggestion," Julie said.

"They're all scared." Andy strode into the living room, picked up a copy of the evening *Herald Express,* and threw it on the counter. "The Nazis taking Czechoslovakia was only the beginning; they aren't going to stop there. There's no holding them back. That ship with all those Jewish refugees? What do you think happened to them when they were refused asylum and sent back to Europe? We're cowards in this business. All people here want to do is read the entertainment rags. They avoid the real news even when it's in the headlines. In four-inch type."

"Not everybody is callous and indifferent," Julie said quickly. "I think at least some people feel it crowding in now. Frances Marion is worried about war. She has sons."

"If we go to war—" Andy stopped and looked at her tenderly. "Julie, we will, you know."

Julie felt a chill travel down her spine. "What would you do?" she asked.

"Just what you would expect."

She turned toward him and briefly rested her head on the shoulder of his jacket, instinctively wanting to hold him tight, against his will. *No.*

He gently pulled away. "Look, we're both down in the dumps. And in case I haven't said it clearly enough, your idea for salvaging that bomb of a movie is brilliant—something will work. If you want to be a writer, you will be."

He was trying to refocus, same as she was. "Thanks for the confidence," she said.

"And I'll do anything I can to help you."

She kissed him swiftly on the cheek, touched. He knew that she wanted to make her own way, that it wouldn't mean the same if he got her a spot as a script girl on this movie or any other. There were many variations of making it in this town. She had chosen the right route for herself.

"Would you like to come watch the final shoot tomorrow?" he asked, breaking into her thoughts. "Not counting retakes, of course. It's going to be a big day."

"With Selznick still rewriting the ending?"

Andy managed a laugh. "Okay, here it is." He cleared his throat. "'Oh, Mammy, he's gone again. How'll I ever get him back?'"

"And Mammy replies—"

"I'm no actor, so, with apologies to Hattie McDaniel, here's the last version I saw this afternoon." Andy cleared his throat again. "'He'll come back. Didn't I say de last time? He'll do it again. Ah knows. Ah always does.'"

"It's a comforting ending," Julie said. She frowned, thinking of the book. "But not an honest one."

"Bingo." Andy lifted his bourbon and drank.

"You think it will be different in the morning?"

"I guarantee it. Vivien and Clark will be reading their final lines for the first time."

CHAPTER 20

he next morning, the soundstage, vast as it was, felt almost crowded to Julie. People were trickling in, slowly at first, then faster—Selznick employees who could manage to sneak away from their jobs, a loyal cadre of David Selznick's friends—and by nine o'clock it looked like a gathering at a Hollywood party. With, of course, many reporters. Julie spied Louella Parsons standing under one of the huge studio lights, nodding graciously, flashing her hard smile. One after another, those who lived or died on what she wrote offered homage. It gave Julie the shivers—all those false, bright faces.

"Dear Louella, she should've been born into royalty," said a familiar throaty voice. "Got herself positioned perfectly for attention, don't you think?"

Julie spun around. "Carole," she said delightedly. "You mean you aren't going over to genuflect?"

"Not me, honey." Carole tossed back her blond hair and beckoned Julie into the seat next to hers. "Glad you came. I usually get bored on the fifth take or so, but Clark wanted me here today." She surveyed the scene around them thoughtfully. "Look at all these jumpy, scared people. If it's a disaster, they're finished, of course. Kind of our town's version of the old-fashioned human sacrifices of the Incas or whoever they were." She glanced down at a copy of the morning *Examiner* someone had left on a chair and paused. "Nothing makes what I just said sound more like pure horseshit than a picture like that," she said, pointing.

Julie looked down. A large photo, above the fold, of a line of people with hungry, haunted faces—Czech Jews, the caption said, being pushed from their homes by the Nazis. One figure, a woman, holding a child in her arms, stared straight at the camera. Not imploring, not pleading.

"Look at her expression," Carole said. "What do you see?"

Julie stared at the photo. "Nothing," she said. "Her face is blank."

"Yeah. That's what giving up looks like." Carole sighed and passed Julie her cup of coffee. "Take a sip while it's hot, honey. This place is cold as a witch's tit. How are your parents?"

"Resigned, pretty much," Julie said, gratefully taking a swallow before handing it back. "My mother keeps talking about Rhett Butler."

"Did you tell them about your idea for a script?"

"No, they wouldn't understand that at all."

Carole cradled the cup. "They will when it works," she said. "No word from Marion yet?"

"No." Even with Carole, she felt anxious talking about it.

"Remember, you've still got a backup job with me. Maybe even with a raise—though, hell, not to three hundred bucks a week."

The noise around them was intensifying. It was more than a buzz; there was shouting.

"That's what Clark was afraid of," Carole said, lowering her voice. "L.B. is making his last stand."

Louis B. Mayer, portly, his face an unhealthy purple, stood under the lights on a raised platform, shouting at Selznick. Like a wave retreating, actors, assistants, and gaffers all stepped back. Only Louella held her ground, her face as alert and sly as that of a ferret. Julie could imagine her burbling in tomorrow's column: Dear, dear, a last-minute fracas, such a pity, heads toppling . . . Along that line.

*

Julie's eyes searched for Andy. There he was, in the middle of it, not shouting, speaking calmly to Selznick, soothing Mayer, looking totally in command of himself—perhaps the only one on the set who did. Mayer began to calm down. Whatever bargaining was going on between the two men was not audible from where she and Carole sat.

Finally, Selznick walked over to Clark and Vivien, who both stood stiffly, in full costume, as if waiting for some kind of execution. He handed them each several sheets of paper. Clark let out a disapproving snort.

"I told Pa not to bother memorizing his lines last night," Carole said. "Here we go, a new final scene. Save these seats. I'm going to get more coffee."

For another twenty minutes, the crowd waiting for the finale of filming what people were calling the most trouble-plagued movie in history clustered in groups, talking among themselves, sneaking glances at Clark and Vivien rehearsing over in a corner.

Carole came back with two coffees and a cheery report. "Ran into Andy," she said. "He said all has been forgiven, and they're about ready to go."

As she spoke, Selznick lifted his bullhorn and demanded quiet. An almost instant stillness fell over all the onlookers in the huge sound studio.

Selznick turned and faced the crowd. His voice was solemn and commanding. "Ladies and gentlemen, I want to point out to all of you that you are about to see us shoot what will be in the near future a historic scene in a historic movie." He paused, looking around. No one could say he didn't know how to frame this speech. He had risked his own health and many thousands of dollars to make this movie, and he wanted the world to know it. "We are going to make movie history!" he shouted. "This will be one of the greatest films ever made!" He whipped around and pointed at Clark and Vivien. "Are you ready?" he demanded.

The pair nodded almost simultaneously. Both were dressed in somber black, Vivien with a single ivory brooch at her throat.

The lights on the set turned low. The cameras moved forward, focused on the set of Rhett and Scarlett's home. As Julie watched, the two actors took their places.

The grand house broods, dark and filled with sorrow. Rhett is packing a valise in his office.

"What are you doing?" Scarlett says. She looks at him, frightened.

"I'm leaving you, my dear. I've tried. If you'd only met me halfway— all you need now is a divorce and your dreams of Ashley can come true."

"Oh no!" she cries. "No, you're wrong, terribly wrong! I don't want a divorce. I love you!"

Clark's voice resonates, imbuing Rhett with the strength of finality. "That's your misfortune," he says, heading for the door.

"Oh, Rhett! Rhett!" She follows him. "If you go, where shall I go, what shall I do?"

Rhett opens the door to a swirling fog outside, then turns back to her, speaking sadly but with full purpose.

"Frankly, my dear, I don't give a damn."

He walks away, disappearing into the fog.

*

"Cut!" bellowed Selznick into his bullhorn.

The room remained briefly quiet, as if all had inhaled at the same time and still held their breath. Then murmurs, then spoken congratulations. Onlookers invited in as Selznick's guests to watch the scene rushed forward and took turns pumping his hand. Jerry Bryant—whose job getting good publicity for this movie never had been easy—was almost jumping with glee as he headed right over to Louella.

"David isn't taking any chances," murmured Carole.

"It was a wonderful scene," Julie said, meaning it fervently. The movie was coming together, pulling her in. Selznick was right. It was still all in pieces, but something grand was being stitched into a whole. Maybe it wouldn't be as much as Selznick wanted it to be, but, oh, he was touching something.

Julie caught Andy's eye. His answering grin was wonderful—relieved, and clearly happy. What a burden he had been bearing. But it *was* worth it, this making of movies; magic could come from all the mundane squabbles and delays and clashing agendas. It was happening now.

Carole was staring at Clark, still cradling her now very cold cup of coffee. Julie expected she would make some joke, probably about how cranky Clark looked as he pulled at his collar, sweating from the long scene under the lights.

"You know something?" Carole said, rolling her words out slowly. "For the first time—watching Clark act?—I almost forgot I was married to him."

"That's quite a compliment," Julie said.

Carole looked at her, a bit puzzled. "You're right, it is," she said.

"Miss Crawford?"

Julie looked up, startled. A tiny, birdlike woman in a perfectly tailored suit with perfectly lacquered hair was standing in front of her, eyes steady in an expressionless face.

"I am Loretta James, Mr. Mayer's secretary," the woman said. "I believe you are in a tryout phase as a writer for MGM?"

Julie nodded, startled. She glanced past the woman and caught a quick glimpse of the fabled head of the studio as he prepared to leave the soundstage.

"Yes, I am," she managed.

"Mr. Mayer would like to see you in his office at three o'clock. I assume you will be available?"

"Yes," she said. What else could she say?

"Fine. Please be prompt; he has another appointment at four." The woman turned and nodded briefly to Carole. "Nice to see you, Miss Lombard," she said in a tone that expressed the opposite.

"Oh, you, too, Loretta honey," Carole said, smiling.

With a crisp nod, Loretta James turned on her heel and walked away.

"Why would he want to see *me*?" Julie asked.

"Poor old Loretta, she's been in the summoning business for too long," Carole said absently.

"Summoning?"

"You know, command performances, casting-couch rumors, you've heard them. But that's not what he wants from you, hon." Carole broke into a grin. "He's seen your script—this could be terrific."

Julie felt herself shaking inside. "Does he have a sense of humor?"

"He's not known for that," Carole admitted.

"Then maybe he wants to throw it back in my face."

Carole gazed at her steadily, seriously. "Okay, it could go either way, right? You'll find out at three o'clock."

*

Julie sat, hands folded, on the white leather couch in Louis B. Mayer's reception room, trying not to glance too often at the large silver clock above the cool Miss James's head. It was almost three-thirty. Did he know she was here? Was he busy with someone else? Had he forgotten? Miss James ignored her completely, giving no information. Julie settled back into the soft leather and stared down at the white shag carpet beneath her feet—the pile was so thick, it half covered the toes of her best black patent leather shoes—trying to appear a little more relaxed.

A door was opening; she heard voices—one a light, melodic woman's voice. Julie looked up and saw a bright-eyed young girl emerging from Mayer's office, the arm of the mogul around her shoulders as he talked in fatherly tones. It was Judy Garland. Ignoring Julie, Mayer walked Garland through the reception room to the outer door, and gave her a big kiss on the cheek and a hug as he said goodbye.

The door closed. He turned to go back to his office and stopped when he saw Julie. "Who are you?" he asked.

"Julie Crawford. You sent for me, Mr. Mayer."

"Oh yes. Come on in."

She followed his barrel-shaped figure through the inner door into the great man's office, trying not to be awed.

The room was dazzlingly white. Everything, even the desk, was white—leather, polished wood, silk draperies. There was something about the color white in Hollywood, Julie thought. It threw light back in the face of the viewers, letting them see only what the occupant wanted seen. It protected the rest, just as sunglasses hid the naked, vulnerable eye.

Mayer had taken his chair behind the desk. He folded his hands across his stomach and stared at her. "So you want to be a writer?" he said unexpectedly.

"Yes, sir, I'm hoping to work for MGM."

He picked up a familiar-looking manuscript. "I've read your prologue and epilogue," he said, giving it a fluttery wave, then dropped it back on his desk. "You think you can get audiences to buy that pile-of-shit movie as a comedy?"

"I think so, sir."

"Do you know how much that damn thing cost us?"

"Quite a lot."

"You bet it did."

It was all or nothing; she might as well try. "It could, if done right, make your niece come off as a great comedienne," she ventured.

"So you knew my niece played in this, God forbid her lack of judgment. Is that why you chose it?"

"No, sir—I chose it to work on because it was the worst movie I could find. Which made it the easiest to spoof."

He resumed staring at her, evaluating. "You're not too dumb."

She wasn't going to say thank you. She bit her lip and told herself again: Don't say thank you.

"I'll think about it," Mayer said, standing up. A broad smile spread across his face as he gestured at the array of photographs in elaborate frames on the windowsill behind his desk. "See my family? Good-looking group, don't you think? Not everybody got the brains." He pointed to the image of a smiling blonde, whom Julie recognized immediately from *Madhouse Nightmare*. "My niece, there. You know, you can get too anxious for success in Hollywood. Maybe she doesn't deserve it."

She said nothing, but tried to offer a neutral smile.

"We'll get back to you in a few days or so," he said.

She hesitated for a moment. He sat down and reached for the telephone—also a gleaming white. No escorting her out: this meeting was over.

"Thank you, Mr. Mayer," she said, and turned to head out the door.

"So what did you think about that ending Selznick shot today?" Mayer asked, stopping her.

There was no use worrying about finding a safe answer.

"I thought it was perfect."

"Well, you better be goddamn right."

She paused again, but this time his dismissal was complete.

CHAPTER 21

 eeks had passed. Julie lay sleepless in her bed at the boarding house, staring at the crumbling plaster on the ceiling. If Mayer didn't want her script, how could she pay the rent for this place after next month? Her father was proving true to his word: no check had arrived. She had no need to worry; she needed to stand her ground. Andy would help, but that would make her feel like some kind of kept woman, and if that was hypocritical of her, too bad. She was still, inside, a Midwestern girl—even if she did curl up in his bed at least a few nights a week.

She turned on her side, trying to blink away the cobwebs in her head. With one hand, she pushed back the covers, already sweaty. The heat was building: another scorching day.

Maybe she was living inside a dream, and none of it was real. She looked across at the empty bed of her former roommate, wishing she were here. Rose had moved out a few days ago, gone back to Texas to plan her wedding. It would be next spring, she'd said. "And you must, must come be my maid of honor—will you do that?"

Julie pulled the covers back over her head, wishing she hadn't been so clumsy with her reply. She shouldn't have stammered and made up some temporizing reply; she should've just been honest.

But Rose knew. "You'll come if you either get a job that thrills you or get married and you're thrilled about that," she offered in her kind, serene way. "I don't have to know right away. But I'm think-ing blue silk for your gown."

Julie pushed the covers away again, this time kicking them with her feet. Get up, she told herself. Go walk on the sand in Santa Monica—to hell with the tar. At least eat something. Pretend you aren't chained to the communal telephone out in the hall, waiting for the call that might change your life. Pretend you're not wonder-ing whether you and Andy could truly get married, pretend you're both wishing that happens, and pretend you're not scared every-thing might fall apart.

She tried to imagine Andy's new routine. "Now we make the real movie," he told her after the last scene was shot. "See you next month."

It wasn't a joke. He was buried daily now, working with Selznick in the cutting room, hunched over 225,000 feet of film printed out of the half-million shot, working to piece together the final product of what would eventually make its way to the movie theaters and be known as *Gone with the Wind*.

When he gave her those numbers, she could hardly believe them. No wonder he often looked wan and gray. And it wouldn't be over for weeks—Andy said Selznick was demanding even more retakes, which would take them through August.

A woman's head swathed in toilet paper and a net to keep her curls in place popped into the room. "Call for you," she chirped. "Don't take too long; I'm expecting a ring from my agent."

Julie ran for the phone. It was Carole. Of course, today was Clark and Carole's move to the ranch. How could that have slipped her mind?

"Okay, I know you're disappointed that it's just me, but you can't sit and cook in the heat in that boarding house all day, every day. Whoa, watch out for that breakfront!" Carole yelled. "Not you, honey; the movers are here. This is the big day, remember? Come up and let's say goodbye to Bel-Air!"

A sudden crash. "They dropped it. Good thing I didn't like the damn thing much anyway," Carole mumbled.

"I don't know if I can come today—"

"And if you don't come today and they don't call, you'll sit and stew tomorrow, too. Julie, if they want you, they will find you."

"I'll think about it—"

"No, you won't. There's a car waiting for you out front right now. Doughnuts and coffee when you get here. No Scotch this time—it's too early."

Julie's spirits were lifting. "Orange juice?" she asked.

"Fresh-squeezed."

"Okay." She hung up the phone and walked back to her room, already feeling renewed. Yes. She didn't have to sit here and brood that her entire life was made up of waiting for other people to decide its direction. If they wanted her, they would find her.

*

"Did you remember who else you were supposed to invite for moving day?" Julie said as she walked in the door.

Carole straightened up from a box filled with dishes, brushing a dusty hand across her face, leaving a streak of dirt on her cheek. Her hair was tied back with a red bandanna, but limp tendrils were working their way through. "What do other people do with their grandmother's dishes?" she asked, puzzled. "I never really went for the stuff that is so delicate-looking you're afraid to eat off of it. Maybe I could leave it on somebody's doorstep, and ring the bell. . . ."

"Carole, you invited Louella, remember?"

"Oh, sure." Carole waved her hand airily. "Big dinner for her at the ranch tonight. We're cooking a deer Clark shot yesterday a few miles from the house. God, I love saying that. On *our land,* waaaay out beyond the house."

"*You're* cooking venison?"

"No, a deer."

"Carole—" Julie started to laugh.

"I know, I know—I just want to see her eyes pop when I ask her if she wants to see the antlers." Carole's eyes were dancing in that impossible way of hers as she threw back her head and laughed. "Let's get that coffee."

They made their way past the movers, a crew of burly men in sweaty tee shirts who, having hoisted boxes on their shoulders, were dodging and weaving past the yapping, darting dachshunds and the highly alarmed Pekingese running in circles. Julie was happy to see old Sammy lying contentedly by the fireplace; he licked her hand when she leaned down to pet him. The cat was curled comfortably on top of the box of dishes. Carole scooped her up as they walked by. "She'll end up in the moving truck if I'm not careful." She sighed. "She wouldn't be very happy."

"You've had some good dinner parties here," Julie said with a smile, looking out into the dining room. "I'm particularly fond of the one for my parents."

"Didn't we play our parts well?"

"You sure did."

"It was a great excuse to reconnect to my Midwestern roots," said Carole as she set a chocolate doughnut in front of Julie; something in her voice didn't sound quite as cheerfully flip as usual.

"Do you ever feel tugged back?"

"Once in a great while." Carole poured some cream into her coffee and stirred it slowly. "I was pretty young when I left, but, hey, there've been plenty of goodbyes since then."

"Your first husband—"

"Yes, that dear, impossible Bill Powell. He's the only intelligent actor I've ever met." She smiled. "With the exception of my husband, obviously." Carole's mood altered as she stared down at her coffee. "I was also in love with a wonderful man, a singer who was killed. A gun accident."

"Russ Columbo," Julie said.

"Yes. Hell, I forget sometimes that just about every nook and cranny of my life has been poked out into the sunlight at one time or another."

"I'm sorry."

"Don't say that, hon. We both know actors' lives are an open book. But I loved him in a way that, for me, was different." Carole seemed to pause and think for a second; then she reached inside the neckline of her blouse and pulled out a tiny gold locket on a chain. "A friend gave me this after his death, and I still wear it." She flicked it open. It held a picture of a handsome young man with dark hair and warm eyes. Russ Columbo. "So why am I showing you this?" she said quietly.

Julie already knew. "To teach me that goodbyes can come around the corner when you least expect them," she ventured. Her voice trembled. She didn't have to say Andy's name.

"I'm not predicting it; I'm saying life holds surprises. And sometimes you hold on—and let go—in different ways."

They sat in silence, neither of them needing any words for the moment. Then Carole stood up, pushing back the bandanna, which had slipped down to her eyebrows. "Let's go feed the ducks. If they start shitting on that wonderful bear rug at the ranch, I'll serve *them* for dinner."

Her laugh was as light and buoyant as ever.

✳

The call came in the form of a telegram from Mayer's office, which was waiting for Julie when she returned that night to the boarding house. She ripped it open as she hurried to her room, keeping her head down, not wanting to convey anything to any observers until she could digest its contents. Close the door, sit down on the bed. Read.

> *You are hereby offered a twelve-week contract at four hundred dollars a week to rewrite the script of* Madhouse Nightmare, *which will be assigned to MGM director Clyde Denton. Your initial rewrite of the original script has promise, although the epilogue needs to more strongly emphasize the screwball role of the heroine. Denton will contact you with production schedule.*

Advise within twenty-four hours if this offer is acceptable or it
will be officially rescinded. Contract will follow.

Louis B. Mayer

She couldn't help it—she let out a happy shout and ran into
the hall, straight for the phone. She could save more money now;
twelve weeks would give her a wonderful cushion. Andy, she had
to tell Andy first. Could she reach him in the cutting room? Her
finger shook as she dialed. Never had the rotary dial taken so long
to click past each numeral. The phone rang several times before a
male voice finally answered. One of the engineers—would he give
the phone to Andy?

Girls were staring at her curiously. "I got a job," she blurted.
"Writing a real movie."

Waiting there, holding the phone, floating in the air, she saw the
mix of responses in the eyes of the girls around her, all the way from
true pleasure to frustration to jealousy; each one, she realized, was
waiting for something. Someone kissed her on the cheek; someone
turned away. She would think about all this, but not now, not yet.

"Andy?" She couldn't contain the excitement in her voice.

"Hey, you're excited. You're hired for *Madhouse Nightmare,*
right?"

"Yes, yes!"

He laughed. "I thought you would be. Congratulations, kid, you
deserve it."

"It's for twelve weeks—"

"That's great. Mayer is giving you a real step up on the ladder,
not that stupid tryout class run by Goldman. Do a good job on this
and you'll be put on another movie." His voice was warm, but somehow distracted.

"When can I see you?"

"I'll be here all night again," he said. He gave a weary chuckle.
"Don't get me started; I'm not going to whine."

She heard somebody shout his name.

"Tomorrow?" she pressed.

There was a brief silence. Then, "Yes, I'll make time." His voice was suddenly tender. "We'll celebrate at Chasen's, okay?"

"No. At your place." Surely he could feel her desire.

"I'll have to go back to the studio after. Is that all right?"

He did feel it; she heard it returned in his voice. "I don't care," she whispered.

"Okay, honey. See you tomorrow. I'll pick you up."

✳

Next she called her parents. She knew they wanted to be happy for her—she could hear it in their voices—but she also heard the doubt, which she tried to push away.

"A farce? You're writing a Hollywood *farce?*" her father asked in a baffled voice.

"What's wrong with that, Dad?"

"But you do serious work. Isn't this temporary?"

There was no use arguing with him, which would only sound defensive, especially since girls within earshot were casting politely exasperated looks at her for monopolizing the phone. Anyway, she had one more call to make.

So it wasn't until she reached Carole at the ranch that she found her mood turning wistful.

"Serious work." That's what her father had said. Yes, she had been writing something he might have been proud of. She thought of her original script, the one she had labored over so lovingly and had dreamed of selling. She had been creating a story she believed in.

"My script—it was naïve, wasn't it?" she asked Carole.

"Oh, honey, it was idealistic; don't berate yourself. And it was damn good, too. You had to do that first."

"This is my first step on the ladder, right?"

"Of course it is. You're going to do great."

Julie realized something. "I'm changing," she said quietly.

"We all do," Carole said. Just as quietly.

*

The next night, they stood together facing the window, Andy's hands cupping her breasts, gazing out over the city; the lights below were scattered like a tapestry of jewels to a black horizon.

"I'm always calm here," she said. "I see now why people want to live in the Hollywood Hills; it all looks . . . glittering, but containable."

"It's an illusion," he said, kissing her ear. "It's really gobbling us up."

"Oh, stop." Playfully, she pushed him away, ruffling his hair.

He pulled her back and kissed her—a long, questing kiss that needed no words. She knew he would not go back to the studio. He would rest in her arms, and she would kiss away the strain in his face, and they both would sleep deeply and together, twisting and twining, inhaling each other's breath, and holding fast.

And later she would remember how peaceful she felt that night, how sure of herself, how safe, and how poised on the cusp of all that was new. She would remember all that for a very long time.

CHAPTER 22

*B*y late August, the rough cut of *Gone with the Wind* was ready; that was the good news. The bad news? It was five hours long.

"That's impossible," Julie protested when Andy told her. They stood together outside the studio offices, whispering hastily in the kind of quick encounter that was the best each of them could manage lately. She had barely a minute to talk. Her head was filled with her own concerns today—Clyde Denton, a reliable veteran of the cadre of MGM directors, was pressing her for some major script changes in the prologue to *Madhouse Nightmare*. She was also worried about Mayer's niece, who didn't like the idea of having her role recast as broad farce. "I'm a serious actress, and I don't do pratfalls," she had said with a sniff upon meeting a nervous Julie for the first time.

"Well, Carole Lombard was the queen of screwball comedies for a long time, and that didn't stop her from being a serious actress," Julie retorted.

Denton had narrowed his eyes, folded his arms, and fired back. "Sweetheart, I can make you a star," he said. "Or you can just go back to your uncle's mansion and suck your thumb and brood about how unappreciated you are by lunkheads like me. Which way, sweetie?"

The girl had looked at him in complete shock. No MGM employee would ever talk to her like that unless Uncle Louie (not that she ever called him that to his face) had given tacit permission. Her eyes darting from Denton to Julie and back, she held in her lethal indignation at such mistreatment until she could decide which one was the weaker. She chose Julie.

"You've never written a screenplay before," she lashed out. "You're not my boss, and if I don't like how you write and cut this, I'll take it right to the top. And you know I will."

She just might. And, depending on Mayer's mood, this could be tricky.

Andy's voice cut sharply into Julie's thoughts. "You think it's impossible? I thought so, too, until we showed it to L.B. this morning."

Julie wrenched her focus back to Andy's news. "How did he react to the length?"

"Completely out of character. He didn't rant and rave—although we had to stop at least five times for him to get up and go to the bathroom." Andy grinned. He looked reasonably relaxed today, standing there in his khakis, hands in his pockets. More like the old Andy. "First time Mayer signaled the projectionist to stop the film, I thought David would have a heart attack. But he likes the movie. We may have to cut another half hour or so, that's all. We'll work tonight."

"Who will sit through a movie that long?" she said, laughing.

"We'll find out at the sneak previews. I gotta tell you, I'm proud of this baby. So how is it, working with Denton?"

He was speaking faster, and Julie felt a little embarrassed. He must have seen her glance at her watch.

"He's fine; it's that spoiled woman—"

"Right, Martha what's-her-name. Not Mayer, right? A couple of marriages, as I recall."

"You know her?" There it was again, a pang of nervous uncertainty. She thought fleetingly of Doris.

"I've seen her around. No, my love, I haven't slept with her. Or even shared a drink with her. But I kind of like making you a little jealous."

"Andy, I miss you."

"We're both busy, that's all." Andy tilted his head up to the sun gratefully. "God, it's nice to be outside," he said. "I'd like to take you to the beach, but can't do it yet. So here's the alternative: Selznick's throwing a wrap party tomorrow; want to come? Everybody's dragging and just dying to get this thing finished, but he wants something festive. Okay?"

"Okay." She didn't care who saw her, and what did it matter? She reached up and kissed him on the lips, then turned to leave.

"Busy lady," he said with a slow smile. "See you tomorrow. Noon."

"Where is it?"

"Where do you think?" He spread his arms. "Right here, outside. On the back lot. Lots of tired people holding each other up, eating hot dogs, and enjoying the sun."

She laughed. "What a glamorous business this is," she called after him as he walked away. "Maybe Clark should be in charge of the barbecue."

*

The day was beautiful, that first day of September, the kind of perfect day that made life something to savor, when hot dogs really were delicious, ice cream was served, and egos were forgotten. Or at least allowed to rest, Julie thought as she watched the many human components of the massive opus called *Gone with the Wind* gather under a very blue sky.

"Christ, I'm glad it's over," muttered one of the engineers as he lifted a can of beer, looking first to make sure Selznick wasn't within earshot. The actors were drifting over from the parking lot to the party. Stripped of their roles, they looked as plain as unbuttered biscuits. But—like the engineer—most of them were relieved to be fading back to who they were before inhabiting the characters of *Gone with the Wind.*

Julie gazed at them all as they clustered around the table of food.

Butterfly McQueen had never been happy with her role, and was still a bit snappy and tense. Hattie McDaniel was joking with Clark, her pal, who puffed on his pipe, so clearly relieved to be finally free of Rhett Butler. Leslie Howard, in slacks and an open shirt, a bit shy and uneasy, looked much older in civilian clothes—too old for Ashley, as he had protested all along. Vivien and Olivia chattered on about a sailing vacation that would involve neither corsets nor retakes nor taking orders from anyone, including David O. Selznick.

"They don't see how good this movie is yet," Andy murmured to Julie. He nodded in the direction of Selznick. "Look at the guy. He is proud."

It was true. The obsessive producer on a daily ration of Benzedrine and thyroid extract to keep him going had somehow vanished today. His other self—the smiling, sunny, brilliant man who could work magic for a movie—stood by the beer keg, grinning at all of them like a benevolent king.

Clark strolled over, clapped Andy on the back, asked Julie how her parents were, then laughed and pointed at his wife standing on the bed of a truck. "By God, she got Selznick to agree to another parade of balloons," he said. He waved and cheered. Carole waved back and continued orchestrating the release of dozens of brilliant yellow and red balloons, starting them on their upward voyage just as an aide came hurrying over from the main office, waving a piece of paper, looking grim.

"What is he saying?" Julie asked, straining to hear. "What is he waving?"

"It looks like wire copy," Andy said as they all moved closer.

"Germany invaded Poland—that's important, right?" the aide announced, looking from one to another, as if waiting for someone to tell him how to respond. "This just came over the wire." He pointed to the large type: "Bombs Rain on Warsaw." "Roosevelt says not to worry, we're staying neutral," he added quickly.

And for a brief moment, they all stared, first at each other, then to the sky, as the balloons floated peacefully, silently upward, catching the wind, disappearing, leaving no trail, no visible last acts.

"So now England will declare war on Germany?" someone asked.

"Of course," Leslie Howard said. He turned to the questioner, a look of contained, almost resigned astonishment on his face. And in that look, Julie saw the reality that she and most people in her vast, protected country were still trying to avoid.

Howard turned to Selznick, frowning, his narrow, melancholy face settling into a resignation that looked permanent. "David, I'm done here; I hope you understand. I will leave for England in the morning."

Clark, standing next to them both, looked down at the grass and said, "You're a good man, Howard. It's been a privilege working with you."

Selznick nodded and said nothing—just heaved a sigh and put an arm around the slender British actor's shoulders. Then the entire crowd walked slowly into the main building, to hear an excited newscaster announce that Britain, France, Australia, and New Zealand were declaring war on Germany. The Royal Air Force was poised to attack the German navy. And soon Roosevelt would address the nation—reassuring all Americans that their country would remain neutral.

"Until they attack us," Andy muttered, his face somber.

Julie leaned against him, closing her eyes. The needle had been lifted from the phonograph, stopping the music. But the record kept spinning, and they all were like dancers still tripping across the stage, performing. What else could they do?

*

"Dancers? Yeah, we're all performers—irrelevant. Maybe mind-less," Andy said when she shared this thought that evening. His happy mood was gone. He slumped deep into the sofa, his face flushed with the day's sun. Or with the liquor. He finished a glass of bourbon, his second of the night?—Julie didn't want to keep count.

"That's not true," she said sharply. "You've got previews coming up—all the early signs show people really *want* something magical to ease their worries, and it's going to be *Gone with the Wind* that does it—please, stop being so negative."

"I don't give a damn if it succeeds," Andy said, staring out at the city below, exhaling, then jamming his cigarette into the ashtray. "There are more important—"

Julie threw a towel at him. "Right, there are more important things going on in the world, but this movie is important, too. And so is the one I'm working on. And being part of it is no mortal sin against—against the needs of the world!" She had to fight his pessimism; she didn't want to see his pleasure in making the movie drain away. Yes, she was worried about war, too, but she was also worried about whether her rewrite of *Madhouse Nightmare* would be successful. Did that make her some kind of vapid "performer"? Filming for the prologue started tomorrow, and she wanted to allow herself to care whether or not Mayer would be pleased. At the same time, she was angry that she cared so much. Because there *were* more important things going on in the world . . . and . . . that damn record she kept thinking about continued spinning, spinning in her head.

Andy started to laugh. "Julie," he said, carefully lifting an edge of the towel over his face. "Next time you throw something at me, will you make sure it's not greasy?" He looked so comical, a smile pulling at the corners of his mouth, that she felt better.

"Life keeps on, you know."

"You're right. It does as long as you're in it. I've been figuring this would happen all the way along. Getting wrapped up in the movie lulled me. So I'm mad at myself. It makes me wonder why I'm here in the first place."

"You're here because you are good at your job and you love it. Isn't that enough?"

He was silent for a moment. "Maybe I've gotten too good at maneuvering in this world," he replied.

Sometimes words just dug deeper holes. Oh, scribble that one down for a script you might write someday, she told herself as she lifted the towel off his head and pressed her lips against his.

"I'll try not to be so gloomy," he said quietly.

"Thank you," she whispered back.

*

Julie tried to relax as she sat on the sidelines the next morning, watching Denton and the hastily reassembled actors of *Madhouse Nightmare* start filming. Rehearsals were quick, and nobody seemed tense—after all, there were no overly hopeful expectations.

Except hers.

Whatever was going to happen was out of her control now, but she hadn't quite expected her reaction on hearing actors read the words she had written. As she listened, enthralled, she felt oddly like a puppeteer, knowing precisely what would come out of each stranger's mouth before he or she spoke.

Andy had given her a hint of how this small taste of power would feel. "You'll fall a little in love with yourself at first," he said. "But you'll get over it."

She smiled to herself now. He was right. Nobody need know, however: she could be professional, and she'd get over it pretty fast. Whatever happened, she was doing just what she wanted to do and enjoying it.

*

The MGM commissary was even noisier and smellier than usual. It was like college, Julie thought, as she pushed her metal tray along the tubed railing, past tired-looking beef stew bubbling in a warming tray, past chopped-up chicken mixed with corn, past custards turned dry and brown. This was leftover day, a good day to settle for a ham sandwich on rye. It didn't go stale as fast.

A week now since Denton wrapped the remake. No word from anybody about anything. Nobody seemed unhappy, nobody seemed happy. What did she do next? She felt a bit like a wallflower, standing around trying to look confident.

"Julie?"

She looked up. Denton had ambled over to the lunch line, a curious smile on his face.

"Heard the news yet?" he said.

"No, what news?" There was a sudden fluttering in her chest as she tried to tune out the clatter of lunch trays and loud voices in the crowded lunchroom.

"We got a distribution deal last night for *Madhouse Nightmare*. Sold for a twelve-thousand-dollar profit. You're gold, kid."

"That fast?" She could hardly get the words out. People in back of her were clearing their throats more or less politely, their message clear: Move on, lady, whoever you are; we're hungry.

"Mayer pushed it through. One screening for distributors, then up or back in the trash bin." His smile was kind. "Didn't know it, did you? You were going to be either dead in this business today or a star."

"And I—"

"Get a good agent. You're in." He turned away, but then stopped. "Oh, and you've got my thanks, too: this helps me. I wasn't doing much lately—and it's hard to come back in this business when you start slipping." He strolled away.

She stood, frozen. Disbelieving. Then giddy.

"Hey, honey, some of us have to get back to work," a voice yelled out. "Can we move on?"

Julie mumbled an apology and stepped out of line. She caused a few heads to turn as she walked, dazed, with a grin on her face, still holding the empty tray, out of the commissary into the hall, a busboy running after her to retrieve the lunchroom property.

*

"Myron. We'll get you Myron," Carole said with a whoop of laughter when Julie gave her the news. "Oh my God, you are *discovered*! I get a percentage of your millions, okay? About fifty sound right?"

Julie laughed. "Who's Myron?"

"David's brother; he's my agent. He'll take you on. This is great news; you'll end up being the highest-paid screenwriter in Hollywood! Close, anyway."

Nothing ever seemed to tamp Carole down, for which Julie was fervently grateful. They sat together in Carole's upstairs bedroom suite, across the hall from Clark's. The suite was immaculate—gleaming marble floors, a dressing table swathed in white silk with mirrored walls, and even a mirrored ceiling. That surprised Julie at first—the Carole she knew scoffed at the pretentions of glamour, so why make her private bedroom a movie set?

"I think it's the most elegant shithouse in the San Fernando Valley, don't you?" Carole said with a happy grin, plunking down on the bed, sinking deep into its cushioned depths. "Clark likes it, he finds it sexy, which means more sex. He needs all the atmosphere I can provide to keep fucking a lot." She sighed. "Poor Pa, he isn't exactly the greatest lay in town. He's too shy. Those ex-wives of his didn't teach him much; they were too old for him. Have you told Andy your good news yet?"

"I didn't want to bother him today," Julie said after a startled pause. "He's coming out here in a few hours."

"Why wasn't he first, hon?"

Julie's answer felt like a betrayal even as she said the words. "He's been pretty sad. He'll be happy for me, but he'll have a hard time pretending he thinks it matters much. He's struggling with whether or not what we do here means anything now that the world is at war."

Carole pulled herself to a seated position; she didn't answer right away. Then:

"That's kind of playing dirty, deciding ahead of time how he'll respond."

She cut to the heart of most everything. "I think I wanted your enthusiasm first. Is that terrible?"

"Oh hell, no," Carole said. But her voice was flat. She reached for the bedpost of the four-poster bed and gripped tightly, her face draining of color.

"What's the matter?" Alarmed, Julie reached for her friend's hand. Carole was sweating profusely, her body shaking. She winced, threw her head back, and clutched at her belly. Julie glanced down and saw a trickling of blood make its way over the white satin bedcover, then, drip by sluggish drip, to the white marble floor.

"Oh God, no," Carole gasped. She reached for Julie's hand. "Help me, please, I think I'm miscarrying."

"Of course I will. Don't worry, I'll get you to a hospital." Julie, stunned, ran to the bathroom for towels and tried to stanch the flow, then grabbed the phone by the bed and with trembling fingers dialed Information. An ambulance, she told the operator who answered. Send an ambulance.

Carole was crying. "I wanted this baby so much," she moaned. "Don't let Louella find out."

Julie cradled her head, smoothing back her hair. A memory flashed—a scene, long ago, in a darkened bedroom; her mother moaning; she, maybe nine years old, standing there, a little girl, smelling the sharp scent of blood before being hustled from the room. Her mother had cried, too.

"I'm so very, very sorry," she said.

"I can't believe it; I was so sure this time," Carole whispered. Her eyes were filled with tears. "Honey, don't give them my name; tell them I'm Jane Peters."

"I did. Help will come soon, really soon; they're just down the hill."

Carole lay still now, like a broken doll, her white hostess gown smeared and crushed. Julie raced back to the bathroom. A washcloth—she needed a cold, wet washcloth to wipe Carole's face.

"Feels good," Carole whispered when Julie laid it across her forehead. She mustered a flash of humor. "Isn't glamour wonderful?"

＊

The emergency room at Cedars of Lebanon Hospital was pitilessly bright as the ambulance attendants wheeled Carole through the crowd of hurrying nurses and health aides to the relative privacy of a cubicle ringed with drab blue curtains. Julie pulled the sheet up over Carole's face as she followed alongside, trying to shield her from recognition.

"I'm not dead, honey," Carole said, trying to grin as she pushed the sheet off her face inside the cubicle. "I've just lost a baby. There, I've said the word." Her eyes began filling with tears again.

The curtain was suddenly yanked open. Clark stood there, his hair wild, eyes wide with fear, as he moved inside and reached for his wife. "Oh, Ma," he said in a shaky voice. "I thought—when I saw—" He sank to his knees next to her and pulled her into his arms.

Julie stepped outside; her own eyes were moist as she tried to make her way through the crowd of people to a quiet corner somewhere. Carole, open about everything, had kept her pregnancy a secret from everybody. The ambulance had arrived quickly enough—Yes, for a woman named Jane Peters; hurry, please—and then she couldn't reach Clark, and the housekeeper promised to send him to Cedars as soon as he got home from the studio. And now she stood in a corner of this raw room of accidents and sickness and cries of pain and rushing doctors, remembering the sight of that tiny morsel of lost life slipping out, how the ambulance attendants had quickly wrapped it in newspaper and put it in a bucket; how Carole had cried; and she thought of how overwhelming a loss was when it caught you unexpectedly and bit you in the neck.

And then Andy was there beside her in a corner of this weirdly lit room which did not allow shadows, his arms encircling her, his breath warm, no words; thank you, Andy, no words; just hold me and now please, tell me you love me.

And he did.

CHAPTER 23

*K*eeping a secret in Hollywood? Impossible.

But maybe not.

Two days went by. Each morning and evening, Julie grabbed the papers from the doorstep of the boarding house before anybody could reach them. She had a plan; Andy had kindly not pointed out its absurdity. She would open the *Examiner* and the *Herald Express,* leaf through the inky pages for Louella's and Hedda Hopper's columns, and scan them, poised for action—any mention of Carole's miscarriage and she would dump the papers promptly into a trash barrel. That was her muddled plan.

But in the gossip columns there were no hints dropped, no lachrymose accounts, no intrusive, coy reports; nothing. She began breathing easier.

"Carole's perfectly capable of taking care of herself," Andy pointed out gently. "Are you off guard duty now?"

"She was devastated. She's my friend."

"Clark is right by her side."

"Do you see what I see, finally?"

"That they're really in love—and not running out the Hollywood marriage clock in the usual way?" he said with a smile.

"Yes."

"Well, let's say I'm considering some adjustments in the standard script."

"Ah, a reluctant concession?"

"Impossible. Don't you know a man always has to be right?"

She laughed. She was delighted with every lighthearted moment they shared these days—anything that cut through the aura of sadness that seemed to hover over him. It wasn't as if he was indifferent to the excitement of each frenetic day spent preparing *Gone with the Wind* for its launching. But there was no escaping the drumbeat of war news now. She would catch him staring into the distance, not quite here, somewhere else. He would be with her, so close—and then gone. By early September, Selznick was finally ready to let the fifty-four cans of film be "pried from his hands," as Andy put it, to be carted off in boxes, stowed in a truck, and taken to the Fox Theater in Riverside for the time-honored practice of presenting a "sneak preview." Expectations were high. An unsuspecting theater full of people was about to be told they were not going to see the movie they came to see, they were going to see *Gone with the Wind,* the movie they had been anticipating for years.

"We haven't told Selznick what theater we're going to. He thinks of nothing else but this movie, and he's totally capable of inadvertently tipping off some reporter," Andy said, wiping his brow, watching as the truck pulled away from the studio. It was searingly hot. He and Julie started to climb into one of the black limousines lined up to follow the van for the two-hour drive.

Publicists and assistant directors and various Selznick aides joined the caravan, joking that they felt like part of some secret initiation ceremony. No actors—that would have given it all away. But Irene Selznick was getting into the auto in front of Julie and Andy's, looking as cool and elegant as ever, unlike her husband, whose jacket was off and whose shirt was already stained with sweat.

It must be hard to be married to such a frenzied perfectionist, Julie thought. Maybe it was her imagination, but there was something sad in the other woman's eyes.

When Julie spotted Doris, looking quite fashionable in sleek pants and a red sweater that might have been molded to her body, she half wished she hadn't agreed to come along. But she had, and if Andy wanted her here, she would be here, even though it meant pulling away for the day from polishing a comedy that the director told her needed some "sparkle." It was another rewrite, yes, but that was okay. The story was fun; it was working. She liked the attention she was getting at MGM; who wouldn't? There were no mornings now when she lay in bed staring at the ceiling; she had too much to do—story conferences, directorial meetings. And Andy *was* happy for her; if anything, news of her workingwoman days at MGM lightened his mood, and that was a relief.

Doris caught her eye suddenly. She gave a small half-smile and lifted her arm in mock salute, then disappeared into one of the automobiles. Julie quelled a spasm of unease. She was in her car now, leaning back against the leather, wishing it didn't stick to her skin.

Her thoughts turned to Carole.

She was doing fine. Julie didn't know how other women recuperated from a miscarriage, but Carole managed it with flair, even though she had to postpone her new RKO movie, *Vigil in the Night.* Bit by bit, day by day, she emerged again. Julie saw her shoulders straighten, watched her once again flinging her hair and rolling her eyes, reading scripts, teasing Clark—who stayed in the hospital room next to hers at Cedars—and poking fun at everything in her usual lighthearted way.

Only once did she talk about what had happened. "I'm not giving up," she told Julie upon arriving home from the hospital, her face still the color of wax. "I want a baby, I want our baby, and I'll be damned if I'm going to stop hoping. Even if I have to give up horseback riding. Got that?"

Julie smiled. "Got it."

*

Andy's voice jolted Julie out of her reverie.

"Three hours and forty-five minutes, that's the length of our final cut," he announced as the caravan pulled up in front of the theater. "Selznick is going to warn the audience, and then he's going to lock the doors. Nobody can come in or leave, just in case they don't get the message that this is a big-time production. The man doesn't miss a detail."

Selznick strode into the lobby first, asking to see the manager. A rumpled little man with rheumy eyes came hurrying out of a back office, hastily buttoning his jacket. This new arrival was obviously an important personage, and he wasn't here to see either *Hawaiian Nights* or *Beau Geste*—you could count on that.

When he heard who his visitor was, and what the men standing behind him were carrying in those canisters, he paled.

"Of course, of course," he managed. The retinue of aides began marching toward the projection room as a few workers at the candy counter watched them curiously. "Mr. Selznick, I must ask a favor—"

Selznick frowned. This was no time for script deviations.

"Sir, I have to call my wife."

"No, we can't allow that."

"Mr. Selznick, you don't understand." His voice was pleading. "If I don't tell her to get over here right away, my marriage will be over. She loved the book; I can't leave her out of the screening." The man was distraught, eyes darting back and forth, bottom lip trembling.

"Jesus, give the guy a break," Andy muttered under his breath.

The exception was made. The wife arrived in minutes, an apron still tied around her waist, flustered, disbelieving, wide-eyed.

"Ladies and gentlemen, we are not going to show our featured film today," the manager quavered as the house lights went up and he ascended the stage. "What you are about to see is a sneak preview of the greatest film ever made."

"What movie is it?" someone shouted.

"I am not free to tell you. If anyone wants to leave, they must leave now, because the doors will be locked throughout the performance. Does anybody want to leave?"

People looked at each other, shrugged their shoulders, settled back. Maybe it would be better than *Beau Geste*.

The doors were locked.

The lights went down, and the film began. When Selznick's name came first in the credits, the crowd began murmuring. Then came Margaret Mitchell's name. The buzz grew louder.

"Here we go," Andy said, leaning forward in his seat, hands clasped in front of him.

The title came next. Julie caught her breath. Each letter of *Gone with the Wind* rolled slowly and splendidly from right to left across the screen, one after another, as the music swelled, bursting out, filling the elegant theater. It was no match for the audience in volume. Men and women began screaming and cheering, jumping up onto their seats, clapping, embracing each other. Yes, now they knew what they were about to see.

Andy sat back abruptly, took Julie's hand, and squeezed it to his chest. She could feel the rapid thumping of his heart beneath her fingers.

"Surprised?" she said.

"Yeah, didn't think it would be so intense. This is great."

"You care, you phony. You care a lot," she whispered.

"You bet I do." He kissed her hand. "Look, Irene Selznick is crying."

"You dope, so are you."

*

No one had seen David O. Selznick look this happy in months. All the way back to the studio, he read and reread the audience comments scribbled out in the lobby and collected in a large, overflowing glass jar. Not a single negative comment, not one. And no complaint about the length. "Keep it long," said one. "Cut the newsreel, don't cut this movie!"

And when the weary but happy group gathered on the steps of Selznick International Pictures in the early evening, even the relentless Selznick, eyes bright behind his thick, round glasses, thanking them for their work and their loyalty, seemed for the first time open to the idea of briefly relishing a triumph.

A great wash of relief had engulfed them all, or so Julie thought.

It dawned on her—as the hour grew late and people kept clapping each other on the back and talking about how they had never doubted this crazy venture would work—that Andy's demeanor had turned curiously flat. And so had Selznick's.

"What's the matter with you and Selznick?" she said as everybody drifted away to the parking lot, still wrapped in euphoria. Only two hours ago, he had been grinning and joking, not even bothering to wipe the tears of joy from his eyes. For that moment, she had felt he was the jaunty Andy she first met on the day of the burning of Atlanta.

"I'm happy, enormously relieved, and"—he paused, kicking at a stone in the path—"bracing for the next crisis."

"What's that?" There were no more scenes to reshoot. And the fight over how to dole out the writing and directing credits would obviously be decided by Selznick.

"The premiere in Atlanta."

Julie knew the preparations for the December launching of *Gone with the Wind* were under way on a grand scale. The governor of Georgia just yesterday announced that the date of the premiere would be a state holiday. There would be a huge parade, and three days of parties and dances for the cast—why, all of Atlanta was turning out to celebrate. "Andy, how can that be something to *worry* about?" she asked.

He cast her an amused glance. "When you're riding a horse as wild as this one, Julie, you *always* have problems. But resolving this is going to be tough. Selznick has worked his ass off gaining support from the Negro press—getting the word 'nigger' out was a huge victory for them—but he learned today what he's facing in Atlanta. Sure, he was told, bring the Negro actors down for the premiere—but white Southerners won't dine with them, invite them to the Junior League Ball honoring the rest of the movie cast, or sit with them in the auditorium. Oh, and no dressing rooms backstage, no bathrooms. Sure, bring them along, if all that is okay with you."

Julie was astonished. "That's outrageous. You mean even Hattie and Butterfly can't be there?"

"Yep. Look how far we've come, and now this. Remember the *Los Angeles Sentinel* editorial that almost paralyzed us?"

Yes, she remembered—so much so, she had it memorized. "They wanted to start a campaign on whether or not—let's see—'some of those who oppose Hitler from a safe distance have courage enough to oppose race prejudice when it may hit them in their careers and in their pocketbooks.'"

"Hey, great memory you've got, kid."

They sat in the car now, staring at each other. Yes, she was disgusted, but then wondered why. She had grown up close enough to the edges and whisperings of the South to know the rules and barriers. A memory from early childhood flashed through her mind—a brief image of a line of people dressed all in white, covered with white hoods, marching down the main street of Fort Wayne. Why were they wearing sheets? Why did they light a bonfire in the shape of a cross? Mother had pulled her away, refusing to answer her questions.

"Selznick was sure he could get them to make an exception, but they won't budge. And you know what that means."

Now she knew. "You're worried about Clark's reaction."

"Yep." He started the engine and put the car in gear. "My job is to keep him from boycotting the whole damn event."

"He can't do that," she said. "Clark *is Gone with the Wind*."

"You know as well as I do that he won't care. So—where are we headed, Miss Crawford?"

"Straight out to Encino is my guess."

He smiled, a slow, lazy smile. "That's why I love you, kid. You know how to tackle a problem straight on."

Julie reached for his breast pocket and pulled a cigarette out of his ever-present rumpled pack of Lucky Strikes. She didn't much like the taste of cigarettes, but right now she wanted one. She lit it, inhaled, and leaned back. Carole was expecting to hear an account of the sneak preview tonight. Good news first.

*

"No Negroes allowed? Are they fucking kidding?"

Clark, lounging contentedly in the silk-and-velvet smoking jacket of Rhett Butler's he had confiscated from the wardrobe department, almost dropped the cigarette from his mouth as he jumped up at the news. Carole reached over, deftly caught it, and put it into a proper ashtray. She did love her bear rug.

Julie felt her collar turning moist with sweat. The living room, usually comfortable and welcoming, felt stifling. Hard to believe, but Carole had a fire going. She wore a sweeping silk hostess gown in pale blue, with a small rim of fur outlining the scooped neckline. Carole believed in hostess gowns, the single item of apparel she firmly declared necessary for entertaining.

"A dumb idea, right?" Carole said, pointing to the fireplace when they first came into the house.

"Yes," Julie said without hesitation. Carole also loved atmosphere, but conjuring it from a roaring fire on a hot day was the wrong way to get it.

The men, both mopping their brows, didn't catch the exchange.

"Selznick found out after the preview. So there you are, from triumph to crisis, in a few hours," Andy said. "He's as angry as you are, and he's done all he can to fight it."

"Not too hard, not if they push back." Clark's face was red. "Damn, I hate the hypocrisy. Hattie deserves to be there—they all deserve to be there. If they can't come, I'm not going!"

Andy stiffened, then spoke in that calm, measured tone he used so well for crises and disasters. "There's no question now, this movie is going to make history. And you are an essential part of it, you know that."

"Don't argue with me, Andy."

"I'm not going to. You're a grown-up. You know how many lives and reputations are tied up in this venture. You know this movie has opened up possibilities for Negro actors. You can figure it out for yourself."

A short silence fell.

"No." Clark's jaw was set tight.

"Well, if that's the way you want it. So you would jeopardize the future of the movie we've all worked so hard on just to make a point?"

Julie bit her lip. She could see how hard this was for Andy to say.

"What would you do?" Clark asked.

"In your shoes? I'd want to kick the whole damn mess out the door, but I hope I wouldn't. Yeah, it's a compromise. Who does it help if you don't go? Not Hattie or Butterfly. Who does it hurt? Figure that out for yourself."

The two men stared at each other. Clark looked away first.

"I'll think about it," he said.

"Scotch or bourbon?" Carole said to Andy calmly. Then, to Clark: "Pa, will you dump some water on that fire? Tonight's a night for tamping things down."

Only Julie noted the quiver of tired relief in Andy's lips. "Scotch," he said. Then glanced at Julie. "Pour it short," he said quietly.

CHAPTER 24

*J*ulie hurried from the small office assigned to her in the Writers' Building, carrying her latest screenplay rewrite assignment, a romance set in Paris that Mayer had decreed a little too sprightly for the times. Calm it down—that's what he wanted—but there must be no mention of war or Hitler or anything dark.

"The usual Hollywood response," Andy said with a roll of the eyes when she told him her instructions.

Coming toward her was a man with long, matchstick-thin legs and a familiar face. Who was he? She remembered—this was one of the screenwriters in Abe Goldman's entourage. She had seen him around. He pretended to be British, and was usually wearing a carefully arranged silk cravat and a testy frown. He gave her a brisk nod, slowing enough to scan the folder in her hands swiftly. She resisted the instinct to clutch it tight, reminding herself that the cover was blank. No name on the screenplay.

He swept on, leaving in his wake an aura of feigned superiority. There was no way he could know for sure that, yes, it was one of his.

"Never put the names of your screenplays on the cover," Frances Marion had counseled. "Men turn hostile if a woman gets one of their scripts for rewrite. You'll make enemies just being here; no need to court them."

"Nice day, Harvey," Julie called out to the man's retreating back. She actually found herself enjoying the sparring of this new game.

"Yes, it is," said a voice. She turned again. Doris was standing in front of her, hair sleekly coiffed, her bright-red lips parted in a wide smile. She wore one of the largest pair of sunglasses Julie had yet seen, so big they tipped forward, exposing part of her eyes. What was she doing on the MGM lot?

"Hello," she managed. "I'm surprised—"

"You're wondering why I'm here," Doris said. "Well, I'm on a tryout for scriptwriting, same as you were. I guess that's what everybody wants to do these days."

"I didn't know you wrote scripts."

Doris shrugged, affecting a jaunty tone. "I'm bored, now that all the whooping and hollering over *Gone with the Wind* is over at Selznick International. Worked for you, right? Maybe lightning will strike twice—you never know." She reached up and took off her glasses.

Julie was taken aback. There was uncertainty in Doris's eyes, not the usual superior scorn. She wondered what to read into that, but did it matter? She no longer felt threatened. She had—she reminded herself—come a long way since their confrontation in Chasen's marble-and-glass ladies' room.

"I never really was a rival of yours, you know," Doris said, almost as if she had read Julie's thoughts. "Though I certainly wanted to be." She smiled almost wistfully.

"Maybe I was too quick at feeling threatened," Julie offered.

"You grew up. You don't seem like a kid anymore."

"I guess that's a positive thing." Julie smiled.

"So now you're in line for the big time. Any tips? Or should we still be thinking of ourselves in competition?" Doris's tone had sharpened slightly.

So here it was, an invitation to dip a spoon again into the tasty pleasure of modest power. "Yes, actually," Julie said, pointing to the script—emblazoned in large type with the title—in Doris's hands. "Always carry your scripts in unmarked folders. You don't want the original writers to see them."

Doris looked momentarily startled. Then, "Okay," she said.

"Good luck." Julie couldn't think of anything else to say. Too many troughs and blind corners. And, she thought as she hurried away, if she was completely honest with herself, she remained intimidated by those long legs.

*

The tempo leading to the premiere was quickening. A million visitors were expected to flood into Atlanta for a grand, dizzying three-day celebration of the opening of *Gone with the Wind*.

Nothing was being overlooked, Mayer was making sure of that. There was to be a grand ball, so MGM sent the original costumes from the charity-bazaar scene to Atlanta for the stars to wear again, along with the original stage set, shipped in segments, to be re-created in Atlanta at a cost of ten thousand dollars. There would be street bands and concerts and parties and glittering guests from everywhere.

Clark remained resistant to the last, as did Victor Fleming, who now had no love for Selznick. They agreed they would not go to Atlanta. But on the day when Clark flatly refused to fly with Selznick and the rest of the cast on a TWA chartered plane, Carole stepped in.

"Enough of this childishness," she yelled at her husband. Julie was amazed at the volume Carole could summon when she wanted to. "I've got a new dress for the premiere, I want to go, and I even took your father and stepmother out and bought them new duds. Get off your ass, honey. This is our party!"

Andy laughed when Julie related the scene. "I love her," he said.

"I was standing in the bedroom, trying on a couple of her gowns for the premiere, when she reined in Clark," Julie said. "But he wins on one front—they're going to charter a separate plane, from American Airlines."

"This is kind of a useless carnival—" Andy started to say.

Julie reached out and clamped a hand over his mouth. "Please, Andy, let's just enjoy," she whispered. "Allow yourself to play."

His eyes were steady as he looked at her, but, for a moment, beyond sad. Where was he going? she thought, alarmed.

Then everything was all right again.

He gently lifted her hand away and kissed it. "Will I be able to unhook that dress easily after the party?" he murmured.

"I'll tell you what," she said. "Just to make it easier? I won't wear anything under it."

"Perfect." He pulled her tight and they kissed, lazily and long.

*

The two planes—each with a stenciled logo on the side reading GWTW—touched down at the Atlanta airfield one after the other, so smoothly it looked as if two planes had been the idea all along.

Julie peered from the window as they taxied after landing. A line of black limousines threaded from plane to terminal, with a uniformed chauffeur standing at attention next to each one. At the very front of the line were two splendid Packard convertibles for the major stars.

"For one long weekend, we're all royalty, rhinestone variety," Andy said. "Did you see what *The New York Times* called us this morning? 'The golden boys and girls of Hollywood.'"

"Will you allow yourself to have fun?" she asked.

"Yes, kid. For you."

"Don't be so self-sacrificing." She felt a flash of annoyance. But that evaporated as they settled into the limousines and started on the seven-mile motorcade to the Biltmore Hotel.

"Jesus, look at the crowds," Clark said with a touch of awe. Only later did they learn that over three hundred thousand people—many of them in vintage clothes from the Civil War era—had lined the path of their journey. Street musicians marched with the caravan, playing "Dixie." Aged veterans—standing straight and proud in their Confederate uniforms—lined the parade route, some holding ancient rifles. The atmosphere was almost hysterically jubilant. At one point, an elegant-looking woman tore off a long white leather glove and threw it to Clark, who ducked, discomfited.

"Pa, I'll bet you a fiver someone throws a pair of pantaloons next!" Carole yelled over the cheers.

"You're on!" Clark yelled back. His dark mood had lifted.

It was as Andy had predicted: any actor receiving this much adulation would have a hard time staying angry, something Selznick knew very well.

They were almost to the Georgian Terrace Hotel, where the premiere gala would be held, when, suddenly, caught like a flapping kite in the breeze, a pair of old-fashioned knickers came flying through the air, landing on Clark's head.

"Pay up, Pa!" yelled Carole. "Close enough to pantaloons!"

*

No expense would be spared, by the city or by MGM, for the weekend. At the lavish ball on Thursday night—as Clark and the others prepared to bring their roles to life for the benefit of Atlanta—Carole, swathed in black velvet and silver fox, held court in a box seat, laughing and joking, scribbling out autographs for the cluster of people gathered around her. And no matter who was pleading, it was clear, from some disappointed looks, that she was sticking to her determination to sign only as "Carole Gable." This was Clark's party, not hers.

Then the high point of the evening—Clark, Vivien, and Olivia swept into the room in full costume, magically transformed back to their fictional characters. The effect was almost surreal. The crowd clapped and cheered.

"I'm not sure if we're all in a movie or not." Julie giggled as Andy took her for a graceful swing around the room. She liked the feel of her body in her new dress, which was quite simple, a column of apricot silk caught at the throat with a small diamond pin once owned by her grandmother. Not expensive. Her paycheck was getting fatter, but not yet ready for designer gowns. The wardrobe mistress had offered to lend her one of the dresses worn by the extras, but Julie was glad she had decided not to try living up to a costume.

"When do you wear the sexy one you borrowed from Carole?"

Andy asked as they took a deft second turn around the glittering ballroom.

"What's wrong with this one?"

"It's beautiful, honey. I'm talking *sexy*."

"Tomorrow, so don't go away."

Andy laughed, holding her closer. He had to be enjoying himself; how could he not? This was all glamorous and fun. She threw her head back, letting her hair swing loose, wanting the dance never to stop. Surely, just tonight, he felt the same way. And tomorrow? She laughed to herself. Well, of course, tomorrow was another day. Thank you, Scarlett.

*

All of Atlanta danced toward the weekend's climax. For the Hollywood contingent, the next day flew by in a blur of lunches and speeches and meetings filled with popping flashbulbs, giggling ladies in their grandmothers' ball gowns, schoolchildren clamoring for autographs, publicists ushering the stars through the crowds that gathered everywhere they went—in parks blooming with flowers, in their hotels, in the restaurants—all straining for a view of the mythical heroes and heroines of their fondly remembered mythical history.

Clark made his way through the day, flabbergasted. "They sure take us seriously," he mumbled to Carole.

Dusk was gathering when, on cue, a dozen monster-sized floodlights placed strategically around the center of town suddenly switched on, sending columns of light cutting upward, to meet in a brilliant, glittering crown above Loew's Grand Theater—where *Gone with the Wind* was about to be presented to the city of Atlanta. December 15, 1939, a day they'd all remember.

Julie peeked out the window of the car as their caravan crawled toward the theater, amazed at the sight that greeted them when they pulled closer. The façade of the grand old theater had been transformed into a replica of Twelve Oaks, the ancestral home of the Wilkes family. It was done so cleverly, Julie could almost imagine walking herself into the library once again. She smoothed down the folds of her borrowed red silk gown, still feeling half naked without underwear, wondering how Carole could be so comfortable about her body.

"Honey," Carole had said as they prepared to leave the hotel, "quit tugging at that dress. You *can't* wear britches with my clothes, so relax and enjoy the feel of the silk on your skin."

She was trying.

They were almost there. Julie saw a scattering of people waving placards and peered hard to make out what they said. GONE WITH THE WIND GLORIFIES SLAVERY, read one. YOU'D BE SWEET TOO UNDER A WHIP, read another.

She had started to point them out to the others when a loud yipping scream rose from the enormous crowds on the sidewalk.

"What the hell is that?" Clark said.

"That's the Rebel yell," a soft-spoken Atlanta publicist said with a nervous smile. "They're welcoming you." Then, proudly, "People are more interested in *Gone with the Wind* than in what's going on in Europe. Isn't that grand?"

Julie glanced swiftly at Andy, hoping he hadn't heard. His expression didn't change, but he seemed subdued—he had been all day, she suddenly realized. Yes, ever since she saw him huddled with Selznick in a corner of the hotel this morning.

Now Clark's attention was taken by something else: he pointed at a slight woman alongside their car on the sidewalk who was hurrying for the lobby, face averted from the crowd, looking like a skittery bird with her long tan coat flapping open. She wore laced-up black oxfords, and her hair was pulled back into a severe bun.

"Ma, is that who I think it is?" he said.

Carole peered. "Well, I'll be damned." She laughed. "Pa, I think you're about to meet the woman who created you. And I sure don't mean your mother."

Margaret Mitchell turned her head at the sound of Carole's voice and stared through the open window at Clark as their car pulled up to the curb. Her lips managed a faint smile.

※

Margaret Mitchell was waiting for them in the lobby, her husband standing protectively beside her. Julie guessed at once that she was not plain and drab, but was trying for some reason to appear so: to be overlooked, to make herself invisible. From what was she hiding, this woman who had written such an astounding book—a book that took her ten years to complete—who wrote seventy chapters, stuffed them into envelopes, and sent them off to a publisher? Who rocked the world of publishing and won a Pulitzer Prize? Who—a Southern belle, Smith College dropout, survivor of several marriages—then shrank back from the public scene but answered every letter sent to her about her book?

Introductions were made, but it was Carole who held out her hand first. "Miss Mitchell," she said, "I have two questions. May I?"

"Yes, of course," Mitchell replied, looking a little nervous.

"Did you really name your heroine Pansy at first?"

"Yes. Terrible choice, wasn't it?"

"Lordy, yes, indeed," Carole said with feeling. "I can't see Vivien playing anyone named Pansy."

"What's your second question?" Mitchell was visibly relaxing.

"Now, this I have to ask. Were you thinking about Clark when you created Rhett Butler?"

Mitchell shook her head quickly. "I keep hearing that, but no, no." She looked at Clark with an almost flirtatious glance. "Sorry, Mr. Gable. But if you do as good a job as I think you'll do bringing Rhett alive, I'll change my story."

"I've done my best," an obviously impressed Clark responded. He actually bowed, looking gallant in his white tie and tails, then took the author's small white hand in his and kissed it.

Julie for a second feared Carole would come up with a wonderful, ribald joke about Clark's true level of devotion to Rhett, but she managed to restrain herself. Fortunately, it was time to enter the theater.

Carole and Clark were ushered in first: Clark, trying not to look uncomfortable in his formal clothes, Carole sinuous and lovely in gold lamé. Vivien, escorted by Laurence Olivier—publicly, now that Selznick had no objections to their liaison anymore—followed, her head held high and her eyes triumphant.

The crowd of guests filled the theater's red velvet seats, chattering, speculating, eyes darting here and there; they were measuring their own importance by assessing that of the others lucky enough to be here at the premiere.

When David Selznick came striding out on the stage, silence fell. Once more, this feared tyrant and perfectionist looked different—eager, excited—and his voice shook with pride and excitement. He seemed smaller, somehow, standing on a grand stage—and yet, to Julie's eye, larger than ever.

The movie began. The splendid, soaring score written by composer Max Steiner—working in twenty-hour shifts to produce the longest score ever written for a movie—exploded into the lofty, elaborately molded interior of the theater, taking Julie's breath away. Selznick hadn't wanted an original score—he had wanted all classical music—but Steiner had won that fight. It was breathtaking music, and Julie found herself again swept up into the world of *Gone with the Wind*.

Her enthrallment was not going away. Strange. Even though she had been part of *Gone with the Wind* only as a spectator, it had soaked through her skin and into her heart. This was what a movie could be. And it hadn't come out of the sky, blazing and perfect. Nothing could soar, could become magical, without sweat and a touch of stardust. This "troubled project," as critics enjoyed calling it, was the result of weeks and months of anger and tensions, of disruptions and mistakes and fears. *Gone with the Wind* was in constant turmoil from start to finish; that was no secret. I mustn't forget that, she told herself. Not if she was staying in this business.

The applause that followed the final scene was deafening. The curtains closed and the lights went up and people stood as one, still applauding.

Carole knew whom they were looking for. She turned to Margaret Mitchell, who was seated next to Clark. "They want you, honey," she said.

"No, no," Mitchell protested, seemingly overcome by the response.

"Here, I'll help you." Carole took her by the hand and led her up to the stage, then stepped back. The applause grew even louder.

Margaret Mitchell looked tiny and frail against the backdrop of the heavy velvet curtains that reached to the rafters. She clutched a handkerchief, twisting it in her hands, then finally spoke. "Thank you," she said. "I am overwhelmed. Thank you all for this movie. I thank you for me and my poor Scarlett."

*

Late that night, lying in Andy's arms in a giant bed that was filled with soft, billowing pillows, Julie couldn't get that moment out of her mind. "Such a big book came from such a little woman," she murmured. "Andy, you've been part of creating something wonderful. You should be proud."

He didn't answer at first. "Honey, I wish it could be that way," he then said.

"Well, why can't it?" She tried to hold back anxiety from her voice. Something was waiting in the wings again.

He was silent for a moment, taking the time to reach for his ever-present cigarettes on the bedside table. He lit one, inhaled, and stared at the ceiling. "I need to tell you something."

She lifted her head, trying to see his face in the darkness. Then waited.

"Selznick wants to assign me to the next Colbert movie as director, with a big raise. Told me this morning."

"Andy!" Julie bolted upright to a sitting position. She was wide awake now. "That's wonderful. This is what you've wanted, isn't it?"

"Well—it forces my hand."

"What does that mean?"

He took a deep breath. "Julie, I realized today—with all this hoopla—I can't do it. I can't live this life, not now. It's not enough to be sending bribe money for French officials and offering sponsor-ships to get people out of Europe anymore. I've got to get into this thing. I can't be happy if I don't."

"I will make you happy." She said it, trying not to make it a cry of dread.

He kissed her forehead. "You do, you do. But I have to get over there. Leslie did it right. He didn't waste a minute. He got the hell out of here. Maybe Ashley Wilkes is a weak character, but Leslie Howard—no matter how he played that part—is a strong man."

"He's British, you're American. This is crazy!"

Andy leaned over and switched on the light. "I've dithered for too long, Julie. It's souring me—I can feel it happening—and I don't want that." He took her hand. "I'm taking a job with the Interna-tional Red Cross in Europe, doing whatever they want me to do, including going as a delegate to internment camps. Somebody's got to monitor treatment of civilians as well as prisoners of war, and they're the only ones who can do it."

The hammer had descended. "You want to find your family," she said.

"That's part of it."

They sat until the first weak rays of daylight crept up in the Atlanta sky, huddled in robes, on the edge of the bed. He told her his plan. It was simple enough. If Germany wouldn't let the Red Cross delegates into their camps, he would volunteer to help at any-thing needed. He could set up auxiliary hospitals, go wherever they would let him go. "Even the British aren't too fussy about accents these days," he said in an attempt at lightness. "They'll take anybody willing to sign up. Even a Yank will do."

"You have this all planned out," she said.

He lowered his head. "I've been thinking about it for a long time," he admitted.

She scrambled to muster arguments. "I need you," she said. "You can't leave, and you don't have to. We're not in this war."

"We will be. I can't wait any longer. And . . . look, you don't need me."

"How can you say that?" Even as she protested, startled, she heard the truth in his words.

"Julie, Julie, remember how outraged you were when I thought you were fragile? That you would sooner or later be defeated here? Yeah, I loved a woman who fell apart, who blamed me for her troubles. I didn't want that again."

She nodded, tears beginning to sting the corners of her eyes.

"Honey, you've proven me wrong." He reached out and gently pushed her hair back from her face. "I'm proud of you. You stand up for yourself, and you're going to knock them out in Hollywood."

"You're just being noble. You're leaving *me,* that's what you're doing. You think I'm too young. It's that old thing about not being Jewish. . . ." She knew she was throwing out wild claims; she couldn't help herself.

"It's none of that, and I think you know it."

"Then let's get married, if you insist on doing this crazy thing."

"Wow, you're proposing to me? How many men have had *that* particular flattery?" He smiled, trying to make it a tease.

"I mean it."

Andy sobered, gazing at her thoughtfully. "Julie . . ." He paused. "Okay, maybe you won't understand. I've thought the same thing. But I can't do that to you. I can't tie you down. I don't know what happens when I get to England; I'm not writing the script from here. Once I go over there, I'm throwing myself into fighting the Germans any way I can."

"What if I *want* to be tied down?"

He slowly shook his head. "You're different. You don't want that, whether you know it right now or not."

"Quit telling me what I think."

"Well, here's what I think. I don't want to settle for being just your first husband."

Julie dropped her head into her hands. He was making too much sense, and, yes, she knew that, too. She dug deep into her heart. Was she actually surprised? Hadn't she been waiting for this hammer to fall?

She lifted her head and, controlling her voice, said, "Andy, I can't stop you. I need to know one thing. Do you love me?"

"You know I do."

"Will you come back?"

"If you want me. If you haven't run off with some sexy version of Abe Goldman."

"When? What happens to the job Selznick is offering you?"

"I told him what I was thinking about this morning. He understood. Surprised, though. Said he would try to get me something good when I come back."

Well, she would have to settle for that. She leaned close, curling as tightly as she could into his arms, telling herself to see clearly, accept what she couldn't change. They fell back onto the pillows, holding each other, burrowed together, and she thought of what Scarlett had finally realized about Ashley, how she had "put that suit on him and made him wear it whether it fitted him or not." She wouldn't do that to Andy. He was gone from her—and from Hollywood—the moment he decided what would truly ease his soul, and if she tried to force anything else, she would destroy all of what was real. The morning sun began to wash through their glamorous suite, touching on the fruit basket wrapped in red cellophane and the gorgeous long-stemmed roses delivered to their door just before the premiere last night, and even kissing lightly the pieces of chocolate wrapped in silver foil left on their pillows, promising—falsely—a gentle day.

CHAPTER 25

This would be a colder Christmas than usual in Los Angeles, whatever was usual. But that's what people were saying, even as they piled fake snow on their Christmas trees, fretting when they had to don anything more than a light sweater. Julie scorned that, but shivered as she headed out with Carole's driver early in the morning to the Encino ranch.

Her bag was packed; she was prepared. The glitter of Atlanta was already fading into memory. It would recede even more when she walked up the steps of the large Dutch Colonial home where she once skipped rope and played with dolls, into the welcoming, tentative, relieved arms of her parents. She could visit now without feeling trapped.

Maybe she was ready for a break. She felt too cranky hearing the familiar tinkle of the Salvation Army's bells, rung constantly by cheery people wearing holiday smiles. They were out of place in Los Angeles; this wasn't Christmas as it should be.

Nothing right now was the way it should be.

"When are you leaving?" she'd demanded of Andy last night. Selznick had spread the news the minute they were off the plane, astonished and a little affronted that Andy was rejecting his promotion. Word traveled fast through the gossip circuit of the industry, even gleaning Andy a congratulatory salute in Louella's column, with just a hint of puzzlement that any Jew would consider making such a move, given the terrible things that rumor had it were happening—no proof, of course. And there were many cheers from backslappers who praised his bravery while thinking him an idiot, then immediately called their agents, wondering whether that director's job Weinstein was offered had been assigned to anybody else yet.

He looked up from a stack of paperwork on the coffee table, distracted. "As soon as I can get things in order; I told you that."

"What about this place?" She swept out her arm, jeopardizing a mug of coffee. This house, which held so many sweet moments.

He hesitated. "I'm renting it out, Julie. No big paychecks anymore."

"That was fast." She couldn't help it: she was angry. "So, I'm asking again, when are you leaving?"

Andy stood and walked over to her, his tread heavy. "I'll go when you head out to Fort Wayne for Christmas."

"I'm not going."

"Yes, you are. You promised your parents; you need the break. Go spend some time with other people who love you." He took her into his arms. "Yes," he whispered. "Yes, I will be back. Quit being so mad."

*

The ranch house with the comfortably faded awnings, shrouded in the early morning haze, was now in view. She couldn't bear all this. Carole would keep her sane.

*

"He'll come back," Carole said as they tromped through slushy mud to the chicken house, in hopes of finding a few eggs for breakfast. "The one I wonder about is you."

"Me? Why me?"

They had reached the chicken house. Carole tiptoed in, lifted the feathers of a bird that immediately squawked and flapped its feathers. "Okay, okay," Carole muttered. "Keep your damn eggs to yourself. I'm never going to make any money off of you anyway."

"Carole?"

"I'm wondering how long you'll stay out here, juggling screenplays, playing the game."

Julie was taken aback.

"I don't know; you'll stay awhile. You'll do great, and then you'll decide to write a book and go back east, all that shit."

Julie tried to laugh. "That is so far from my plan," she said.

"You know—since Atlanta?—I've been thinking about it. We're all going to die, but not that movie. You can feel it—it's huge. When we're dead, *Gone with the Wind* will be going strong." She shook her head. "Isn't that the limit?"

"What a strange definition of eternity," Julie said. "Showing *Gone with the Wind* nonstop forever? With the rest of us underground? That's gloomy."

"Well, something has to stick around. Might as well be a movie."

"Do you believe in God?"

"Jesus, who's being gloomy now? You're worried about Andy getting killed, aren't you?"

Julie didn't even try to blink back her tears. "I love him, I'm afraid," she said. "It chews at me, it makes me want to hold tight and"—she shook her head, she had to get these thoughts out of her brain—"and at the same time push him away. He's brave, maybe too brave? He's Jewish, Carole. He'll be a target. Where will God be when Andy needs saving?"

"Honey, I don't know where God is. Whether with you or me or Andy or Clark. But it's all here—in the mountains and the desert. It's where we are, in our everyday living. You can find it anywhere. Including Europe."

"How do you manage to stay so sensible?"

Carole had no chance to answer. The chicken who hadn't wanted to be disturbed began squawking loudly. Carole dived for its nest, hoisting the startled bird up in the air. "Well, I'll be damned," she squealed delightedly. "An egg!" She peered closely. "Come on, try again, push hard now."

And then a second egg plopped out of the bird on the next nest, and they both cheered.

Carole picked the eggs up carefully, cradling one in each hand. Holding them in front of her, she looked directly at Julie and said quietly, "Let him go, honey. That's all you can do. You can't hold on too tight."

Julie smiled; she had found what she came for. "Neither can you, if we're going to have any breakfast."

Carole looked at the eggs in her hands and gave a devilish grin before flipping one egg in the air and then the other, catching them both. "Taking chances makes you braver," she said.

*

Julie lay in Andy's arms, breathing in the warmth of his skin, feeling the beating of his heart. It was their last night together in the little house perched on a cliff overlooking the town of her dreams. She felt newly calm.

"Please don't think I'm abandoning you, honey." He stroked her hair, mussing it lightly, teasingly. "My loving little redhead," he murmured.

"It's not red, it's auburn."

"Nope, you're my feisty, tempestuous redhead."

She giggled, pulling his hand away and kissing it. If only time could stop; if only it could stay like this. "I will miss you and wait for you," she whispered.

"Sweetheart, I hope you understand," he said. His voice was hoarse, almost cracking. "I've been ashamed of myself. Why wasn't I doing anything? That's made me cranky, acerbic—a royal pain in the ass. You know that's true."

Of course she did. And she'd felt flashes of annoyance; and now he had found a way to unstick himself. That was true, too.

"I've blamed this wonderfully crass business. Blamed Selznick. Blamed the United States government. Began wondering if I'd become too good at fooling myself. From there it was easy—just toss down the bourbon and wonder why I was here in the first place. Don't you see? When I got tired of blaming everything and everybody else, I would end up blaming you."

She kissed him, touching a finger to his lips. "It's okay," she said slowly. "It's taken me a long time, but I understand. You know why? Because you finally let me inside."

"I would've told you sooner, but I wasn't sure myself. Now I'm anxious to get into it."

"You have to go."

"Yes."

"You know what Carole said? She said taking chances could make one braver. That's what you are doing. I know it now."

"You mean it?"

She made one more foray into her heart to find the true answer. "Yes," she said. "And you know what? I'm proud of you."

"Frankly, my dear"—he chuckled—"I fervently give a damn."

＊

Her flight to Fort Wayne was scheduled to leave the next morning at nine o'clock. Andy drove her to the airport, and they talked very little. But it was comfortable—nothing further needed to be said. Julie glanced up at one turn in the winding road to the airport and caught sight of the HOLLYWOODLAND sign. It was indeed a jaunty symbol of glamour lifted high above the city, filled with promises and expectations. What would the future here hold for her? For Andy?

He walked with her, down a narrow path separated from the field by a high wire-mesh fence, to the gate where her plane waited. He leaned forward and kissed her tenderly. His lips were soft and strong; she shivered.

"Please don't cry," he said.

"I won't."

She could do that much for him, couldn't she? She managed a smile and stepped away, turning toward the wire fence, then trudged to the steps of the plane. She turned again and waved. Andy, to her bleak satisfaction—hands stuffed into his pocket, hunched forward—looked miserable. Then it was up the stairs, handing her ticket to the pretty blonde stewardess, having the absurd thought that, you know, this could be Andy's old girlfriend.

She made her way to her seat and opened her purse. She stared at its interior, at the one comforting thing she had placed there this morning: a new script, pinned to a new contract. When she came back after Christmas, that would see her through.

Julie closed her eyes. One year ago, she had come stumbling into this town, dreaming of glamour and work and love, and she hadn't been denied. She and Carole were true friends, and how did that ever happen? And now a page was turning. She had finally accepted that yesterday, as they walked together early in the morning, in the swirling low-hanging fog that rolled across the meadows at the Encino ranch.

*

The propellers began to turn, filling the cabin with noise. As Julie peered out the window, she remembered she hadn't told Andy about that conversation—or that one of those hens finally laid two eggs. He would've laughed at that. Maybe, in a few months, where he was going, doing what he felt he had to do, nothing much would seem funny anymore. Maybe she had missed the chance to hear that loose, easy, warm laugh of his just one more time.

But he was already gone. She saw his receding back; that was he, wasn't it? Maybe not. But he was gone.

Her fingers curling around the contract, she thought, I wish he had waited until the plane took off. But the figure she thought might be Andy turned just as the plane lifted from the tarmac and roared up into the sky. He was waving.

She waved back.

Maybe it was corny. But, yes, she still believed in the possibility of happy endings.

EPILOGUE

Gone with the Wind grossed twenty-six million dollars in its first six months; the equivalent amount in 2014 dollars would be more than four hundred million. The movie received eleven Academy Award nominations. As it swept across the major cities of America, it was met with raves. "The mightiest achievement in the history of the motion picture," declared *The Hollywood Reporter.* Indisputably, America fell in love with *Gone with the Wind.*

Reaction was indeed mixed among black Americans. Many loved the movie as much as white audiences did, but others felt as did the reviewer for *The Chicago Defender,* who called the movie a "weapon of terror against black America." Yet it did pave the way for African American actors and actresses—including Hattie McDaniel, who won the first Oscar awarded to an African American in motion-picture history for her performance as Mammy. When she was called an "Uncle Tom" by the NAACP for playing the role, she said, "I'd rather make seven hundred dollars a week playing a maid than seven dollars being one."

At the Oscar ceremony on February 29, 1940, *Gone with the Wind* won Best Picture of 1939 and swept the top performance awards, with the exception of Best Actor. Clark Gable did not win for his performance as the dashing, unforgettable Rhett Butler.

The war in Europe was closing in on the United States, and Hollywood studio moguls—so shamefully in collusion with the

Nazis to preserve their overseas profits—were about to stop playing dodgeball. War movies would soon emerge from the movie industry. It wasn't long before France fell to the Nazis, in the spring of 1940, shaking up the Western world. Winston Churchill announced in the House of Commons that the battle of France was over, adding, "I expect that the battle of Britain is about to begin."

The world was slipping into war. And Hollywood began changing fast.

Leslie Howard did return immediately to Britain to help with the war effort when England declared war on Germany—he was no vacillating Ashley Wilkes. He died at the age of fifty, in 1943, when his plane was shot down by the Germans, leaving unresolved questions as to whether he had been on a secret spy mission for Britain.

Carole Lombard threw herself into the war effort after Pearl Harbor, giving it her all, pretty much the way she did everything. She traveled around the country selling war bonds, and was in great demand, until tragedy struck.

Carole was returning home to Hollywood after speaking at a war-bond rally in 1942 when her plane slammed into a mountain. All aboard died in the fiery crash, including Carole and her mother. The actress—at that time, one of the highest paid in Hollywood—was only thirty-three years old.

To switch off my writer's cap for a moment, I must admit I became very fond of this woman, who has lived all these months in my imagination—and I mourn her.

Clark Gable was devastated by Carole's death. I find myself imagining how he might have received the news. I see him in a darkened room, head down, sitting alone, unable to cry, unable to rewrite the script that had snatched his wife away.

Clark was known as a womanizer, but his marriage to Carole was clearly a happy one. And the key to that was Carole. She had recognized for some time the diffident, shy man inside the glamorous shell of Rhett Butler as someone who craved love and honesty, and she set out to give it to him. When she died, a shield that kept Clark safe was surely gone.

Shortly after her death, he joined the U.S. Army Air Forces and flew several combat missions. He married twice more, and died of a heart attack at the age of fifty-nine.

Vivien Leigh—who married and later divorced Laurence Olivier—went on to a stellar career, but also, plagued by health problems, died in her fifties.

As of May 2014, Olivia de Havilland remains the last surviving member of the legendary troupe of actors who made *Gone with the Wind* one of the most memorable films in history.

And I add a salute here to Frances Marion, a brilliant, trail-blazing screenwriter, whose name is barely remembered today. She and Mary Pickford were partners in the making of many Pickford films, and her humor and desire to help other women in the business of screenwriting deserve more recognition. She died in 1973, at the age of eighty-four.

About Carole and Clark. It's no secret that Hollywood marriages spun out of fantasy tend not to survive in reality. But I will risk this observation: even though they did not have a long marriage, they shared both the ability to laugh at themselves and a certain common sense about life, traits that might have given them a better chance to endure than many other Hollywood couples of that time—or any other.

That may be *my* fantasy. But, after all, this is about Hollywood.

As for my fictional characters? I think Andy would throw himself into rescue work and go wherever he could feel his efforts were worthwhile. I like to think he would possibly have been able to save some in his family, and to survive. And I believe he would do his best to return to Julie.

And Julie? Julie is one version of Everywoman—that girl in any generation at any point in history who strikes out with a small arsenal of choices and expands them to search for—if not always to find—what she wants. She grows, she changes. And at a certain point, the reader salutes her on her journey, and wishes her well.

Hope so.

I do.

Kate Alcott

AUTHOR'S NOTE

This is a work of fiction, with invented details and characters, and I have taken liberties with some facts and time sequences—although the central structure, many anecdotes, and key dates are accurate. Also, descriptions and dialogue from the actual filming of scenes from *Gone with the Wind* have been compressed. As for quotes, Carole was a wonderfully colorful talker, and much of what she actually said has made its way into my book. Thank you, Carole.

I also owe thanks to Catherine Wyler for lending me her mother's unpublished memoir. Margaret Tallichet was befriended by Carole Lombard and given a screen test for the part of Scarlett O'Hara, and her remembrances of that time were a delight to read. She later married producer and director William Wyler.

My grateful thanks to Judy Silber, the daughter of Sam Jaffe, a legendary agent and producer in Hollywood, who lent me her father's delightfully juicy memoir, an oral history now in the archives of the Academy of Motion Picture Arts and Sciences.

And once again, a salute to my treasured manuscript readers, who keep me from falling on my face: Mary Dillon, Ellen Goodman, Irene Wurtzel, Judy Viorst, Margaret Power, Lynn Sherr, and Linda Cashdan.

Esther Newberg, you have been behind me every step of the way for a long time. Nobody could ask for a better agent.

Melissa Danaczko, as my editor, you wield your red pencil with intelligence and care—always tuned in to what I am trying to do and finding ways to help me say it better.

And always, my thanks to my husband, Frank Mankiewicz, who grew up in that house on Tower Road in Beverly Hills. With both a pencil—drawing the layout of his family home for me—and his memories, he helped bring me back into that time between the wars when Hollywood shone so brightly and brilliantly.

It's been a privilege and a pleasure to visit there.